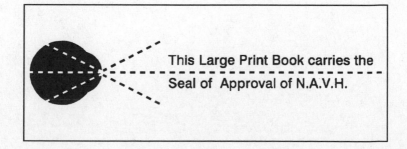

This Large Print Book carries the
Seal of Approval of N.A.V.H.

Fatal

FATAL

JOHN LESCROART

THORNDIKE PRESS
A part of Gale, Cengage Learning

GALE
CENGAGE Learning·

Farmington Hills, Mich • San Francisco • New York • Waterville, Maine
Meriden, Conn • Mason, Ohio • Chicago

GALE
CENGAGE Learning®

LIBRARY OF CONGRESS CATALOGING-IN-PUBLICATION DATA

Names: Lescroart, John T., author.
Title: Fatal / John Lescroart.
Description: Large print edition. | Waterville, Maine : Thorndike Press, 2017. | Series: Thorndike Press large print core
Identifiers: LCCN 2016053155 | ISBN 9781410496775 (hardback) | ISBN 1410496775 (hardcover)
Subjects: LCSH: Married people—Fiction. | Adultery—Fiction. | Large print edition. | Psychological fiction. | BISAC: FICTION / Thrillers. | GSAFD: Suspense fiction.
Classification: LCC PS3562.E78 F38 2017b | DDC 813/.54—dc23
LC record available at https://lccn.loc.gov/2016053155

Published in 2017 by arrangement with Atria Books, an imprint of Simon & Schuster, Inc.

Printed in the United States of America
1 2 3 4 5 6 7 21 20 19 18 17

This book is dedicated to Lisa Sawyer
— muse, best friend, and true love

What extraordinary vehicles destiny
selects to accomplish its design.

— HENRY KISSINGER

■ ■ ■ ■ ■

PART ONE

MAY 12–MAY 19

■ ■ ■ ■

1

Kate Jameson and Beth Tully walked west at the bayside edge of Crissy Field.

The lines of the Golden Gate Bridge materialized in haphazard fashion through the fog in front of them, but neither paid much attention. This was a view they encountered nearly every time they walked together, and they usually tried to do that once a week, so none of it really registered — not the choppy gray-green bay sloshing to their right, the bridge looming ahead, the kite-boarders, the sailboats, the joggers passing by — all of it swathed in the ubiquitous, wispy fog.

They'd been roommates twenty years before at the University of San Francisco and though their lives had taken different turns, they were still close friends who rarely ran out of things to talk about. The walk, from Ghirardelli Square to the bridge and back, took them about an hour, and usually

11

the first half of that got devoted to discussing their offspring — Kate's two and Beth's one, all teenagers.

There was never a dearth of material.

When they finally arrived at the bridge and turned around, they'd usually chitchatted enough about *les enfants.*

They had several mutual acquaintances, mostly from the old days, and also some recurring personalities from the greater worlds of the kids' schools or sports teams or their domestic lives, and the normal walk back to where they'd begun was all gossip — laughter, agreement, connection.

But today, not even halfway to the bridge, Beth said, "And so finally there was Ginny" — her seventeen-year-old — "sitting inside the refrigerator with a pork chop on her knee." Getting no response, she kept walking for a few more steps and then stopped mid-stride. "Earth to Kate. Come in, please."

"What? I'm sorry. What were you saying?"

"Well, the last minute or so I was just making stuff up, wondering if you'd notice. Which I have to say you didn't. Are you all right?"

"Sure." She hesitated. "I think so."

"But something . . ."

"No. It's nothing."

"That old elusive nothing."

"Maybe. Should we keep walking?"

"Unless you want to head back."

"No. I'm good. I'm sorry. Let's keep going."

Falling in step together, they covered a couple of hundred yards in silence before Beth reached over and touched the sleeve of Kate's workout jacket. "You can tell me, you know," she said. "Whatever it is."

"I know. But that's what I'm saying, or not saying. It really isn't anything. At least not yet." She shook her head, once, emphatically. "It shouldn't ever be anything."

"That sounds ominous enough." Beth paused, then said, "Tell me, please, it's not Ron."

Kate reacted almost as if she'd been stung. "No! No no no. Ron's great. He's always great. It's not him."

"But it's somebody? Something?"

A nod. "It's something." They had come up beside a bench that bordered the path, and Kate stopped, hands deep in her pockets. "Maybe we could sit a minute."

"Sure."

They both sat and Beth waited.

Kate finally started. "I don't know what happened, exactly. We went over to Ron's partner's house for dinner on Saturday. Do

13

you know Geoff and Bina Cooke? No? Well, it doesn't matter. It wasn't them. But there was another couple there we didn't know. Nice people. Kind of normal. Like us, really, I mean like me and Ron. Lawyer husband and sweet wife, two kids, house payments, all of the above."

"Okay. And?"

"And so we had this nice dinner and sat around talking afterwards, finishing our wine the way people do, you know. Nothing groundbreaking, just relaxed and easy. Then we all said good night and went home."

A rogue gust of wind swept by them, trailing a small cloud of dust and debris. When it had passed, Beth turned to her friend. "Did I miss something?"

"I know. Right? I told you nothing happened."

"Except whatever it was seems to have your attention in a major way."

Kate pushed her hands more deeply into her jacket pockets. "Ron and I came home and went to bed, and an hour later I was in the living room, wrapped up in a comforter, wide awake. I couldn't get the idea out of my head that I was going to have to have sex with this guy. I mean, it was right there, large, like this massive . . . I don't know, *need.* I couldn't get rid of it, and I've been living with it ever since. It's like the idea is totally consuming me. I can't think of anything else. It's making me a crazy person."

"Maybe you're just horny, girlfriend."

Kate shook her head. "It's nothing to do with horny. Ron and I have been . . . well, three times in the past week. I promise you that's not the problem."

"Did something happen between the two of you — you and this guy — at the dinner?"

"No. Nothing. That's the thing. We barely talked to each other. There wasn't really even any reason that I would have noticed him, or him me. He's no better looking than Ron, and his wife is kind of cute."

"Well, you're a little more than kind of cute, Kate. I'm sure he noticed you."

"Okay, maybe. But basically he's just another guy. A really normal, average guy who I've just gotten fixated on." She turned on the bench, put her hand out on Beth's arm. "And don't think I don't realize how ridiculous this is."

"You haven't done anything, have you? With him?"

"No. God no. I couldn't . . . I mean, not that I ever would. It would kill Ron and mess up the kids' lives. I know that, of

15

course. I couldn't let that happen. I probably shouldn't even have told you, but I don't know what to do here. I've never had anything like this happen before, not since I've been married anyway. I love Ron. I really do. And I don't know anything about this guy. I wasn't really even consciously aware of him. But then, somehow, after we got home, the idea was just there and it was . . ." She brought her hands up to her forehead, then brought them back through her hair. "I don't know what it was. Or is."

"Well, I do, Kate, truly. It's dumb and dangerous."

"I know. That's probably why I'm telling you. Because I want to hear you say that."

"Okay. I've told you," Beth said. "And do you hear me?"

"I do."

"Good. Because I'm dead serious here, Kate. This is nothing to play around with. A little fantasy, maybe, okay. But take it out on Ron if you've got to do something about it."

"That's good advice."

"Damn straight it is. We're not in high school anymore. Acting on this is the kind of thing that ruins lives."

"I got it. Really. You've convinced me. I'm not going to do anything about it. Which

16

will be easy, since I don't even know the guy's last name or how to get in touch with him."

"Good. Keep it that way."

"I will."

"Promise?"

"Swear to God." Kate made a sign over her chest. "Cross my heart and hope to die."

Two days later, Thursday, Kate went out grocery shopping in the morning while Carmen was cleaning the house. On the way back, she found a parking spot in front of a coffee shop on Fillmore around the corner from her home on Washington Street. Killing time, anything to keep her brain away from its ongoing preoccupation with Peter, she ordered an espresso and a croissant, and then came back outside. The sun had broken through the clouds and it was warm for a jacket, so she shrugged out of it and hung it over the back of her chair, then sat at one of the sidewalk tables.

Catching a quick glimpse of herself in the coffee shop's window, she felt a small jolt of satisfaction. The reaction surprised her, since she did not usually think of herself as beautiful.

She was wearing her favorite old jeans, hiking boots, and a high-necked, ribbed white sweater that flattered both her ample bosom and her thin waist. Her glistening dark hair was just short of shoulder length and around her neck gleamed a gold chain necklace that held a *kachina* charm from Santa Fe that Ron had given her two months ago for her forty-fifth birthday.

Now she cast another glance at the window, looking for some sign of the low-voltage electricity that had been her constant companion since the weekend, since that moment she'd been putting away the dishes at Geoff and Bina's and a pair of hands — Peter's hands — had gently but firmly settled on her shoulders from behind and most politely moved her to one side.

"Excuse me. Just need a dish towel. Sorry."

Carmen had finished up with the cleaning and gone home.

No one else was around.

After sitting at her kitchen counter as ten minutes slowly ticked by on the wall clock, Kate took out her cell phone, pushed her Contacts button, and brought up the Cookes. But seeing their name printed out on her screen seemed somehow irreversible, and she returned the cell phone to her purse.

"Come on," she said aloud, to no one. "Really?"

With an air of impatience, brushing her hair back off her forehead, she abruptly stood up and crossed to where they had their landline telephone at the end of the hallway. Picking up the receiver, she listened to the dial tone for a few seconds, then — before she could change her mind again — she quickly punched in the numbers.

Bina picked up on the first ring. "Hello."

"Hola, amiga. It's your space case friend Kate."

"Hola yourself. What makes you a space case?"

"I just looked in my purse and realized that I'd forgotten to give back your keys for Incline and the boat, which I had specifically brought over on Saturday and then promptly forgot."

"Oh, they don't matter. We're glad you get to use the cabin, since Geoff and I so rarely get to. And the boat for that matter. There it is, just down in the marina and it might as well be in Scotland for all that we use it. And you may as well just keep the keys, rather than having to borrow them again. We've got our own set, after all. Consider them yours."

"You're the best. Thanks." Kate knew that

19

she could stop now, no harm done, but somehow she could not. "But returning to the space case theme," she said, "I also just now realized that I hadn't called you to thank you for the wonderful evening the other night. Fantastic food, stimulating conversation. We always have such a great time with you guys."

"You're welcome, and we did, too."

"I think it's kind of magic, don't you, that our men get along so well? Especially after Ron and Geoff spend their whole week slogging out their work together, but then we show up for dinner and there they are, pals."

"I know. They're lucky. Partners and friends both. Doesn't come around every day. But I guess that's what happens when you're forged in war, Kate. I marvel at it still, after all these years. These Desert Storm boys. Eighteen months over there together. Can you imagine how heavy that bond is? I'd say we're pretty lucky, you and I, to have both of them."

"We are. We do manage to have a lot of fun, don't we?"

"Every time."

"Well, next dinner date, it's our turn. Not negotiable."

"Well, if you're going to play hardball. You pick the day and we'll be there."

"I'll just check our calendars and get back to you. Oh, and I also wanted to tell you, we really liked that other couple, too. Peter and . . . ?"

"Jill."

"Jill. Of course. Jill. I am so the worst at names. Jill Jill Jill. Got it now, though. Do they have a last name?"

"Ash. It's Peter Ash, anyway. I think she's hyphenated — Corbin-Ash? Something like that. Though she doesn't use it all the time. Probably Ash would work fine."

"Well, in any event, I was thinking we might ask them to join us again if you'd be okay with that."

"Of course. That'd be nice. They're really starting to be friends. You might have noticed that Peter and Geoff have a little mutual interest on the wine front."

"I think I do have some faint memory of that."

"Plus the Giants. Plus fly-fishing. Golf. It's like ten years since Geoff's met somebody like Ron where they've got stuff in common and then, all of the sudden — wham! — he's got a new friend. It's kind of neat to see."

"How'd you meet him?"

"Up in Napa a few months ago. They were tasting at the same place we were — have

21

you been to Handwritten in St. Helena? It's awesome. Anyway, they were there and we just clicked. Really what we need," she added, laughing, "another excuse to drink wine."

"So if we invited them over next time with you, you'd be good with that?"

"Totally. Although we love you guys by yourselves, too."

"Of course. That goes without saying. So you've got a number for them?"

"I do. You ready for it?"

"Hit me."

Of course Peter Ash was on Google. Kate knew that Ron had never even looked at her laptop and in all likelihood never would. Still, she didn't leave Peter on the screen for long, just long enough to get his work phone number to go with the number Bina had given her. And to see that he was a partner in the downtown law firm Meyer Eldridge & Kline. For deniability's sake — if Ron ever *did* glance at her iPad history and notice, Kate could claim that she just had a burst of curiosity that had led to some innocent computer stalking — she also checked on his wife, Jill, and discovered that she worked as a Realtor.

But now that she'd discovered some of

these details, what was she going to do about them? She had the laptop open. Her screen saver was a picture of Half Dome in Yosemite. She could close it up and never think about her searches again.

Up until this point, she knew that she had done nothing even remotely wrong or irrevocable. Possibly she should have resisted the impulse to share her thoughts with Beth on their walk the other day, but the two of them had long ago proven that they could keep each other's secrets.

Was she moving toward doing something? Acting out around this fantasy?

Stupid, and yet it felt inexorable. She was going to have to do something.

Why, she wondered, had this come up? She knew that what she'd told Beth had been the absolute truth. She did love Ron. He was a great man, a rock-solid provider, a more than adequate lover, and about the best father she could imagine — to say nothing of being her best friend, much closer to her than Beth or any of her other girlfriends. What was she thinking?

She opened the laptop again, stared at Half Dome, closed.

She had taken this far enough. It was ridiculous. She wasn't going any further

down this path and that was all there was to
it.

2

At a few minutes after two o'clock, Peter Ash picked up the phone at his desk. His secretary had told him that the caller had given her name and said it was a personal matter, that she and Peter were friends. But he was deep in the transcript of a deposition he'd conducted in the middle of the previous week, and he couldn't place the name Kate Jameson, although it sounded vaguely familiar.

"I'm sorry," he replied after the woman had come on and said hello. "Theresa said it was a personal matter, but I'm afraid I'm blanking on where we know each other."

"Last weekend, at the Cookes'? Geoff and Bina's. Me and my husband Ron?"

"Oh yes, of course, I remember now. How can I help you?"

"Well, this is a little awkward, I admit, since we barely know each other. But I'd like to talk to you privately, about a legal matter, if you could spare me an hour or two."

Peter hesitated. "Not to jump to conclusions," he said, "but I don't do much private legal stuff. My work is pretty much all corporate. I don't do divorce, although if that's the issue, I could suggest you get in touch with one of my partners."

"It's not divorce," she said. "Ron and I are fine. I don't mean to be mysterious, but I don't want to go to Ron or even Geoff or anyone else in their firm. It's more in the line of a secret that I'd like some advice with from a legal perspective."

Another silence. Then, finally. "Mrs. Jameson . . ."

"Kate, please."

"Kate, then. I must say that this is one of the rather more intriguing phone calls I've ever received in all my years in the law. How much of my time are you talking about?"

"What I said earlier. Not much more than a couple of hours, I shouldn't think."

"More mysterious all the time."

"I don't mean to sound like that. I'm just trying to keep something more or less private, and all the other lawyers I know, and I know lots of them . . . well, they all know each other, too. So I thought I'd reach out to you as someone a bit out of our personal loop, that is, if you can spare the time. If it's not too much of an imposition."

"There's no question of that. I'm flattered you thought to call me. I'm sure I could block out an hour or two. When would you like to come in?"

"That's the other thing."

"What's that?"

"I'd just as soon avoid coming down to your office, if you wouldn't mind. You're at Embarcadero Two, aren't you?"

"Home, sweet home," he said.

"Well, if I came by there, there's a fairly decent chance I'll run across somebody I know, and I'd rather avoid that."

"This is starting to sound really cloak and dagger. So where would you like to meet?"

She drew a breath. "I've got a room at the Meridien." On Battery Street, the hotel was less than two hundred yards from Peter's office. "Eight twelve."

"You mean right now? This minute?"

"I hope so. I thought I'd take the chance. It's really quite important. If you could please just come by." After about ten seconds of silence, she spoke up. "Peter?"

"You're scaring me a little, I must say."

"There's no danger. I promise you. I just don't want to be seen."

"Okay. Give me a few minutes to wind

things up here. Room eight twelve, you say?"

"Yes."

"All right." A last hesitation. "I'll see you in ten."

Whatever this was all about, it was fascinating, Peter was thinking. And even if it were a total waste of his time, it had to be better than the deposition work in which he'd been immersed. Better than all the other work he did, too. Something out of the boring ordinary at last, saving the remnants of his day. If for no other reason than that, he thought, it was worth walking over and finding out what was going on.

Closing the folder on his transcript, he pushed himself back from his desk and stood up.

Kate Jameson had promised him that there was no danger associated with her unorthodox request, but he spent a minute or two considering whether in fact there might be the possibility that he was walking into some kind of trap, some desperate situation.

Try as he might, he simply couldn't imagine it.

He had no trouble remembering Kate Jameson from Saturday night, but his memory of her, his *sense* of her, did not include

28

anything sinister. Although it did include beauty. He remembered that well enough. She was a fucking doll, the absolute complete package. But as a person, she came across as what she was — a happily married, well-adjusted mother of two.

She was, he told himself, not a CIA spy or an FBI agent. And he had no secrets and no hidden agenda with a foreign power or terrorist organization. Kate Jameson was not going to have henchmen in the Meridien with her who would drug him or hold him for ransom.

But still, even though he was smiling at these absurd scenarios, he stopped at his office door, telling himself that no matter how intriguing this whole situation was, if he were smart he would stop right here and go back to his regular work.

What was he thinking? He couldn't just get up and leave the office for a hotel assignation in the middle of the day with a woman he barely knew.

The idea was preposterous.

He should call her back, and if she wanted, he would tell her that there was still time for her to walk over to his office and have a regular business interview with him, or she could find herself another lawyer. Of which, she admitted, she knew several.

He asked himself again: was he only going over to *Le Méridien* because she was so attractive? No, he told himself. That had nothing to do with it. She was a damsel in some kind of distress and for whatever reason, she'd come to him to help her out. She was probably — in fact, obviously — a bit frightened herself.

Of something.

He'd just swing over to the Meridien, hold her hand, give her whatever legal advice she needed, send her on her way.

There was certainly nothing for him to worry about.

Theresa looked up from her desk expectantly as he came out of his office.

"I'm just going out to get some sunshine and clear my head," he told her. "I ought to be back in an hour, maybe two."

His secretary's face clouded with concern. "You're going out? Are you all right? You never go out."

"Today I am," he said. "I've got the deposition transcript blues. If I don't take a break, I'm going to kill somebody and that would be bad luck, wouldn't it?"

Only on the way down in the elevator did he realize that he'd lied to Theresa.

Why had he done that?

■ ■ ■ ■

By the time he got to the door to room 812, his heart was a jackhammer in his ears. He felt so dizzy with the rush of adrenaline that he found he needed to hold himself up, his hand against the door jamb.

What he was doing was not just unusual, he was thinking. It was — somehow — wrong. He shouldn't be here. It made no sense.

Taking a deep breath, for another moment he considered simply walking away, but then, almost as though he were watching himself from some distance above, he saw his hand come off the jamb and rap twice sharply on the door.

"One second."

He heard her steps approaching, then her voice through the door. "Peter?"

"Yes. It's me."

She pulled the door open, inward toward her. "Thank you so much for coming over. Sorry for all the secrecy." Standing in the short, dark hall that led back into the suite and backlit by the room's windows along the far wall behind her, she wasn't much more than a very shapely silhouette. Her face was mostly hidden in shadow, even as she backed away, holding the door. "Come in. Please."

He closed the door behind him.

The unlit hallway passed a similarly dark bathroom to his right as he followed her further into the suite, past the king bed and the large bureau that held the television set that separated the bedroom from the seating area — on the right, a small desk with two chrome and leather chairs, and on the left, a glass table with two more chairs.

On the table sat an unopened bottle with a corkscrew and a couple of wineglasses. At a glance Peter recognized it as a Napa Valley Silver Oak, perhaps half a step below cult status but by any standard a superb bottle of wine, although what it was doing here at this meeting was another mystery.

Though perhaps it had become less so.

Peter couldn't seem to stop himself, putting one foot down after the other, following a couple of steps behind her.

With the floor-to-ceiling shades open, the bright sunshine out the windows lit up this back half of the suite. He could not fail to notice how sensational she looked from behind. At the Cookes' on Saturday, she'd worn jeans and flat shoes and a bulky, nearly formless sweater, looking good because of her natural attractiveness, but not so good that she'd stop traffic. Today, her two-inch heels accented a pair of very shapely legs that disappeared into a black leather mini-skirt, above which she had tucked an emerald-green silk blouse.

But the view from behind her as she walked through the suite, seductive as it was, did not adequately prepare him for when she turned around just beyond the table. She wore no bra and the outline of her breasts pushed at the fabric of the blouse. She'd undone the top two buttons.

Mesmerized by the look of her, he couldn't move.

She now had turned all the way to face him, and she broke a smile, her green eyes sparkling and playful. "Before we get down to what I've asked you here for, I thought we might start with some wine, if you'd do the honors. Is the oh seven a good year?"

"Silver Oak," he said. "They're all good years."

"That's what I thought, too." She held the corkscrew out for him. "Do you mind?"

And suddenly he was holding the cork-screw, reaching for the bottle. "I'm afraid this is a little out of the ordinary for me. I don't usually drink in the afternoon. It puts me to sleep."

"I'll cut you off at a half glass." Her smile

urged him on. "Though I might have a whole one. Or even two. Really." She touched his hand. "It's all right. Promise."

For Peter, it did not feel all right. It felt at this one moment like the end of something, of the constant awareness of the existence of Jill and the twin boys in his life — the life he'd chosen and committed to — while at the same moment he was plunging the sharp end of the corkscrew into the cork and beginning to twist it down.

"Oh, while you're getting that," she said, brushing by him — touching his shoulder, the lightest of contacts — heading back past the king bed, down the short hallway to the door. "Excuse me one minute."

He heard the room's door open, then close. Then she was coming back toward him.

He popped the cork.

"That sounded perfect," she said.

He held the cork to his nose. "Smells right," he said. He held it out to her.

She took it and gave it a sniff. "That'll do," she said.

"Where did you just go?" he asked.

"I put the 'Do Not Disturb' sign on the door," she said. "You can take off your jacket, you know. Get comfortable. Here."

She helped him out of it, draped it over

the chair in front of him, then turned and put her right palm flat against his chest.

"Your heart is going crazy," she said.

Then, "Mine is, too." She lifted his hand up and held it against her breast. "See?"

3

The actual experience matched Kate's fantasy in all respects.

After the first kiss, Peter had pulled away, fighting her persistence as well as his own conscience, but in the end he couldn't summon the strength to resist her.

Once she put her hands on him, the sex became its own thing and carried them each to two climaxes in the next ninety minutes.

It was by far the most satisfied she'd been in her memory, maybe in her whole life. She hadn't even been aware that she was so desperate.

And she was sure it had been the same for him.

Now sated, still warm under the covers, Kate listened to the shower running in the bathroom, heard it stop. After another minute, he came out with a towel around his waist. With a kind of rueful half smile, he said, "I'm afraid I'm not too clear on the etiquette right now."

She scooched back against a pillow, against the headboard, pulling the sheets up to cover her breasts. "I think you get dressed and probably go back to work."

"And what about us?"

"What about us?"

A moment of hesitation. "Well, for example, are we going to do this again?"

"I don't know. I never have before, you know."

"No. I didn't know that. How would I?"

She waved that off. "The point is, it's all new to me, too."

After a couple of hesitant breaths, he sat down on the edge of the bed. "I'm not sure I even know what happened."

This brought a small smile. "Oh. I'm pretty clear about that."

"That's not how I meant it."

"No." More seriously now. "No, I understand."

"I don't know what to do with any of this. I mean, how does it fit in our lives?"

"I'm not sure it does. I really don't know that."

"So we leave it where it is?"

"I think so." She reached over and gently touched his leg. "I don't want to complicate your life. Our lives."

He broke a little laugh. "I'm thinking you're a couple of hours late on that. But let's agree at least that we don't tell our spouses. How's that sound?"

"Of course not."

"And you're good? We just forget this?"

"If we can. Consenting adults. One afternoon. It doesn't have to be any more than that."

"All right then." He reached out his hand. "We've got ourselves a deal."

She took his hand and shook it. "Deal," she said.

She took an Uber car back from the hotel to her house.

She had her own Uber account, paid through her American Express, with which she'd also paid for the hotel room. Since she had gone paperless, the record of her expenditures was only available online with her password.

She handled the household bills, essentially aware of every cent either she or Ron spent, except for the cash expenditures from his fifteen hundred dollar monthly "allowance." By contrast, Ron had very little contact with their expenditures. Kate had set up an elaborate system that automatically paid most of their household expenses from their checking account — mortgage, car payments, gas, electricity, various insurances, telephone, television, tuition for the children, and so on. What remained — credit cards, groceries, house cleaning, yard maintenance, clothing expenses — had over time evolved into Kate's province as well.

Kate held a degree in business from Stanford. After graduating, she'd put in two years at Deloitte, then another three with a local venture capital firm, after which Ron — five years her senior — was doing well enough in the law to allow her to quit working to start their family and to be a full-time mother.

Most days, both of her kids were at their respective schools until after 5:00 and didn't make it home until at least 6:00. So she didn't have to worry about them running into her by mistake. By the time the Uber car dropped her off in front of the house, the last chance that one of her neighbors could possibly see her, she'd put on the plain tan overcoat that covered the miniskirt and the green silk blouse and light leather jacket. The heels were in her purse, replaced by ballet-style slippers.

In any event, she didn't see anyone and she doubted that anyone saw her. Though still clear and sunny, the evening had gotten cold and the wind out of the west had scoured Washington Street of pedestrians.

Upstairs, she changed into her jeans, her hiking boots, and a Stanford sweatshirt. After Peter had left her at *Le Méridien,* she too had taken advantage of the hotel's shower, and now she spent a few minutes in her bathroom with her hair dryer, making sure no dampness remained. She hung up the miniskirt and jacket in her closet, dropped the blouse into the hamper, then ran a small load of laundry that included the underwear she'd worn to the hotel.

In the kitchen, she opened a bottle of Francis Coppola claret and splashed it into a glass, which she then dumped into the sink to wash it away. Pouring another inch or so into the glass, she put the open bottle back down on the counter and took the glass with her into the living room, where she sat in her favorite reading chair and put her feet up on the ottoman.

Finally, closing her eyes, she allowed herself a breath of relief.

She was home, safe, undiscovered.

Let them all come now — Ron, Aidan, Janey. She was ready for them. Ready to go back to normal life, to real life.

Jill Ash checked the kitchen clock when she

heard the garage door open. 8:45. She dried her hands, having just finished the last of the dinner dishes for herself and the kids.

When Peter came in, she walked over, went up on tiptoe, and planted a kiss on his cheek. He looked exhausted, his eyes bagging, his shoulders slumped. "How do you work thirteen hours and still smell so good?" she asked. "Or is that a trace of wine I detect?"

He put his heavy lawyer's briefcase down on the floor next to him. "Jerry opened a bottle to celebrate something, and I had a half glass going out the door. Silver Oak."

"My, my. Must've been a big one."

"Must have. But I didn't even ask. I'd been downtown long enough." He looked up at the corners of the room, then met his wife's eyes. "Some nights it is just so good to be home."

"It is. I know. And good to have you home. I hate it when you're this late. Even when you call, I worry."

"That's why I call. So you won't."

"I know. But I still do. Have you eaten?"

"I'm afraid I didn't get around to it."

"You know what we tell the kids, about the body being a machine and it needs fuel?"

"I know. If I would have thought of it, I

41

would have."

"That's what they say, too. But luckily we've got about half a lasagna left, still warm."

"You are my savior," he said. "Come back over here a minute."

She took a step into his embrace and felt his arms tighten around her. He kissed the top of her head. "I love you."

"As well you should." She gave him a squeeze and another quick kiss, this time brushing his lips. "Okay, now sit. A little more wine?"

He pulled out his chair. "I don't see how it could hurt."

At the kitchen table, Jill sat across from Peter with her own glass of wine.

The boys, Eric and Tyler, were off hanging out with some friends — it was all suitably vague. They were both seniors at Lowell and had already been accepted into the fabled "college of their choice" — Eric to UC Berkeley and Tyler to Chico State — so their full-time commitment to academic excellence was in the waning stage. Peter and Jill both understood that they were probably not out studying.

"I just don't want to see them flunk something in this last semester," Jill was saying, "and get their acceptances rescinded."

"That's not going to happen," Peter said. "They'd have to kill one of their teachers to get less than a B, or burn down the school. Something along those lines, anyway. The general understanding is that standards for seniors relax a bit, like if they show up and hand in their work, they pass."

"Yeah, but that whole showing up thing . . ."

"I haven't heard about them missing classes. Is that going on?"

"No."

"Well, then. They're good kids, Jill. They've made it this far. They're not going to blow it now with a month to go."

"Let's hope not." She let out a sigh. "I just wish they weren't out every single night. Maybe we should tell them they need to come home earlier."

"Sweetie, they're eighteen. In six months they'll both be living on their own, out of our house. They're going to run loose a little, or even a lot. We might look on this as good training for us as well as for them."

"Well, I don't like it. I don't know why they can't have their friends all come over here, even just to hang out, instead of them going out who knows where every night."

"You really want a half dozen teenagers

43

over here every night? Or more? Be careful what you wish for."

She nodded, picking up her wineglass. "I know. You're right. Okay, enough." She indicated his plate. "Not hungry?"

"I guess not." He glanced down at his plate and carefully put down his fork. "You know," he said, "now that I think about it, I think I might be coming down with something. I don't feel good at all."

"You're working too hard. Getting home at almost nine o'clock. That's too long a day, even for an associate, and you're a partner, if I recall."

"I am." He shrugged. "And I even agree with you, but we all know that's the job sometimes. In fact, not to be a party pooper, but would you mind if I just went up now? I'm about done in."

With a frown of concern, Jill stood up and came around beside him, putting her hand to his forehead. "No fever."

"No. Just general wear and tear."

"Sure. Go on up. Do you want me to come up and tuck you in?"

"Thanks, but I think I can manage. I should be fine in the morning."

"Well, if you're not, you're staying home."

"I might, but let's wait 'til we get there. Meanwhile . . ."

"Go," she said. "Get some sleep."

By the time Jill slid into bed next to him, the digital clock read 10:45, and he hadn't even dozed. Nevertheless, he rolled over to face her and, pretending he was just surfacing from deep sleep, reached an arm around her, held her a moment, then let his arm fall slack.

When the boys got home together at 12:43, he swung out of bed in his t-shirt and gym shorts, went back down, and met them in the kitchen, where they were raiding the refrigerator.

"Hey, guys."

"Hey, Dad." In unison.

"Isn't school starting at the normal time tomorrow?"

The twins, busted, looked at each other.

"Just sayin'. A little late for a school night, huh? I know you think your mother and I don't worry, but when it gets close to one, guess what?"

Eric took the lead in their defense. "Now you're going to say that nothing good happens after midnight. I think we've heard that before once or twice."

"You know why? Because it's true."

"Come on, Dad, we're home now. And we'll be fine tomorrow," Tyler said.

"I'm sure you will," Peter said. "But really, maybe we can shoot for midnight on school nights, as I believe we've discussed a few times before. For your mother's and my sake, if nothing else. Do you think that would be doable?"

"Probably," Tyler said.

"Probably's a start," Peter said. "Eric? How about you?"

"Your house, your rules," Eric said with an elaborate shrug.

Peter yearned to shock his surly bastard of a son one time by popping a hard jab off his arm, but instead he simply nodded, his face set. "That's an acceptable answer," he said. "See you guys in the morning."

It must have been sometime after 3:00. Peter hadn't even flirted with sleep. Now he lay under an afghan on the leather couch in the dark television room behind the kitchen.

Since he'd first come upstairs, he had relived the afternoon continually. He still could not believe that it had actually happened, that he had been part of, and a willing participant in, the whole thing. He traced the steps that had led them there one by one: the bizarre telephone conversation that he should have ended in the first seconds; the lie to Theresa; the walk over to

46

the hotel; knocking at the door. Waiting for her to open it.

So many opportunities for him to have bailed out, and none taken.

And why not? What had he been thinking?

Okay, when he'd been younger, just out of Desert Storm, he'd gone wild for a time. After what he'd been through over there, he figured the world owed him. So he messed around when he could — which was often — and even kept that behavior up for a while after marrying Jill, especially after the twins arrived, when she was always either too tired or flatly uninterested. He hadn't thought it was that big a deal, but when she'd caught him at it and threatened to take the house and half his money, he'd cut it out, reached a tolerable, even good, sexual accommodation with her, forced himself to live with it, convinced himself that it was enough. This was adulthood. He was a father, played the role model to keep things smooth at his home.

That other stuff, he had to shut it down.

If he didn't, there was no doubt that Jill would wipe him out — financially, professionally, any way she could.

And today, Kate Jameson.

How, he wondered, how could he have been so stupid to allow this threat to enter his world?

Or maybe it hadn't been stupid, after all. He had put in the time, supported his wife, raised his difficult sons. Maybe the world still owed him.

He had given his all, his energy and his passion, and for what?

He had met Kate less than a week before, and now, suddenly, she was by default among the most important people in his life. He had no control or leverage over who she was, what she wanted, or what she did. He had given her the power to wreck everything he'd ever worked for and cared about. Actually, even worse, she'd made him realize that he didn't care about it, the life he was living. Maybe he'd simply outgrown it.

That could never be undone. But could it stay buried and unmentioned forever? He couldn't imagine it, not least because he could not seem to control one recurring thought: regardless of what she had said, he knew he had to see her again. The graphic scenes after that first kiss, playing and replaying in his mind, trumped all of his qualms.

He turned on the couch and an unconscious moan escaped.

"Peter?" Jill, standing in the doorway, a silhouette. "Are you all right?"

48

"Just not sleeping," he said. "I didn't want to wake you up."

She came around the couch and sat. "First you can't eat and now you can't sleep."

"I know. Not a good night."

"Can I do anything, get you something? Maybe some tea?"

He let out a heavy breath. "I don't think so. I've just got to slow my brain down."

"You think it's work?"

"Probably. Mostly."

"These people, whoever they are, they're your clients, not your life. You know?"

"I know that. I'm trying."

"I'm sure you are." She touched his face in the dark. "I'm not criticizing you, babe. I'm just saying." After a minute, she said, "If you want to come upstairs, I could rub your back."

A deep sigh. "That might be good."

"At least better than tossing down here all night."

He sighed again. "At least that."

"All right." Reaching for his hand, she pulled him up. "Come on, then," she said. "And no discussion. I'm turning off the alarm."

4

Sergeant Beth Tully knew that guns didn't kill people; people killed people. First as a patrol cop, and now and for the past eight years as an inspector, she had always been a gun fan. She loved her Glock. She liked going to the range and keeping up on her skills; she enjoyed sitting around with her fellow cops and shooting the shit about different makes and models and bullet payloads and muzzle velocities. Though she had yet to draw her gun in the line of duty, she felt comfortable wearing it every day, wouldn't know how she'd feel without it, and really didn't want to find out.

Nevertheless, she had to admit that guns frequently seemed to contribute a little something extra to the volatile mix of variables that often played a role in domestic homicides. A husband and a wife in the middle of a fight might resort to blows, or blunt objects, or plates or other dishware, or even kitchen or butcher knives, but only relatively rarely did these weapons — grabbed at random and used in the heat of anger — produce a fatal result.

On the other hand, if a gun in the house came out during an argument, the odds of somebody getting all the way to killed went up significantly.

She didn't buy any argument she'd ever heard for gun control. In her opinion, every law-abiding citizen in the country had an absolute right to bear as many arms as they wanted. But sometimes, as for example this morning with the Rinaldis, she was telling her partner Eisenhower "Ike" McCaffrey that she couldn't help but think that if they hadn't owned a gun, both of the Rinaldis, instead of neither, would in all probability still be alive.

Ike, a forty-two-year-old skinny redhead with an acne-scarred face and pale blue eyes, didn't agree. "No. She just would have stabbed him or clubbed him instead. Once she decided she was going to kill him, she would have found a way."

"Okay, him, maybe. But then done herself?" she asked. "What? Hit herself on her own head with a rolling pin? Stabbed herself in the eye? Come on. All I'm saying is that without the gun, at least she's still alive.

51

Maybe both of them are still alive."

"Yeah, okay. As if being alive is a positive in this case. So this way, one quick and painless shot to her own head and she saves everybody the trouble and expense of a trial. Whereas without the gun, we're talking three squares and a cot for ten years or more, which ain't cheap. So this way, the fact that they owned a gun and that she used it so effectively . . . hey, she saved the state's good taxpayers like a million bucks, maybe more if it turned out she got sick in prison and they had to treat her for some slow degenerative disease instead of just let her die of old age. With dignity of course."

"Of course," Beth said. "Goes without saying, especially from a sensitive soul like yourself."

They were standing on the balcony of the Rinaldis' apartment, four floors above California Street out in the Avenues, not far from Beth's own home on Lake Street. The Crime Scene investigative team was inside, memorializing the apartment where earlier this Friday morning Shannon had apparently first shot Frank in the bedroom and then herself in the kitchen.

The gun still lay on the kitchen floor, several feet from Shannon's body.

Ike took a step over to the sliding door,

glanced around at the inside scene, and came back to his partner. "So what do you say?" Ike asked. "Philosophy aside, we about done here? No question what happened, right?"

"Damn little," Beth said. "Gun violence."

"That, too. But the fight itself?"

Beth thought it was so textbook that it was a cliché. Men who got shot by their women in the bedroom were inevitably unfaithful. "She shoots him in the bed, Ike. We're dealing with symbolism here. Gotta be he was playing around on her and she found out. He's probably calling the girl-friend every half hour. We check his cell phone, you watch, we'll find out the same thing."

"That obvious, you think?"

"Pretty much." Beth shrugged. "Not you, of course, but generally," she said. "Guys are pretty dumb."

But guys, Beth believed, didn't have a monopoly on dumbness. Not even close.

And after her somewhat disturbing discussion on her walk with her best friend Kate just last Tuesday, she took the Rinaldi situation as a case study of what could go wrong with a little bit of symbolic overtone. It wouldn't hurt, and it might actually help, if she passed some of the karma of that case along.

Because sure enough, as she had predicted, Frank Rinaldi's cell phone when they finally got a look at it had a single recurring telephone number that appeared under his "Recents" list roughly a million times in the past month. When Beth punched in that number on Frank's phone at 10:30 that morning, the voice of a young woman answered with the words: "Frank? Where have you been? I've been so worried about you."

After which Beth had introduced herself as a cop and given her the bad news.

Now, atypically shaken after the young woman, Laurie Shaw, had broken down and sobbed for five minutes on the phone, Beth sat at her desk in the wide-open bullpen on the fourth floor of San Francisco's Hall of Justice, holding her phone in her hand. Ike was out picking up Chinese food for lunch, giving her a window of time where she probably wouldn't be bothered, and she was going to take advantage.

Kate sounded upbeat and happy, but after Beth's first couple of syllables of reply, her friend obviously picked up something in her voice.

"What's wrong?" Kate asked. "Something's wrong. Tell me."

Beth sighed, relieved not only at Kate's directness, but — surprisingly — at the opportunity to unburden herself of the load of sadness she'd apparently and all but automatically taken on. "It's just sometimes the world. Or the world I'm in. Not that I haven't asked for it. I'm not saying that. But sometimes it's just so sad."

"What was it today?"

She gathered herself, let out a breath, and started in. "I called this girl about an hour ago because her number was on the cell phone of a man who'd been killed. It turns out he was her boyfriend, and his death just totally destroyed her. He was the love of her life. They were going to get married just as soon as he could break up with his wife —"

"The shithead."

"I know. Really. But in any event, she believed him."

"Of course she did. They always do, don't they? Any kids?"

"No."

"Well, thank God for that."

"Anyway," Beth said, "did I tell you it was the wife who killed him? Shot him in bed, then shot herself."

"My God, Beth. And that's your morning? I don't know how you can stand it. I

55

mean, you see all this in person, don't you? It's not like you hear it on the news."

"No. It's not like that, not even a little. It's a lot more real." Then, delivering her not so subtle message. "People don't seem to realize that this infidelity stuff has consequences."

Kate did not reply.

Beth pressed on. "But anyway, this girl was so sad. It was like the end of her life, too. She couldn't stop sobbing, couldn't believe that this had really happened. I wanted to tell her she might have considered what she was doing before she decided to sleep with somebody else's husband, but she'll come around to realizing that soon enough, I suppose. She didn't need to hear a lecture from me, not now. But she might have thought . . ." She let the sentence hang.

"It's just so sad," Kate said. "And so avoidable."

"Heartbreaking," Beth said. "And now here's my partner showing up with my lunch. Do you want to walk next week?"

"Tuesday?"

"I'll book it. And Kate, thanks for listening. Sorry to lay all this on you."

"Don't even think about that. I love you, you know, and part of why I do is because of how you feel things."

"Love you, too," Beth said. "See you Tuesday."

Peter finally made it out of bed a little before noon.

In an old pair of Dockers and a gray Nike t-shirt, he came down the stairs to an empty house. On the counter in the kitchen, Jill had left him a note that said: "I absolutely forbid you to go into work. I also absolutely love you. There's frittata in the fridge. Love (again), Jill-Bug."

Briefly, he wondered if there was any way she could know. He couldn't imagine how, unless he'd talked in his sleep. But even then he would have plausible deniability. Early in their marriage, she'd called out in the middle of the night a couple of times for Jimmy, one of her former boyfriends with whom she'd ended things long before.

Or — the thought came unbidden and he wondered now, for the very first time — had she, in fact, ended things? Who could say that Jill hadn't cheated on him at some point?

"Right," he said aloud, disgust in his voice. "I'm sure."

He wasn't going there.

And here, almost taunting, right in front of him, was a solution. A pen and a pad of paper. He sat down at one of the counter stools, picked up the pen, pulled the pad close.

No. He couldn't write it.

He would tell her in person. He owed her at least that much. Call her at work right now, ask her to come home, tell her that he would move out, go to marriage counseling, whatever she wanted. He would make it up to her if he could. Somehow. He had no excuse other than he was weak and he had just fucked up. He couldn't ever express to her how sorry he was.

Except that this was not really remotely how he felt. It was the habit, he realized, acquired by living day to day in the shadow of guilt.

Or, of course, he could save everyone from the pain and simply not tell her, ever. Just put the whole sordid, stupid thing behind him. Kate Jameson was never going to be part of his life. She wasn't going to pursue a relationship with him. She'd all but said it. He was positive that she didn't want to ruin her own domestic life any more than she wanted to ruin his. And if neither of them ever talked, and it never happened again, then no one need ever know.

No pain for Jill. That was worth everything all by itself.

But that was another habit. Did he want to live protecting Jill from reality? What about his own happiness, his own needs? What about feeling alive?

And with the silence, after he'd grown accustomed to the silence, he would spend the rest of his days making it up to her. He'd never have to tell her why he had become a better husband, provider, father, lover, person. He would recommit here and now to their new life together. And he would never threaten that again.

But then, of course, the lawyer within him argued, everything would be based on a lie. Could you build a good life on a basic falsehood?

No, you could not. That would be impossible.

He had to tell her. It was the only way.

He got up off the stool and walked over to the phone. He started to punch up Jill's work number, then stopped and put the receiver back down.

Do nothing, he told himself, until he'd considered the consequences, short and long term.

He couldn't make another mistake. He had to think about it some more, make sure he did the right thing. Not ruin everything with one (more) stupid move.

He must avoid resorting to any desperate acts.

Everything depended on that.

Kate and Ron had a tradition on First Fridays that went back to the first weeks after Kate had quit the venture capital day job and now, seventeen years later, the enclosed booth for two at the back of Sam's Grill had their names inscribed on a little brass plaque on the side wall. It was a low-key source of pride for both of them, and when Kate slid into her place, the first thing she did was kiss her fingers, then touch them to the plaque. Ron, sipping from his stemmed martini glass, nodded in acknowledgment, silently letting her know that he'd already performed the same ritual.

Putting down his glass, he asked, "You realize what today is?"

"I need a hint."

"Minor milestone."

"Hmm." Reaching across, she lifted his glass and took a small sip. "How minor?"

"Medium, I'd say. Medium minor. But real nonetheless."

"One more hint."

"Okay. You and me, not the kids."

She sat back, crossed her arms, and put on what she knew was her cute pout. Finally, she met his eyes, lifted her finger, and pointed. "The plaque," she said.

"You are good," he said, impressed. "What about it?"

"Big number anniversary."

Breaking a grin, he nodded in admiration. "Would you believe two hundred?"

"I would," she said, "except I can't believe we're that old."

"Ah, but you forget that time spent at Sam's doesn't make you older, so we save almost half a year right there."

"Well, then, I suppose it is marginally possible, age-wise."

Their favorite waiter in his tuxedo, Stefano, arrived and they placed their order for a half-bottle of Roederer sparkling wine to mark the occasion. When Stefano left, closing the curtain behind him, Kate popped up quickly, leaned across the table, and kissed Ron. "Hi," she said.

"Hi yourself. One more."

"It better be a good one," she said.

He put his hand up behind her neck and held her there a moment. "How was that?" he asked when he let her go.

"Adequate. Quite decent, actually." Smiling, she settled back into her place, indicated the plaque again. "What was your methodology figuring this was number two

61

hundred?"

He smiled back at her. "Do you have any idea how great it is to be out with a beautiful woman who uses the word 'methodology' correctly?"

"Fun?"

"Fun would be part of it, yes."

She had her left hand stretched out along the side of the table and he took it.

"Methodology," she said.

"Coming right up. We start with a few assumptions," he said, and began laying them out for her — averaging twelve lunches a year for six plus years before Sam's had put the plaque up, then eleven years after that, minus about one miss a year due to one thing or another, they were either at two hundred or pretty damn close. "So I say we declare it a minor milestone and celebrate."

"Minor milestone it is."

"And in light of that . . ." He reached down into his jacket side pocket and took out a small maroon felt box, holding it out to her. "To my partner at two hundred First Fridays."

Her eyes glistened as she reached for the box and opened it to reveal a black pearl with a golden chain. She shook her head back and forth. Sighing, she said, "You are too much, you know that? How did I ever get to keep you?"

"Must be clean living." Ron shrugged. "I saw it in a window downtown and it spoke to me. You don't have any other black pearls, do you?"

"You know I don't." She was fastening the chain's clasp behind her neck. "I'm never going to take this thing off."

After lunch, harboring a slight buzz from the sparkling wine, Kate walked around downtown, winding her way among the skyscrapers in the financial district, then at last cutting through the Embarcadero buildings that she knew were home to Peter's firm.

Eventually she found herself at the Ferry Building.

Midafternoon on a warm sunny Friday, the place was alive with sightseeing tourists and locals getting a jump on their weekend gourmet shopping. Kate browsed the aisles at Sur La Table, stopped at booths for extra virgin olive oil, dried mushrooms, locally cured prosciutto. At the Golden Gate Meat Company, by now having defined her mission to make a special dinner by way of thanking Ron again for the black pearl, she picked up a large filet of venison, Ron's favorite. With the blood-rare meat, she'd serve mixed roasted vegetables — carrot, fennel, fingerling potatoes, leek — and a bottle of Silver Oak.

Or, no. Not the Silver Oak.

Given everything, maybe a Bordeaux would be a better choice.

She didn't expect to see Peter here, but the slight possibility lent an edge to the day as she negotiated her way through the milling crowd. Someone who might be him — but turned out not to be — appeared in the periphery of her vision nearly every time she turned a corner; the anticipation at least as powerful as the now-dimming effects of the champagne. All but unaware of it, every couple of minutes she would press her hand to her stomach and reach for a breath.

The Jerusalem artichokes looked excellent, too, and would perfectly complement the other veggies, she thought.

Laden now with her purchases, she headed for the restroom, thinking after that she would go sit outside in the sunshine overlooking the bay and have a cappuccino before Ubering home. But as she turned into the corridor, on the wall she noticed what was probably one of the last public telephones in San Francisco; certainly Kate could not place another one.

In a black tank top and cut-off jeans, a

heavily tattooed and pierced young woman with bright pink hair and a ring in her nose stood with the handset to her ear, her laughter shrill enough to draw disapproving stares from the passersby.

Outside at her tiny table, the coffee was delicious and the weather fine, almost impossibly so, she thought, here right on the edge of the water, where usually an afternoon breeze or, more commonly, afternoon gale, would originate.

While she sipped, one of the ferries arrived and disgorged its load of mostly enthusiastic and happy passengers. Whoever had been at the table next to her had left behind part of a croissant-like something, and suddenly a large seagull swooped down right over Kate's head, grabbed the morsel, and took off, only to be attacked immediately by another pair of birds, with much squawking and avian drama.

At about the same moment, the pink-haired girl who had been using the pay telephone came out of the building. She noticed Kate glancing at her without any sign of judgment and gave her a small acknowledging smile and a nod before she continued out onto the pier, around the corner and out of sight.

Kate savored the last of the coffee, super-sweet with the last of the undiluted sugar. Checking the time, she saw that it was three o'clock, almost exactly the time she had called him yesterday. There was still plenty of time if . . .

The tiny shining bubble of anticipation, barely noticeable when she'd sat down with her coffee, had expanded so that it seemed to fill all that she was made of.

Gathering up her stuff, she pushed back from the table and stood.

She would not call him on her cell phone. That just got too risky. The pink-haired girl finishing up with the pay telephone, on the other hand, just behind her on the wall inside the building, was so obviously a sign that it could not be ignored.

In any event, she could not ignore it.

But she would leave it to fate. If somebody else was using the phone when she got to it . . .

"Hello. Can I please speak to Peter?"

"He's not in the office. May I take a message? Or would you like his voicemail?"

"Do you know how I can reach him?"

"I'm sorry, I don't. But he checks his voicemail frequently. He should get back to you right away."

"All right. Thank you. Voicemail would be fine."

"Just a minute. Here you go."

As soon as he told her hello, Theresa told him that he sounded terrible.

"Thanks," Peter said. "That's nice to hear. I feel like shit, too. No sleep."

"Problems with the depo?"

"I suppose. Anyway, here I am, dutifully checking in. Anything I need to know about?"

"No. It's pretty slow. But have you checked your voicemail?"

"Just before I called you. I didn't have any."

"Hmm. That's funny."

"What?"

"Well, you got a call from a woman asking for you about twenty minutes ago. I put her through to your voicemail. She didn't leave a message?"

"Apparently not. Did she say who she was? What it was about? If it was important."

"No, none of the above, but she sounded a lot like the woman yesterday who said she was a personal friend of yours. You're sure she didn't leave anything on voicemail?"

"I'm sure. Nothing."

67

"Oh, well. If it's important," Theresa said, "I suppose she'll call back."

5

In nothing like their fine and playful moods at lunch at Sam's that day, Ron and Kate waited in the living room for their kids to get in from school. It was a few minutes past six. Kate stood at the wide windows at the front of the house, watching the street through the plantation shades. The sun was low in the west, casting the whole street in a warm yellow glow.

The lovely quality of the light didn't translate indoors.

Ron sat in his reading chair. Kate had come in a minute before and handed him a heavy glass half filled with Scotch, then gone over to look out the front windows.

From behind her, Ron said, "Maybe you should go back out and make another one of these while I pound this one down."

Turning back to him, she said, "Finish that one first, and then we'll talk about the next one." She went over to him, sat on the chair's arm, and fingered the black pearl on her necklace. "I'm still in a bit of awe about this thing, you know," she said.

He looked up. "Changing the subject isn't going to help." He took a good pull of the drink. "Although I'm glad you like it."

"I love it." She put a hand on his shoulder. "And I've got a great dinner planned. We'll be all right."

"Maybe not."

"Of course we will. It's just a client. You've lost clients before."

"Not like this one. Ten million in billings last year, twelve the year before. You don't just make that up in a couple of weeks. And fucking Geoff . . ."

"It's not Geoff, Ron, it's . . ."

"It's fucking Geoff, don't kid yourself. Geoff's still got Tekkei, my fucking client, because it wasn't him that screwed everything up. It was me. Except I didn't screw anything up. I did everything right. Considering what I had to work with — these people just refused to believe that US law forbid what they were doing. I don't give a shit if it flies in Japan or China. Price fixing is a crime here. So considering that, I saved them. It was a resounding success, the best result possible. The best."

"I'm sure it was, Ron, but . . ."

"But meanwhile," Ron on a full-blown rant now, "because of my shame and loss of face, I have to bow to fucking Mr. Hiroshi and tell him I need to resign. When in actual fact I won the goddamn case and kept him personally out of prison. So what if three of his guys are looking at time? It's so much better — two years max — than it could have been on any level. Hiroshi himself was looking at twenty years. And you know who saved his ass? You want to guess?"

"No," Kate said. "I know it was you. Everybody knows it was you."

"Ask Geoff that."

"Geoff knows, too, Ron. He does."

"And what good does that do me? What good does it do us? Geoff should have stood with me and let them go take a flying fuck. Instead, he graciously agrees to take over their representation and just keep me out of it. Oh, and since he'll be putting in the hours on Tekkei and I won't, his points go up and mine go down. And never mind that my compensation tanks and his flies — what the hell do I do with my associates? Or with my own shares, for that matter?"

"What would you expect him to do, Ron? Tekkei is still with the firm, with you guys. Geoff can't give up ten million a year."

"Sure he can! Bina's a bazillionaire on her

71

own. He's still got a great book. He could have stood by me instead of tossing me to the wolves." He took another long drink, finally calming a bit. "Maybe I'll leave the firm. Start up again on my own."

Kate gave his shoulder a buck-up squeeze. "Well, let's see what shakes out," she said. "We don't have to make any decisions today."

Getting up again, she crossed back to the shutters and looked out. "Meanwhile, here are the kids. Finally. Thank God." She paused for a short breath. "I don't think we want to start this out by yelling at Aidan."

"No." Ron tipped up his drink. "God forbid we show any anger at our little fucking darlings when they've helped pretty well shoot this day all to hell."

She shook her head. "It won't help."

"It might. I'd sure like to try it one time and see how it worked. Who knows, maybe we've been doing it wrong all these years with all of our peace, love, and understanding."

"We've been doing fine. Aidan's a good kid. We'll get to the bottom of this. Yelling doesn't teach him anything except how scary you can be."

"How about if I want him to see how scary I can be?"

She crossed to him and went down on her knee in front of him, her hands on his arms, leaned up and gave him a quick kiss. "You don't want that. You want them to love and respect you, and if you yell, they'll just think you're an asshole."

Ron closed his eyes and let out a deep sigh. "I know, I know," he said at last. "Of course we'll be reasonable. Of course we'll discuss everything. But I would so like to get permission to vent once in a while. My dad vented at me all the time."

"And you still think he's an asshole."

"Yeah." He broke a small grin. "But not all the time."

"It'll be all right. You'll see. The firm stuff and this with the kids." She kissed him again and stood up as they heard the back door open behind the kitchen. "Is that both of you?" she called out.

Janey was in eighth grade and the yearbook editor at Holy Name of Jesus, and Aidan was a junior varsity baseball player for the Wildcats at St. Ignatius. Kate and Ron identified themselves as agnostics — neither had gone a day to a Catholic school — but the schools were a good fit for both of the children; both parents agreed that there was no way either of the Jameson kids were going to a public school in San Francisco.

Aidan's voice had dropped most of an octave in the past five months. "Yeah," his voice seemed to reverberate off the walls and hardwood floors.

"Well, before you get comfortable, your father and I would like a word with you."

Another rumble, some mumbling back behind the kitchen, then both the children appeared under the arch leading into the living room, Janey a step behind her big brother but the first to wade right into it. "Hi, guys," she said, all innocence. "What's going on?"

"That's a good question," Ron said. "So good I'll shoot it back at you. Aidan, what the hell is going on?"

"What do you mean?"

" 'What do I mean?' he asks. As if he has no idea. Are you really sure that's the way you want to go with this? Pretending you don't know what this is all about? Because let me tell you up front: we do know."

Ron looked imploringly across at his wife, who picked up the thread. "Father Silas" — dean of men at St. Ignatius — "called your father at work this afternoon, checking to see if you were feeling all right since you hadn't been in school for the last two days.

74

And you weren't answering your cell phone or texts either. Two days, Aidan! What in the world were you thinking? What is going on?"

"Don't be mad at him," Janey said. "It's my fault."

"It's not your fault," Aidan shot back at her. "I did it on my own. It was my decision."

"What's not her fault?" Kate asked. "Aidan, what was your decision?"

"Cutting."

"You cut school? That's the whole answer, you cut school?" Ron asked. "And did what?"

Aidan shrugged. "Just hung out. Drove around."

"Just hung out and drove around? What for?" Ron threw his hands up in front of himself, brought them down, and stared at his son in disbelief. "Do you realize you only have a month or so to go until you're done and school's out for the year? If you fall off the bus now . . . well, you know this is the most important semester if you want to get into college . . ."

"I don't care about college."

"Of course you do," Kate said. "We've all been working toward college for both of you since kindergarten. When did this start?

What is it all about?"

"It's about Mr. Reed," Janey said.

After a long beat, Kate spoke into the silence. "Mr. Reed, your yearbook supervisor? What about him?"

"He's gay, you know."

"Yes, we know that," Ron said. "Or we thought we did. But either way, so what?"

"So what, Dad, is that he's afraid they're going to fire him."

"For being gay? In San Francisco? I don't think so, sweetie. And what's that got to do with Aidan anyway?"

"Mr. Reed is gay and teaching in a Catholic school, Dad, and you know the archbishop's got everybody thinking that's the next step, and you can't blame them. Didn't you read the pastoral letter?"

This was a letter that the archbishop of San Francisco had written a few months earlier to the Catholic high schools in the diocese, reiterating what he believed to be the true teaching of the Church: i.e., it opposed same-sex marriage, homosexuality, birth control, and abortion. The letter specifically forbade educators to "visibly" contradict these teachings, and many believed that this was a thinly veiled threat to dismiss teachers who could not support the Church's stand on these issues.

Ron nodded to his daughter. "Of course, I glanced at it, but it was so reactionary, I couldn't take it very seriously. Really? Gay issues aside, and that's bad enough, but the Church is also against birth control? Still? Your mother and I both thought it was ridiculous. But haven't we all discussed this already back when it was news? And far more than it deserves? Mr. Reed isn't going to get fired, Janey. He'd sue and win, and after all the pedophile stuff, the archdiocese is not going to survive another round of lawsuits."

"And I still don't see," Kate said, "what this has to do with Aidan. Unless . . ." As though coming to some profound under-standing, she brought her hand up and covered her mouth.

"Jesus Christ, Mom!" Aidan exploded. "I'm not gay, all right! Really! Maybe you haven't noticed I've had a girlfriend for the past two years . . ."

"Well, that doesn't necessarily mean . . ."

"It does in this case! Jesus! I'm sure."

"All right, all right, everybody. Calm down." Ron was out of his chair, on his feet. "We're just trying to get to the bottom of this." He faced his son. "Nobody's saying anybody here is gay. And since that's not it, I still don't get what cutting school has to do with anything."

"They're a bunch of hypocritical cretins," Aidan said.

"Who's that again?" Ron asked.

"The teachers, the administration, the whole bunch of 'em. None of them have the guts to stand up on the record and say, 'Hey, we're not on board with this stuff. We're not doing it.' Either that, or they're actually in favor of all this medieval shit. And whichever it is, I don't want any part of it. That just makes me a hypocrite, too. Going to their school."

"That's exactly what I told him," Janey said. "And he decided he had to do something."

"Wait a minute," Kate said. "Did you cut, too?"

"No. But if they fired Mr. Reed, I would."

"She's in eighth grade," Aidan said. "Grade schools didn't get the letter, so there's nothing to react to. But SI is different," Aidan said. "The high schools got the letter and should have blasted back at it, but instead they — or at least *we*, SI — just wimped out. So if I don't want to be associated with that, and I don't, I've got no choice. I've got to quit."

"I think it's the right thing, too," Janey said.

"Well," Ron said, "it's arguable and idealistic, for what that's worth. But what I don't understand is why you didn't come to your mother and me and talk about this. We talk about things in this family, do we not?"

Aidan snorted. "You would have just said don't do it."

"That's so not true," Kate said. "We would have talked about it just like we're talking now."

"And finally decide I shouldn't do anything."

"Or maybe something a little different, maybe that wouldn't make you lose a semester."

"In other words, nothing."

"Not really, no, not nothing. Maybe an open letter of your own to the *Chronicle* or the archbishop. Or we — all of us — could go down to SI and tell the administration that if they don't take a different stand, we're pulling you out of school for your senior year. And that's just off the top of my head. I'm sure we can come up with other options that might work, too. But we can't have you just cutting school and disappearing for a day or two, Aidan. It's too hard on your mother and me. Okay?"

"I don't know, Dad. I don't know what I'm supposed to do."

"Well," Kate said, "we've got the whole weekend coming up. That gives us a little time to figure something out. How about that?"

His face clamped down, Aidan shrugged. "All right, I guess."

"All right, he guesses." Ron's second drink nearly finished, he spoke quietly so that the kids, now off somewhere in the back of the house, couldn't hear. "Give me a break."

"That's just how he saves some face with us."

"Do you think I care if he saves his precious face? This is about where he goes to college, that's what we're talking about. That's the only real issue here. Not whether they fire some teacher because he may or may not be gay. I mean, really? That's an issue? How about the half million or so we've spent on their private educations, so that — follow me here — they have a chance in a mega-competitive world to get into the right college? Haven't we made that pretty fucking abundantly clear by now?"

"They know that, Ron. They know the bottom line."

"Well, I would have said so a few days ago, but now I'm not so sure. Now I see this self-righteous moral posturing and I'm asking

myself, 'These are my kids? Putting everything we've done for them at risk?' Don't
they get it, really?"

"They get it, Ron. They'll come around.
They're trying to do what they think is
right."

"How special for them."

"They'll come around."

"They'd better," he said.

6

Beth found the name Laurie Shaw beneath one of the six mailbox slots just outside the entry to the lobby of the building, a reasonably modern, nicely kept up place on Green Street. She pressed the button over the name and waited.

Laurie was the woman who'd been having an affair with Frank Rinaldi, the murder victim from this morning. Beth knew that although she was nothing like a suspect in the Rinaldi murder-suicide, she had been the victim's lover. As such, suspect or not, an interview with homicide inspectors was definitely in her near future.

Beth knew that what she should have done was call Laurie and invite her down for a nice, cozy interview in a videotaped interrogation room. Two inspectors and a videotape. It's the way things were done. But the case was such a clean murder-suicide that Beth convinced Ike that she could get an interview done with Laurie — check off that box — on her own before dinner.

In fact, she couldn't have elucidated any clear reason why she felt that she wanted to speak personally to this woman, so suddenly bereft. The phone call she'd made that morning, where she had inadvertently been the one to inform Laurie of her lover's death, had stuck with her for the whole day, and some sixth sense told her that the woman might benefit from another woman's empathy. Beth had lost her own husband, Denny, seven years before and knew about the pain of loss.

The buzz sounded. "Yes?"

"Laurie Shaw? Inspector Tully with the police. If you've got a few minutes."

Nothing else came from the squawk box, but the door clicked and Beth pushed her way inside. When the elevator stopped and its door opened, she crossed the hall to number 5 and rang another doorbell.

Laurie was somewhere in her twenties, with oversized blue eyes and a body that bordered on anorexic. She'd obviously been crying. The skin around her eyes was puffed and reddened. Her shoulder-length dark hair was a mess. Barefoot, she wore faded denim jeans and a man's white dress shirt that hung on her.

"Laurie? Inspector Tully. Beth. We spoke on the phone this morning."

Nodding, her face vacant, she pulled the door inside and stepped back.

Beth crossed over into her apartment and followed her down a short hallway that on the right led to a spacious, beautifully appointed living room and a kitchen. The door to the bedroom was open on the left, the bed quite a bit more disheveled than just unmade — blankets and pillows on the floor and piled on the mattress.

Three large windows made up the back wall of the living room — the rear of the building — and looked down on this clear late afternoon over Union Street, then the Marina District, and finally the bay.

In front of Beth, Laurie simply stopped walking and stood facing those windows. Without turning around, she said, "He was moving out this morning. I told him to just stay here with me. We could . . . he could pick up his clothes later. Or just buy new stuff. He didn't believe she would be violent, but she owned her own gun." She turned around. "What does that tell you? You don't own a gun if you're not ready to use it sometime, do you?"

"Did Frank have a gun, too?"

"No way. Frank wouldn't shoot anybody.

84

He thought everybody, including Shannon, was like he was that way." As though the thought must have just occurred to her, she asked, "Do you want to sit down? Can I get you anything?"

"I'm good, thank you." Beth crossed over to the kitchen table and pulled out a chair. "But you go ahead." She watched Laurie cross the kitchen, where she free-poured half a juice glass of vodka from the bottle on the drain, then filled the glass with orange juice from the refrigerator. Turning around, she came back and pulled her own chair out from the table. "I'm drinking," she said redundantly, and took a serious slug, swallowed, shivered, and shook her head. Then, putting the glass down, she broke into tears. "How can Frank be just gone?" she asked between sobs. "How can this be happening?"

Beth found herself getting up and crossing around the table, putting her arms around her. She'd never done anything like that in the whole time she'd been a cop. She'd counseled victims and the families of victims, yes, but never before had it felt so personal. She couldn't figure it out, and somehow it didn't matter. She had felt this woman's pain in their phone call this morning — not that she thought Laurie didn't share some of the blame — and that was enough.

The young woman's arms came up around her. Beth held her and let her cry it out. When she was done, Laurie said, "Thank you. I'm sorry."

"There's nothing to apologize for. You're allowed to cry."

"I don't know what I'm going to do."

"Nobody would expect you to. Do you have someone you can stay with for a while? Or who could stay here? It would probably be better if you weren't alone."

She nodded. "My brother Alan is coming over when he's finished work. He's taking the weekend off."

"Good. That's a good idea."

"Meanwhile, don't you have to ask me questions?"

"I should, yes." Beth took out her tape recorder.

"So how am I supposed to help you?" Laurie asked.

The doorbell interrupted her.

"That'll be Alan." Laurie walked back down the hallway to buzz her brother in. Beth heard some muffled words, another small sob, then a male's deep, consoling voice. She stood up and turned around as they came out of the hall and Laurie introduced them.

Alan appeared to be in his late thirties, quite a bit older than his sister. He was a big man — six feet four or five. His hand completely enclosed Beth's when he shook it, but though his palms were rough, his touch was gentle. His words when he heard she was from Homicide, however, were not. "I'm sorry, but I'm afraid I don't really get why you need to be here."

"I was just in the process of trying to explain that to your sister."

"Did you mention to her that when she talks to cops, she ought to have a lawyer?"

"Alan! She's —"

He held up a hand, cutting his sister off. "She's a cop, Laurie. There's her tape recorder. She's not here on a social call. I promise you."

Beth spoke up. "Laurie's not a suspect in her boyfriend's murder, sir. I'm interviewing her as a witness. She's not under investigation."

"But you just have a few questions. Is that it?"

"Yes, I do." Beth blew out in frustration. This was why, she knew, you didn't vary the protocol. Whatever your motivations, they were misunderstood. "I haven't asked her any questions yet, other than how she's holding up. I just want to establish what we both know to be true — that she had a relationship with Frank Rinaldi that might have played a part in this incident. I thought it would be easier on her, under the circumstances, to talk to her here rather than ask her to come down to the Hall of Justice. That's all."

Laurie said, "Alan, she's not interrogating me. She really just wanted to make sure I was okay. Please, Beth, just stay another few minutes. Ask your questions. I'm so glad you came by. I don't want you to feel like I'm throwing you out."

Beth looked from one sibling to the other. "Well, one way or the other, Alan, Laurie is involved in a murder-suicide. So you can see that there are questions that are going to get asked. But I really did come here because when I talked to her on the phone this morning, she sounded really upset. And I thought that under the circumstances, this would be easier than some of the other options."

"That's the truth," Laurie said. "You need to apologize."

Alan still didn't look like he bought it. "I'm sorry, but you don't hear too often about cops making condolence calls."

"It doesn't happen every day," Beth said.

"Laurie's situation here struck me as just particularly tragic. So I thought she could probably use a little support."

"Well, you'll pardon me for being protective of my little sis."

"Of course. Truce?" She put out her hand and he took it.

Again, gently.

7

Jill's book club had been meeting on the usually inconvenient Friday night once a month for more than five years, and the meeting night wasn't going to change now. Tonight, because Peter had had such a hard time yesterday — couldn't eat, couldn't sleep, obviously working too hard — she offered to stay home if he felt he needed the company. She would make him a strong martini, cook him dinner, open a good bottle of wine.

"No. Get out of here. Have fun. I've just got some low-grade thing. I'll probably be in bed by eight."

After she left, he ate take-out Chinese with the desultory twins. Tyler and Eric, until recently his golden boys, were the enemy camp. He was seeing them now with unblinkered realism. Both of them were entitled slackers — although Eric was worse than Tyler — who with their incessant needs had robbed him of so much of his emotional, not to say sexual, life with his wife. The pathetic truth, which he'd somehow come to accept as his lot in life, was that Jill only had time for him when everything was peachy with the boys.

Which was almost never.

To say nothing of the unending financial drain — about to get much worse since they were starting college in a few months — that would eat up eighty grand after-tax dollars a year minimum for the next four years.

Shit. It was unbelievable. When he was eighteen — their age — he moved out of his parents' house and never looked back. Paid for his own college, did ROTC, went to war, got his law degree, all on his own dime.

Every part of that was a foreign concept to these spoiled rotten kids.

But if he called them on their bullshit, it would only lead to conflict, to an argument. And he just didn't have the energy. Or, he suddenly felt, the will. He didn't really care, didn't want to get into anything unpleasant, so he kept his tone civil. "So where are you guys off to tonight?"

Both of them doing the eye roll thing with each other. As if he wasn't even there, as if he couldn't see it. But he pushed on. "I've got a dead night since Mom's got her book club. I thought maybe we could all go out and catch a flick."

"A flick?" Eric said, setting a new record for derision in two words.

"Uh, it's Friday, Dad," Tyler said, trying to undo some of the damage. "We were just going to hang."

" 'Hang' doesn't really tell me much," he said.

"You know," Tyler said, "just with the guys."

Peter didn't know. He didn't have a clue. But he kept up the front, mild and understanding. They'd go do what they did, which would probably be stupid and perhaps dangerous, but nothing he could do would stop them. "Sure," he said. "I just thought. No big deal."

Ten minutes later they were gone.

In another life that suddenly felt like very long ago he'd been reading and as far as he remembered very much enjoying a book called *Stuff Matters*. It was right where he'd left it on the table next to his reading chair in the living room, but now when he picked it up and leafed through it, he had no idea how much he'd read, where he'd stopped, anything. He looked at the front cover for a minute, read over the flap copy on the back.

Had he actually started it? It seemed impossible.

His next stop was in front of the television, where he might be able to kill a couple of hours, and perhaps deaden his mind, watching a ball game. The Giants were playing the Cardinals at AT&T Park and he normally loved listening to the banter between Kruk and Kuip, but after half an inning, he shut off the damn thing, went up to his bedroom, stood there flat-footed and empty-brained for some immeasurable time, then turned around, went down the stairs, grabbed a jacket from the hall closet, and walked out the front door and into the night.

McCarthy's in West Portal wasn't more than half a mile from Peter's house in Saint Francis Wood. He had passed by it a hundred times but hadn't been inside in years, ironic because as soon as he opened the door, he remembered it as his kind of place, or at least the kind of place he'd frequented, often with Jill, when they were younger.

Prime time on Friday night, people packed all the tables and crammed the bar. Peter stood just inside the door, wondering if he should just turn around and try another watering hole. Before he'd moved, though, a burly, bearded guy right in front of him pushed back from his place at the corner of the bar and stood up. Turning, he saw Peter standing there and made an extravagant gesture, offering up his seat. "Kept it warm for ya."

"Thanks."

Taking the stool, Peter shrugged out of his jacket, draped it behind him, and suddenly the bartender was in front of him. The ball game he'd turned off at home was playing on three of the television sets to the accompaniment of Dire Straits, loud but not ear-splitting.

He ordered Hendrick's gin on the rocks.

Next to him, a husky female voice insinuated itself just above the music. "I don't know Hendrick's. I can't believe it's better than Sapphire."

He turned his head, noticing her for the first time. "Maybe not better," he said, "but different for sure. Roses and cucumbers."

"Sorry?"

"The botanicals they use," he said. "Hendrick's is all rose petals and cucumbers. The Sapphire is all about the juniper. You taste them together, it's pretty obvious."

"Rose petals? Really?"

"Really."

"I've got to try myself some of that while the night's young and I can still taste it."

94

The bartender was coming back toward them. He placed Peter's drink in front of him.

"Stan," she said, pointing at his glass. "You want to mix one of those up for me, too? Hendrick's." She met Peter's eyes. "Rocks, or up?"

"Good either way."

She nodded to the bartender. "Stan, you decide." Placing her Sapphire drink in the bar's gutter, she said, "but let's hold onto that if the Hendrick's doesn't work out." She came back to Peter. "I can't let myself forget the basic problem with gin."

"What's that?"

"Same as with breasts," she said. "One is not enough and three is too many."

Peter chuckled. "I've noticed that."

"You've known women with three breasts?"

Now he laughed. "No. I didn't mean that. I meant three is too many gins. Although, I suppose, that goes for breasts, too, of course, now that you mention it."

She made a small show of looking down at herself, one side then the other. There was plenty to see on both sides. "Whew," she said, and they both laughed.

She put out her hand. "Diane."

8

Geoff and Bina Cooke had no children and had evolved as a couple to where they either went nearly every night to something culturally rewarding — live music, theater, the opera, a lecture, occasionally a movie — or they dined in or out with friends.

To keep this organized lifestyle humming along, early on in their marriage, in fact within a couple of months after Bina's miscarriage, they began scheduling a semi-formal meeting for the two of them at their Pacific Heights home for Saturdays at lunchtime. This was their time together every week, almost invariably preceded by sleeping in (9:00 a.m.!) and then making love. After that, they were out of bed, dressed, and ready for business by noon. This schedule had served them well now for over ten years — it wasn't broken, and they weren't going to spend any time trying to fix it.

Now — a rare treat in warm, windless sunshine — they sat outside at their picnic table on the glass-enclosed deck that looked over the Marina District, the bright sparkling bay and Marin County in front of them, the Presidio and Golden Gate Bridge off to the left. On the table were bagels, three kinds of smoked salmon, cream cheese, capers, thinly sliced red onions, fresh squeezed pineapple-orange juice, and a Keurig coffee machine. They'd already scheduled the coming week, and it looked to be a great one — Yoshi's had Norah Jones coming in, Isabelle Allende was speaking at the Commonwealth Club, they had a wine-pairing dinner at Piperade. The magic that was San Francisco went on and on, into the next week, and now finally they were talking about Friday night two weeks hence.

"Is it too soon to redo last week with Ron and Peter?" Geoff asked. "It will have been three weeks by then, and last time seemed to be an absolute home run."

"It was, I agree. But I don't know if I told you that I heard from Kate last week when she called to thank me and she insisted that next time we all get together at her house."

"Did she have a date in mind?"

"She didn't mention one."

"Well," Geoff said, "snooze, you lose.

97

Maybe Peter and Jill would want to go out someplace. Just the four of us."

"We could do that, but I'd feel bad not including Kate and Ron. Especially after she kind of went out of her way to say how much she liked them. She even asked for their number. So I thought she'd be putting something together with all of us pretty soon."

"And yet she has not done so."

"And yet she has not."

Geoff sighed. "I suppose it's not the end of the world to leave a few open dates. Maybe I should try to get a tee time tomorrow and see if Peter's free."

"You like that guy."

"I do."

"Okay. How about this? Maybe I'll just call Kate and tell her we don't mean to be pushy, but we really would like to get everybody together again, so we're planning another dinner Friday after next, and if she wants to overrule me and have it at her place, she can. But if not, we would love it if they could come."

"An elegant solution, Bean" — his term of endearment for her — "and worth a try. But let's check with Peter and Jill first, make sure that day works for them. How's that sound?"

■ ■ ■

"Hey, babe." Jill lowered herself onto the bed and leaned over, barely whispering. "Are you awake?"

Peter rolled over and his head appeared out from under the blankets. "What time is it?"

"About one o'clock. The boys are making some deli sandwiches, and since they're your favorite . . ."

"I'll get up."

"What time did you finally get to sleep?"

"I don't know. Two or three, somewhere in there."

"I'm starting to worry about you."

A mirthless chuckle. "Join the club."

"Do you know what this is about?"

"I wish. Something subconscious." Subconscious, my ass, he thought. He knew pretty damned exactly what it was, but he wasn't about to fall into her trap again, where she was kind and understanding and forgiving and he would apologize and amend his behavior to avoid any marital unpleasantness. Or spontaneity. Or fun. "Maybe work, but I can't figure out what exactly."

"Not us? You're sure?"

He reached out and put his arm around her. "Nothing to do with us."

"I mean, if there's anything you need me to do . . ."

"It's not you, hon. I promise. Just a particularly nasty bout of insomnia."

"This from Mr. Fall Asleep Anywhere Anytime."

"Maybe not so much anymore. Although I wouldn't mind having that fall-asleep guy come back. I miss the hell out of him."

She hesitated a moment. "When you weren't here when I got home, and no note, no nothing, I was worried sick."

Here it comes, he thought. The Third Degree. He sighed. "I didn't know I was going to be out so long. I just needed to get out of the house and started walking. Next thing I know I'm at McCarthy's, then it's midnight. Then it closes. I'm so sorry. I should have called or something. I don't know what happened."

"So. What? You blacked out?"

"No. I don't literally mean I don't know what happened. I didn't black out. I watched the game, had a couple, talked to some guys. Maybe had a couple more, thinking they'd help me sleep. And we know how well that worked."

She sighed. "It makes me uncomfortable,

you feeling like you have to leave the house. I don't know what that means."

"It doesn't mean anything. It's just something that happened."

Normally he showered in under five minutes, but today, after a tense and quiet lunch with the rest of the family, he let the water run down on him until it turned cool. Stepping out, he dried off and, tying the towel around him, went back into his bedroom to find Jill seated there by the door in what she called her book chair, though she didn't have any reading material in her hands. Instead, she had her arms crossed and was staring down at the floor.

"Hey," he said.

She almost swallowed her response. "Hey."

He sat on the bed across from her. "Are you all right?"

She took a deep breath, glanced up at him, then looked back down.

"Jill?"

After a long moment, she said, "Did you hear the telephone ring while you were in the shower?"

"No. Who was it?"

"Jerry Hobbs. He said he needed to talk to you about one of your cases."

"Today?"

"That's what he said."

"Okay. I'll give him a call."

Jill went back to studying the floor.

"Is that it?" he asked. "Is something wrong?"

She brought her eyes up and looked at him. "I don't want to be a nag, Peter, but yes, I think something is wrong. Clearly something is wrong. Look at how you've been the last couple of days. You don't have to say anything." She held up her hand. "After I told him — Jerry, I mean — that you were in the shower and couldn't talk at the moment, I mentioned that I'd heard that congratulations were in order and he asked me what I meant. So I reminded him of the bottle of Silver Oak that he'd broken out on Thursday after settling whatever it was. But he just laughed and said that must have been another Jerry because it definitely hadn't been him." Leveling her gaze at him, she asked, "What the hell is going on, Peter? Why did you lie to me?"

It took him a long moment to respond. This was his opportunity, he knew. He could just tell her that he'd had enough of the way he'd been living, of the flat suburban nature of their lives together. A stone had been turned deep in his soul. He'd been unfaithful to her now, twice in two days, and in his heart he didn't care what she felt about it. He could tell her now and everything would change.

But glancing at her face, expectant and fearful, he couldn't yet make that sudden leap. He did not picture himself a cruel man. He didn't want to hurt her, and he didn't have the simple energy to go through it all now. So he took the easy way, the usual path. The convenient lie. "I guess I just . . ." He hesitated again. "Maybe it's just that I didn't want you to know that I'd been drinking during the afternoon at work."

"*Maybe* that's it? You don't know for sure?"

"No. That's it for sure."

"You drank a bottle of wine at work?"

"Most of it, yes."

She nodded as she took in this information. "Has this been going on for a while? Are you telling me you're an alcoholic? Do you think you need to get into some program? How much did you drink last night?"

"I don't know. Six or eight gins, maybe a couple more."

"More than eight?"

"I don't know. I didn't count them. And I knew I wasn't driving. It's not like it's every day. It's just sometimes when I get started . . ."

"You don't stop."

Peter looked down in chagrin. "I didn't want this to be something you had to deal with. I've been working on it on my own."

"Peter. Listen to yourself. You're saying you had a whole bottle of wine on Thursday." Her voice now had taken on equal parts of its usual reason and sympathy. "And eight or more gins last night. Is that what you mean by working on it? And if it is, I'd have to say it sounds like it's not working."

Their eyes met.

Peter wasn't going to be able to take much more of this. He was no more an alcoholic than he was the Queen of Sheba. But until he was ready to tell her the truth, he thought, let her think alcohol was the problem. That would cover a multitude of sins.

He was the first to look away.

He answered all of Jerry's legal queries on the phone, but when he hung up, it was a believable and simple excuse, so he told Jill that there was a small crisis at work and he had to go down to the office for a while — probably not more than a couple of hours.

The main thing was to get away again.

Away from the house and Jill and the boys. When they'd all been eating lunch together, he'd found himself growing not more guilty and ashamed as he might have expected, but increasingly angry at the judgment he knew lay dormant in the hearts and minds of his family.

How dare they?

So he told his wife another lie — easier than the one before — and got in his Z3 and put the convertible top down and backed out of his driveway and drove a half a mile to Diane's apartment building, where he pulled over to the curb across the street and kept watch over the entrance for five long minutes. It was a little before 3:00, another atypically warm day, and the sun beat down, glaring off the street and the cars around him. He put on his sunglasses, then a Giants cap, and sat there in the sun.

At last, he unclipped his cell phone and put in a call to Jerry Hobbs, whom he knew would still be at the office. "Hey, dude," he said. "I've got a favor to ask. I'm out trying to buy a surprise present for my lovely bride, and to do so I had to make up a reason to get out of the house, so I told her I was going in to work for a couple hours. But it's not impossible that she might try to reach me on the office line. And if she does,

105

I wanted to ask you if you would pick up and tell her I'm in the bathroom or something, then call me on my cell so I can call her back."

"I could do that. But why would she call you?"

"I don't know. She probably won't, but she might want me to pick up some groceries on the way home or something. It's been known to happen. So I can count on you?"

"Done. Of course. Hey, by the way, who was the Jerry you had the Silver Oak with the other day?"

Peter forced a chuckle. "I have no idea where she got that."

Jerry either did not notice that this was no answer or chose not to pursue it. "Because if you are opening fine wine in the office, I know somebody who'd be happy to share."

"You're the first one I'd call, Jerry. Really. If that ever happens."

"So what are you going to get her?"

Peter almost asked, "Who?" but caught himself in time. "Probably something in a little fuzzy box. That usually seems to do the trick, present wise."

"You're making the rest of us cheap husbands look bad. You know that?"

"Not my fault. You guys just need to step it up a bit. So . . . you got the phones?"

"Roger."

"All right. Thanks. See you Monday."

Closing the phone up, he sat back, squinted into the sun, and let out a breath.

Another lie.

He glanced again over at the building across the street. Diane's apartment was on the third floor facing the street, and in the window he saw a shadowy movement.

She was home.

But then he realized he hadn't driven here to see her again. Last night, Diane had been a substitute for the real thing. Pressing the Start button, he pulled away from the curb and took a right at the first corner. Twelve minutes later, he found a parking space on Washington Street near Fillmore.

He put up the top of his car, got out, and took his bearings.

The Jameson house was on the other side of the street, five driveways down. He and Ron had exchanged contact information at Geoff's place last week, and armed with his phone number, Peter had no trouble finding the address from the reverse directory when he'd gotten back to the office after the tryst.

Hands in his pockets, his baseball cap and sunglasses still on, he strolled down his side of the street past the large, well-maintained, two-story Victorian that looked all closed up — window blinds down, darkness within. When he got to the end of the block, he turned and retraced his steps. But this time, he stopped directly across from Kate's address and leaned up against a convenient mailbox, arms crossed.

"Can I help you?"

He jumped at the intrusion.

"Oh, I'm sorry. I didn't mean to startle you."

He held his hand over his heart and broke a small, embarrassed smile. "That's okay. When my heart starts beating again, I'll probably be all right."

She was a well-preserved, attractive woman of indeterminate age. "You looked like you were looking for something."

"Just scouting the block, hoping one of the properties might look like it's coming up for sale," he told her. "But I don't suppose these houses turn over too often, do they?"

"Not too, I'm afraid. It's a lovely street, isn't it?"

"Beautiful." He offered her another smile. "Well, I guess I'll keep looking."

"Good luck. It's a little bit of a tough market nowadays."

"I'm getting that picture, but we'll find

something, I'm sure. Have a nice day."

"You, too."

Shaking, his heart pounding, another lie notched in his belt, he made it back to his car. He hadn't even heard her coming up behind him. She could have been anybody. Even Kate. And for that he would have been completely unprepared.

What was he doing here?

9

The school crisis with Aidan kept Kate distracted over the weekend.

She and Ron weren't about to have their son jeopardize his otherwise excellent chances to get into one of his chosen colleges — he had a 4.3 grade point average and was thinking at the Stanford, USC, Princeton level — by dropping out of school with less than a month to go in the last semester of his junior year. On the other hand, they both professed to be very proud of him for his principled stand. They made it a point to tell Janey that they were proud of her, too, for prodding Aidan into taking the big step.

They weren't as delighted with the fact that the kids had gone out on their own and kept all these decisions from them.

In any event, by Saturday morning, she and Ron had decided that they needed to shake up their scheduling to underscore the seriousness of the situation. Their kids were the priority. Always, always, always. Therefore, they would put everything else on hold for the weekend and take off to the small town of Occidental, up in the redwoods, where they would eat large quantities of Italian food at one of the family-style restaurants there and come to some decisions about how they would handle the situation.

That's the way the Jamesons did things: as a family, working together, talking things out, coming to an enlightened consensus.

On Sunday night, in their bedroom, Ron asked her, "So what do you think? Was that worthwhile?"

"Definitely. It will at least keep him in school until the end of the semester and buy some time. Then if it comes to it, he transfers out next year, but he's still covered with his applications. Plus, I'm proud of you, too."

"What for?"

"I think it's pretty brave of you to volunteer to go talk to Father Silas."

Ron shrugged. "He's a reasonable guy. My guess is he considers that pastoral letter bullshit, too. I flatly can't believe that in this town they would even make a small move toward firing any teacher for being gay. Or for preaching tolerance. But they've got to pretend they're on board with all this mumbo jumbo so they don't piss off the archbishop. It's a thin line and Silas is probably trying to walk it."

"And we know Aidan will be able to make up the missed days and work?"

"It's only two days, and there's no reasonable doubt about that."

"Says the lawyer."

"Well, yes, I will certainly make an impassioned argument on that score. And God knows, beyond that, we've given that school enough money . . ."

"Maybe it's not that."

Ron frowned. "Don't kid yourself. It's at least some of that. And maybe this is a blessing in disguise after all. If Janey also wants to opt out of Catholic education for high school, it's probably worth looking into. And it could even save us a bundle, which we might wind up needing in a big way if we restructure the firm."

"Which is not —"

He held up a palm to stop her. "Plus," he said, "last but not least, that was kind of fun up there in the redwoods. It does us all a world of good to get out of the city now and then, don't you think?"

"I do. Except I think I must have put on

five pounds in lasagna and cannoli."

"Well, if you did, they went to all the right places." He patted the bed. "Why don't you come on over here and we can check it out, see where everything settled."

The next morning, the family was up early and ate breakfast together. Aidan was back to his routine, taking Janey to school and then driving himself to SI. Ron had his appointment with Father Silas. Kate had a hair appointment at 11:00.

As she rinsed the dishes, she was humming Pharrell Williams's maddeningly addictive song "Happy." The fog was socking in the backyard out the kitchen window.

Life was back to normal.

All that other madness last week. What had that been about? What had she been thinking?

"Hello."

"Hello, Kate."

He didn't have to identify himself. It could not have been anyone else.

She went silent, then reached over and put the handheld wall phone's receiver back into its place above the kitchen counter, cutting off the call.

In under a minute, the goddamned thing

jangled again.

Once. Twice.

She picked up, unable to form any words.

"Kate? Are you there?"

Finally. "How did you get this number?"

"Your husband gave it to me at Geoff's."

"You can't call here. This is my home."

"All right. I won't call there again. Give me your cell, then."

"You can't . . . I can't . . ."

"Sure we can. We have."

"That's not funny."

"I wasn't trying to be funny."

Another silence.

"Kate? Are you still there?"

"I'm here." A breath. "What do you want, Peter?"

"I think that ought to be obvious. I want to see you. Or at least talk to you."

"We're talking now."

"Not like this."

Her phone's receiver had a coiled cord that unraveled to twelve feet, and now Kate stepped away from the counter and turned, wrapping herself in it, then turning again, releasing her. This took time. At the end of which, she said, "Peter, listen. I thought we decided that we weren't going to do this."

"And what is it we were not doing?"

"Anything else. We had the one time and

114

that would be that."

"We decided that? I don't remember deciding that. Didn't you call my office on Friday?"

No reply.

"Didn't you?"

"Yes."

"All right, then, what was that about?"

"I don't know. I wanted to hear your voice. I wanted to see you."

"But you don't now?"

She didn't answer. Finally, she said, "It's different."

"What's different?"

"Everything."

He broke a brittle little laugh. "At least we agree on that."

"I don't mean it the way you do."

"So how do you mean it? Everything being different?"

"I don't . . . I just . . . I think it was a mistake."

"Then it was a mistake on Friday, too? Calling me. So now, suddenly, it's Monday and let's forget all that?"

"Yes. I'm afraid so. Yes."

"How about if I can't do that? If I don't want to do that?"

"Peter . . ."

"So what happened over the weekend?

Where did you go, by the way?"

She took a moment. Then, "How do you know I went anywhere?"

"I know you weren't home."

"You didn't try calling here, did you? God, tell me you didn't leave a message on voicemail."

"No." He paused. "I walked by."

"You walked by my house?"

"A couple of times. Saturday and again on Sunday."

"Oh my God, Peter. What were you thinking?"

"I was thinking I wanted to see you. Not really visit. Just get a glimpse."

"At my house? Not at my house!"

"I wasn't going to knock at the door or anything like that. I just wanted to see you again."

"Shit, Peter, shit. How were you going to see me if you didn't knock or anything like that?"

"I didn't think it out. I thought if I was just there, in the course of your day you might come out. And frankly, I don't see a big difference between that and you calling me on Friday. I thought after Thursday, I don't know, we were in each other's orbit somehow."

"That was never the plan, Peter. It was

116

just a thing."

"And now it's not?"

"I didn't mean for it to hurt anybody. I mean you especially."

"Past tense already? Just like that?"

"I don't know what else to say. I'm sorry." She waited a moment. When Peter didn't speak, she said, "I'm going to hang up now."

And she did.

"You can't just . . ." he finally said.

But she was gone.

Peter, his knuckles white gripping the receiver, looked down at it until he heard the dial tone kick in, and then he placed it back in the cradle and let go of it.

He was sitting with his back straight on the front half of his chair behind the desk in his office, his hands now clasped in front of him. The door to the room was closed, and he'd even thrown the deadbolt to make sure Theresa or someone else couldn't barge in unannounced during the call. Behind him the fog clung to the enormous windows, obscuring the world around and beneath him.

This was unacceptable.

Kate had upended his world, his entire vision of who he was. Because of her — or the changes she'd forced him to acknowledge in his psyche — he had put his family and possibly even his career in jeopardy. Had it all really been nothing but a whim on her part? How could he have let her have that much power?

He cast a glance at the telephone as though it might somehow be a living thing. Reaching out, he put his hand on the receiver yet again. He knew, though, that if he reached her, she would simply refuse to talk to him, probably would hang up immediately. Beyond that, he had nothing more, nothing different, to say.

He stood up and crossed over to the windows, looking out and down into the enveloping whiteness. Turning around, his eyes came to rest on the framed photograph of Jill and the boys on his desk. The shot was unfeigned, the three of them goofing around, their faces alight with joy, all wrapped in each other's arms on the beach in Kapalua. Peter had taken the picture three years ago, over the Thanksgiving vacation, and at the time it had seemed to capture the very essence of who they all were — solid, together, trusting, happy.

If he, in so many ways, did not belong in that picture, at least he had been comfortable, complacent, generally satisfied with his life. Most of the time.

He walked over, closer, and picked up the frame. He had always found Jill's smile particularly attractive. But looking at that smile now, he felt nothing but sadness and — worse — pity. What he had done would destroy her if she ever found out, and yet he knew that if he managed to keep it hidden from her, he would never be able to think of her in the same way again. She would be someone he was able to fool, to make a fool of.

In fact, she already was that person.

Staring at that smile, frozen in time, he realized that it was already too late. He would never truly love her again. Not as his equal; not as his partner in life. The bare fact that she might never know what he'd done, might never figure it out, in a fundamental way diminished her.

This was unfair to her, of course, but what could he do? He felt the truth of it in his gut.

And what of the boys?

In a sudden fury, he threw the picture down and it exploded on the floor.

He was still standing over the wreckage when Theresa tried the doorknob and, finding it locked, knocked on the door. "Peter, are you all right?"

"Just a second." He glanced at his desktop

119

and moved a prop or two. Then, stepping around the broken glass, he got to the door and opened it. "I'm such a klutz," he said.

"What happened?"

"I pushed a binder out of my way on the desk and wasn't paying attention, and it knocked my favorite picture off."

"Don't worry about that. We can get it reframed, good as new. Are you all right? You look like a ghost."

He shook his head. "Just pissed off." Letting out a deep breath, he said, "Sorry. It's been a tough couple of days. And now this."

"There's nothing to apologize about. Not to me, anyway. Let me call the janitor and get that stuff all picked up. Meanwhile, why don't you take a break? I can get you some coffee."

"That might be nice. Thanks."

But she hesitated, shifted her weight from one foot to the other. "Not to be nosy," she asked, "but is this connected to that personal matter you've been dealing with? The woman?"

He flashed her a quick smile. "No. God forbid you're nosy. She's a family friend. It's not that." He gestured to his desk. "It's all this." Then, "Why would you think it's the woman?"

"I don't know. You locked your door, for

one thing, which you never do."

"I just wanted to discourage interruption. I'm a lot more behind than usual."

She held up her hands. "No judgment. Just sayin'. But in all seriousness, maybe you need to take a break. A real break, Peter."

"Yes, well, you may remember I took off all of last Friday, which just means I was a day further behind when I came in today. It'll pass. I'll get it all done."

"There's never a doubt about that, but you really seem a little bit burned out, and I worry."

"That's why you're the world's best secretary. I'm fine, I promise."

"All right. But I'll be watching you. Meanwhile, janitor and coffee. And don't step on the broken glass."

10

Tuesday, a reversion to pure winter.

The June fog, two weeks early, blanketed the city and knocked the temperature down to the low fifties. With the wind chill, the "real feel" was 41.

Kate and Beth didn't make it much beyond their first turn off Washington north onto Fillmore when a couple of biting gusts cut through them and they decided to turn around and give today's walk a pass. Instead, Beth suggested that they take her car and drive down to the Ferry Building, where they could pick up some specialty groceries and then get a light lunch at the Market Café. Kate, who had after all just been to the same location four days ago — it was where she'd placed that stupidly spontaneous last call to Peter Ash — nevertheless didn't want to have to explain her reluctance to go there again, so she agreed.

By 11:00, the women had finished their

shopping and were sitting at a warmish inside booth at the Market Café, their coffees on the table in front of them. All of the other seats in the restaurant were taken as well. Though it wasn't as crowded inside the main building as it had been on Friday afternoon, the place was still filled to near capacity with shoppers and tourists.

Peter waited until it was nearly lunchtime before he got up and told Theresa that he was going down to the Ferry Building for lunch and he'd be back in an hour. He'd come in early to catch up on the work that he'd been all but ignoring, but he had accomplished essentially nothing, whipping his frustration into a near frenzy.

Five minutes after he'd left his office, he arrived at his destination, entering by the northern doorway, and though it was cold and blustery, he stopped to get an ice-cream cone — salted caramel had become the world's ubiquitous flavor in the past year or so, not long enough ago that he'd been able to develop a resistance to it. Savoring the taste, he strolled out to the deck area that looked out over the ferry landing gate and the bay.

The ice cream slowed him down and while he ate it, some of the edge seemed to come off the low-level panic with which he'd been living since he'd left the hotel and Kate.

He took a breath, let it out slowly. He could beat this thing, he thought. Just put it behind him. Chalk it up to boredom. Temptation was sometimes irresistible, and he'd given in to it once, then again. But that could stop. He could make it stop. It didn't have to defeat him.

Last night at home had been proof of that. They'd all sat down to dinner together, him and Jill and the boys, and they'd talked about the Giants and school and the movie *Interstellar* and afterwards, when the kids had gone out, he had helped Jill with the dishes and then they sat next to each other on the loveseat for two episodes of *Blue Bloods,* to which they were addicted. He'd had a couple of glasses of wine, and nobody had said a word about alcoholism. They had made love, and he'd thought neither of Kate nor Diane until they were done. But then, almost immediately he'd fallen asleep. No stress, no drama. That could be his life again. He could reclaim it.

Finishing the ice cream, he threw his wrapper in a trash can and wandered outside down the back of the building until he came to Sur La Table, where he decided to stop in to see if he could find some kind of

124

knickknack that Jill would like for the kitchen. After a couple of minutes, he walked out into the main pavilion with a small low-tech vacuum device that promised to keep opened wine fresh for weeks.

Crossing the hall and looking in at the Market Café for a free table, he saw Kate — unmistakably Kate — against the back wall and sitting sideways to him, talking animatedly to another woman. Thinking that this must be a cosmic existential test of some kind, he steeled himself and kept walking until he was outside again, at the far end of the building, then across the Embarcadero and on his way downtown.

Kate and Beth had already covered the drama with Kate's kids and the archdiocese, and after a short lull, Beth drew in a breath and started in on another topic. "So there is one kind of weird thing happening with me," she said. "Do you remember that girl I told you about on Friday? The one who got involved with Frank Rinaldi, which in turn got him shot by his wife? Her name is Laurie Shaw."

"Sure. I remember. I think that's maybe the first time you've ever really talked about actual details of your work with me. What about her?"

"Well, it's not so much her, as she's got a brother."

"She was sleeping with her brother, too?"

Beth laughed out loud. "No. She was not sleeping with her brother. But she was so upset when I called her on Friday that I went by her place as much to see if she needed anything as to get her statement. I thought maybe she could use some help with coping. Or maybe I could recommend a professional. Anyway, somebody to help her get through this."

"You are such a nice person."

Beth shrugged. "I don't know about that. In any event, there was no question of her being a suspect — the Rinaldis were a definite murder-suicide, and she was just this poor mixed-up woman who'd made a bad decision and now she believed — and she wasn't all wrong — that she was responsible for her boyfriend's death. Anyway, long story short, I went by to see her when I got off on Friday, and I'm there about fifteen minutes when her big brother, Alan, shows up. Did I say 'big'?"

"I believe you did."

"He is. Big as Denny was."

"And?"

"And, we didn't start out so great — he didn't like that I was there to question

126

Laurie about the murder. But by the end, I'd been there an hour and we were all just talking and getting along and he wound up asking me if I had a card. Which of course I did. Anyway, bottom line is he called me on Sunday and it looks like we're going out tonight."

"Tonight? Moving fast."

"Well, I don't know. We'll see. But it was just so strange how the whole thing came about. He's over there to take care of his sister, and I just happen to be there, too. And the next thing you know, no effort on my part, I've got my first romantic date in years. How does that happen?"

"Karma. A good sign, anyway. What's he do?"

"Construction, I think. Something physical anyway. Salt-of-the-earth guy."

"Very cool, Beth. That's perfect for you, since you're a pretty salt-of-the-earth person yourself."

"Well, I'm trying not to load too much expectation onto it. I mean, it's one night, and speaking of which . . . ?"

"What?"

" 'What?' she asks." Beth lifted her cup and sipped. "I'm really, sincerely hoping you took my advice last week and did not pursue anything to do with your fantasy guy. What was his name again?"

"Peter." Kate tried a dismissive smile, gone in a flash, then shook her head. "No." She lifted her own cup, drank distractedly, replaced it carefully on its saucer. "Of course not."

Beth hung her head, then looked back up. "My God, Katie. What are you thinking?"

"I said nothing happened."

"Yes, you did. But you may remember that I'm a trained investigator and if there's one thing I'm good at, it's knowing when someone isn't telling me the truth." Beth sat back in her chair, eyeing her friend in disappointment and even anger.

"No, I . . ." Kate began.

"Please, stop. Don't even start."

Kate played with her cup.

"This isn't like when we were teenagers, Kate. Or young adults. Or whenever it was when we played around. What about Ron? What about your kids?"

"It wasn't anything. There isn't going to be any fallout around Ron or the kids. And okay, you were right. I mean, it was a mistake. I wish now I hadn't done it. I really do."

"And the guy? What about him? He just went along with it?"

Kate gave her a knowing look. "You just

said it. He's a guy, Beth. You know how guys are. What do you think?"

"He's a married guy, and I think that's depressing as hell."

"Well, maybe it is if you think of it that way."

"I don't know any other way to think of it. It's just when I'm marginally entertaining the idea of putting my foot in the relationship waters again, I hear about this and go 'What am I thinking? Am I an idiot?' "

"You're not an idiot. This was one guy. And he probably regrets it, too."

"But not enough to have stopped him from doing it in the first place." Beth found herself getting more and more worked up. To slow herself down, she took a long sip of her coffee, then with exaggerated control lowered it into its saucer.

"I —" she began.

But suddenly, from outside in the main hallway came the booming sound of an explosion, followed quickly by two others, and then a volley of pops, like strings of firecrackers.

Both women turned toward the restaurant's entrance where now they heard another enormous explosion, then more of the popping sounds, accompanied by the completely unexpected, terrifying, and unmistakable noise of people screaming.

Then Beth was on her feet, reaching behind her back for her service weapon, which she realized too late that she never carried on their walks. Swearing, she turned, looked back at her table. "Get up! Get up!" she yelled at Kate. "Let's go!"

But another explosion — a grenade blowing up outside the restaurant's front door, close enough that they felt the impact — froze them where they stood. All around them now, people were out of their seats, pushing, yelling, rushing to the exit, to the outside seating and service area. The shots — for they could be nothing else — rang out in bursts inside the pavilion amidst the by-now continuous screaming and mayhem, as thick smoke wafted its way into the room.

Another volley of shots sounded just outside the restaurant's door that led to the main indoor pavilion. The giant window by the check-in station shattered and people who hadn't made it to the exit went down in front of it like sheaves of wheat.

A man in green camo, his head completely covered and his face concealed by a black mask, now appeared in the doorway. Much to her horror, Beth saw that he was holding an assault weapon, leveling it at chest height.

Kate and Beth stood next to each other, together, twenty feet in front of him. Beth turned, intending to tackle Kate and get them underneath the line of fire.

11

The word reached Tadich's before Peter got
his sand dabs and it had no sooner registered than he left some cash on his table
and queued up to get outside, although
right from the start it was terribly slow going. When he finally made it out to the
sidewalk, he realized that all traffic westward
was at a dead stop, so he turned up north
with the idea that he could get to his firm's
office and find out what was going on from
the relative safety of the high-rise.

But whatever plans he tried to make felt
like a jumble. He wasn't able to get control
of his thoughts.

*Christ! Was Kate dead? Could she just die
randomly like that? Out of any context, simply
here then gone?*

Without a doubt, she had still been in the
building when the attack had begun. Even
at a quick glance, he thought it had been
obvious that the two women had settled in.

132

But even if they'd called for their check when he'd seen them, there was no chance that they could have paid it and gotten out in the very few minutes between when he'd left and the firing started.

People all around were using the word *terror* in all its forms. Here in San Francisco? It was, he thought, unimaginable.

But they had no doubt thought that in Paris as well. As they had in Mumbai. And New York. And San Bernardino and Orlando. And everywhere else.

Sirens — an uncountable number, an endless wailing scream — were cutting through the noise of the crowd and blending with the thwack of helicopters overhead.

Cutting through the crowd, Peter made decent progress. He got to his building in six minutes by his watch and was surprised to encounter people fighting their way out. Against that current, he finally made it to an elevator in which he was the only passenger going up.

The reception area was deserted, although around the corner in the hallway he could see that some of the secretaries were still in their cubicles, glued to their monitors.

Down to his left, Theresa wasn't at her station. Peter half-ran down to his office, where the door stood ajar, and stepped inside.

Theresa was standing by his floor-to-ceiling windows, outside of which the sky had gone black with smoke.

Hearing him, she turned, bringing her hands up to her tear-stained face. "Oh God, thank God," she said, and in three or four steps crossed the office to where Peter stood, where he'd closed the door behind him. She put her arms around him, and he held her for a long moment until she pulled away enough to look up into his face. "I thought you were down there. You said you were going there, didn't you? The Ferry Building?"

"I changed my mind. I went to Tadich, and I'm fine. Any word on what's happened down there?"

She backed away a step. "They're saying it was a terrorist attack. At least four men with hand grenades and assault weapons. Lots of dead and injured. And come over, have you seen this?" She went back to the window, to the three round depressions in the thick, reinforced glass.

Following her, he took in the bullet holes. But scary and immediate as they were, they didn't prepare him for the view down below, where the Ferry Building was still enveloped in black smoke and the occasional lick of bright orange flame.

"I am so afraid," Theresa said. She turned back into his arms.

One of the paralegals in Ron and Geoff's firm came running down the hallway, yelling. "Somebody's shooting up the Ferry Building!"

Seconds later, Ron was out in the conference room with most of the rest of the firm. The television set was already on, and everybody was straining to see and pick up details amid the smoke and the panicked throngs along the Embarcadero.

Second nature, he pulled his cell phone from his belt and punched up Kate's number. The call went straight to her voicemail. Of course it would, he remembered, since this was her day to walk with Beth. She wouldn't have her phone with her. He checked his watch. It was 11:21. They probably wouldn't be done yet, and even if they were, they sometimes went out to lunch after. Nevertheless, he tried their home number as well, left another message asking Kate to call when she got it, no matter what. Just to make sure he reached her — she often left her phone on in her purse but didn't pick up — he texted her as well.

"Please call immediately. Urgent."

Wherever she was, when she heard about the Ferry Building, she'd call him anyway. He was sure of that.

Something like twenty eternal minutes passed with no response from Kate. Telling himself that there was no reason she would have been at or anywhere near the Ferry Building, Ron finally thought to put in a call to Beth's cell phone, where again he left a message and then a text. He then tried Beth's number at work, but the police phone lines were jammed.

Out in his reception area again, the news was not good. Apparently, the four assailants had all taken their own lives after blowing through their grenades and ammunition; not counting them, the casualties numbered fifty-four dead and 141 injured. Both numbers were expected to increase.

The television commentators were urging people to stay away and give the emergency teams and vehicles room to access the scene and do their work. Nevertheless, it was utter chaos everywhere the cameras looked, massed humanity on the sidewalks and the streets blocked with cars well into the city proper.

He tried his wife again, left messages with both of his children for when they got out of school that he was all right, but that they should call him as soon as possible and come straight home after their classes. He didn't want to panic them by asking them if they'd heard from their mother. He tried to convince himself that the silence from her end was due to the unusual amount of traffic on the phone lines, clogging the cables or the airwaves.

Or something.

By the time he tried to take the elevator down to the building's garage, it was jammed with people leaving work. Standing behind the mob in the packed hallway, he watched the doors open and close in front of him four times before he gave up and walked down the twelve flights. In the stairwell, the nervous shoulder-to-shoulder herd probably wouldn't let him get to the garage any faster than the elevator, but at least this way he was moving.

When he pulled out of the parking garage entrance, he was stopped by cars immobile in the street, some of them seemingly abandoned, people walking between the lanes. After an interminable wait — ten minutes? fifteen? — he finally squeezed into an opening and made a right turn toward his home way out near Fillmore.

It took him another twenty minutes, the

traffic slowly thinning as he got farther away from downtown. Scanning the cars parked on his street, he caught sight of his wife's green Volvo in its usual spot. Which didn't mean anything except that it might.

He pulled into his driveway, ran up to the front door, first knocking on it, then letting himself in with his key. Inside, he listened to their landline voicemail on the kitchen phone and only heard himself asking Kate to call him soonest.

The cell phone buzzed at his belt and in his haste to pull it from its holster, he lost control of the damn thing. It fell out of his hand and onto the floor with a clatter.

"Shit! Just a second." Finally, he had it. "Kate?"

"No. Dad? It's Aidan. Isn't Mom with you? Is she okay?"

"I've been trying to get to her. She was out walking with Beth and probably doesn't have her phone."

"But you haven't heard from her?"

"Not yet, no." Best, he still thought, to appear unconcerned. "They're probably halfway across the Golden Gate Bridge, oblivious to any of this. Have you gotten in touch with Janey?"

"Yeah. I'm on my way over to get her now."

"Good. Then straight home, okay? Both of you."

"Got it. Dad?"

"Yes?"

"Is this really happening? I mean, we've been watching it at school . . ."

"Yeah," Ron said. "It's happening. Just get home, would you?"

"Will do."

To Ginny Tully, Beth's daughter, her mother's absence when she got home from school was not by itself a matter of grave concern. After all, her mom was a cop, and the terrorist attack at the Ferry Building was going to lead to a mass call-up of law enforcement. Ginny had no doubt that's what was going on. Her mother was on emergency duty.

What felt vaguely wrong to Ginny was that her mother had left neither a note nor a phone message telling her what was up. Of course, Beth knew that her daughter would figure it out without any message from her, but it wasn't like her not to give her one anyway. Usually, even if she'd just gone shopping, she would let Ginny know where she was and roughly when she would get home. And at least, her mother would check her phone and text messages from Ginny and get back to her, but that hadn't happened. Not yet, anyway.

Still, after she got home she sat in dead-eyed shock, mesmerized by the TV and the horrific images. The good news was that it seemed that all of the assailants were now dead, and with every minute that passed, the likelihood decreased that there would be another attack in another location in the city.

But the bad news, far outweighing the good — the death toll was now up to sixty-seven, not including the four terrorists, with a hundred and fifty-six injured. To Ginny, these seemed impossibly huge numbers, although she knew, somewhere in her brain, that the number of dead was smaller than in the Paris attack. On the tube, the first responders — cops, firemen, ambulances, and paramedics — filled the screen from every angle. Of course, that's where her mother would have gone, where she probably was right now, helping out, securing the crime scenes.

Still . . .

Although the practice was heavily discouraged, putting in a call to her mother's partner was acceptable under certain conditions, and Ginny finally decided that this was one of them. Steeling herself, she tore herself from the television and punched in Ike's number.

"McCaffrey." From the ambient noise in the background, he was in the middle of it, too.

"Hey, Ike, it's Ginny."

"Who? Talk loud. It's bedlam down here."

"It's Ginny, Ike. I'm trying to locate my mom. Have you had any word from her?"

"No. I thought she might have gone down to pick you up at school. She's not with you?"

"No. And she's not answering her phone."

"I know. I've been trying her all day." He paused. "But I wouldn't jump to conclusions. The phones are all whacked out. And it's crazy down here."

"Are you at the Ferry Building?"

"Just outside. But she could be right across from me on the other end and I wouldn't know it. Today's her day off, right? Remember?"

"Okay, but it's not like her to be off her phone. Especially with something like this going on. She'd want me to know she was okay. And vice versa."

"Yeah, well, all right. I'll try to hook up with her down here, and I'll make sure she gets back to you the minute I reach her. But it might really be a while, Gin. We barely have a command center set up down here. The structure's kind of fallen apart. She'll turn up. You just stay cool by your phone. And hey, if she gets to you, have her call me, too, huh?"

Alan Shaw was working on a remodel out in the Avenues. The residents had moved out while that process was going on and today he'd sent his two subs on this job — Ryan and Felipe — over to another site while he finished up the taping on the new drywall they'd put up around the living room. Alan considered one of the big pluses about working alone was that he didn't have to listen to the radio blasting all day long. There was something profoundly peaceful and satisfying in just going about your work, making sure you got it right, without the blast and bleat of music or political commentary.

He finished up today's work at a few minutes past six, drove his F-150 home through dense fog to his cottage out on Forty-First, almost to the beach and the Cliff House. His place shared half of a lot with another tiny house that stood in front of it, closer to the street. After showering and shaving, he put on a clean pair of jeans and an ironed shirt, then after a moment of

142

hesitation grabbed one of his two sports jackets. On the way back out to his car, he noticed that the roses along the path from the driveway to his door were in full bloom, and he took out his Swiss Army knife and cut half a dozen perfect specimens, all red, whittling away the thorns.

Ten minutes later, seven o'clock sharp, he found a miraculous parking spot on Lake, the same block as Beth's duplex, and backed into it. Checking his watch for the tenth time, he grabbed the roses and opened his door.

He still didn't have a clear idea of what he and Beth were going to do. He'd just asked her if she'd want to go out and she'd said yes and he'd supposed that he should probably take her someplace for dinner where they could talk and get to know each other a little bit more. A quiet place with decent food.

But he was seriously out of practice — he hadn't had a date in almost a year, and the last one had been a complete disaster with some stoner who'd asked him out, or rather in, since she'd tried to snare him into her bedroom before they'd said more than a few dozen words. Which in her case he did not find to be a turn-on. So tonight he was nervous about the etiquette, whether, for example, Beth might see even the roses as too presumptuous or silly or something.

Well, he'd find out soon enough.

Beth lived upstairs in a duplex that looked like every other one on the street. Double checking the address at the bottom of the steps — this was the place — he huffed out a quick breath and hit the steps. Pushing the button by the door, he heard the chime echo in the house.

But nobody came.

He rang again, heard the chime again, waited, then knocked tentatively. "Beth?"

No answer.

His watch said 7:06.

He waited until 7:30, then double-checked his cell phone to see if she'd texted him, or even called — maybe he'd left the phone on vibrate and he'd just missed her.

But no, nothing. He sighed and placed the roses on the welcome mat before walking back across the street to his truck.

■ ■ ■ ■

PART TWO

NOVEMBER 11–NOVEMBER 13

■ ■ ■ ■

12

Ike McCaffrey sat double-parked on Funston, his flashing bubble lit up on the roof of his city-issued Plymouth. He'd picked up a couple of go-cups of green tea and a bag full of pork bao from Tong Palace, the dim sum place down the street on Lake, then texted his partner that he was five minutes away. He'd meet her in the street in front of her place.

But she hadn't made it down yet by the time he showed up. That didn't bother him. She moved slowly all the time now, albeit getting more mobile by the week. But he knew that the fact that she was moving at all was in the realm of divine intervention.

Outside, it was about as cold as it ever got in San Francisco, a bright and sunny mid-November Wednesday morning, but in his warm car, redolent with the terrific smell of the Chinese buns fresh out of the oven, he halfway felt he could be content to wait all morning.

After all, being late wasn't going to matter to the body they were going out to see.

She appeared at the landing by her front door, and he leaned over a bit in his seat, surreptitiously, to watch her start navigating the stairs.

Slowly.

Under normal circumstances, there was zero chance that Beth would have been cleared for duty in the condition she was in. Theoretically, every cop on duty has to be able to chase a miscreant through backyards and over fences. And Beth could barely walk.

But in the wake of the total chaos that had surrounded the terrorist attack last May — six months earlier — SFPD had gone to all hands on deck. There was work for anyone who had a pulse. And cane or no, they were glad to see Beth. A few weeks ago, she had ditched one of the canes before the doctor had really recommended it. In fact, he'd flat out forbidden it — she'd been hit, after all, in both legs, and her doctor believed that neither one of them was ready to bear the full weight of her body on its own. But that, Ike knew, was how Beth was. Tough. She now stood at the top of the stairs, and he saw her hesitate. Then, tucking her cane under her arm and taking hold of the railing with both hands, she stepped down, lowering her second foot in a separate movement. One step, pause, bring the other foot down next to the first one.

She'd done this three times when, raising her eyes, she must have just seen their car parked waiting for her because she straightened up, took her left hand off the banister, grabbed the cane with it, made her plant, and dropped a foot onto the next step.

One at a time.

It took her most of a minute, after which he leaned over and pushed at the passenger door. She pulled it all the way open and grinned over at him. "Oh my God," she said. "It smells like heaven in here. You got pork bao!"

The usual caveats surrounding the treatment of a dead body did not apply in this case, primarily because this was pretty obviously not where the crime had occurred. The 911 call had come in just after dawn, when it was still almost dark and in any case in full shadow under the huge, the simply enormous, overhanging rocks that had planted themselves eons ago in the sand below the Cliff House Restaurant. John Morgan, the sixty-four-year-old striped-bass fisherman who'd made the call, at first thought it had been a seal that had washed up, but something about the coloring had looked wrong even from a distance, and as he got closer, it was plain that it was a person with some clothes still clinging to him — what was left of a long-sleeved sweatshirt, most of a pair of casual khaki pants.

The techs had pulled the body from the water and up onto the hard sand beyond the surge waterline, and this was where Ike and Beth now stood, hands in their pockets, looking down on the badly damaged corpse. The man's shoes and socks were gone, as was most of the left foot, pieces of his arms and legs and most of his face. He did wear a wedding ring, which had somehow escaped the carnage. The left-hand thumb also appeared unscathed, which meant they could soon have a fingerprint, and probably an identification.

Barefoot with alligator shoes in hand, Lennard Faro — the city's always well-dressed head of Crime Scene investigations — came up to the homicide inspectors and wished them good morning, then told them that he was on his way back downtown. He was already too cold and there wasn't much to be gleaned from this location. Clearly, judging from the shape the body was in, the victim had been in the water for at least a couple of days, perhaps longer.

"Any sign of what killed him?" Beth asked. "He drown?"

"We haven't mentioned that yet?" Faro replied. "Sorry about that. No, maybe he drowned. The ME will tell us that soon enough, but it doesn't really matter because if he did, it was after he got himself shot in the chest." They moved down nearer to the body and Faro leaned over and pointed to a perfectly circular indentation just to the right of the man's left nipple. "Miracle if it didn't go through the heart," he said. "There's a pretty clean exit wound in the back, too, probably a jacketed bullet, certainly not a hollow point. I'm guessing something north of a nine millimeter or forty caliber."

"Any reports of missing persons?" Ike asked.

Faro shook his head. "I haven't heard. I figured we'd let you guys get on that stuff."

"Somebody will notice he's gone," Beth said. "If he's still married, especially."

"You'll know soon enough. The fingerprints alone . . ."

Beth nodded. "I hear you."

"So." Faro tempered his brusque tone to

151

one of sympathy. "How are you doing, Inspector? That's a long walk down here in heavy sand."

"And back," she said. "But I'm fine, if still just a little banged up. I should be dancing by Christmas."

"That'd be Christmas, next year," Ike put in.

"Well, whatever," Faro said. "I'm glad to see you back up and around. I heard it was pretty close."

Beth shrugged. "They always say that when there's a lot of blood. It fools people. But I appreciate the thought. In truth, I was one of the lucky ones."

"That's one way to look at it," Faro said.

"It sure is." She took a last glance at the body. "Well, we'll get moving on this right away, Len. Have yourself a good one."

"You, too."

Halfway across the beach, on the way back to their car, both of them slogging slowly through the deep dry sand, Ike said, "You know the other thing that fools them? When there's a lot of blood and all?"

"What's that?"

"Arterial bleeding. That whole spurting thing. People get all fooled and think it's serious."

"Nah. Who needs those details? Just

152

makes people feel sorry for you."

"And we wouldn't want that, would we?"

She threw him a sideways glance. "I won't dignify that. Oh, and by the way . . ."

"Yeah."

"It's not Christmas next year. It's Christmas, this year. Dancing, I mean."

They checked Missing Persons upon their arrival downtown and struck out. Nobody was wondering about a missing adult male.

Then the fingerprint came back, a positive identification, delivered to their office in under three hours. The murder victim was Peter Ash, a lawyer with the firm Meyer Eldridge & Kline, offices in Embarcadero Two.

At Beth's desk in the open bullpen area where she worked, her fingers flew over her keyboard and when they stopped, she was frowning. She also must have made some kind of unconscious sound, because her partner looked up from his desk across from hers.

"What up, dog?" he asked her.

"This is a little unusual. This guy Peter Ash has been missing at least two, maybe as many as three or four days, right?"

"Yep."

"Okay, so he's got a full-time job. His driver's license says he's local. And nobody's bothered to note or comment on or question his absence over the last few days?"

Ike shrugged. "Maybe he was supposed to be traveling. Maybe he disappears with regularity and people who know him don't worry about it anymore. Maybe nobody wants to appear panicked, and they'll give him a few more days before they report anything."

"Maybe."

"That's what I said. Three times even. I could probably come up with more if you give me thirty seconds."

"I'm sure you could. And they're all possibly true, Ike, but it makes me wonder. Meanwhile, we need to go check out where he lives. Lived."

"I had a feeling you were going to say that next."

"Mind meld," she said. "It's what makes us such a good team."

"I don't suppose we can just let the pros do it. Break the news that he's dead, too."

"We are the pros, Ike."

"I knew you were going to say that, too."

"Come on," she said. "We've got his address. Let's roll out of here."

"Now?"

"As opposed to when?"

154

"Oh, I don't know. Say after we get a warrant?"

Beth made a face. "Who's the warrant duty judge today, Sommers?"

"I think so, yeah."

"Look. Even if he's back from lunch, which is unlikely, and even if he's sober, which is impossible, do we want to kill this whole afternoon sitting in his courtroom until he gets tired of playing video games in chambers and deigns to review our affidavit?"

"I'm guessing you don't."

"Correct. And neither do you. So the warrant duty changes over at six. Let's go do a knock and talk now and hope whoever catches the duty then is less inclined to waste our time."

Peter Ash's current driver's license address turned out to be apartment number 4 on the second floor of a three-story, six-unit building at Grove and Masonic, in the shadow of the University of San Francisco. As soon as they hit the block, both of the inspectors felt it was unlikely that this was the primary residence of a big-time downtown lawyer, but they rang the outside bell and waited on the stoop anyway, got no answer, and were just turning to head back

155

to their car when a heavily bundled-up young woman with a backpack stopped in front of them. She held a set of keys in her mittened right hand and backed up a step, as though perhaps the two serious-faced adults made her nervous.

"Can I help you?" she asked tentatively.

Beth gave her a tight smile, dug in her purse, and flashed her identification. "Maybe you can. We're police inspectors looking for Peter Ash, in number four. He lives here, right?"

"Peter? Yes. But wouldn't he be at work this time of day? What did he do? Is he in trouble?"

Ignoring her questions, Beth asked, "Would you mind telling us your name, please?"

"Sure. Monica Daly." She pointed at the mailboxes. "I'm in number one."

"Do you know Mr. Ash well, Monica?"

"Not really. I mean, to say hi to. But we don't party with him or anything."

"We?"

"The rest of us. We're students, the whole building. He's like, old, so he kind of sticks out, you know. But otherwise, he seems okay. He buys for some of the guys if they ask him."

"Buys?" Ike asked.

"You know," she said, "beer and stuff. Liquor. Not everybody here is twenty-one. But he's cool, he doesn't worry about that stuff."

"The law, you mean?" Ike asked.

She let out a little laugh. "Well, *that* law anyway."

"Has he lived here for long?" Beth asked.

"I don't know, really. Since I got here anyway, but that's only a few months. So what did he do, anyway? What did you want to talk to him about?"

Monica Daly turned out to be the only student at home in the Grove Street apartment building in the middle of the day. And without a warrant, they weren't going to get a look inside the victim's apartment. Not that day, at least.

So Beth called back to her office, and they got a previous address for Peter Ash, where he'd lived before he moved to the apartment on Grove. Of course, they should have checked for previous addresses before they left downtown, just as they probably should have gone to Judge Sommers and gotten a search warrant for Ash's apartment, even if they'd had to wait for it. But as with any fresh murder, they'd been in a hurry. Enough time had already passed since the crime had taken place, and the Rule of Forty-Eight was that after two days, the odds of finding someone's killer approached zero.

Movement, even in the wrong direction, sometimes felt like progress.

Ash's former residence turned out to be a large dark brown bungalow on Paloma Avenue in Saint Francis Wood. He'd resided down here in the Wood Hood for seventeen years before he'd moved out. Both inspectors knew that was about as clear cut a sign as you could get that Peter Ash had been either divorced or was in the process of getting there.

They pulled up on the wide, empty street and parked directly in front of the address. A flagstone path bordered with wilting impatiens and pansies on one side and a low but overgrown hedge on the other bisected a wide lawn that was clearly at least a few weeks past due on its last mowing. More visible signs of a marriage on the rocks.

Before they reached the front door, they could hear the sound of a vacuum cleaner inside. Ike waited for Beth's slower gait to get her to the front door, and when she'd come up next to him, she nodded and he pushed the doorbell. A deep gong echoed from inside, the noise from the vacuum ceased, and in a moment the door opened about six inches until the chain stopped it.

"Yes? Can I help you?"

Ike took the lead, flashing his ID. "We are inspectors with the police department. Are you Mrs. Ash?"

"No. I go by Jill Corbin now, but Peter Ash was my husband. Or is, until the divorce is final. Is he all right?" Through the door, they could see her put her hand over her heart. "Oh my God. You said 'police'? Is he dead? He's dead, isn't he?"

"I'm afraid he is," Ike intoned. "We're very sorry."

Standing behind Ike, Beth made a mental note that Jill had immediately assumed her husband was dead rather than injured or in an accident or anything else.

Jill stood on the other side of the door, making little mewling sounds — Beth considered moments like these the absolute worst part of her job. After a few seconds, she leaned in. "Jill — Ms. Corbin — could we please come in for a minute?" Giving the grieving something to do, no matter how slight, sometimes helped them get through the first horrible seconds.

The door closed, the chain rattled behind it. The door opened all the way.

Jill was medium height and build. Her dark hair stopped just below her shoulders. She might have been pretty under normal circumstances — she appeared to have good skin and regular features — but both of her eyes and the top of her nose were swollen and bruised as though she'd taken a serious beating in the past few days. Stepping back from the door into the foyer, she held her right hand up to her mouth in what seemed almost a caricature of grief.

Mute sorrow.

The vacuum cleaner stood by itself on the hardwood floor in the archway that led into the large living room, which was now well lit by the cold afternoon sun through the picture window.

Beth closed the front door behind them.

Without a word to the inspectors, Jill turned. She took a few steps into the living room, then lowered herself onto a wing chair. Beth and Ike took seats on the facing couch.

Jill wore faded blue jeans, white tennis shoes, and a tan USC sweatshirt, the sleeves rolled up to her elbows. Eventually, she came back to the inspectors. Then, as though settling something in her mind, she asked Beth, "What happened to him? Can you tell me?"

"We haven't gotten the medical examiner's report, but we are looking at the possibility that somebody killed him."

"What do you mean? Do you mean murdered him?"

"We don't know that," Beth said. "Not for certain. The body was in the bay, but he might have been injured before he went into the water."

"Well, then, maybe it was an accident? Oh my God, do you think he might have committed suicide?"

"It's not outside the realm of possibility," Beth said. "Why? Do you think he was suicidal?"

Jill shifted her gaze over to Ike and again came back to Beth. It was almost, Beth thought, as if she wondered why these inspectors were really in her house. She drew in a breath, her hands clasped on her lap, then exhaled as her expression went almost completely blank.

"Jill," Beth prompted her.

She looked across, met Beth's gaze. "He's really dead? This really is the end, then." She brought her hands up to her forehead, seemed to press into them.

"The end?" Ike asked. "The end of . . ."

She lowered her hands. "Everything. Every thing. Us." Meeting Beth's eyes again, she got her voice under control. "I can't believe this. Peter is just dead? Just like that. That's it?"

Beth nodded and said, "I'm sorry."

"You mentioned the possibility of suicide," Ike said. "Do you think that was something he'd be capable of?"

Jill shook her head. "I really don't know what he was capable of anymore."

"Anymore since when?" Ike asked her.

"I don't know exactly. This is going to sound a little weird, but since he changed."

"Changed in what way?" Beth asked.

"In every way imaginable. It was just like he woke up one morning and was a different person. One day he was a good husband and father and lawyer, then, suddenly, he just wasn't anymore."

Ike came forward on the couch. "When was this?"

She scrunched up her face, remembering. "Late May, I'd say. Right around the time of the terrorist attack."

"Related to that?" Beth asked.

"I don't think so, no. I can't imagine how. It started before that, I'm pretty sure, but not too long before. But after that, it just got out of control."

"What did?" Ike asked. "Specifically?"

"Well, drinking for starters. And then."

She paused. "Then all the women."

"He had affairs?" Beth asked.

Jill shook her head, her lips tight. "I don't know if you'd call them that. I don't think there was any real relationship with any one woman, although I may be wrong there. He just started seeing other women. Getting drunk and going home with them. I don't have any idea what that was about. But the bottom line is that we seemed to be going along fine, all of us, having a normal life, and then this . . . this *thing* started, and within a month he just got more and more unpredictable, more irrational, and then he just packed some stuff one day and told us he was moving out."

"And you don't think this had anything to do with the terrorism?" Beth asked.

"I don't know. I know that screwed up a lot of people. Maybe the attack made whatever it was get worse. I just don't know. Nothing really seems the same since then, anyway. San Francisco is a small town. Everybody you meet was there or was shot or knew somebody who was shot. Everybody's world is just different now. It's like everything you thought you knew about people was a lie. It's like finding out your husband cheated. You suddenly doubt everything else you thought you knew." She

163

brushed at the air in front of her face. "I don't know what I'm saying. Nothing makes any sense. You guys must see that a lot, I'd bet."

Beth again nodded, noncommittal.

Ike asked, "So he moved out in June?"

"June tenth. Just gone."

Beth found her voice again. "Have you seen him since then?"

Jill nodded. "I wanted to go to a marriage counselor, and he agreed at first, but it didn't take. He just didn't want to work anything out anymore. He said he was done with the whole life we'd . . . we'd put together, and after three appointments he just said it was a waste of time and he stopped going."

"And you stopped seeing each other?" Ike asked.

"I haven't seen him in about two months now. Last time was our sons' birthdays. Which was another disaster, maybe the worst one actually."

"I'm sorry," Ike said. "Your sons' birthdays? Was that one or two of them?"

"Two of them. Same birthday. September sixteenth. They're twins, both nineteen now. Eric and Tyler. Good boys, although this whole experience with their father has really messed with their heads. And now, with

164

this . . ." She looked plaintively at the inspectors. "Now there's no fixing it, is there?"

After a beat of silence, Ike broke it. "So what happened on the birthdays?"

Jill hesitated another second or two. "Well, the short version is that Peter got drunk and decided it would be a good day for him to come by and touch base with us all again. He seemed to think that maybe we could all just move ahead and forget that we used to be a family, and since he didn't have any hard feelings, we should feel the same way. It just hadn't worked out, the whole family thing, and if it bothered any of us, we should just get over it."

"And how'd that play?" Beth asked.

"Not so good, as you might imagine. Peter got about halfway through this truly ridiculous pitch, trying to get us all to understand that he hadn't really deserted us and blah blah blah when Eric just had enough and basically jumped him and started swinging . . . not that Peter didn't deserve it, but it was the worst. Tyler and I had to pull them apart, everybody was bleeding. It was just awful."

"I'm so sorry," Beth said. "That must have been very hard on you."

"I don't know what happened. He just

became a terrible man."

"Where are your boys now?" Ike asked.

"Both off at school. Eric's at Cal and Tyler's at Chico. Oh my God, how am I going to tell them this? Those poor boys." Abruptly, she stood up, brushing her hands against her pants. "I've got to call them. I can't have them hear about it on the news or in the paper."

Beth and Ike got to their feet. When they got back to the front door, Beth reached for the doorknob and then stopped and turned. "I've just got one last quick question if you don't mind, Jill. Please don't take offense, but what's happened to your face?"

"My face . . . ?" She brought both of her hands up to her cheeks. "Oh!" She seemed to breathe a sigh of relief. "I had a rhinoplasty last week. A nose job. And an eye tuck, if you want to know. I figured if I wasn't pretty enough for Peter anymore . . . maybe if I changed how I looked . . ." Her shoulders gave an inch and suddenly to Beth she seemed about fifteen years older. "Stupid," she said. "Just stupid vanity." Then, "I'm sorry, but I've got to call the boys."

"Of course," Beth said. "And we won't bother you further. But before you do call them, could we trouble you for Peter's cell phone number? We'll need to get the records to try to figure out where he was and who he was with on the night he died."

"Well?" Beth asked as they pulled away from the curb. They'd been partners for over two years and Ike didn't need her to explain what she was asking about.

"One to ten," he said, "with ten meaning she absolutely did it, I'm giving her a two, maybe a one. In fact, she might even be a zero."

"Have we ever had a zero before? I don't remember one."

"I don't think so. I'd eat my badge if she turns out to be his killer. We just totally blindsided her. She had no idea."

"I agree."

"But I wouldn't mind talking to the boys before she did."

"Yeah. Well, that's not happening." Beth chewed her cheek for a minute. "You noticed," she said, "that the one at Cal — Eric — he's closer, a BART ride away. Plus, he's the son who went at him. Physically assaulting your dad is no small deal."

Ike looked over at her with a half-grin in place. "Eric at Cal, the one who attacked his dad. You remember that? What are you, a detective or something? It'd be interesting

167

to know if Eric had a gun, or a car, or both."

"I'm sure we're going to get to find out."

"Plus, it would be good if we could narrow down a time of death, within a day or so."

"Plus that, yes. That'd be nice."

They drove on in silence — one block, two blocks. They pulled up to a stop sign and stayed stopped an extra six or eight seconds. A longish time.

"Okay, I give up. What?" Beth finally asked.

"What what?"

"Whatever it is you're pondering. You want me to drive so you can think harder?"

"Hey. I'm doing great, multitasking here." He looked left, then right, then pulled out into the intersection. "What do you think happened that he changed so much all at once?"

"I'm going to *chercher* some *femme* here, Ike. I'm thinking he got himself a girlfriend."

"Evidently, according to Jill, more than one."

"Well, we don't know about that. One could have done it."

"But on the other hand, getting out from under the family might have just set him free. You think it could have had something to do with the terrorism, after all?"

Beth considered, her mouth set. "Those sons of bitches." She went inside her head for a moment, and then she shook out whatever it was. "I'm not ruling out anything in terms of reactions people had to that day. But Jill said whatever it was, it had started before then. Not that it couldn't have been exacerbated . . ." She went silent. Then, "I can see the drinking. Especially if he was close to where it happened, or even in the Ferry Building. His firm's in Embarcadero Two, right across the street. He could've been there."

"And that pushed him over some edge?"

"If he was teetering, it couldn't have helped. And let me tell you, if I wasn't a monstrously strong woman trying to raise a super-sensitive daughter all by myself, I might have become a common drunk. Or addicted to Oxy."

"I don't think so. Not you, under any circumstances."

"Well, thanks for saying so. But I don't think I slept for six weeks. And it wasn't all the physical pain. So yeah, I could see Peter Ash starting to act out after the attack, especially if he was anywhere near it. Bottom line is I'd be shocked if it didn't play some role, get him into some reckless behavior, and that in turn might have helped get him killed."

"You think?"

"Honestly, I don't have a clue, Ike. For all we know, he was killed in a random street robbery and dumped in the ocean."

He looked skeptically across at her.

"Not my first choice, either," Beth said. "Because if there's no connection between Ash and whoever killed him, we won't solve this thing. It would be like trying to find out who the fucking terrorists were by knowing the people they killed. So if we're going to be doing anything at all, we have to assume a connection between Peter and his killer. But if he was any kind of victim of what went on that day down at the Ferry Building, I'll tell you what."

"What?"

"He's got my full attention."

13

The single bullet that had taken Kate out passed through her body, just missing her heart and her backbone, but nicking her left lung, causing it to collapse. After the initial internal cleanup, she then developed some serious medical problems relating to her resistance to the standard antibiotics they were using, and by four days after the attack, they had had to move her into the intensive care unit with a dire prognosis of imminent death. To make matters worse, she then developed pneumonia in her damaged lung, which somehow spread to her other lung as well. Her injuries and these complications finally made it necessary to get her onto a breathing machine in the ICU, where she remained for two more weeks. During that time, she flatlined twice, and both times they were able to bring her back.

And then, miraculously, the treatments in

the hospital started to work. On July 1, Ron came down and picked her up and drove her to their home on Washington Street, where she was still mostly bedridden, although even on that first day, she could get up and walk to the bathroom on her own. With physical therapy, she had regained more of her mobility day by day. Without further medical complications, the consensus had been that she would be completely back to normal within another couple of months.

And this turned out to be the case. Physically, she seemed to be recovering.

Although saying that the rest of the family was completely back to normal would not be accurate. Ron and both Aidan and Janey, great communicators all, treated her with concern and kindness, but much more as though she were a visiting invalid instead of their wife and mother, respectively. She had been physically healed for three months now, and here it was October and she and Ron still hadn't restarted anything like their love life.

Now, on the day after Peter's body had washed up under the Cliff House, Kate sat at the kitchen table, drinking coffee, with the *Chronicle* open before her. The kids had dutifully eaten their healthy breakfasts in the same kind of nervous peace that had characterized the house's atmosphere ever since Kate had come home from the hospital. They had both kissed her and gathered their books and backpacks and driven off to school.

As had become his custom since she'd become mobile, Ron stayed upstairs while Kate and the kids had breakfast. He would come down a few minutes before he left for work, and drink a civilized cup of coffee with her. But he'd drink it quickly, covering the day-to-day logistics of the house in his organized, kind, understanding, distant fashion.

Waiting for him today, the news about Peter on the front page of the newspaper, her stomach was already churning. She thought it was possible she was going to be sick.

Their house telephone rang, and she was pushing herself up to get it as she realized that Ron had picked up the extension in the bedroom. She heard his muffled voice echoing down through the house.

She settled back down in her chair, reached for her coffee, and took a sip. Folding the paper closed, she pushed it out into the center of the table. She rubbed the scar left where the bullet had gone in.

Ron was still on the phone, but she really

couldn't make out what he was saying. When the words stopped, his footsteps sounded on the stairs, and then he was standing in the kitchen doorway.

"Who was that?" she asked with a blithe false gaiety.

"Geoff," he said. He glanced at the newspaper. "He had some pretty horrible news. You might have seen it already in the paper. It looks like somebody killed Peter Ash."

She swallowed. "I did see that. It's unbelievable."

"It is." He gestured toward the counter. "Let me just get some coffee."

"Do you want to eat anything? There's still some bacon and an English muffin."

"No, thanks. Coffee's good."

Filling his mug, he stayed where he was, hovering over the machine, hands planted on the counter on either side of him.

"Are you all right?" Kate asked.

With another heavy sigh, he turned, waited another second, then crossed to the table, and sat down. "Do you have anything special planned for this morning?"

"Just the usual. Physical therapy, then grocery shopping for dinner. Why?"

"I just thought . . ." he began. Looking over the table at her, his body seemed to come to a dead stop. "I think we need to have a talk."

Ron wore what Kate called his brave face.

Carefully calibrated midway between an understanding smile and a glowering frown, his brave face signaled to Kate that Ron was near the end of his emotional tether. When Aidan had been in the car wreck when he was twelve, Ron had broken the news to her wearing his brave face. Likewise, for when he had to tell her when those bastards at his previous firm, Crandall and Dodd, had laid him off just after Janey's birth, over Christmas vacation. And again when he'd had to bow out of the Tekkei representation.

Now, his hands cupped around his coffee mug, his eyes unfocused somewhere across the room, he cleared his throat and finally looked at her again. "First off, I want you to know that I love you. We all love you. No matter what, nothing is going to change that. We're all just trying to deal with it in our own ways, make sense of it, understand what it was all about."

She cocked her head to one side, an inquisitive bird. "I don't know what you're talking about, Ron."

He nodded as though that was the answer he expected, then after a beat came back to her. "I know, Kate," he said. "Don't you understand that? *I know.* And I wouldn't be surprised if the kids have figured it out as well."

She set her jaw, stared across at him.

"Not everything," he went on. "Maybe not even most of it, but the basic facts are pretty much beyond dispute."

"The facts," she said, dismissively.

"It wasn't like I was snooping, trying to find something. But of course, with you in the hospital, who else was going to have to take over paying the household accounts if not for me? And opening the mail?"

She turned her coffee cup on the table, staring at it. A quarter turn. A quarter turn back.

"I got the customer satisfaction survey," he went on, "addressed to you, and asking how you had enjoyed your stay at the Meridien. So then I checked that date against the AmEx bill and there it was. And as I looked some more, also the Uber rides to and from. The bottle of Silver Oak. So I went back and checked our calendars, thinking maybe I'd forgotten something, or maybe we were putting somebody up at the hotel, one of your old friends coming into town I'd forgotten about?"

"It wasn't —"

Ron raised his left hand, palm out.

176

"Please. Let me go on. I might even have let all that go, except that life around the house here got a little crazy when we all thought you might not survive. It became clear that something serious beyond your condition was bothering the kids — we were all talking about real stuff most of the time you were in the ICU — life and death, as you'd imagine. Anyway, you know both of them have this rarefied moral sense . . ."

"Okay."

"Okay, so you'll remember those days Aidan didn't go to school last May. Well, he didn't just go and hide out someplace. He went down to the Embarcadero — you know, Pier 39, the restaurants, and guess where else? The Ferry Building. The towers. And he saw someone that looked like his mom go into the Meridien. But Aidan hadn't ever seen you dressed that way before — in his words, like a hooker. And with nothing else to do, he followed, just in time to see you check in."

"And he told you this? Did he say what he thought I was doing?"

"He didn't know. He and Janey couldn't figure it out. So I covered for you."

"And how did you do that?"

He held his right fist out on the table in front of him. A slight tremor traveled up his arm. A muscle worked on the side of his jaw. "I told him that you sometimes took luxury days for yourself, went to a hotel or a spa or someplace just to break up the routine at home. If you'd gone to the Meridien that day, that was why. And they both seemed to buy it. But, of course, I knew that it wasn't true. I knew you'd gone to see somebody, though I didn't know who."

Kate sat still as a statue, her hands still clasped around her coffee mug.

Ron nodded at her, weariness all but leaking from his pores, his anger under control now, leached out. "But then a few days later when we all came down to the hospital to visit one night — you were still pretty out of it — who did we run into just outside the door to your room but a guy who looked a little familiar to me, and who turned out to be Peter Ash. Clearly embarrassed to have run into us, making up some story that he was down there visiting somebody else and had seen your name on the door and remembered it from the time we'd all met at Geoff's and he looked in. As excuses go, this one was ridiculous on the face of it, but it brought everything around full circle for me, and, I think, for our brilliant kids, too. We didn't have to say a word to each other. After that, we just knew. All of us."

"That doesn't seem like a lot of evidence to come to any real conclusion, Ron."

"No? Maybe not." Sighing, he went on. "But for the record, after Peter left that night, the nurse told me he'd been to look in on you a few times, right from when you were admitted. And afterwards I looked up where he worked, a whopping couple of hundred yards from the Meridien." He waved that off. "But that's not the point, either. I don't want to argue about any of this with you, Kate. I know what I know."

"Well," she said. "That doesn't mean . . ."

"Enough, Kate. All right? Enough. I'm telling you this so you can understand if the kids are distant, if it's tense around here, why that is. And if I'm not really all here, either, all the time, it's because this is a new world we're all living in. And trying to adjust to it."

"And what if your assumptions aren't right. What if —"

Ron brought a flat palm down, hard, on the table. "I called him up, Kate. I confronted him about it."

"What did he say?"

"He said it wasn't his fault. He said you called him . . ."

She kept her eyes down, staring at her hands. "That liar," she said. "That fucking

179

liar. As if I . . ." Raising her gaze, she looked him in the face. "That is just so not what happened. It was . . ."

"It doesn't matter," Ron said. "I don't want the details. I don't care about them. What I do care about is that I can't trust my loving, faithful wife anymore."

"And now he's dead and . . ." She paused. "And now you think I might have had something to do with his murder?"

He sat back straight in his chair, as if stunned. "I never said that."

"But the thought creeps in."

"Don't go there, Kate. I'm with you here, whatever you've done. What I said at the beginning when I sat down here is true. I love you. I want to be with you. I want our family to stay together."

Anger simmered in her eyes. "And you're ready to forgive me? Is that it? Just as long as I admit I've been a bad girl?"

"Do you want to fight about it? How I feel?"

"It's clear to me how you feel, Ron. I've fallen from grace, and you're going to take the high road and try not to punish me."

"Actually, not, Kate. That would be pretty condescending, wouldn't it? It's not like I haven't made some bad mistakes as well. Some serious fucking errors. Nobody's

180

keeping score here. I just wanted you to know that I'm on your side. I've never not been on your side."

Finally, she settled back in her chair. She rubbed the scar at the top of her abdomen. Her eyes shone with incipient tears. "Whatever it was, it had nothing to do with you, Ron. With how I felt about you."

"All right. I can accept that."

"And I had nothing to do with his death."

"Of course not."

"I'd like it if things could go back to the way they were." She let out a deep sigh, raised her eyes to meet his. "If we could trust each other again." A tear broke and ran down her cheek until she wiped it away. "I am so sorry, Ron. I never meant to hurt you."

He spun his coffee mug slowly around. "I think if we had a contest about who's dealt with more pain in the past six months, you'd win."

"It's not the same."

"No, but close enough. Maybe we could just let it go. Call it square. That's all I wanted to tell you."

"You know," she said, "it might be a lot easier in some ways if you were more of a cold bastard. Then we could just break up, and that'd be the end of it."

"I don't want that. Do you want that?"
"No."
"Well, then. Let's not go there."

14

Beth sat at her desk in the Homicide detail. It was a few minutes after 9:00 a.m. and Ike had already called, saying he was running late. His six-year-old, Heather, was throwing up with a fever of 102 degrees. He told her he thought he might be a while. She told him she'd manage without him until he arrived, and then she hung up and her phone rang again and a deep male voice said, "Hello. Sergeant Beth Tully?"

"This is Inspector Tully."

"Inspector, this is Alan Shaw. I don't know if you remember me, but . . ."

"I remember you, Mr. Shaw. How can I help you?"

"Well, it's not me. It's my sister, Laurie. I'm not sure if you remember, but . . ."

"Mr. Shaw. That's two things in a row you didn't think I'd remember so far. So how about moving forward we go on the assumption that unless I ask you a question about it, I remember whatever it might be you're talking about. What's the problem with your sister?"

"She's dying, I think. The anorexia she's been fighting . . . ?"

"I don't remember that. She was too thin, but I didn't see that as her main problem."

"Yeah, well, it is now. Frank Rinaldi getting himself killed was bad enough, but they think — the counselors who've seen her — they think the terrorist thing so soon after that must have pushed her around the bend with post-traumatic stuff. And lately it seems to have gotten the better of her, especially the last couple of weeks. She just got back from the clinic where she seemed to put on some weight and be pulling it together, except when she got back home . . . anyway, long story short, she blew me off when I wanted to come see her and check out how she was doing, until finally I got a bad feeling and I just went by her place a couple of days ago. She . . ." The voice faltered slightly, then went on. "She's a mess, Inspector. She can barely move around. She looks like a skull. I told her she needed to go back to the clinic and get back on some kind of feeding schedule, but she said she was done with that. What was the point? So now it's like she's forgotten how to eat and her body seems about to give up."

"I'm very sorry to hear that," she said, very clearly remembering the night she and Alan — Mr. Shaw — had spent consoling Laurie after Frank Rinaldi's murder, "but I'm not sure what you have in mind that you'd want me to do."

"I don't know exactly what, either, to tell you the truth. But I'm about at the end of my rope here. And I know that you seemed to really care about her . . ."

"I did care about her. I still do."

"Well, okay. I'm counting on that. But my point is . . . I mean, I know this might feel a little awkward — I know it is for me — me calling you again out of the blue, since I never got my act together last time around you and me."

"Last time?"

"You remember we had a date?"

"Let's keep assuming I remember things, shall we?"

"Okay. But when I came by, you weren't there."

"You came by my house?"

"We had a date. I thought you just blew me off."

Beth was gripping the telephone so tightly that her knuckles hurt.

She had thought of Alan many times during her recovery, but as the days went by and he had never called, never tried to contact her again, she had finally written him off.

He was going on. "The next day I realized of course that you were probably slammed at work about the terrorist thing, so I thought I'd leave you some space. But then that space just got bigger and bigger and pretty soon a couple of months had gone by and I never pulled it together to try calling you again. All things considered, it just felt too awkward, like I'd be butting into your life when you had more important things on your plate. I should have picked up the phone, but I never did, and I'm sorry."

"That's a done deal, Alan. It doesn't matter. And now? This call?"

"This isn't about me, or me and you. This is about Laurie. I don't know who else to reach out to. To me, it looks like my sister's given up. I don't know what to do about her, and I'm afraid if I don't think of something fast, she's going to die. In any event, I feel like you could help her more than I can. At least there's a chance she might listen to you."

Beth didn't know if that were true, but she didn't feel like she could ignore Alan's desperate request. "Does she live in the

186

same place?" she asked. "I've got some time this morning I could swing by and talk to her. You're sure she'll be there?"

"The question is can she make it all the way to the door."

"I'll give her a lot of time."

The bitter cold wouldn't relinquish its grip on the city.

Beth stood in bright sunlight on the sidewalk on Green Street and waited for Laurie's response to the doorbell. She wasn't wearing gloves and since she'd rung the bell had blown into her cupped hands three times, resting her walking stick against her hip. If Alan hadn't warned her that Laurie might be moving pretty slowly, she might have already started pushing the doorbells of the other residents, to at least get inside the building so she could pound on Laurie's door, when at last she heard the young woman's barely audible voice on the intercom.

"Hello?"

"Laurie. This is Beth Tully. Sergeant Tully. I wonder if you could spare me a couple of minutes?"

No reply for two or three seconds. Then, wearily, "What for?"

"Your brother said you might be in need

187

of a little company."

"Alan called you?"

"Just this morning."

"He's just . . ." Beth heard her sigh in the squawk box. "Oh, all right."

The buzzer sounded and the door clicked and Beth pushed and was inside.

Laurie opened the door barefoot. Although Beth thought that she had prepared herself for her first glimpse of her, in the event she found that she wasn't ready. If anything, Alan might have underestimated his sister's condition. Her wrists, hands, and feet were all bones, as were her neck and face. Her hair, still long, had thinned dramatically, and it didn't look as if a brush had touched it recently. Bruises shaded yellowish blotchy areas at her jawline and under her eyes.

Beth took this in at a glance and obviously failed at hiding her reaction, because Laurie said, "I know I don't look too good, but I'm trying to work on things. It's not as serious as Alan thinks. Do you want to come on in?"

"Sure."

Laurie backed away, then turned and led the way in a gawky gait, as though her hips were not working correctly. Her orchid print pajama top seemed to hang straight down from her shoulders. When she got to the end of the hallway, she moved to one side, and as Beth reached her, she asked, "What happened to you? The cane? You didn't have that last time, did you?"

"No. It's a new addition." She reached the closest chair and let herself down onto it. "The short version is that I was in the Ferry Building when it got attacked."

"You're kidding me. You were there?"

Beth nodded. "One of the lucky ones, as it turned out. A lot of people got a lot worse."

"Of course. I know, but it's just . . . I didn't suspect that someone I knew was in there. It must have been terrifying."

"Very. Mostly it was just weird and so completely unexpected. Since then, I'm still not the best at public spaces."

"I'd think not. I don't know if I'd be able to go out at all."

"Are you?"

"Am I what?"

"Going out? Seeing anybody? Even just some friends?"

"Not too much, no." She shrugged. "I just don't see the point somehow."

"The point?"

"You know. Going out. Doing things. I mean, after Frank it was bad enough, but then the Ferry Building . . . hey, you'd know it more than me. You were there. What's the point of caring about anything when in a second it's all wiped away?"

Beth glanced over and out through the back windows, the northern edge of the city sprawling down to the bay. "Laurie," she said gently. "Have you eaten anything recently?"

She shook her head with a small show of petulance. "I haven't been hungry. I don't really have much of an appetite anymore. It ought to come back, I think. I'm not trying to starve myself or anything like that, regardless of what Alan thinks. It's not like I really have anorexia, the disease. But if I started to listen to how much my body wants me to eat, and then went ahead and did it, I'd look like a pig."

"You're a long way from that, Laurie."

A bitter little laugh. "Not really. Not if I really started."

"But you don't know the last time you ate?"

"Well, I was at the clinic . . . I know I had some soup there. There was always soup. I actually got a little bit sick of it. But I ate enough of it to get me back to the weight they let me in at."

"And when was that? When did you check

out of the clinic?"

"Four days ago."

"And you haven't eaten anything since then?"

"No, that's not true. I had a box of rice crackers when I got home and I think I've eaten most of them. And some yogurt. So it's not like I haven't had anything at all."

Beth got to her feet. "Laurie, do you mind if I poke around in your kitchen for a minute? Alan was worried that you might not have enough on hand to keep you going. I'd feel better if I took a look, and then if you need some groceries, maybe I could go out and help you stock up. Meanwhile, do you know if by any chance you have some tea? I could use a cup of tea and maybe some honey while I'm opening the cupboards."

"I think I have some of that." Laurie got to her feet. "But I don't really need anything."

"Well, let's see."

While Laurie put on a pot of water, Beth opened the refrigerator, the shelves of which were all but bare — two eggs, some condiments (ketchup, mustard, pepper jelly, soy sauce), a moldy half block of cheddar cheese, four single servings of plain yogurt, half a jar of pickle relish, one onion in the vegetable drawer. The two pantry shelves above the counter were similarly bare. She had a third or so of a package of dried angel hair pasta, a four-ounce can of julienne beets, two cans of tuna, three packages of Top Ramen.

"You know," Beth said, "this ramen looks great, and I didn't have much of breakfast this morning either. When that tea water gets hot, maybe we could mix up a couple of bowls of it. How does that sound?"

Maybe Beth imagined it, but Laurie seemed to consider the possibility for a moment before she shook her head. "I'm not really that hungry," she said, "but you go ahead if you want. Maybe I'll have a spoonful."

But when the ramen was ready, Beth filled two bowls and pushed one of them, with a fork and spoon, in front of where Laurie sat at the table. "So do you have a specific counselor?" she asked. "Somebody you could call if you got weak, or found yourself in trouble somehow?"

"Well, no. I mean, you can. There's plenty of people there. They're all really professional. It's a good place if you're really sick, like if you've got actual malnutrition. But that's not my case."

"It's not? Was that their diagnosis?"

"Not really, no. They think I'm too skinny, of course. I mean, that's why I went there in the first place. Alan thought I needed some counseling and stuff. If they only knew how I can eat, how fast I could get fat if I gave in to that, they'd know they didn't have to worry. So I don't need like one individual counselor. And besides, it's not what you'd call cheap. So I went there to get Alan off my case mostly, but it's not like I need counseling day to day. I'm fine." She tried a smile, but it broke and her eyes glistened. "Except, okay, I'll admit I'm having a hard time dealing with the whole thing with Frank still. And the world."

"Do you have anyone who comes by to see you from time to time?" Beth pointed at the bowl across the table. "Meanwhile, a bite of that won't put too much weight on you, Laurie. I promise. Why don't you try it?"

Laurie lifted the spoon, dipped it into the broth and brought it to her lips, made a face as she delicately slurped it, then swallowed. "I know I should see people," she said. She put the spoon down. "I know I'm a total bummer to be around. I probably do need to get out more. But I don't really see the point. I mean, you were in the attack, right?

193

You must know a little how I feel."

Beth twirled ramen on her fork. "Maybe a bit. But I had my daughter. I had to take care of her."

"I don't have anybody like that. To take care of."

"What about your brother?"

"Alan?" She shook her head. "Don't get me wrong. He's a good guy, but he doesn't need me. I'm just a burden to him."

"I didn't get that impression this morning. He really cares about you."

"Well, okay, sure. But it's . . . there's no real comparison."

Beth forked noodles and pointed again at Laurie's bowl. "Your ramen's getting cold."

Laurie sighed, picked up her fork, and brought a small portion to her lips. This time, no face. Leaning in over her bowl, she loaded up her fork again and brought it to her mouth, closing her eyes in what looked like pleasure. "Maybe I was a little hungrier than I thought."

"Maybe." Beth took another bite, too. "So what are we going to do here, Laurie? Should I take you back to the clinic? You know, if you look at this rationally, you can't go on like this much longer. Do you want to die alone here in your apartment?"

"I don't think I'm . . ." But she stopped,

hung her head, and shook it slowly.

Beth pressed. "How about if I come back tonight and we eat together? I could pick something up, plus a few basics to put on your empty shelves."

"What about your daughter? Don't you have to be home with her?"

"I could bring her with me. We could have a girls' night. You'd like her."

"I'm sure I would."

"All right, then. Let's call it a plan."

15

Manny Meyer of Meyer Eldridge & Kline sat across the huge conference table from the two inspectors in the enormous corner glassed-in room that overlooked the Ferry Building as well as a good portion of the rest of the Bay Area, glistening now below them in bright sunlight. Meyer was sixty-four years old, large and florid, with an over-the-ears silvery mane of hair. He gave the impression of being a guy who laughed a lot, although he was not laughing today.

Hands clasped on the table in front of him, Meyer seemed like a man who'd just been knocked out of his saddle and was trying to figure out where he was. "Everybody here knew that Peter was going through a difficult time the past few months, but I don't think anybody saw anything like this coming."

"Like this?" Ike prompted him.

"You know. Getting to the point where

he'd . . . want to end things."

"You're saying that you think he took his own life?" Beth asked.

"Let me ask you one, Inspector. Have you found something to indicate that he didn't? I had just assumed. When I heard . . . the news. It was the first thing that came to my mind, that he shot himself. But now are you saying he didn't?"

Beth shook her head. "Not entirely. We haven't completely ruled out anything." She kept her tone neutral, patient. It was possible, she thought, that Meyer might be in some degree of shock. He looked from Beth to Ike and back again. "So you're saying he was murdered?"

Beth nodded. "Is that so hard for you to imagine?"

"That somebody would want to kill Peter? I'd have to say yes. Almost impossible. At least, for someone who knew him."

"And why is that?"

Meyer considered for a moment. "Because he was such a . . . I know that this might sound a little out of context, but you had to know him. He was just a charming man, a truly sweet guy. I can't believe that he'd have an enemy in the world, much less someone who hated him so much they'd decide to kill him."

Ike asked, "So what about all these troubles in the past few months?"

Meyer made a brushing movement with his hand. "His marriage was breaking up, and I know that took its toll. But he and Jill were still talking, maybe even still trying to make things work. I know that they'd gone to counseling together."

"We spoke with Jill yesterday," Ike said. "The divorce was going ahead. They probably weren't going to be working things out."

Meyer nodded at the sad reality. "That's probably true. But you don't think Jill . . . ?"

"We don't think anything at the moment, sir," Beth said. "We're just starting to talk to people that knew him, see where it takes us."

"Is there anyone at the firm here with whom he was particularly close?" Ike asked. "Maybe somebody he saw outside of the work environment?"

"Well. Me. We were in a wine-tasting club together. We met every month or so. My wife and I would get together with him and Jill for dinner or the theater or a concert three or four times a year. But as I say, it wasn't just us. Peter was super-friendly. Everybody liked him."

"How about his clients?" Beth asked.

"That's why they were his clients," Meyer said. "They loved the guy."

"So no turnover there? No dissatisfaction? He didn't just lose a big case? Anything like that?" she asked.

Meyer shook his head. "Nothing that hit my radar, and I'm certain that it would have. But you know, if you want to go down that road, maybe you should talk to his secretary, Theresa Boleyn. She's been with Peter since he came on board. In fact, he brought her with him. If there are any hostile bodies among the clients, which I doubt, she'll know where they're buried. I could have her come on down here in a couple of minutes, unless you need anything more from me." He stood, seeming to slump in his navy blue pinstripe suit, and looked from one of them to the other. "This is such a tragedy. Such a terrible loss."

Theresa did not come down to the conference room in the next few minutes because she had not come into work at all that morning. When Beth and Ike got to her apartment in a thirty-unit building on Market Street way up under Twin Peaks, she opened the door before they'd even knocked and invited them in. "Too cold to be standing around even for a minute," she said.

In spite of the warm welcome and the breezy tone, once everyone was inside, Theresa visibly slumped. She was a naturally attractive young woman, Beth thought, who, with deep-set blue eyes, shoulder-length blond hair, an unblemished complexion, and prominent cheekbones, with minimal effort might transform herself into a true beauty. But, this morning at least, she wasn't making any effort in that direction. No lipstick, no mascara or other makeup. Unflattering granny glasses.

Leading the way to the island in the kitchen, Theresa slid onto one of the stools. That morning's *Chronicle* lay open in front of her and she glanced at it, then pushed it as far out of the way as she could. She nervously rubbed her right hand over first one cheek, then the other. Her eyes were heavy and shot with red. "I'm sorry," she said.

"What about?" Beth asked.

Theresa shrugged. "Everything. I'm not sick, I guess you can see. But I just couldn't go in today." Her expression seemed to seek absolution.

"There's no need to apologize," Beth said. "Thanks for seeing us on such short notice."

"There's nothing to do down there anyway, now with Peter . . ."

Ike cut her off. "Did you just find out from the paper this morning?" he asked.

"No. One of my friends saw it on the news last night and called me. I don't know if I believed . . . but then I saw . . ."

They gave her a minute. Beth pulled another stool around and boosted herself up onto it.

"I'm sorry," Theresa repeated. "Really, I'm just . . . you never expect." She wiped at her eyes again.

Ike seemed uncharacteristically impatient. "When was the last time you saw him?"

The abruptness of the question broke her from her reverie, and she fastened on Ike, her mouth a tight line of concentration. "What's today? Thursday. Then Wednesday, no. Tuesday. It must have been Monday. It *was* Monday. It was the only day he was in this week."

Ike kept it going. "Did he work a full day Monday?"

"Yes. Well, for him, lately. Although he left before I did. I could check, but probably around four thirty."

"Did he have an appointment?"

"Not that I know of. It wasn't calendared, if he did."

"So he didn't come in on Tuesday at all?"

"No."

"Was that standard?"

"Well, there wasn't really a normal routine anymore. He usually came in, except when he didn't. He worked whatever hours he wanted."

"He didn't tell you where he was going to be?"

"Most of the time. Yes."

"Did he have appointments on Tuesday or Wednesday?"

"Yes. He had a depo scheduled at another firm in town on Tuesday, and he was supposed to go to LA on Wednesday."

"But he didn't make either of those?"

"No. Neither one."

"And did that worry you?"

"Of course. Not showing for Tuesday's depo was bad to the level of inexcusable. I was really worried by Wednesday. I tried to call him a number of times on his cell. No answer. But I still thought he'd just turn up the way he tended to."

"Did it occur to you to call the police?"

"Not really, no."

"Why not?"

She shrugged. "Because this kind of thing had happened before. More than once, actually. He would have killed me if I called the police to look for him after a couple of days of just not checking in. I mean, it was more my job to cover for him, not call attention to when he was acting . . . you know, being irresponsible. Figuring stuff out."

Finally, Beth put in a word. "Did you have any indication of what that was, that he was figuring out? Specifically?"

She shook her head. "He didn't really confide in me on that kind of stuff."

"So, what?" Ike said. "You were supposed to read his mind?"

A small smile. "If you look up legal secretary in the dictionary, Inspector," she said, "that would pretty much be the job description."

"And he didn't give you a hint about what was on his mind? What he was doing?"

"Well, I knew his schedule, of course. I kept his calendar. So in theory I knew where he was supposed to be all the time. But then if he blew off a meeting or an appointment and I'd ask him, he was all like, 'Don't worry about that. That's my job. I know what I'm doing.' He acted like it was all some game he was playing."

"And that didn't bother you?" Ike asked. "Didn't you call him on that?"

She thought for a while before answering him. "You've got to understand. He was a great boss. He took me with him when he came over to Meyer, eight years ago. I make a really good salary, probably more than I'm worth, and it was all because of Peter. I figured his problems were mostly about his marriage breaking up. Kidding around with me was just his way of letting go of some of the pressure. What was I going to do, scold him about it? Tell him he ought to take his work more seriously? Come on. If I couldn't flow with it, I didn't deserve his trust. I figured that when everything settled down, and it would, he'd revert to his old Type A self, and then we'd go back to being the way we used to be. But until then, how could it hurt to humor him?"

Beth had no answer for that, so she moved on. "So what about the marital problems?"

This question sparked what looked to Beth like a guilty response. Theresa's eyes darted from one inspector to the other, finally settling back on Beth. "I don't know any details about them," she said. "His marital problems. As I said, he didn't confide in me about his personal life."

Ike followed up. "All right. But you did notice this change in his behavior. His wife told us that it came on all at once, or at least over a very short period of time. Would you agree with that?"

She thought a minute, then nodded. "I guess I'd have to say yes."

"Do you remember anything specific?" Ike asked. "About exactly when that might have been, or what might have brought it about?"

Theresa scratched at the counter. "I don't, I mean, nothing I could swear to."

Beth said, "Nobody's asking you to swear to anything, Theresa. Whatever it is you're thinking, even if it's just a vague impression, it might be important. Was it something to do with a client, maybe? Mr. Meyer told us you'd be the one to talk to about if Peter had had some negative run-ins with one of his clients."

"No." She was shaking her head again, still picking at a spot on the counter. "I mean, none of his regular clients. They all loved him."

"But . . ." Beth prompted her.

Theresa finally let out a breath. "It might have been . . . I thought she might be a potential client."

"She?" Ike asked.

"I mean, this is so unlikely . . ."

"Go ahead," Beth said. "Unlikely is good."

Theresa drew a breath, let it out, then finally gave an emphatic nod, committing to what she was about to say. "Sometime back in the spring, when all this started, he got a

205

call from a woman who didn't identify herself when I asked her. All she told me was she needed to talk to Peter and that it was extremely important."

"A legal matter?" Ike asked.

"She didn't say, but what else could it have been?"

"Right. Of course. Go ahead."

"Well, she was very polite, but she wasn't taking no for an answer, not from me, anyway. So I asked her to hold and I punched up Peter, and he said he'd talk to her, and I put her through."

"And then?" Beth asked.

"Well, I don't even know if this is related or not, but after a few minutes Peter came out of the office and said he was going out to clear his head. He said he'd be back after a while, but if he ever came back, it was after I'd left. That was the first time he broke his schedule." She looked pleadingly from one inspector to the other. "But he really did have a depo that was eating him up. It might have had nothing to do with the woman and her phone call. But now, thinking about it . . ."

"It might have had something to do with it after all," Ike said.

"Well, that's the other thing," Theresa said.

"What's that?" Beth asked.

"A couple of days later, that same woman called again."

"No name? No identity?"

"No, I'm sorry. Normally, I try to find out on these types of calls, of course, but . . ."

"That's all right," Beth said. "Did she say what she wanted that second time?"

"No. Just that she needed to talk to Peter again. But he wasn't in the office, and I sent her to his voicemail, but she didn't leave a message."

"And you say that this was right around when Peter started behaving differently?"

"Yes." Theresa furrowed her brow and looked over at Ike.

"What are you thinking?" he asked.

"I just remembered the time of it more exactly. The woman's call, I mean. It was the week before the terrorist thing at the Ferry Building. On the day of the attack, Peter had told me that he was going to lunch there, but then he changed his mind and went to Tadich instead. And I remember being so glad that he hadn't gone where he said he was going, and how out of character that change of plans would have seemed until just recently, which I guess is why it stuck with me. Anyway, in my mind, this mystery woman seemed somehow connected to when he started changing. If you could find out who she was . . ."

"That could be helpful," Ike said. "We'll look into that." He glanced at Beth as though he was going to say something else, but in the end came back to Theresa. "Thanks for your time and all this information." He handed her his business card. "And of course, please contact us if you think of anything else."

"What do you think?" Ike asked Beth as he pulled into the Market Street traffic heading back downtown.

"As in 'Do I think she was sleeping with him?' "

"Right."

"Did you pick up anything that indicated she was?"

"Nothing except she's thirty-ish, single, and has been with him for eight years."

"Don't you think it's possible that they have a friendly and solid professional relationship and that's all?"

"Definitely. I'm sure that happens all the time with a lot of people."

"But . . ."

"But my intuition tells me they were doing the bonero."

"What an elegant turn of phrase," Beth

said. "But I thought, being the woman in our partnership, I was the one who was supposed to have the intuition."

"And you don't have a feeling with Theresa?"

"Not really, no. She seemed like a loyal and dedicated secretary to me. Besides which, if she gets involved with him romantically and they break up, it threatens her job. A woman living alone doesn't want to risk that. So I'd say it's unlikely. And even more unlikely that she killed him."

"Why's that?"

"Same reason. Killing him is killing her job. And again, if she was romantically involved with him, why is that a reason she would have killed him?"

"Easy. He started this fling with her, which of course she didn't think was a fling. And then he either dumped her outright or moved along to the next one. Which made our Theresa crazy and jealous and she blew him away, job be damned. What do you think?"

She shot him a sideways glance. "I'll try to keep an open mind."

16

Geoff Cooke washed his face in the firm's bathroom sink, then dried it with one of the paper towels. He stared into the mirror, shocked at the gimlet tint his eyes had taken on.

He'd been sick on and off all through the day, ever since he'd read about it in the paper in the morning. Breakfast had come right on up at him, and he didn't even try to get down any lunch, instead locking his office door and trying to grab a nap on the couch in his office. That effort had been futile as well.

He hung on with busywork for another couple of hours. A bit after 4:00, he gave up entirely, told his secretary the truth, which was that he felt like he was getting the flu — she probably shouldn't expect him to come in to work tomorrow either — and left the office. Wearing a heavy tan cashmere coat against the chill, he considered getting his car from the garage and driving up to the Marina — an hour or two out on the bay with his sailboat generally worked for his peace of mind no matter what it was that ailed him.

But today, somehow, that didn't appeal.

Instead of going down to the garage for his car, he started walking around the downtown streets, strolling really, his mind empty except for the swish of vertigo from the sick-making emotion that seemed to wash over him every couple of breaths.

But otherwise, without a plan.

Fifteen or so minutes later, he found that he'd crossed Market and was on Fifth, heading south, a destination vaguely forming in his mind.

Straight out of law school, long before he'd even dreamed of going into private practice, Geoff had worked for two years as an assistant district attorney in the city. He still maintained relatively current friendships with a couple of the guys he had known back then.

There, a block over to his right, he made out the massive bluish-gray monolithic structure that was his former workplace — the Hall of Justice — home to Superior Court, the Southern Police Station, the district attorney's offices, and assorted other smaller local bureaucracies. When he got to it, the front of the building was as inviting as it had always been, which is to say not. Several homeless people lay in their sleeping bags by the struggling foliage on either side of the glass-and-plywood front doors; a line of fifteen or so desultory and mostly poorly dressed citizens blew on their hands as they waited to slowly move forward into the building proper, where they would eventually encounter the security checkpoint and metal detector before finally gaining admission.

Checking his watch, 4:45, Geoff thought his timing would be pretty good for his unannounced visit. It was near the end of the workday, and though the assistant DAs often put in long hours, the courts were generally closed up by now and the office work took on a more relaxed character.

Which was, apparently, not shared by the guardians at the front gate.

When he finally got inside and made it to the security checkpoint, Geoff dutifully emptied his pockets, putting the contents into the plastic saucer provided to hold them, but the heavyset white cop at the desk stopped him before he was cleared to walk through the metal detector. "Hold up!" he said, extending his hand. "What's this?"

Geoff looked around behind him to see who the guy was talking to, then realized with some surprise that it was him. "I'm sorry," he said. "Me?"

The cop pointed. "Yeah. You. Is this what it looks like?"

Geoff looked. "My keys and my Swiss Army knife."

"Not allowed."

"What's not allowed?"

"No knives."

"But it's just a —"

"It's a knife and it's not allowed, sir. You can either leave the line and bring it back to your car or wherever you want to keep it, and return without it, or I confiscate it here and now. No knives allowed in the building."

Geoff drew in a breath, let it out slowly. "Look, Officer," he said. "I promise I'm not going to stab anybody with the knife. It's not that kind of knife. Can't you just keep it in a drawer in your desk or something until I'm finished my business here and then I pick it up on my way out? How would that work?"

"Wouldn't work at all," the guard said. "You can take it out of here or I can take it and it goes in the confiscated pile. Those are your options."

"Really?"

"Really."

"Jesus!"

Behind him in the line, somebody raised her voice. "Hey! Let's keep the show on the road up there. We're waiting all day and freezing back here!"

The guard eyed Geoff with a terrible flat affect. "Your choice, but let's make it right now, sir."

Geoff shook his head, then nodded in frustration. "Keep the damn knife."

"Thank you." The guard picked the offending weapon out of the saucer and with no ceremony dropped it into a trash container to the side of him. "Next," he said.

On the other side of the metal detector, Geoff stood a moment, considering the odds if he reached into the trash container and just grabbed his knife. Maybe stab the guard. But already the people behind him in line were moving him forward, so he simply reached for his keys and kept moving, into the lobby and over to the elevators.

"And they haven't gotten any quicker — the elevators, I mean — in the last twenty years, either," Geoff said.

"Nothing's gotten quicker," Don Cordes said. Bald and muscular, Cordes had his

214

jacket off, his tie loose. "There's no getting around it. Entropy is on the rise. Things are slowing down and we're all doomed. I am sorry, though, about your Swiss Army knife. But if it's any consolation, I don't think there's anybody who has to come to this building often who hasn't lost at least something to the Gestapo down there."

"Do they really just confiscate that stuff and then throw it away?"

"That's the word."

"They could auction them or something, couldn't they?"

"Probably not. Somebody would stab somebody with one of the knives and then the victim would sue the city for providing the weapon. But if you want, you're a big-time fancy lawyer now. You could write a letter with that suggestion, put 'em in the police auction, I mean. Although it wouldn't work, because nothing does."

Cordes was doing homicides now and so had to share his office with only one other person, who wasn't there at the moment. Surrounded by dozens of file boxes lining the walls, he sat at one of the two facing desks, leaning back in his chair, his feet up. "Why don't you take off your coat and stay awhile?" he asked. "I'm guessing you didn't drop by your old stomping grounds to talk

215

about how we keep the building safe, fascinating though the topic is. So what's up?"

Geoff gave him a sad look, let out a breath, then shrugged out of his overcoat. "I'm all fucked up," he said. Crossing to the facing desk, he hung the coat over the chair behind it, then sat and brought his hands together on the desktop. "Are you following the story of the lawyer they pulled out of the ocean yesterday?"

Cordes nodded. "Peter Ash." Not a question. "What about him?"

"Well, it's him and me, actually."

Cordes cocked an eyebrow. "Are you coming out to me here, Geoff?"

Geoff snorted in derision. "Fuck you, Don. Give me a break."

"Hey, you say it's you and him. What am I supposed to think? This is San Francisco. It's not like I haven't heard it before."

"Well, this isn't that."

"Fine. What is it, then?"

Geoff started in again. "I met him six, eight months ago, somewhere in there. We got seated together at this wine tasting up in Napa and it was just like click city between the two of us. We've read the same books, we like the same music. The guy knows every fact in the world. Plus, I'm laughing so hard my cheeks hurt. Anyway,

216

long story short, by a week or two later, it was like we'd been in each other's lives for twenty years."

Cordes nodded. "Bromance."

"Maybe. Call it what you want. But it was pretty cool."

"Okay?"

"Okay, so now somebody shot him and dumped him in the ocean."

"How do you know that?"

"That's what the paper had this morning."

"It had somebody dumping him? I don't remember that."

"Well, they pulled him out of the water at the beach. So I assumed that if he's shot, he didn't walk there, not from any distance, anyway. Somebody must have put him in."

"Not necessarily, but all right. Let's say that was it. Where do you fit in?"

"I'm pissed off, Don. Maybe it's as simple as that. I'm just royally fried that somebody took out my best friend. And I know for a fact that I was the closest guy to him in the past six months. In that same period of time, among other things, his marriage started to break up. In any event, he was going through a ton of shit, and I was the one he was confiding in. We were hanging out with each other a couple of times a week. And then somebody shoots him? Why? I mean, what the fuck? How does that make any sense?"

"You don't have any ideas?"

"None. The guy was a pure sweetheart. But then again, I realized it's possible I might know something important and not realize it."

"So you want to talk to Homicide?"

"I imagine I do. I think that's probably why I came down here. I don't just want to insinuate myself into a homicide investigation if they've already got a suspect and it turns out I'm wasting their time. I don't really have anything concrete to offer. I'm just, as I said, pissed off. I feel like I ought to do something, but I don't know what the hell it's supposed to be."

Don Cordes tugged at his lower lip. "I haven't heard word one about a suspect, so I'm thinking they'd love to talk to you."

"Do you want to help me set that up?"

"I could do that. Or, since you're here at this very moment, how'd you like to take a walk upstairs, see who's hanging around?"

Ike's daughter's fever was spiking again and he'd gone home, so Beth was alone at her desk in the Homicide detail when she looked up and saw Don Cordes coming her way with another man in tow. Cordes was Homicide and she was Homicide, and they saw quite a bit of each other in the normal course of their business, so it wasn't unusual to have him come to the Homicide detail. What was unusual was that he was bringing someone along with him.

And unusual was a good thing, since it might mean that something had broken outside of her routine.

From halfway across the large room, Don pointed at her and gave her a nod — yes, he was coming to see her — so she pushed back her chair, forced herself not to wince as she got to her feet and not to limp as she came around the desk. She said hello to her colleague and shook hands with Mr. Cooke, an old friend of Don's and a former ADA himself. As part of his introduction, Cordes dropped the short version of Beth's ordeal on the day of the terrorist attack, and when he'd finished, Geoff took her hand again. "So I'm meeting a true hero," he said.

Embarrassed, as she always was by this sort of thing, she shook her head. "Hardly," she said. "It was my day off and I was having lunch with a friend. I couldn't do a damn thing to stop it. If some real cops hadn't been around and stepped up just in time — the real heroes — I would have been killed for sure."

"What a terrible day that was," Geoff said. "I have another friend who got caught in it. She almost died, too."

" 'Almost' being the key word. I hope she's all right now."

"Getting there. She's back home, anyway. Thank God."

But enough of this, Beth thought. This goes nowhere except back around to herself. And she wanted no part of that. "So," she said, "you were ADA back in the day. Whatever made you leave all this glamour here?"

"I'm afraid it was the pursuit of filthy lucre."

"Well," she said, "if you've got to have a reason, I suppose that's a good one."

"Mr. Cooke also has a pretty good reason for wanting to talk to you," Cordes said.

"Geoff, please," he said. "Mr. Cooke was my father, may he rest in peace."

As subtly as she could, taking the weight from her weary legs, she boosted herself onto the desk behind her. "All right. Geoff it is. What can I do for you?"

With a look that came across as mostly apologetic, he nodded. "I may have some information on Peter Ash."

"And that is my cue to disappear." Point-

220

ing at each of them in turn, a characteristic gesture, Cordes said, "Geoff, lunch. Beth, later." Then he turned and headed for the exit.

Beth didn't hesitate for a second. "What kind of information?" she asked Geoff.

"That's just it, as I was telling Don. And I'm assuming the killer knew him, by the way, because if this was random street violence, all bets are off. I don't even know if what I know rises to the level of relevance. Peter and I were good friends, really good friends. I know we confided a bit in each other. I thought maybe if you had some gaps in your knowledge about him, I might be able to fill in some of them. Whoever did this to him, I want to help you find him. Or her."

"Thank you. But basically, I've got nothing but gaps. I know next to nothing about him except that he seemed to have had some sort of existential breakdown over the past few months and started acting erratically. We're going on the theory that in his altered state, if you want to call it that, he did something that finally got him killed. If you know anything about that, one way or the other, it might be a good place to start."

"Well," Geoff said, "I'll start by saying that he didn't seem to be in any kind of altered state to me. I mean, in the sense of truly crazy, or high on drugs, or anything like that. He didn't act like a dangerous person that you'd recognize from a distance and steer clear of."

"But still, somebody decided they had to kill him."

Geoff picked at the fabric of his overcoat.

Beth broke the silence. "A minute ago," she said, "you indicated that you wanted to help us find whoever killed Mr. Ash. You said you wanted to help get him, or her. Do you have any reason to think it might have been a woman?"

He broke a slight, crooked smile. "Only about a hundred of them."

"He was seeing a hundred women?"

"I don't have any idea of the real number, and I wouldn't call it 'seeing' them, as in more than once. But it was a lot of different women — he'd meet me for a drink after work a couple of times a week, and half the time he had somebody new on his arm. Either that, or he was heading out to hook up. I'm talking a few times a week with different women."

"And you think one of them may have killed him?"

"That makes more sense to me than one of his guy friends."

"Well, that's worth looking into. Did the two of you talk about his dating habits?"

"Sure. It just seemed so out of character, especially when he told me he was getting divorced, breaking up his family."

"You were critical of him?"

"Well, I didn't completely understand it, I can say that. I think I made that clear."

"And how did he take that? The criticism?"

"Frankly, it rolled off his back. It didn't bother him at all."

"So this sexual behavior, it was a change from when you originally met him?"

"It was dramatic. Hard to imagine, really."

"So what happened?"

"Actually, from what Don just told me, I think you might understand better than I do."

"What's that?"

Geoff took a beat. "Well, like you," he said, "Peter was at the Ferry Building that day."

Beth narrowed her eyes at him, not sure of what to make of this. But, in Geoff's defense, he seemed to share whatever obscure thing it was that she was feeling.

"He left before the attack started," he said, "but evidently he missed it only by a few minutes. He should have been killed, he thought. There was no reason he'd been spared when so many others had died. So then suddenly, after that, and I mean right away after that, he decided he'd had enough of the way he'd been living — working hard, the good husband, the devoted father. What was the point, right? If it could all end so randomly, so meaninglessly?"

"I felt the opposite," Beth said. "I wanted to live, to see my daughter grow up and have children of her own, to be a better cop, to make what was left of my life mean something more."

"That sounds like a healthier reaction than Peter's," Geoff said. "He felt that somehow the straight and narrow he'd been on had cheated him of his best years and he was going to make up for them now, all at once. He was going to indulge his sexual appetites, which he'd been sublimating for years. His kids were all grown up and didn't need him. His wife would, frankly, be better off without him, since he felt no more passion for her. She'd be happier with some new guy who wanted to share her boring life. His characterization, not mine."

Beth waited, content to let another silence grow between them.

Finally, Geoff went on. "Anyway," he said. "That's where Peter was coming from these

last few months. I wouldn't be surprised if he broke a few hearts along the way."

"Or angered a few husbands or boyfriends?"

A nod. "Probably, just given the odds."

Beth glanced up at the wall clock behind Geoff and realized that she needed to get home for Ginny, especially if they were going to Laurie's later on. She made an apologetic face. "This has been very helpful, Mr. Cooke, except now instead of none, I've got a hundred suspects to find and interview. Do you know if there was anywhere that Peter tended to meet these women?"

"Not for sure. He joked about some of the online sites, where he said it was so easy it almost took the fun out of it. He preferred bars. I know he liked North Beach in general, and a semiprivate club called The Battery, up by Broadway. But otherwise, he was pretty eclectic."

"Good to know. And at least it gives us some direction. Thank you."

"My pleasure." He reached for his wallet and extracted a business card, handing it to her. "If you want to get in touch with me," he said. "Anytime. In case I know something I don't know that I know." He sighed. "I really loved that guy. I can't believe some-

body killed him."

"Yes, well . . ." She glanced at his business card and her face clouded for a moment.

"Is something wrong?" Geoff asked.

"No." A small hesitation. "No. Everything's fine. Thanks again for coming by. If anything relevant comes up, I'll give you a call."

"Anything I can do," he said.

"Got it," she replied. "Thank you so much."

17

Ginny Tully wasn't really into her mother's idea of paying a courtesy call and sharing her famous eggplant parmesan with this Laurie Shaw person — some victim's girlfriend? She had been planning to stay home and finally get going on the term paper that was due on Monday. If she didn't put down some pages tonight, she would wind up spending Friday night and then at least part of the weekend getting it finished, and that was not in her game plan at all.

But now that looked like what she would have to do. It was so not fair.

On the other hand, she knew that her mother wouldn't have asked if she didn't believe it was important. Laurie obviously had bigger problems than either Beth — with the continuing slo-mo recovery of the use of her legs — or Ginny's term paper.

Beth almost never made requests of Ginny's time.

The two of them had had to become mutually independent after her father, Denny, had died when Ginny was ten — a joyriding teenager named Jonas Wilder had run a red light and T-boned her dad's Honda Civic, killing them both.

At the time, Beth, a fourth-year cop without any other family, didn't feel she had an option other than to keep her job. After a short, unpleasant, and expensive succession of nannies and au pairs, the mother-and-daughter team decided that Ginny would just have to make do on her own — get herself to and from school, help with the housekeeping and cooking, become a functional adult before she was even technically a teenager.

And somehow the accommodation had worked for both of them. Most of the time, it hadn't even been that hard.

But sometimes . . .

In the passenger seat, holding the eggplant parmesan in her lap, Ginny consciously and dramatically exhaled and this time, finally, her mother shot a look her way. "You know," she said, "this isn't exactly what I had planned for tonight either, in case you're wondering. Sometimes stuff comes up and you just have to do something."

"Really? Does that sometimes happen? I

thought everything worked out for the best all the time." Ginny didn't really like the snotty tone she heard coming out of her own mouth, but there it was, so she tried to notch her reaction down a bit. "I'm sorry, but meanwhile I'm here, aren't I? Dutifully going along."

"Yes, you are, and thank you very much. But just so you know, I could do without so many theatrics."

"How am I being theatrical?"

"I think you can figure that out. A couple more sighs as deep as that last one and you might pass out. Are you sure this is about your term paper?"

"What else would it be about?"

"Oh, I don't know. A seventeen-year-old girl might have a couple of other things on her plate."

"It's not that." They rode in silence for another block, and then Ginny said, "Well, maybe that's what it is after all."

"What?"

"That there isn't much on my plate. 'Much' as in anything. Not to whine, but sometimes you wonder when something's going to change and get better instead of change and get worse. You know what I mean?"

Beth worked a muscle in her jaw. "Yes,"

she said. "I've got some general idea."

"I know," Ginny said, now truly repentant. "I didn't mean . . ."

"No, it's all right. I know what you're saying. It's a valid point."

"I hate it when I get this way. Why does this happen? Where does it come from?"

"You want some of your own time. I understand that. Maybe I shouldn't have tried to include you tonight. Except I selfishly wanted to be with my daughter."

"But it's really me who's being selfish."

"Maybe both of us, a little." She patted her daughter on the leg. "We don't have to stay long. I just want to make sure she's going to be all right until she can get some more counseling. We'll see how it plays."

"We can stay as long as we need to, Mom. I don't mean to be difficult. It might actually do me some good, get my mind off myself for a while."

"I wouldn't say you have that problem, hon."

"More than I should."

"Well . . ." Again, Beth reached over and patted Ginny's thigh. "I wouldn't beat myself up over it. You're here with me now, for example, on an errand of mercy."

"Sure. Kicking and screaming."

"Not really so much that after all."

"I don't know what gets into me. I should have more empathy."

"We should all have more empathy, Gin, but meanwhile, I'd say you're on the right track."

The first order of business after the introductions was getting the eggplant into the oven. That done, Beth put together a tray of brie and crackers and herded the two younger women back into the living room while she went back to rummage in the kitchen. Her idea was to set a nice table in there so that the meal might have a resonance as an event of sorts — something you sat down for and could take a while enjoying.

Somewhat to Beth's surprise, Laurie had some Pottery Barn plates, a full set of flatware, flowery yellow and green placemats, cloth napkins. In a couple of minutes, she was done with the table, but stayed in the kitchen to put away the grocery bag full of stuff that she'd picked up on the way home: eggs, ramen, pasta, spaghetti sauce, a bottle of red and a bottle of white, cheese, bread, milk, juice, yogurt, and java chip ice cream.

The girls seemed to be having a real conversation in the other room. They'd put on what Beth recognized as Taylor Swift's *Red,* and the music played quietly in the background, intimate and enveloping.

Reluctant to interrupt the mood in the living room, she opened the red wine, poured herself a glass, sat down at the kitchen table, and waited for a lull in the chatter.

"This is the best-tasting thing I've ever put in my mouth," Laurie said. "You made this yourself?"

Ginny nodded. "It's my specialty."

"She's actually got at least ten specialties," Beth said. "Not that this isn't one of the most special specialties, but you should try her lamb meatballs with mint jelly gravy. Talk about to die for."

"That sounds really good."

"It's amazing," Beth said. "Potentially life altering."

Laurie swallowed. "Do you guys eat together every night?" she asked.

"Whenever we can," Beth said. "Although sometimes I'm late getting in from work. But then usually Ginny waits up and she has a snack while I heat up whatever she made."

"That must be nice," Laurie said. She looked from mother to daughter. "Do you think I could have some wine?"

"May I see your ID?" Beth deadpanned.

Momentarily nonplussed by the question, Laurie finally chuckled.

"I guess we can let it go." Beth reached for the bottle and poured.

Laurie took a tentative sip. "You really eat like this every day?"

"Whenever we can," Ginny said.

Laurie sighed. "Well, no offense, and you both look great, but I know if I ate like this every day, I'd weigh a ton. Although if I had something like this to look forward to . . ." She cut a tiny bite of the eggplant with the side of her fork and brought it to her mouth.

"You could," Ginny said.

"No," Laurie said. "You'd have to plan it, and I never think about fixing anything good."

"Maybe that's because you're by yourself. Nobody likes to eat alone. Not even me, and I'm always thinking about food."

"Well, I can't," Laurie said. "I really have to watch out."

"Or you'd get fat?" Ginny asked. "Do you think you're fat now?"

Laurie shook her head. "Not really. A little, I guess. But it's always close. You know. If I slip up."

"Well." Ginny showed a bright grin. "You

233

know the awesome thing about this eggplant parmesan? Besides how great it tastes?"

"What?"

"You can eat as much as you want and never gain weight. Mom and I have experimented extensively and it's absolutely true."

"She's right," Beth said. "It is."

Visibly perking up, Laurie said, "In that case, I think I could probably eat another bite. Would that be all right?"

"That's what we're here for," Beth said, cutting another slice and putting it on Laurie's plate. "Some sourdough? Salad? Similarly delicious, I promise."

Laurie nodded, sheepish at her enthusiasm. "Might as well. My brother should see me now," she said. "He thought I was never going to eat again."

"You should tell him about tonight," Beth said. "Does he come to see you often?"

"Every couple of days," Laurie said. "He worries."

"Maybe you could invite him by," Ginny said, "and I could make another one of my specialties."

"No. I couldn't ask you . . ."

"Are you kidding? How fun would that be? Lamb meatballs, Greek chicken, paella, my famous duck breast with blueberry . . ."

"Duck? I don't think . . ."

234

"Duck is the best meat on the planet, Laurie. Trust me. Well, maybe squab, super rare."

"Come on!" Laurie now laughed freely. "Do you really cook all that?"

"And so much more. I love it. So we start with the easy stuff, like this eggplant . . ."

"This was easy?"

"Piece of cake. Fifteen minutes' prep, half hour cook. Done. And the meatballs are easier. I could show you the inside moves. You'd love it."

"I don't know. I've never . . ."

"You can. We could do it together. It would be a blast."

Laurie pondered for a moment. "Maybe Alan would relax a little. He thinks I'm . . . I mean, I know he's worried." She turned to Beth. "Would you be free to come and help, too?" Then to Ginny. "Would that be all right?"

Beth shook her head no. "I don't know if that would be . . ."

"Mom!" Ginny said. "Of course you're coming. You started all this." Then, to Laurie. "Fine with us," she said. "Let's book it."

Eric Ash didn't understand his mother at all. Or his brother Tyler, for that matter. All of their weeping and gnashing of teeth over his asshole father's death.

Hey! Wake up! He wanted to yell at both of them. If anybody in this world fully deserved to be murdered, Peter Ash — betrayer of biblical proportions — was that person.

But now here they all were, the second night in a row, sitting around the kitchen table at Mom's place, rehashing all the whys and wherefores, the whens and ifs and hows. Talking talking talking, and then getting on to details about the funeral next Monday, when the reality was that they didn't have to talk about fucking Peter Ash and his motivations and his troubles anymore.

He was gone.

And if Eric had had any real guts instead of just an inchoate anger, his father would have been gone long ago, certainly within a couple of weeks of when Eric had bought his unregistered, completely untraceable gun from those gangbangers in Oakland with every intention of using it.

But no sooner had he taken it home and hidden it than he'd been paralyzed with paranoia about what would happen if the cops got any hint of what he'd done, as — he thought — they surely would. Especially after his and his father's fight in September, wasn't he too obvious a suspect? Maybe the most obvious one? He could imagine the interrogation, and the idea of it scared him to death.

It's no secret you hated your dad, right?

Yep.

You've told your mother and your brother that you intended to kill him.

Yep.

That he deserved to die.

Absolutely.

And so you bought a gun. Illegally.

I did? Prove it.

And maybe they could.

So, gutless and frustrated, he'd waited. And waited.

But now it had turned out for the best. His dad was just as dead as he would have been if Eric had acted in September. And no one — no cops anyway — had even mentioned the fight.

If suspicion fell upon him, it would be a drag. The idea of getting charged, of going to jail, terrified him. But he was pretty sure they could never prove that he'd bought the gun. And that was the only thing he might have to worry about.

"What are you thinking, Eric?" His mother's voice broke into his thoughts. "You're hardly saying a word."

"What's to say?" With a flat stare at his mother, he said, "Good riddance to bad rubbish."

Jill brought her hands up to her face. "You don't really believe that."

He slammed a flat palm on the table, and his mother started in her seat.

"I don't believe that?" he screamed. "Are you shitting me? I totally believe that, Mom. How can I believe anything else? The man was a colossal fraud who ruined all of our lives."

"He wasn't . . ."

"Yeah, he was! You know what I can't believe? I can't believe that we're sitting here talking logistics about how we're going to handle things at the goddamn funeral. Would it be too awkward to have people over for cake and cookies? Who should be on the guest list? Yeah, I guess I'm not paying attention, when the real question is why we're even talking about going to the funeral at all. Fuck the funeral is what I say. And fuck him."

"Don't be such an asshole, Eric," Tyler said. "Mom's trying to keep this together, in case you haven't noticed. You want to punish her more?"

Eric shot an angry glare at his brother, gathered himself, then turned to his mother, his voice softening. "What I'm saying is that you ought to stop punishing yourself, Mom. You didn't do any of this. He did it."

"I know that," she said. "We all know that. But I was his wife. I must have had something to do with it, whatever it was. He had a breakdown and I never saw it coming, so how much attention was I paying to him? I should have seen something."

"Wrong," Eric said. "Not your fault at all. Not our fault, either. Dad did all this by himself. It doesn't matter why."

"It does to me," Jill said, dabbing at her eyes with her napkin.

"All right, Mom," he said, forcing a gentler tone. "What do you want me to do?"

"I'd just like you to be part of this, with me and Tyler. So it doesn't seem as though the whole family has collapsed."

Eric wanted to tell her that it already had, but the sight of her tears reined in his hostility and impatience. "And how would I do that?" he asked.

"Maybe try to stop hating him. Maybe forgive him."

"I can't do that, Mom. Either one. I can't believe that you think you can."

She reached over and put her hand over his. "He's *dead,* Eric. Somebody killed him. Whatever he's done, he's paid for it now."

His mother — she'd let him call her Jill-Bug, she'd just gotten her face "fixed" — was hopeless. Eric exhaled. "All right, Mom," he said. "I'll go to the funeral."

Then added, to himself, but only to watch him get covered over with dirt.

18

It turned out that Ike's daughter didn't have a simple fever; Heather had spinal meningitis. She'd been admitted to the emergency room last night and then immediately got transferred to the ICU, and that was where she remained this morning, on fluids and meds. Ike told Beth that the prognosis was uncertain — the strain of the disease was bacterial, not viral, and so it responded to antibiotics — but it was still a very dangerous situation, and he wouldn't be coming into work at least until they released his daughter from intensive care.

So on this Friday morning, four days after Peter Ash's death, Beth sat at her desk in the Homicide detail, catching up on administrative paperwork. Through some disruption in the fabric of the universe, she and Ike didn't have any other active homicide cases that required her attention right at this second except Peter Ash's. And waiting for Ike, she hadn't yet worked out a plan on that investigation for today, although first on the list was to apply for a warrant to search Peter Ash's apartment. She realized now that she probably should have done that two days ago. But she hadn't wanted to hassle with the warrant judge, which probably — because there were few if any probable cause issues related to searching the domicile of a deceased person — would not be as bad as she'd imagined. And then Ike's daughter had gotten sick, and she'd been stuck in the field interrogating people. Excuses, excuses.

In any event, Judge Sommers signed off on the warrant in ten minutes.

And now Beth was filling out some other forms — the city owed her for eighty-six hours of overtime and, all things being equal, she'd rather have it than not.

On the other hand, the city was claiming she owed a far less, but still galling amount — $312.40 — for traffic tickets she and Ike had accrued during the normal course of business conducting homicide investigations. This expense was an ongoing cause of frustration in the Homicide detail.

It seemed that the normal city traffic cops couldn't grasp the concept that homicide investigations assumed a life and rhythm of their own, and sometimes inspectors had to park or double-park their (clearly marked) city-issued vehicles (with their police IDs visible on the dashboard) on streets or sidewalks or in otherwise illegal parking areas while they interrogated or pursued suspects in murder cases. Almost invariably, or at least with regularity, they would return to their car and find a parking citation under the wiper blades. Astoundingly, these were not just summarily dismissed, but got entered into the system and then billed to the offending inspectors, who then had to fill out a special form to negate the fine or else pay it.

Beth looked at the small stack of forms and decided that she had more important work to do. It meant some walking inside the building without the aid of her cane, and she knew that that would be both tiring and painful, but she'd made that bed by faking her recovery so convincingly. She pushed herself to her feet behind her desk, then checked her balance and discomfort level moving from foot to foot.

Doable.

A minute later she breezed by the lieutenant's office on her way out of Homicide and stopped at his door.

"Ike's out with a sick kid," she said. "I'll

be around the Hall on Peter Ash."

"Any leads?"

"Half a dozen. We're hoping to winnow the number down some. Ike should be back in by Monday, but I might get lucky today. I've got a few stops."

He hesitated for a second. Then, "You're moving pretty well."

"Thanks." She considered adding a bit of embellishment but decided to keep it simple. "Getting better every day."

She wasn't exactly sure about where she might find the information she was seeking, but figured she could do worse than begin with the Crime Scene Unit.

Her good karma was holding, and Len Faro was out in the bullpen with a few of his staff gathered around one of the desks, with everybody seemingly talking all at once. As she got closer, it became obvious that they were engrossed in the coming weekend's football schedule; whether a simple pool or a fantasy league was impossible to tell.

But Faro saw her as she approached and straightened up, waving her to follow him as he made his way back to his office. "It's a particularly immature group," he said by way of explanation as soon as she'd gotten settled. "But there's a lot of brains out there and they work better if they get some playtime. So what can I do for you? Although I should say that if it's on Peter Ash, the pickin's are slim."

"Nothing unexpected on the body?"

"A tattoo with the perp's name, perhaps?" He shook his head. "You saw him. He got pretty mangled before he washed up. No wallet, no ID. Have you seen the autopsy?"

"Pretty bleak."

Faro nodded his head. "No kidding. The bullet was through and through and then gone. Touched nothing except the heart, which didn't much slow it down. No stippling, no tattooing. Crime Scene says no GSR" — gunshot residue — "on the clothes. No alcohol or drugs on board. Not much there."

"And," Beth said, "I noticed, not much of an indication of time of death. Which means all we've got is the last person to see him."

"And who was that?"

"So far, his secretary, Theresa. Monday afternoon." Beth shrugged. "You know, Len, on TV, you'd have cracked the case with something forensic by now, with time left over to sell Subarus and Viagra."

Faro made a rueful face. "Yeah, I am bitterly and constantly aware of that shortcoming. So given that, how can I help you?"

"Well, I was thinking. Assuming he didn't fall into the water when he was shot, his killer probably moved and dumped him, right? And we know where he got found."

"And you're wondering," Faro said, "if we could check the tide tables or something and get an idea of where he entered the water."

"You read my mind."

"It's not a bad thought," he said. "And we even kicked it around a bit."

"Did you get anything?"

"Short answer, no. He could have gone in anywhere — just offshore from where we found him, or on any of the northern beaches, or — my favorite — off a boat."

"A boat?"

Faro held up a hand. "The wildest conjecture on my part. But there were no drag marks as if somebody pulled him across a beach or a parking lot or even in some shallow water. The real answer is it could have been almost anywhere. And almost anytime after Monday."

"But maybe not that," Beth rejoined. "Maybe closer to Monday than Tuesday."

"Why do you say that?"

"Because he got chewed up pretty well, didn't he? He washed up Wednesday morning. Could that degree of damage happen in one day?"

"Possibly not. But if he happened to drift into a Great White or a particularly hungry pod of Dungeness crab, I couldn't rule it out."

"Put it like that," Beth said, "I'm going to hold off on seafood for a few weeks."

"Probably not a bad idea," Faro said.

San Francisco's new medical examiner could not have been more different from his predecessor, John Strout, who — pushing the city's mandatory retirement guidelines to their limits — had finally called it a career last year at the tender age of seventy-nine. The new ME, Amit Patel, was thirty-six years old, although he appeared to be a decade younger. After a general residency at Columbia, a PhD in endocrinology from UC San Francisco, and six years of research with Big Pharma (he would not reveal the actual company), it finally dawned on him that his problem with medicine was that he didn't like working on living people. Terrible though it might sound (although he made no apologies for it), he hadn't gone into the profession to save lives or ease pain, but to philosophically and theoretically understand the incredibly complex systems and cool structure/living mechanism that was the human body. So he went back and got his boards in pathology, and when the medical examiner position opened up, he'd jumped at it.

He also had more than a little bit of Sherlock Holmes in him.

Beth had met him on a few cases when he'd first come on, although it had now been several months since they'd seen each other. No sooner had she sat down in his antiseptic office when he templed his fingers at his jaw and said in his wispy voice, "I hope you're in a physical therapy program and aren't just hoping the legs will get better all by themselves."

"Not anything regular. Other than working out most days."

"Most days?"

She shrugged. "Walking anyway. My doctors said that walking is critical."

"No doubt. It is important. But you also need a PT program if you don't want the muscles to atrophy. Pardon me for insinuating myself."

"You can tell?"

Patel shrugged. "The right thigh is the worst, I see. You want to isolate and exercise the problem area if that is possible. Walking may help, of course, but it will take twice as long, and may not get you all the way back to where you were." Nodding in a self-satisfied way, Patel pushed back from his desk and crossed his legs. "But I'm sure you will do what is best. Meanwhile, you have a question on the Ash autopsy?"

She couldn't help teasing. "Are you sure you don't want to tell me what the question is?"

"I would think it might have something to do with whether or not he had sex on the night he was shot. And the answer, sadly, is that I cannot tell."

She had to laugh in admiration, since he'd nailed the exact question she was going to ask him. "How did you . . . ?"

With a self-deprecating gesture, Patel said, "Some of the staff were speculating. Rumor had it among them — where they hear these things, I never know — that he was known to have a promiscuous lifestyle. And of course, you as a homicide inspector would be interested to know whether he had sex shortly before his death since his partner, if any, would be at least a person of interest. But as I say, alas . . ."

"Understood," Beth said. "Was there anything of that general nature?"

"Such as?"

"I don't know. Might there have been

female DNA, for example? Or any other DNA?"

"No. Really nothing."

"All right. Let's forget the sex for a moment, unless something else about it occurs to you. How about the time between when he was shot and when he went into the water?"

The question made Patel sit up and frown. "I don't understand the question."

"All right. Could he have still been alive when he went into the water?"

"He was not. He would have drowned, then, with saltwater in his lungs. Of which there wasn't any."

"So he definitely did not drown?"

"Definitely. He was shot through the heart and died instantly, or very close to instantly. But why do you care about that?"

She held up a hand. "Bear with me. If we knew this, how long it was between when he was shot and when he went into the water, it might narrow down where it happened. On or near one of the beaches. Maybe on a boat."

Patel came forward, his fingers intertwined on his desk. "I don't think I can help you with that, Inspector. He was shot, then sometime later, he was dumped into the water. There is no telling forensically how long a time passed between the two events. I can say that it probably wasn't days. But that's the best I can do."

"I was afraid you would say that. But if anything else should occur to you . . ."

"It goes without saying," Patel said.

"She's responding to the antibiotics," Ike was telling Beth on the phone. "That's about all they'll give us. They don't want to get our hopes up, God forbid. But I guess it's better than not responding to the antibiotics."

"Way better, Ike. Believe me. Is her fever down?"

"Slightly. One oh three."

"Better than one oh five."

"No question, Pollyanna. So, what have you got?"

She told him about her morning, which had yielded so little, concluding with, ". . . so I thought next I'd check out Theresa's phone calls back in May, the mystery woman."

"Good luck with that," Ike said. "Sorry I forgot to tell you, but I've got nothing but wait time here, and I called Manny Meyer this morning and asked if he could take a look at their phone records and let us know if there were any numbers — calls Ash made

251

— that he couldn't identify."

"Good. What'd he say?"

"Not so good. He said he didn't think he'd be able to supply those records because there might be a conflict."

"With what?"

"Who knows? A couple of Ash's clients? Some chance they might compromise the attorney-client privilege in some way. The point is, Meyer's not comfortable letting us look at the records, unless either we get a warrant with a judge's sign-off and a special master . . ."

"You've got to be shitting me. This is a homicide investigation, Ike. And we don't want to know what anybody actually said on these phone calls. We're just talking about the fact that Ash made the calls."

"I know. But in this case, without a judge, we lose."

"This noncooperation just sucks," Beth said. "You know that?"

"I have some sense of it."

After a moment, Beth suggested, "Maybe we can get something out of Theresa?"

"I don't know," Ike said. "I still like her as our killer."

"I know you do. But let's see if maybe I can get her to help out with these phone calls before we get too excited," Beth said.

"I'd be careful if you go that way."

"Of course. Careful is my middle name. And listen, Ike, Heather's going to be okay."

"Your mouth to God's ear," Ike said. "I've never been so scared in my life."

"I hear you. Hang in there."

"Nothing else to do," he said. "Talk to you."

19

Dressed in perfectly tailored work clothes that flattered her figure, and with her face made up, an unexpectedly lovely Theresa Boleyn sat alone against the side wall on a chrome-and-red-plastic chair in the windowless coffee break room at Meyer Eldridge & Kline, a mug in front of her on the small table. When Beth entered, she turned her head and nodded uncertainly, as though she couldn't place where this woman came from. When recognition dawned a moment later, she let out a sigh. "Inspector," she said.

"Do you mind if I sit down?" Theresa gestured at the chair cater-corner to her. Behind the coffee mug was a crumpled wad of Kleenex. Close up, Beth could hardly fail to see the swollen redness around Theresa's eyes. "How are you holding up?" she asked after she'd sat down. "Doesn't look as though you're getting much sleep."

"Not too much. I just can't seem to get my head around the idea that Peter's gone. Everybody always says they want finality or closure or whatever you want to call it, but I wish they'd never found his body. Then maybe I could believe he just ran off to Tahiti or someplace, instead of . . . instead of what happened." Suddenly, she focused and looked sharply over at Beth. "Have you discovered something?"

"Nothing groundbreaking."

"Well, then, no offense, but why are you here with me again? I've told you everything I could think of that might help."

"We appreciate that," Beth said. "But I thought of a few things you might be able to clarify."

"Okay," Theresa said uncertainly. "However I can help."

"Great. Thank you." Beth took a small tape recorder from her breast pocket and put it on the table between them.

"What's that?" Theresa asked.

"Usually we tape witness interviews." Beth pushed the Record button. "Do you mind?"

"Not really." Her face, however, was clouded with doubt. "But you didn't do that last time, did you? Did something change?" She hesitated, then let out a few notes of nervous laughter. "Am I some kind of suspect now? We're surrounded by lawyers here, you know. Should I call one of them?"

"Of course, that's your absolute right. As to you being a suspect, at this point, most of the whole world is in that category. If you're more comfortable with a lawyer in here with you, by all means invite one in, but if the advice you'll get is not to talk to me, as in not say one word, that isn't going to get us any closer to finding who killed Peter. But it's your call."

Theresa pondered for a second. "I just don't understand why you didn't tape me before."

"Last time my partner, Inspector McCaffrey, kind of ran away with the interview and I didn't think to slow him down and get a tape running. My bad, but there you go. It happens."

With a sigh, Theresa looked down at the little red dot that meant the machine was recording. "Okay," she said with resignation. "What do you want to know?"

"Well, a couple of things. First, the last time we talked, you mentioned this mystery woman who called Peter's office sometime around the Ferry Building attack."

"Right. I thought you said you were going to check our phone records and see if Peter maybe called her back so you could identify who she was."

"Well, that's the issue. We haven't had any luck getting information about any calls Peter made. So I thought I'd ask you if you could remember anything else about that call or the woman who made it. Even the smallest detail."

Theresa frowned, leaned back in her chair, closed her eyes, and crossed her arms over her chest. After a few breaths, she opened her eyes. "I think she asked for Peter, not Mr. Ash. That's why I thought there might have been something personal in it. Just the way she asked for him." A pause. "You said the smallest detail."

"No. That's fine. It's something. If there is any information at all that you think of or that comes to your attention, it would be a big help." Beth figured that this was as far as she could go, especially on tape, to nudge Theresa to take it upon herself to look up the phone records. "Meanwhile, I've got another question for you that might be easier."

"Shoot."

"This was just Monday, Peter's last day. You said he left work around four thirty."

"That's right."

"Do you remember, was he in business clothes? Suit and tie?"

This time, it took her only a couple of seconds. She nodded and said, "Yes. I joked with him and straightened his tie when he came out of his office on the way out. He loosened it up again and said he was off for the day and he could undo his tie if he wanted to. So definitely, he left work in his business clothes. Why is that important?"

"Because he wasn't wearing a suit when we found the body. Which means if he was killed Monday night, he changed after work first."

"Which means he went home," Theresa said.

Or someplace else where he kept a change of clothes, Beth thought. But she only said, "It might mean that." Once again, Beth wished she had some information about Peter's sexual activity, if any, in the last few hours of his life. But the clothes situation had occurred to her soon after she'd left the medical examiner's office that morning. "It's something to consider about the chain of events, in any case," she said. "Can I ask you another one?"

"As many as you'd like."

"Did you know a friend of his named Geoff Cooke? He's another attorney in town."

Theresa didn't even have to think about

it. "Sure. I mean, I didn't know him well personally, but he came by here and picked up Peter for lunch or sometimes dinner or whatever. They were buds. Why? What about him?"

"I don't know. Probably nothing. I was hoping maybe you could tell me."

"You want to give me a hint?"

Beth shrugged. "Really, I don't know anything about him, other than he came by my office yesterday and asked if he could help us. He basically corroborated most of what you told us about Peter's change of behavior over the past few months, but he said he might know something that he didn't know he knew. If there's a hint in there, it's all yours."

After a couple of beats of reflection, she said, "Nothing's jumping out at me. They hung together pretty regularly — lunch, dinner, ball games, golf — just guy stuff. Sailing."

The word sent an electric buzz down Beth's spine, but she kept her voice in check. "Sailing?"

Theresa nodded. "Geoff has a small boat in the marina. I don't know if they actually went out a lot. I gathered it's where they broke out the cigars and Scotch."

"That would have been when Peter wasn't

dating, I presume?"

Theresa narrowed her eyes, tightened her mouth. "What do you mean, when he wasn't dating?"

"Well, I don't know about you, but I don't consider Scotch and cigars the world's strongest aphrodisiacs."

"No," Theresa said with great firmness. "They weren't seeing women, if that's what you were thinking. Maybe the one, the mystery woman, back in May. But even she, whoever she was, was out of the picture the last few months. Absolutely."

"So all this bad behavior with Peter, breaking up his marriage, all of that . . . it wasn't about him running around or being unfaithful to his wife?"

Theresa shook her head. "Peter was not seeing other women, Inspector. I never heard anything about that, and I would have. The craziness was all about drinking and the breakdown over the stress with work and his family and everything, but . . ." She shook her head in utter conviction. "No. He was confused, but he wasn't out playing around. I'm sure of that. That's just not who he was."

The temperature had come up about ten degrees, though it was still under fifty, the sky bright blue, the sunlight glaring everywhere. Beth sat in her Jetta, parked illegally at a bus stop, talking to her partner about his sick daughter. Heather continued to improve, although Ike didn't think he'd make it out into the field today.

Eventually they got around to the job.

"So did she come through?" Ike asked. He was still fixated on Theresa somehow getting them the phone records.

"No. I just planted the seed. I didn't want to ask her straight out since, as you point out, that would be unethical. It'll either come to her in a vision or it won't. But meanwhile, you're not going to believe . . . Peter Ash wasn't sleeping around."

"Yes, he was."

"That's what I thought, too. It's also what Geoff Cooke believed, unless he was lying, which he was not. He actually saw our boy Peter with not just a few but many of these alleged women . . ."

"They weren't alleged women, Beth. They were real women who were Peter's alleged lovers."

"Spare me that unclear antecedent bullshit, Ike. You know what I meant. But Theresa says that didn't happen — he wasn't sleeping around. She was positive. Defensive, even, on the general topic of

261

Peter's connections with other women."

Ike was silent for a couple of seconds before saying, "Peter lied to Theresa."

"Or," Beth said, "it was what she wanted to believe and never asked. One of those two or she was lying to me. I take door number one."

"Me, too. So why would he conceal messing around with other women?"

"Because he and Theresa were having an affair, and he wanted her to believe that she was the only one. Which she dutifully does believe. Right up until last Monday night when she finds out that she's actually not his one true love, but one of many, and it gives her all the motive we could want for her to shoot him. So I'm thinking you might have nailed it, Ike."

"It's a modest talent," Ike said. "How was she otherwise? Emotionally."

"A wreck."

"Because she loved him."

"That's how I read it, too. This is not your average mourning over a dead boss, even if he was the best boss there's ever been. She's devastated."

"So what was she doing Monday night?"

"I didn't ask her. Not yet. I didn't want to spook her because I'm still hoping she'll pull those phone records for us. Whipping out the tape recorder was bad enough. So maybe next time. But let's remember it's not definitely Monday night, either. Could have been Tuesday morning, maybe Tuesday afternoon. Meanwhile, though, a couple of other things did come up."

"They must be good if they beat Theresa."

"They are. At least a tie, anyway."

"So hit me."

She did, starting with the most provocative: Geoff Cooke, Peter Ash's best friend, owned a boat berthed at the marina that the two men frequently used; also, sometime between 4:30 and when he got shot, Peter Ash had changed out of his business suit and into the casual clothes he'd been wearing when they'd found him under the Cliff House — the most obvious conclusion from that being that he went home, although of course he could have gone to another place — Theresa's apartment? — and changed there. Did he meet a sexual partner at whatever location he chose? Did he, in fact, have a sexual partner on Monday night?

When she finished, Ike said, "You've had a productive morning."

"I'm not done yet."

"No," Ike said. "I figured you weren't."

20

At Peter Ash's apartment building on Grove Street, Beth went with the tried and true shortcut approach and pressed all six buttons under the mailboxes in the outside entryway. After about ten seconds, even though it was long after the waking hour for most people, a sleepy male voice came over the crackly speaker.

"Yeah?"

She identified herself as a cop, and without any more ado, he buzzed her in.

She couldn't help thinking: What if she was not a cop but rather a mass murderer armed to the teeth? Or a terrorist?

Sure, don't bother looking first, she thought. Don't check any IDs, just buzz whoever it is right in.

The trusting nature of human beings still blew her mind. But she pushed at the door, opening it, and was still holding the knob when another voice, this time female, came through the speaker. "Who is it?"

"San Francisco Police with a few questions about Peter Ash."

"Just a second," the voice said. "I'll be right down."

No buzz this time, which was marginally better, Beth thought as she heard the footsteps descending the stairs. But still relatively stupid.

She didn't remember if she'd thought this way before the Ferry Building attack.

A young African American woman bounced down the last few steps into the lobby and stopped, frowning. "How'd you get in already?"

"One of your neighbors buzzed me first. But thanks for coming down."

"Jesus," she said. "That was Ned, I bet. He's up in six and doesn't want to come all the way down, so all you need to do is ring his doorbell and it's open sesame. Are you really with the police?"

With a small smile, Beth said, "I am." She held up her ID. "I'm investigating the death of Peter Ash. Did you know him?"

"Sure. From around the building."

Beth reached into her breast pocket and flicked on her tape recorder. "Can I ask your name, please?"

"Holly. Conley." She spelled it out.

Holly was both short of stature and slight of build. Medium-length dreadlocks. No makeup because her pretty face didn't need it. She was wearing blue yoga pants, a tan fisherman's sweater, and hiking boots. "I'm in three," she continued, pointing vaguely behind her at the stairs. "Up one flight right across from Peter. I couldn't believe when I heard about what happened. None of us could."

"It's pretty much always a shock, someone getting killed."

"I mean, it makes you think . . . it could be you, me, anybody. And anywhere. He's here one day and next thing you know, he's gone."

"That's often how it happens. Do you remember the last time you saw him?"

"I think last weekend. I know he was around. He kept some pretty flexible hours. But Sunday morning, he was coming in when I was going out. We said hi on our landing."

"How about Monday?"

After a beat, she shook her head. "I've got a full day of classes on Mondays and then a bio lab from six to however late it goes. I didn't get back here 'til eleven and then I crashed."

"And you haven't seen him since then?"

"I don't think so." She considered another moment. "I'd have to say no."

"You didn't hear him go out on Tuesday or Wednesday morning?"

"No. I'm sorry."

Beth shrugged. "If you didn't see him, you didn't . . ."

More footsteps on the stairway stopped her. A young man with long, blond, disheveled hair, barefoot in shorts and a ragged Bob Marley t-shirt, jumped down the last couple of steps to join them in the cramped vestibule. "Hey! Everything cool here? You good, Holls?"

"Fine, Ned. Peachy. But you buzz people in, you might want to see if they're who they say they are next time. Or every time even. Haven't we talked about this before?"

"Yeah, okay." Ned pouted, but the expression didn't hold. "But hey, I'm here now. And she rang me. I thought she'd be coming up to my place." He pointed at Beth. "You are the cop, right?"

With a tolerant look, she held up her ID. "That's me."

Point made, Ned said, "There you go."

"She rang me, too," Holly said.

"I rang everybody," Beth confessed. "And Holly's right, you know, that probably the smarter thing would be to come down and

267

check out who's ringing your bell, Ned. I could have been anybody out there."

"Yeah, well, I can't live with all that paranoia. Life's too short. Anybody wants to get inside bad enough, they can just kick the door in anyway, or blast it open. I'm not going to worry about it."

"You would if you weren't a guy," Holly said.

Ned gave the two women a flat stare. "Okay. I get it. No more free buzzes. Scout's honor. Meanwhile, how about we move along? This has got to be about Peter, huh? Poor guy."

Beth nodded. "We've been trying to get a handle on where he was Monday night. Specifically if anybody had seen him after he got home from work."

"Monday night?" Ned took another second, then nodded in certainty. "He was here."

"You're sure?"

"Yeah. Positive."

"On Monday?" Beth repeated.

"Unless they had *Monday Night Football* on another night."

"What? Did he watch that with you?"

"No. But he . . . he was around."

Suddenly, Beth recalled the first woman who lived here, whom she and Ike had talked to out on the sidewalk. Beth said, "He bought you beer for the game."

"I don't want to get him in trouble," Ned said. "Or anybody."

"Peter's pretty well beyond trouble like that, Ned. And I'm a homicide cop. How people get their alcohol isn't my concern. So you're saying that Peter bought you beer on Monday before the game?"

"Yeah."

"Do you know what time this was?"

"Not really. Exactly, anyway. Five thirty, six, somewhere in there."

"Right after he got home from work?"

"I don't know where he was coming from. Maybe. I was listening for him to come in because we needed the brew and he was usually good for it."

"Okay, so when you saw him, was he wearing a business suit?"

Ned closed his eyes, gave it a second, then opened them. "Yeah," he said.

"So . . . did he watch the game with you?"

"No. He didn't even have a beer with us."

"Was that unusual, I mean when he bought you beer?"

"Sometimes," Ned said. "He'd stay around or not. There wasn't any usual."

"But that night he didn't?"

"Right."

"And did you see him after that? I mean that night?"

Ned flashed a quick, disappearing, somewhat embarrassed grin. "Uh . . . no. Not really."

"What does 'not really' mean, Ned?" Beth asked with some exasperation. "It's a yes-or-no question. Did you see him later or not?"

"Not see him. No. But you know, I'm right above him."

"You heard him."

Ned nodded. "Everybody heard him. And he was having a better time than we were."

"He had someone with him?"

"Mos def."

"A woman?"

"Sounded like that."

"Do you know who she was?"

"No. I never saw. But from the sound of it, it was pretty obviously what it was."

Beth hesitated. Then, "How many people were watching the game with you?"

"Four other guys."

"Did any of them leave your apartment during the game, or maybe see Peter and whoever was with him when they were coming in? Did anybody say anything about it?"

"No."

"I'm going to want all their names."

Ned hesitated. "Umm."

"Relax, Ned. No one's in any trouble here. I just want to ask if they saw or heard anything that can help. And while I'm at it," Beth went on, "would either of you be able to get me the contact information on your landlord? I'm going to want to have a look at Peter's apartment, see if it tells me anything."

Holly said, "They're just down the street, on the next corner. I can give you their phone number."

"Thank you." She came back to Ned. "Meanwhile, those names? Your guests for football?"

"I don't know about last names, but I've got all their emails."

Carol Lukins was about Beth's age and about her size — five foot six, a hundred and thirty pounds. Even dressed heavily against the cold — fleece and sweater, a woolen skirt, black leggings — she could not camouflage the likelihood that she kept to an exercise regimen. Her long hair, in a French braid, was pure white; her eyes a pale green flecked with yellow; the face was a bit overlong, reminiscent of a Modigliani model. The general effect was an aggressive, even harsh, beauty.

She'd come down within five minutes of answering Beth's call to her, and now, the key in her hand, she paused in front of the door to Peter's apartment, number 4. "I have to tell you that I'm not comfortable doing this. It feels like I'm intruding on him."

"Look," Beth said, "I don't mean to be heavy-handed, but you've seen the search warrant. If you don't open the door, I'll just get somebody to force it open. You don't have any choice in this, if it's any help."

"I'm not sure it is. Any help, I mean." In spite of the physical strength she seemed to exude, the landlady carried herself with a tentative air, as though something — the presence of the police? — spooked her. "Well," she said to herself. With an almost palpable act of will, she huffed out a breath, inserted the key, and pushed at the door.

After the dimness of the second-floor landing, the apartment itself seemed to bask in brightness. Beth poked her head into the kitchen, the first door off the hallway on the right. Another step or two down the short hall, and directly in front of the women, two large windows in the far wall let the early afternoon light into the spacious living room. On their left, in the bedroom, more light cascaded from three more windows.

The double bed wasn't formally made but did have its sheets and blankets pulled up, its two pillows unfluffed and piled against the headboard.

Beth took a couple of steps into the room and stopped. Behind her, Carol said, "I'm sorry, but suddenly I'm not feeling very good. Do you mind if I wait outside?"

Turning around, Beth saw that her already pale face had gone bloodless.

"No, that's fine," she began. "Are you sure you . . . ?"

As Beth watched, Carol's eyes abruptly turned upward and almost before Beth knew what was happening, she found herself lunging across the space between them. She caught Carol under both arms as the landlady's legs went out from under her. The weight of her as she went limp was too much for Beth's own not-yet-full-strength legs, and both women fell to the floor.

A moment later, Beth had gotten out from under her and propped her up against the wall. Carol had already opened her eyes, but they didn't seem to be focused yet. Beth gently slapped the side of her face a few times, then left her, ran back into the kitchen, took a glass from the cupboard, and filled it with water. She also checked to make sure that her tape recorder was func-

273

tioning and turned on.

Getting back out into the hall, kneeling in front of the other woman, Beth met Carol's eyes and saw that consciousness had returned. "Carol?"

"What happened?"

"You fainted."

"I'm so sorry." She closed her eyes, let out a deep breath. "I've never fainted before. I don't remember."

"That's all right. Nothing to be sorry about."

"How did I get down here? Did I really fall?"

"Yes, but I caught you, so no bruises or bumps on the head, which is the big thing you want to avoid."

"Thank you. But I don't . . ." She started to push against the floor to get up.

A hand on her shoulder, Beth held her back. "Let's wait a sec, okay? Have a sip of this." She handed her the glass.

Lifting the water tentatively to her lips, Carol took a tiny drink, closed her eyes again, then opened them. "Wow," she said in a wondering tone. "I really fainted?"

"You really fainted."

"I still feel pretty light-headed."

"Right. That's to be expected. You're probably going to be unstable for a little while.

Just sit back. Give it a minute."

She followed orders, taking another sip of the water, bringing her eyes back to Beth and then taking in the surroundings. She brought a hand up to her face. "Oh my God," she said.

"What?"

She shook her head, took a long beat. "Nothing, I guess."

"That's not a real enthusiastic 'nothing,' Carol. If you don't mind my saying, it sounds more like a 'something.' "

She closed her eyes again.

"Carol?"

She opened her eyes, looked straight at Beth. "I don't know what happened right then. Why I fainted. It's just so surprising. That's all."

"Okay." Beth, down on one knee, leaned back and folded her arms over the other one. "You just had an unexpected emotional reaction. It's not unusual. Did you know Peter well?"

"No." She cast a quick glance behind Beth, as though someone else might have been back there, listening. "I barely knew him at all."

"Really?"

"Why do you ask that? Of course, really. Did somebody say I did?"

275

"No. I was just asking."

"Well, I didn't. Know him too well, I mean. He was just another tenant."

"Okay."

"Don't you believe me?"

"Why wouldn't I believe you?"

"I don't know. Maybe because I fainted."

"Maybe, if it seems slightly hard to believe that you didn't have any feelings for him, that's the reason for it," Beth said in mild agreement. "People don't usually faint for no reason. Maybe it's just that you walked into this apartment with me a minute ago and suddenly, obviously, something upset you enough to make you faint."

"I just wasn't expecting . . . I mean, he . . ." She threw Beth a glance, perhaps hopeful that she'd provide an answer for her.

She didn't. Instead, she said, "He's dead."

Carol caught a breath in hesitation. Then, "Yes."

"Just the shock of realizing that he was walking around these rooms a week ago and now he's gone. That could be terribly upsetting."

Carol nodded. "It is. I'm sure that's what it was."

"Do you remember the last time you saw him?"

276

"I don't know why I would. He was basically just another tenant, that's all. Maybe in the coming and going, sometime. But it doesn't stand out."

"So. He was nothing special?"

That characterization seemed to frustrate her. "No," she said. "Not exactly that. He definitively had something more going on, this kind of vibe. Everybody would tell you he could be charming."

"That seems to be the consensus."

"I mean, of all the people — my tenants here — he was just so much more alive. So to come in here and realize that . . . that he's just gone . . ."

"He's not just gone, Carol. Somebody murdered him. That's why I asked when you'd seen him last. Ned, upstairs, told me he saw him early Monday evening — Peter bought him beer for the football game — but if anybody had seen him later than that, it might be super helpful. You're sure you didn't run into him or see him leaving the apartment or anything like that? This is just last Monday we're talking about."

"Why would I be over here to see him? I don't even live in this building. Did somebody tell you that they saw me here? Because if they did, it's not true." Her eyes again began to take on a slightly glazed look.

"I might have come by early in the day," she went on, in Beth's view protesting far too much. "There's always something that needs fixing in one of the units, but by Monday night, I would have been done with whatever it might have been. But I don't think there was anything. Not on Monday, anyway."

"That's a lot of denial, Carol. When actually nobody's even suggested you were here."

The hint of rebuke seemed to take the wind out of her. "Well, but if they do, I'm just saying they must have the day wrong."

"I hear you," Beth said. "So do you recall the last day you did see him?"

"One day last week — I want to say Thursday or Friday — I ran into him as he was coming in from work." She paused, then said, "No, it was Friday, because he asked if I had any great plans for the weekend. That's the last time I specifically remember."

"Good." Beth saw nothing to gain in pushing her any further at this moment. But Ned's account and Carol's reactions all along made Beth reconsider her original idea of doing a manual search of Peter's apartment rather than having the Crime Scene Unit process it for trace evidence.

Whoever was in that bed with Peter last Monday might have been the last person to see him alive, and Len Faro might find fingerprints or DNA to identify that woman. And Beth now had Carol's DNA on the glass she'd been sipping from, and if the landlady had been in Peter's bed four days ago, there was probably matching DNA there as well.

Meanwhile, Beth needed to back off, end this interview, and preserve the sanctity of the scene. Particularly, she didn't want Carol to go into the bedroom at all. So, standing up, she put out her hand down to where Carol still sat on the floor. "Do you feel okay to move?"

"Better, I think, yes." She took Beth's hand and pulled herself up. "I still don't know why I had that reaction. And thank you again for catching me."

"All in a day's work," Beth said. "But let's not you and me take any more chances. I might not be near enough to catch you if it happens again, and I really don't need to take any more of your time. I'd be more comfortable poking around here on my own anyway."

"You're sure?"

"I am. Thanks for coming down and letting me in."

"No problem. I'm glad I could help." She hesitated. "I hope you catch him."

"So do I, Carol. So do I."

With Beth feeling very much like an extra wheel, staying out of the team's way as it moved from room to room, Len Faro and his Crime Scene Unit spent the better part of three hours at Peter Ash's apartment. In the end, they left with his bedsheets and the drinking glass that Carol had used. They also took Peter's laptop and an iPad, but they encountered no sign of a telephone. They tested for gunshot residue and blood spatter evidence, but there was none of either. They collected fingerprints. Peter had ten business suits hanging in his closet, along with sixteen dress shirts, a coat hanger full of ties. Underwear, socks, t-shirts, sweaters, and casual pants in the dresser. In the refrigerator, they found a bottle of Hafner chardonnay, half of which was gone, and they bagged it to bring to the lab. If Peter and his guest had been drinking that on Monday, this was another possible source of either fingerprints or DNA. There were also two unwashed wineglasses on the counter, the dregs dried up in the bottom of each of them.

Faro's team was thorough, but it didn't

find much. Maybe one or both of the computers would reveal something about Peter's personal life, but that was a big maybe. Also, if they couldn't get a DNA match with Carol Lukins — that is, if she had not been Peter's sexual partner on Monday night — then Beth thought it unlikely that the search exercise would have produced anything of substance.

Taken together, the condition of the room and Ned's testimony indicated that Peter had come home from work, bought beer for his young neighbors, then had a woman stop by, with whom he apparently drank some wine and then had sex. Afterwards, he changed into more casual clothing and, assuming he hadn't been shot in this room, he must have gone out. Which left a couple of unanswered questions: Did his sexual partner leave right afterwards on her own, or did they leave together? And if he left alone, did someone then pick him up? Or did he drive himself?

Where was his car?

Leaving Faro to his colleagues and duties, Beth excused herself, left Peter's apartment, and crossed the landing to number 3, where she knocked, hoping to get the cooperative Holly, but no one answered. Her legs killing her, Beth trudged up the next flight to

281

Ned's apartment where, much to her surprise, she seemed to have succeeded in waking him up again.

"Man," he said as he opened the door, squinting through a haze of marijuana smoke. "Really?" He had removed his shorts and stood on one foot in the doorway in his tighty-whities and his Marley t-shirt while the man himself was singing "No Woman, No Cry" in the apartment.

"Really, Ned," Beth said. "Tough day at school?"

He shrugged, grinned stupidly. "I fixed my schedule so I don't do Fridays. Is that great, or what?"

She shook her head, not particularly sharing his thrall. "Do you know Peter Ash's car?"

"Sure," he said. "A Beemer Z3 convertible. Totally awesome machine."

"The ultimate driving, if I'm not mistaken."

Clearly not getting the reference, Ned's face slipped further into vacancy.

Beth moved along. "So do you know where he would usually park it? Does this building have some designated spaces?"

"Are you kidding? Parking is like the biggest hassle there is."

"So where did he park?"

282

"Wherever he found a space, and good luck with that. It could take twenty minutes circling the block, sometimes more. A total drag."

"Do you know what color it was?"

"Purple."

"Okay, Ned. Thanks a lot. And by the way, how're you doing on those email addresses you were going to get me?"

"I haven't gotten on that yet. Today's kind of not my main workday."

"I'm picking that up," Beth said. "I could wait and you could go rustle them up right now. How long could it take?"

Sighing deeply at the tremendous infringement on his personal liberty and busy schedule, Ned said, "Give me five." Leaving his front door open, he disappeared back into the apartment.

Beth leaned back against the railing by the stairs. She thought if she got randomly tested for drugs in the next hour or so, the pot smoke she was inhaling would show her positive for THC. She backed a couple more steps away from Ned's door.

It actually took him less than four minutes. He came back to the door — still no pants — and handed her a sheet of paper. "They were all here the whole time," he volunteered. "Nobody would have seen anything."

"Well, I'll just double-check to be sure. Thanks for your help."

"No problem," he said.

"No," she replied. "I didn't think it was."

Faro and company were finishing up as she passed Peter's unit on the way down. Her legs were shot, her right thigh especially — catching Carol Lukins as she'd fallen, then standing around in the apartment, finally walking up and down the long flight of stairs three or four times — had taken their toll. Still, she forced a regular gait as she passed Faro on the landing. Lennard wasn't a gossip, but he had six officers with him, and you just never knew what people, even her law enforcement colleagues, saw and what they'd comment on.

Outside the building, she turned left and with the cold sun at her back walked down four blocks to Broderick, where the neighborhood decidedly changed its character, from mostly students to mostly ghetto. Peter Ash wasn't likely to have parked his BMW convertible any further east than Broderick, not if he wanted it to be there unmolested when he came back to it.

She found the car with a handful of parking tickets under its windshield, at McAllister near Lyon. She called it in for towing to the city lot behind the Hall of Justice.

■ ■ ■ ■

"So what does that tell us?" Ike asked her. "He didn't use his car. So what?"

She was sitting in her car, the heater going as the sun went down, parked where she'd left her ride within half a block of Peter's apartment, in front of a fire hydrant on Grove. Miraculously, she thought, this time her dashboard ID seemed to have worked and the traffic Nazis hadn't cited her. "So one of two possibilities," she said. "Either he went walking around in the dark, or somebody came by and picked him up, which is the money bet."

"Whoever picked him up must have called him first, wouldn't you say? I'd kill to get my hands on his cell phone records."

"Me, too, but that's probably not happening."

"Fucking terrorists."

"Right. Again, now and always."

"If the FBI hadn't put in a request for basically all the phone records in the city . . ."

"Yeah, but they do," Beth said, "and the phone companies are backed up to forever. A couple of low-rent homicide inspectors like us will be lucky to see anything within a month."

"Okay, moving on," Ike said. "This land-lady, she's cute, right?"

"Quite a bit more than that."

"And she truly fainted? What's up with that?"

"I think Carol had a rendezvous with our victim on Monday night and coming back to his apartment with a homicide inspector in tow literally knocked her out. She thought she could power through how she'd feel and she got it wrong. We'll find out for sure, I hope, if we match some DNA from Peter's place, but I'm giving big odds she and Peter got it on."

"So . . . Theresa's out."

"Not necessarily. It still could have been Theresa who picked him up afterwards. Or anybody else. Carol's husband comes to mind, for that matter."

"She's married?"

"She's got a ring. So I assume."

"Okay. You think it's time we got Theresa's alibi?"

Beth took a moment. "I was hoping to keep her thinking she was on our side until she gave us the phone numbers from Peter's office, but you might be right. It would be nice to eliminate her entirely if we can, or reel her in."

"Well, you've been doing all the work lately. Maybe I should give her a call, pitch the phone records again, then either way find out what her Monday night looked like."

"I'll leave that decision up to you."

"Got it. I'll let you know something as soon as I do."

"Sounds good. And whatever else, hug your little girl for me."

"Will do."

21

Kate Jameson waited until 5:00 o'clock sharp before she opened the bottle, poured herself a generous glass of Rombauer chardonnay, and moved to the reading chair in her living room to watch the dusk advance across her front lawn.

She'd been craving that first drink all day, but today she wasn't going to start early as she had the day before.

Yesterday, with the shock of Peter Ash's death right there in the newspaper and minutes later in the wake of Ron's confession that he knew about her and Peter, she'd started in on the wine at lunch and had had to summon all of her will and physical strength as she struggled to act sober enough to put together dinner for them all. And as soon as they'd finished, she had pleaded a headache and had been essentially passed out in bed by 8:00. She didn't suppose Ron, who missed nothing, had been

fooled by her feigned sobriety.

Settling back into her chair, she took her first small sip.

It was ironic, she thought, that it had taken Peter's death to prompt Ron into admitting that he knew about them. Because without that admission, Ron made it clear yesterday morning that he didn't think there was any chance for the two of them to move beyond her betrayal as a couple. He was furious, of course, but he knew and he truly forgave.

Ron had had to let her know that he knew, and she had to know and believe that that knowledge would not and could not break them up. Not ever. The irony was that in reality, there had been almost nothing between her and Peter except the one day, and even that one time had been before she'd been shot and her whole world had changed.

Today, as she sat sipping her wine, she reflected that from the day of the Ferry Building attack until yesterday, when the news of Peter's murder had appeared in the *Chronicle,* she hadn't felt an ounce of desire for him even once. She had, in fact, rarely thought of him in any context at all. She certainly had never known that he'd come to visit her at the hospital when she'd been in her coma. She had no idea why he'd done

that. And even now, with the memory of him refreshed, she felt nothing for him as a person.

She only wished that she could erase the one day, wished that she had not betrayed Ron, not hurt the children.

But the consequences from that, thank God, were behind her now, behind all of them. The sense of dislocation was over. There were no more secrets. The rupture had healed and her family had survived.

The doorbell startled her out of her reverie. She could barely remember the last time they'd had anybody stop by unexpectedly. She looked up and was surprised to see that outside, it had grown perceptibly darker. She got up and flicked on the light over her reading chair — "Just a second!" — then hit the room and hall and front porch lights as she walked to the door, saw who it was, and opened it.

Smiling at her — beaming really — was Beth Tully, who had struck a sassy pose, hands on her hips. "Girlfriend," she said. "It's been way too long."

And in fact, the two friends hadn't been together since the Ferry Building. Both of their respective recoveries had carved out new priorities, schedules, regimens. Beth

had to regain her strength, mobility, and balance and get back to work, while for a long time, with all the complications, Kate fought for her life.

They had talked on the phone a few times in the past six months, just touching base, but it had felt forced and awkward, and even after Kate had finally left the hospital and come back home, somehow the idea of picking up where they'd left off — relatively carefree as they power walked in their free time for exercise — had never come up.

But now, sitting at the counter in the kitchen, Kate had refilled her wineglass and poured Beth a large glass of iced tea. "So here's to us, huh?" she said. "Would we ever have believed we'd be together like this again?"

"Probably not," Beth said, "but I'm so glad we are."

"I am, too. Before you rang the doorbell just now, I was thinking that it felt like life was finally getting back to some kind of normal at last. And then you drop by, it's icing on the cake."

"Hardly that."

"More than you know. Just that you've got the guts to do things . . . every time I go out, which is as little as I can get away with, I'm scared to death and can't wait to get back home."

Beth nodded in understanding. "It's definitely something to work on."

"Apparently not for you, though."

"Au contraire. I fight it every step of the way. Any crowd bigger than about three people and I get nervous. I think it's just something we're always going to have to live with. But on the other hand," she added brightly, "since we've already been in one, what are the odds of getting caught up in another terrorist attack? Very, very unlikely, wouldn't you say?"

Kate clearly wasn't convinced, but she forced a smile. "That's a good way to look at it."

A shrug. "Well, it's one way. The other thing keeping the fear away is my work."

Kate's eyebrows went up. "Don't tell me you're back working? Full time? In homicide?"

Beth chuckled. "That's the job."

"And it makes you feel *safer*? Chasing murderers."

"Well, first, there's very little real chasing involved. Which is lucky, since don't tell any of my fellow inspectors or my lieutenant, but I've slowed down more than a couple of steps. But the other thing is here I am, already shot up once. So it's like the odds of being in two terrorist attacks. Shot twice? No, I don't think so. It's like insurance."

"Getting shot as insurance against getting shot again?"

"That's it."

"I'm pretty sure there's some kind of flaw in your logic there."

Beth shrugged, smiled, sipped at her tea. "Whatever. But I think if we've learned anything, it's that we don't have much say in the matter of what happens next. All in all, I've come to believe that we're the lucky ones. Certainly as opposed to all the people who died or aren't ever going to get better."

"I can't argue with that. You're so right. I just haven't been looking at it that way."

"Sometimes I haven't either. Not all the time, anyway. But when I get to there, it seems to help. At least, along with the job, it gets me out of the house."

"I still just can't believe that you're back on the job."

Beth stalled for a moment, taking another sip of her tea. "Actually, speaking of the job, it's full disclosure time."

"About your job?"

Beth nodded. "I've been meaning to stop by and see you for the last few weeks or so, but didn't want to feel like I was pushing you if you weren't yet up and about and didn't feel like seeing anybody yet. Particularly if that somebody was a reminder of what you'd been through. Like, say, me."

"Come on, Beth, I never felt —"

"I know. But I wanted to give you more time to recover if you needed it. Now I see it could have been sooner, but as I say, I didn't want to push. But then yesterday, I got an excuse."

A perplexed look on her face, Kate said, "You don't ever need an excuse to come by and visit. But I don't understand how this excuse was about your job. Are you saying you're investigating something about a murder that has to do with me?"

"Not you," Beth said. "Your husband. And only tangentially at that."

"You're talking Ron? Involved in a murder? That's absurd, Beth. He's —"

Beth held up her hand, stopping Kate's response. "He's not really it, either. But I'm assuming both of you know a guy named Geoff Cooke."

Kate straightened up and sat back in her chair, almost as if Beth had taken a swing at her. "Sure, we know Geoff. He's one of Ron's partners in the firm. He's the nicest guy in the world, Beth. I mean, we see him socially all the time. You can't really think

he's got anything to do with killing somebody."

"No. I don't really think that. But Mr.
Cooke came by Homicide yesterday wanting to talk about a murder victim named
Peter Ash, and when we'd finished our
interview, he left me his business card,
which told me that he worked in the same
firm as Ron."

"I just told you, they're partners. Does
that mean anything?"

"I don't know. Probably not. But when I
investigate, I try to get a handle on the
victim, on anything that might have led to
his death, and it occurred to me that Ron
might have known Peter Ash, too. If nothing else, it gave me the excuse I was looking
for to see you."

"But you know you don't need . . ."

"Whatever. I thought it was possible that
maybe Ron went out a time or two with Ash
and Mr. Cooke and had found out something about Ash, what made him tick, or
what he was going through. Something like
that, just to add to the picture. Maybe, like
Mr. Cooke, Ron knows something about
Mr. Ash but doesn't see its significance."

"What does Geoff know?"

"That's just it. He doesn't know if he
knows anything either. He just offered to

help, and then I find out he's in Ron's firm, maybe they all know each other." Beth shrugged. "At least it's another avenue to explore. And any connection to the victim is worth following up. Even if it's as tangential as this one."

"Well, you'll pardon me for saying so, Beth, but that seems a bit of a reach. Geoff knows, or knew, this Mr. Ash? And therefore he's connected somehow to Ron?"

"Don't be mad."

"I'm not mad. I guess I'm just surprised you think that there could be something in this."

"So you guys didn't know Peter Ash?"

Kate went still. "So what is this, now? We're suspects? I'm under investigation?"

"No. Not at all, Kate. There's no reason to be defensive . . ."

"Except maybe Ron, who tells me everything, maybe he's got information on this murder victim and somehow Geoff comes to you but Ron doesn't. So why is he hiding what he knows? And while we're at it, why am I hiding what I know?"

"That's not it at all, Kate. Nothing like that."

"I wonder why it seems like it is, then." She gulped a mouthful of her wine, her eyes alight with affront. "Since you asked, though, the truth is we didn't really know Peter Ash. We saw him once at a dinner party, and even that was months ago. I hadn't even thought of him recently until I saw the article in the paper about him dying. Before that, I don't think I'd heard his name in months. But you can ask Ron and make sure. Maybe," she added with heavy sarcasm, "he and Geoff and Mr. Ash went out for lunch last week and all got drunk together and Ron just forgot to mention it to me. And then one of them killed him."

Beth sighed. "I'm sorry. You're right. I'm just fishing because the case is frustrating and I know nothing. I should never have brought it up."

Kate, her hands shaking holding her wineglass, took a deep breath, then another. "I'm sorry, too."

As she drove home, Beth was thinking that she was losing her touch and her intuition.

In the course of the afternoon, she'd interviewed three women, and not even in a particularly threatening manner, and all of them — Theresa, Carol Lukins, and her best friend, Kate — had reacted far more violently, and defensively, than she would have thought possible. She wondered if it was just because she herself had become im-

297

mune to the power of her badge. In her mind, she was still a woman (and even a mom) first, cop second, and she more or less expected that other women would view her the same way.

But judging from today's reactions, she was dead wrong.

And now, almost against her will, as she negotiated the myriad streets and turns to her home, she found the cop in her analyzing what she'd drawn out from these women: Theresa's apparent utter ignorance of Peter Ash's profligacy around sex, Carol Lukins's protesting far too much about the last time she'd seen her tenant, and Kate's going ballistic at the mere mention of the possibility that her husband had even the slightest familiarity with Peter Ash.

Why, she wondered, were these reactions so strong? Was it just the fact that they viewed her as a cop first, and so her questions, no matter how benign, carried an emotional wallop? Might they all, in different ways, actually feel legitimately threatened? And why would there be all that smoke, she thought, unless there was a flame somewhere?

Beth might understand the feeling of threat in the case of Theresa, if she was in fact having an affair with her boss.

Or with Carol, who was almost certainly, in Beth's mind, another of his sexual partners/conquests.

But Kate . . .

Although her reaction had in some ways been the most defensive, besides the random social occasion, there was no evidence that Kate had ever had anything to do with Peter Ash. Beth tried to give her the benefit of the doubt   after an incredibly difficult time while she recovered from her injuries and infections, she was simply super sensitive trying to protect her husband and her family. But still, her reaction could only be viewed as somehow provocative.

And something nagged. Something intimately connected to the two of them — her and Kate — and to the day they'd both been shot. The connection flittered back and forth across her subconscious, a ghost of a memory almost totally obliterated by the violence and destruction they'd endured together on that day.

And now, bubbling up from some cauldron of repression in the wake of the disaster, Beth tried to recall: in the seconds before the shooting began, they'd been talking about Kate's dalliance with some guy . . . had it actually happened? Had Kate admitted . . . ?

Beth remembered now. She had just told Kate about her upcoming date with Alan Shaw, Laurie's brother, and Kate had tried to cover up that she'd gone ahead and hooked up with the guy she had been fantasizing about. Beth had called her on it. Or had she? Had they gotten that far? Beth knew that she had drawn the conclusion, but had Kate confirmed the conjecture?

The answer was right there, just out of her reach.

Stopped at a red light, she closed her eyes for a moment, trying to recapture the conversation, the telling details . . .

Suddenly behind her came the familiar *whoop whoop* of a patrol car. At the same moment, flashing red and blue lights exploded in her rearview mirror.

"Shit!" Slapping her steering wheel, she pulled over to the curb and waited. When the officer appeared at her window requesting her license and registration, she opened her wallet to her badge. "I'm sorry," she said. "I'm afraid I wasn't paying enough attention. What did I do?"

"You sat through an entire green light cycle. If people do that, even if they don't turn out to be inspectors, I like to see if they're all right."

"I'm sorry," she repeated. "I'm fine,

except I guess I've been thinking too hard about a case. I should be paying more attention to what I'm actually doing."

"That's a good thought." He handed back her ID. "Do you need an escort?"

"I don't think that will be necessary. I'm on my way home. It's only a few more blocks."

"Okay, then. Please drive carefully."

"Thank you. I will."

She waited until the officer had gotten back to his car before hitting her ignition and pulling carefully back out into the street. Drawing a deep breath, she shook her head in disgust even as her brain returned, seemingly of its own volition, to the question that had been nagging at her: hadn't Beth mentioned a name? She and Kate were sitting and talking seconds before the attack at the Market Café, and then . . .

Suddenly there it was, the name of the man Kate had slept with. It finally settled down out of the miasma shaking around in Beth's skull with total clarity.

The name, she now remembered, was Peter.

22

Laurie wasn't sure what exactly had gotten into her, but she wanted her whole apartment, and especially the table, to be particularly nice.

Last night, with Beth and Ginny in her kitchen, using real plates and utensils, eating food that had flavor, it was all still so odd, something she vaguely remembered from another era that now, late but maybe not too late, was making an unexpected reappearance in her life.

If she had to say what it was, as she had tried to describe it to Alan when they'd talked in the morning, she felt as if she'd come awake after a long sleep. The feeling had lasted all day, bolstered by two meals — she'd scrambled an egg for breakfast and ate some turkey — a slice and a half — sometime in the middle of the afternoon.

Oh, and a spoonful of the java chip.

The feeling was still with her, a kind of

hopefulness that felt as though in some way she was regaining some of the strength in her muscles.

Beth and Ginny would be here again in a few minutes, and she checked herself in the bathroom mirror. She'd put on jeans that weren't too loose and a bright red pullover that bulked her up somewhat. With a little makeup, the blotches disappeared, a touch of mascara brought her eyes to life, some gloss gave a clean definition and fullness to her lips.

She realized that in spite of everything she'd put herself through, all of the eating problems, the psychological trauma, she still looked good, reminiscent in fact of how she'd looked when she and Frank . . .

With something of a shock, she realized that she hadn't once thought of Frank all day, not even when she'd been outside buying the bouquet for the table at the place he'd always stopped to get flowers for her.

She walked into the kitchen. The bouquet was in a vase in the middle of the table, which she'd set with great care. It was full of fall foliage, large and flamboyant and the orange and yellow in it matched the placemats and made it look as though somebody lived here.

Somebody could live here.

■ ■ ■ ■

"Okay, I've got one," Ginny said.

Laurie swallowed a bite of lamb meatball. "Go."

Beth didn't let on, but she was taking an inventory of the food that Laurie was eating and thus far, it looked promising. That was also the way Laurie herself looked. Not that she'd gained any visible weight since yesterday, of course, but she was carrying herself differently, with what struck Beth as confidence that hadn't been there before. She'd also told them about her meals during the day, if you wanted to call them that — a slice of turkey and an egg — but Beth realized that any eating was a bonus.

There was no question about whether she loved the meatballs. She was on her third one, smothered in yogurt sauce. Plus, two relatively big servings of rice pilaf, two stalks of asparagus. One whole piece of pita bread. More importantly, without dwelling on it she seemed to simply be enjoying the food, the experience of eating.

And beyond that, the younger women were clearly having fun. They'd spent almost ten minutes howling over some app on Ginny's cell phone that gave the wrong, but invariably hysterical pronunciation of common, or sometimes not so common, words. Such as synecdoche — syna kyna dotie chotie! When Ginny had first discovered the app, Beth herself had laughed until she'd cried more than once.

That had led to a few rounds of riddles, Laurie stumping Ginny with, "What never leaves the corner and yet travels around the world?"

Beth having to supply the answer — a stamp.

And then Ginny jumping in with, "So Donald Trump and Sarah Palin are both drowning in the pool right in front of you, and you know there's only going to be a minute or two before one or both of them goes under. Here's the question: What kind of sandwich do you make?"

Laurie laughed out loud. "That's awful," she said.

"It is, a little," Ginny agreed. "I feel bad every time I tell it, but not bad enough to stop."

As the two girls continued laughing and generally yucking it up, Beth got up from the table, took a few steps over to the refrigerator, and pulled the java chip out of the freezer so it would soften up a bit before she served it. She had just placed it on the counter by the sink when the doorbell rang. "I'm up. I'll get it," she said. "Are you expecting anybody?"

"Not really. It's probably just Alan." At Beth's fleeting, questioning expression, she raised her palm as though taking an oath and said, "Unplanned, I promise. Sometimes he just stops by."

The younger girls had gone into the living room with their ice cream and they'd put on some music, someone Beth didn't recognize. She and Alan stood by the sink, and she handed him plates to dry as she finished washing them. "The thing I'm so surprised about," she said, "is how young Laurie is. Tonight she seems almost like Ginny's age, which is eighteen. When I first met her, I thought she was closer to thirty. Of course, that was the day she heard about Frank Rinaldi's death, and that could put a few years on a person."

"She's twenty-three," Alan said.

"So? What? You're in your twenties, too?"

He chuckled. "Hardly. I was nineteen when she was born."

"Same mom and dad?"

"That's their story and they're sticking to it. Or did, at least, until they died."

"Oh, I'm sorry to hear that, Alan."

He shrugged. "It was a long time ago. She was ten when Dad passed — heart attack. Then Mom with cancer a couple of years after that."

"Who'd Laurie live with then?"

"Me, until five years ago, when she moved out for college."

"You supported her? By yourself?"

He downplayed it. "If you don't count the two hundred grand my parents left us. That helped a bit. Still does."

"But you raised her during those special teenage years?"

"I don't know if I'd call it raising her. We lived in the same apartment. She was pretty much on her own, with me working. But she mostly kept herself out of trouble. Until this food stuff started, which like an idiot I couldn't even see."

"And you blame yourself for that?"

He shrugged. "Somebody else might have recognized the signs earlier, that's all. Gotten a little more proactive." A sudden burst of laughter came from the living room. "That's a good sound to hear," Alan said. "I haven't heard very much of it lately."

Beth handed him another plate. "They're getting along." Then, "It's good of you to come by and check on her."

"It's good of you," he replied, "to come

307

by at all." He indicated the kitchen, the table, the food. "And bring all this."

"Well, you said it was serious, and I agree with you. I don't know exactly what should happen next to get her some help, but meanwhile I've got a case that's eating me up and my partner's daughter is sick in the hospital, so I . . . I mean, there's nothing else I can do until . . ."

"Hey hey hey. Stop. No apologies. You're here. Your daughter's doing more good in there than any shrink or doctor on the planet. I haven't heard Laurie laugh out loud in a year, maybe more. Whatever the prize for being a great person is, you've already won it, so I don't want to hear about you not doing all you can. This is half a miracle right here, to say nothing of all the food she told me you'd brought over. And speaking of which" — he put down the dry plate and reached for the wallet in his back pocket — "what do I owe you for all that?"

"Don't be ridiculous."

"I'm not being ridiculous."

"Well, you're not giving me any money, either. This has been my pleasure. And listen to them." She cocked her head back toward the living room. "My daughter's having a great Friday night and maybe getting herself a new friend in the bargain.

That's worth a lot more than a bag or two of groceries."

"Maybe. But it still doesn't feel right, not paying our own way."

"It feels right to me. So how about we don't fight about it? Just say 'Okay, you win,' and we let it go at that."

He took in a frustrated breath, cast his eyes around the kitchen, came back to her. "Okay, you win," he said, then added, "but I owe you." A beat. "Maybe a dinner, if you'd like to try that again."

"I might," Beth said. "But not because you feel you owe me anything."

"That wouldn't be it."

"Well, we'll see." Her shoulders settling, she put down the last washed plate and turned off the water. Turning, her arms now folded over her chest, she looked up into his face.

She met his eyes again and drew a breath. To her dismay, she felt her eyes begin to fill with unexpected tears, and she quickly, almost angrily, brushed at them before they overflowed onto her cheeks. She didn't want to play any part of this for sympathy.

"Twice?" he asked.

She nodded. "Two bullets. One per leg. I thought you might have noticed me walking a little funny as you followed me down the hallway."

"I noticed you walking, all right. Way more graceful than funny."

She gave him a no-nonsense look. "Let's not get all silly now. I'm still a couple of light-years from graceful."

He shrugged. "Just sayin'. I saw graceful. And so what happened?"

"What do you mean, what happened?"

"I mean with you. You're shot twice. What happened? What did they do to you?"

"More like 'for me.' They shipped me down to Kaiser in Redwood City, and I'm not even a member, but you probably know that every bed in the nine counties had a shooting victim or three." She shrugged. "They triaged everybody, and I wasn't by any stretch one of the priority people. It was a pretty chaotic time."

"I remember following it all on the news, but it never occurred to me that you . . . I mean, I knew that you were a cop, but it never occurred to me you were one of the victims." He pulled around a chair and sat on it, shaking his head in disgust with himself. "I tell myself that if I'd have known that, I would have made a bigger effort. I am so sorry I never followed up," he said. "But the reality of what you were going through never even crossed my mind. I never even looked around for another explanation, when it was right there in front of me. What an idiot."

"Well, it's over now. And let's remember that I could have called you anytime to explain where I was and what had happened, but then I figured you had probably just decided that on reflection you weren't really interested."

"That wasn't it at all."

"I believe it if that's what you're telling me now, but that's what I told myself then." She gave him a rueful smile. "Well, we sure make a great pair, don't we?"

"Fantastic," he said, breaking a grin back at her, "if just slightly pathetic."

23

Theresa Boleyn didn't get to sleep until sometime between 2:00 and 3:00 a.m., but at 6:20 she came fully awake. She considered lying back down — someone had poured concrete into her eyes and they didn't want to stay open — but after fifteen minutes of tossing back and forth, she gave up, put on her bathrobe, and went into the kitchen to make coffee.

Light was just coming up, but after a week of bitter cold and clear high pressure, this morning thick fog blocked any view out her back window.

That suited her.

Though eating was the furthest thing from her mind, she set her regular breakfast on the kitchen island out of habit — orange juice, granola with sliced bananas, fresh blueberries, and nonfat milk. While the coffee dripped, she went out to the front door and got the newspaper.

Back at the kitchen island, coffee cup in her hand, she did a quick scan through the pages. No mention of Peter, of the investigation into his murder. Nothing.

When the first cup was empty, she put it down. She had no memory of having eaten the cereal, but it was gone. Going through the *Chronicle* a second time, she read more slowly, not really sure of what she was hoping to find. If they had a follow-up story, how would that help in any way? It wouldn't, of course. She didn't know why she was looking for it.

She poured another cup, then unplugged the charger from her cell phone on the counter behind her. Turning the phone on, she saw that she had one voicemail — Sergeant McCaffrey had called her last night.

But she'd already turned off the phone on the chance that she'd fall into a deep sleep.

What was with these cops? Was this the harassment you heard so much about? She'd already talked to them several times now and told them everything possibly relevant that she knew about Peter, although of course she hadn't told them about their true relationship, at least their relationship over the past months, ever since the hug they'd shared after seeing the bullet holes in his office window had led to their intimacy, which she knew had nothing to do with his murder.

McCaffrey's voicemail asked her to call him at her earliest convenience today. He had just a few more questions that he'd like to clear up.

She really doubted that.

What she did believe was that Inspector McCaffrey was going to try to rile her again by not so subtly dropping more false accusations of some kind about Peter. She was pretty certain that this was the strategy that his partner, Inspector Tully, had attempted with her yesterday by dropping those comments about Peter's supposed infidelity with other women.

When Theresa didn't believe for a minute that he was seeing anyone else but her.

She didn't know what the inspectors hoped to gain by these innuendoes about the man she loved. Maybe they thought that Theresa actually did have something to do with his death. That, she knew, was absurd, but maybe they were getting desperate to solve the murder and just needed to get their hands on a suspect, any suspect.

On the other hand, she did know Peter better than almost anyone else. Why wouldn't she want to cooperate with the police to help find who had killed him?

What about the mystery woman, anyway? Maybe that's who the cops wanted to find out about. What had been the real story behind her calls? When she'd asked Peter that very question just after they'd become lovers, he'd not exactly been evasive about her. The woman wasn't a romantic interest, but clearly something she'd done — he'd hinted at blackmail that would threaten his career — had played a huge role in rewiring Peter's vision of who he was, including his decision to divorce Jill.

But hell, Theresa told herself, she was a big girl. She didn't have to let the insinuations of police inspectors get under her skin. As if anything they could imply could be as devastating as the pure fact of Peter's death. Whatever meaning she'd made out of her life, or hoped to make with Peter, was gone now, thoroughly washed away, but that did not mean she could not be cooperative. That was, after all, how her parents had raised her — dependable, perhaps uninspired, but unfailingly polite and helpful.

She was the perfect secretary.

It was almost 7:30. Still fairly early, but McCaffrey's voicemail had said to call anytime.

She hit his number on the screen, and he

picked up on the second ring. "Ms. Boleyn. Theresa. Thanks for getting back to me."

"No problem. I'm sorry if it's early. But you said you had a few questions."

"That's all right. I've been keeping some odd hours the past few days myself." He hesitated. "There is one thing we haven't covered, but I don't want it to offend you."

"I'm not that easy to offend, Inspector. How can I help you?"

"Well, this really falls under the heading of general housekeeping. Do you recall what you were doing last Monday night, say after nine thirty?"

In spite of her resolution not to react to exactly this kind of question, one obviously intended to upset her, she felt her stomach turn over and her head go light. "I did not kill Peter, Inspector," she said, "on Monday night or any other night."

"And I don't think you did, either, Theresa. But it would completely eliminate you from the picture . . ."

"What picture is that?"

She heard his sigh in her ear. "Possible suspects, which I think Inspector Tully told you was pretty much the whole world."

"Not me, I promise you."

"And I believe you. But if you were with someone that night . . ." He gave her a short speech about alibis.

Absurd, she was thinking when he finished. "After nine thirty on a work night," she said, "I was home, probably reading or watching something on television. I'm usually asleep by ten thirty. I'm sure I was that night, too. I did not see Peter after he left work early. I'm sorry if that doesn't help, but you really shouldn't be thinking about me. Honestly. And that said, I still may be calling you later on that phone issue."

"I would appreciate that."

"But no promises. I'll try, that's all."

"I understand."

"All right, then. Good-bye." Fully depleted, perched on her stool, Theresa ended the call. Her hand went to her churning gut. "It doesn't matter," she said to herself. "It doesn't matter. It doesn't matter. It doesn't matter."

Bina was at the tiller of their 24-foot sailboat, the *Mary Alice,* named after Geoff's mother. She and Geoff were almost out to Alcatraz, close to half the journey on their way to lunch at the Anchor Cafe in Sausalito. They'd left the marina as the fog was starting to lift, and though it still clung to the western side of the city, above them all was blue. A sweet following breeze coming

317

in through the Golden Gate, still cold but balmy in comparison to the past few days, was pushing them along nicely, but in spite of that, the bay itself was a flat pewter plate, a very good day for sailing.

Geoff had told Bina all about his meeting with Beth Tully at the Hall of Justice, his offer to help with the investigation if she could think of something he might be able to do. He didn't know what, if anything, that might be. She hadn't called him yesterday with any ideas on that score, though, and now he was telling Bina that he really didn't think she would reach out to him today or tomorrow or ever because he had nothing specific to give her.

"Maybe," she said, "that's all to the good."

"Why do you say that?"

"Because I've been thinking about it, Geoff, waiting for a good time to mention it to you, and I think that now we've come to it. Has it occurred to you that you probably don't really want to let yourself get too involved in a murder investigation?"

"Why not? Back in my DA days, as you'll remember, I was in murder investigations all the time."

"Right. But back then you were dealing with guys who were mostly already locked up in jail and weren't any threat to you."

"So you're saying that someone's a threat to me now? Who would that be?"

"Well, if we knew that, we'd probably know who killed Peter. Wouldn't you say that's true?"

"Mostly. Probably. Yes, I suppose so."

"So this something that you have this vague feeling you might know about — this fact, this clue, whatever it might be — even though you don't yet recognize its significance, let's say you suddenly realize what it is. Not the murderer, just some indication that points in a certain direction. What do you do with that information?"

"That's what I'm saying. I call Inspector Tully."

"Okay. But just let me play this out a bit. You call Tully, which sets her on the right track. She goes out and questions our suspect, who turns out to actually be a cold-blooded murderer. And somehow in the course of her interrogations of this guy —"

"Or girl."

"Okay, or girl. Either way, it comes out that you're the source — maybe the sole source — of this damning information . . ."

"How does that happen?"

"It doesn't matter. Fluke, luck, mistake, whatever. The point is, it comes out. And in fact, it comes out that you're the only witness to it, whatever it may be. Then guess what? No, let me go on. All of a sudden this is nothing like the murder cases you were part of back in the day, when your suspect was safely locked away in jail. Instead, you are the only person threatening our killer's freedom. Which makes you not just a prime witness, but a prime target. Do you not see this?"

Geoff ducked under the spar and shifted to the other side of the boat as they came about. "I don't think it's impossible," he said. "But neither do I think it's too likely."

"I don't think it's likely either, my dear, but 'not likely' is a far cry from 'impossible.' And especially since we're talking about you getting killed here — by, let's remember, someone who has already killed before — I'd be much more comfortable with the 'impossible' scenario. Which is why, really, I'd just let this go. Tully probably won't call you and that's a good thing. If the magic something you might know — whatever it is — comes to you, write her an anonymous note, but really really, hon, you don't want to be part of this thing. It's too late to help Peter, anyway. Let Tully do her work, and while we're on this, here's the flip side of the coin. Let's hope she doesn't decide to come looking at you."

"At me? What for?"

"What else?"

He huffed dismissively. "Get serious."

"You don't think I'm serious?"

"How in the world could that happen? Come on. I loved Peter. I came up and sought out Tully on my own so I could tell her what I knew."

"Granted. But you and I both know that it wouldn't be the first time somebody's tried to get up close and personal to an investigation so that he could keep tabs on how close it was coming to home."

"Tully isn't going to think that. That was so clearly not what I was doing. I'm still a DA in my heart, and she knows I'm on her side. How could she think I killed Peter?"

"Okay, since you asked. First, she doesn't have another suspect yet. Second, Peter got dumped in the ocean and you've got this boat. Third, let's say she hears that your best friend Peter came on to your wife . . ."

"Except that he didn't."

She pulled her sunglasses down and looked at him over the rims. "Easily rebuffed, with no hard feelings," she said. "But a different woman might have been a different story."

"Are you kidding me? When did this happen? Why didn't you mention this before?"

"Because nothing happened. Nothing was going to happen. I played it that he was joking and he dropped it. But what if he wasn't joking? Which — not to flatter myself — I don't think he was."

"That son of a bitch!"

"Well, my point is . . . you see my point. Watch it," she said. "Coming back about."

"So that's pretty much the gist of it," Ron said.

The family was gathered in the television room at the back of the house. Ron sat next to Kate on the love seat, holding her hand in tight solidarity. Aidan hunkered, sulking, on one of the leather ottomans, and Janey had flopped herself into the wicker Papasan chair, which nearly swallowed her whole.

Aidan looked out from under his heavy brows. "I don't really get it," he said. "It doesn't make any sense. Somehow, because you and Mr. Cooke work together, you're supposed to know something about this other guy, the dead guy?"

Kate cleared her throat. "Let's not all of us pretend we don't know who we're talking about, Aidan. Your father and I have discussed this. We want you both to know that there are no secrets between him and me, and I don't want there to be any with us, either. The dead man's name is Peter Ash. And yes, your father and I both saw him socially. We knew him." She looked at Ron and squeezed his hand.

Janey's voice carried more than a hint of whine. "Do we have to talk about him? And about this? It makes me feel sick."

"I'm afraid we do," Ron said. "It's the only way we're going to get this behind us."

"Why don't we just forget about it if he's been killed?"

"Because, Janey," Ron said, "it looks like it might not be completely over. After Beth's talk with Mom last night, it looks like we're going to have to hear more about it. I don't know what, precisely, but I think we can count on that."

Aidan looked to his mother. "But I thought Beth was, like, your best friend."

"She is," Kate said.

"So why is she hassling you?"

"She's not. She's just doing her job, asking some questions. Not even hard ones at that. And what happened last night, I think, is we haven't been seeing each other too much lately and I suppose we both got off a little bit on the wrong foot."

"So now she thinks . . . what?" Aidan asked.

"That's not clear," Ron said. "She may

think nothing about any of this. After all, as you said, so what that Geoff Cooke and I both had social dealings with Mr. Ash? Big deal, right? The only connection with me and Geoff is that we work at the same firm and we're pals."

Kate said, "I'm sure that Beth didn't mean to imply that she had anything as strong as a suspicion. She was just following a trail and it seemed to run through your father's office."

Janey sighed theatrically. "I hate this. I don't know why this all started."

"I know, baby," Kate said. "It's confusing. And I'm so sorry we're all having to deal with this."

Ron reached over and put a hand on Kate's knee. "That's enough. We all just need to turn the page and move on. Do you all think you could do that? Janey?"

Another sigh. "I'll try."

"Aidan?"

"Yes."

"And Kate, you, too. All right. Enough. You getting upset with your friend Beth isn't the worst thing in the world, even if it might make her feel like she needs to involve us somehow in her investigation. We're all fallible. We all make mistakes."

Kate looked from her husband to her

children and nodded. However Ron called it, she was on board with him, and the kids needed to be as well.

"Okay, Dad," Janey pleaded. "Can we just be finished now?"

"Almost, sweetie. But there's one other thing we have to be crystal clear about as a family. Why we're having this talk this morning, all together. And that is we tell the truth. Always, about any of this, about everything. If any more questions come up with Beth Tully or anyone else, especially about Peter Ash, we don't evade, we don't make up answers. But let's remember that 'I don't know' is an acceptable answer. We just say what we know, whatever that may be."

"But we don't know anything about Peter Ash getting killed."

"Right," Ron said. "And that's why whatever happened between your mother and me and Mr. Ash is irrelevant to his murder. They're saying he was killed on Monday night, and all of us know where we were when it must have happened, and so it couldn't have been any of us. Easily proven, with witnesses. Mom and Janey doing that term paper. You, Aidan, at your play practice. Me at my endless deposition.

"So we can't get in any trouble if we just

stick with the truth. And you probably won't even get asked, but if you do — just remember honesty, honesty, honesty. Though I know that neither of you would ever lie anyway, and your mother and I are so proud of that, of who both of you are." He looked to his son, then his daughter. "End of lecture. Does anybody have anything else they'd like to say?"

No response, save the shaking of heads. "Okay, then," Ron said. "Let's call it a wrap."

24

Beth's morning work had entailed trying to assimilate a lot of her thoughts and notes. Ike's call telling her not only about Theresa's lack of success with Peter Ash's phone records, but Theresa's own lack of alibi for Monday night, made her decide to step back and try to get some perspective on where the case stood.

Which was pretty much nowhere.

She had three women — out of perhaps dozens? — whom she assumed Peter had slept with in the past six months, and who might therefore in theory provide some kind of primary or ancillary motive for his murder: his secretary Theresa Boleyn, his landlady Carol Lukins, and the mystery woman, who might very well be Kate Jameson.

But with all three of these women, there were problems.

In spite of Ike leaning toward Theresa as

Peter's killer, Beth intuitively didn't believe it, and over the years, she'd very much come to trust her intuition. Theresa was heartbroken, obviously, and probably had lied about her true relationship with her boss, but that did not make her a murderer. Beth knew that they could try to get a warrant to search her apartment for the murder weapon, if she had been unwise enough to keep it. But they had no probable cause, and this meant that no judge would sign off on the warrant. Period.

Carol Lukins might have been intimate with Peter on the night he got shot, but that was just a hunch on Beth's part, based mostly on Carol's too strenuous denial that she'd even seen him that night. But until Beth got her DNA report, she didn't even have the bare fact of any relationship at all between Carol and Peter. And therefore, any theory of his murder stemming from that could only be the wildest of conjectures.

This left Beth with the mystery woman, who perhaps had something to do with Peter's apparent breakdown, and — Beth didn't want to believe it, but also didn't want to fool herself — who might in fact be Kate. But even if this were the case — and how, even as a cop, could she ask her again without threatening their friendship? — the last known contact between this woman and Peter had been six months ago, so why would she have suddenly killed him last week?

But talk about intuition: Beth had known Kate her whole life, and she was the type of woman who caught spiders in her house and released them outside rather than dispatch them. No matter what Peter Ash may or may not have done to her, Beth found it hard to believe that Kate could have killed him. And certainly in her present state she did not kill him and then haul his body somewhere near the ocean or the bay and throw him in.

Meanwhile, there were other avenues they hadn't even really begun to explore. Peter's immediate family — Jill and the twins, Eric and Tyler — whom he had abandoned to their rage and grief; the unusual volunteerism of Geoff Cooke; Peter's professional acquaintances, including his clients, because say what one will about how much his clients loved him, in the world of high-stakes litigation, sometimes things went badly and quickly awry.

It was nearly a four-mile walk from Theresa's apartment down to where Market Street ended at the Ferry Building, but it was almost all downhill, and she thought the exercise would do her good. Even as she told herself — again and again — that it didn't matter, that nothing really mattered anymore.

She wore fitted jeans, a ribbed green pullover, and hiking boots, and now in the sun had removed her light windbreaker and tied it around her waist. Since her affair with Peter had started, she'd grown her blond hair longer, and now it hung a few inches down her back in a ponytail.

Because she often worked irregular hours and even on weekends, her card key let her onto the elevator and into the firm's main work space at all hours. Today, the usual Saturday group of red hots — attorneys, paralegals, secretaries — toiled away in their cubicles and offices. She said hello to a few of her colleagues as she walked down the hallway, finding it surreal that no one seemed to think it odd that she was there.

Or even acknowledged that Peter was gone.

Most of them had already shared with her their condolences — they were so sorry, and wasn't his death the saddest, most tragic thing? But that appeared to be about the extent of their sympathy or concern.

Bypassing her desk, she opened the door

to Peter's office and then closed and locked it behind her. She walked over to the window and looked way down to the Ferry Building, now back to its normal bustling weekend self. Putting her hand out, she pressed it against one of the indentations left in the glass by the bullets, all three of which had been left unrepaired by decree of Manny Meyer as a memento of that terrible day.

This room, the door locked behind them, was where it had begun, when the desperate platonic hug they'd shared had lasted and lasted and had become something emotional and raw and more, something terrifying and wrong and perfect as the black smoke from the fire below had curled around the building and Peter had lifted her onto his desk and taken her almost before either of them could process what was happening, what had happened, what it might mean.

Now she was back out in her cubicle. She just sat at her desk, her hands folded in her lap. It wasn't loud in the office by any stretch, but the industrious worker bees all around her were creating an ambient white noise — a telephone ringing, a copy machine spitting out work product, the random beep of a computer, disembodied voices — that she suddenly found to be all but intolerable. She wanted to stand up and scream and get everybody's attention and remind them that Peter was *dead,* goddammit, murdered less than a week ago, and what the fuck were they all doing in here pretending that nothing had changed?

Finally, shaking, really wanting to scream, she got up and went into the bathroom, not to use the facility but to get her bearings. She threw several handfuls of water onto her face, wiping her eyes, then her cheeks with the harsh paper towels.

Outside, she stood still in the hallway. The noise hadn't abated. One of her fellow secretaries, Cheryl Padilla, undoubtedly on her way to the bathroom, gave her a quick, automatic smile and a "Hi, Terri," before she stopped in a double take and asked if she was all right.

"Fine."

"Sure?"

"Fine. Really."

A questioning look, then, "Okay."

She didn't speak to anyone else on her way out. Riding down the elevator alone, she left the building just as the clock on the Ferry Building struck noon.

Most of the pedestrians on Market were heading toward the water and the farmers' market and the ferries, and she went along

332

with the flow, through the artist exhibits where Market met the Embarcadero.

To her left, skateboarders were cutting their way through the light crowd moving across the Justin Herman Plaza with its hideous dry fountain.

Pushed along by the thronging masses, Theresa found herself in the first line of people waiting for the light at the curb. Again, noise seemed ubiquitous — plastic-can drummers, steady honking out in the traffic, an auto alarm going off in one of the pay parking lots, the sudden squawking of a flock of gulls overhead. It was suddenly unbearable, all of this cacophony reverberating inside her brain, the jarring street noises and now the pounding bass of a rap track from one of the passing cars, the clang of the F Market historic streetcar descending on the crosswalk where Theresa stood in front of the other pedestrians right at the curb.

Clang. Clang! *Clang clang clang!*

Still a hundred feet from its next regular stop down at Mission Street, the streetcar rumbled heavily on its tracks, now nearly to where she waited, her eyes fixed on the bright façade of the Ferry Building, looming there across the double-wide street, right in front of her.

Clang! Clang!

The trolley was rapidly closing the last few feet between them.

Without any hesitation, Theresa stepped off the curb and out onto the tracks.

PART THREE

NOVEMBER 14–NOVEMBER 27

25

"I should not be doing this," Beth said. "I should be working."

"When I called, didn't you tell me you'd already been working all morning?"

"That's true."

"So this is a lunch break in your regular workday. They let you eat lunch, right?"

"It's more or less encouraged, actually."

"Well, there you go. Besides, when your daughter showed up with that sandwich from Lucca that she was going to split with Laurie, I realized she hadn't bought one for me, which probably meant nothing doing in the lunch realm for you, either. It didn't seem right."

"So you wound up staying at Laurie's overnight?"

Alan nodded. "I keep a toothbrush there at all times. So I asked Ginny what you might be up to this fine day and she said she thought you'd be working. She also said you probably wouldn't mind if I called you."

"God bless that child," Beth said. "And by the way, this is the best sandwich I've ever had in my life."

Another nod. "I once lived on them for a whole year. Two thousand twelve I think it was. I'm still not sure why I stopped."

They were out at the table on what Beth euphemistically called her back deck — six feet on a side with stairs leading to the postage stamp lawn two stories below. The sun was actually bright enough that she had put the table's umbrella up over their heads. Behind the facing backs of all the surrounding buildings, the early afternoon was dead calm.

"So Laurie didn't mind Ginny coming by with more food for her?"

"I'm knocking on wood," Alan said as he reached over and did just that on the railing. "Evidently, Ginny primed her for it last night, and Laurie was actually looking forward to food when she woke up. I haven't seen a sign of that in months. I think if your daughter keeps that up, coming by and just being Laurie's friend who eats like a normal person, she might really pull her out of this. And it is so good of you to let her do it."

"It's not me," Beth said. "Ginny's doing this all on her own. The two of them just

338

connected."

"True, but they wouldn't have if you hadn't thought to put them together."

"Okay, maybe that. I'll take a tiny bit of the credit."

"Good. That's settled, then. And while we're settling things, I wanted to let you know that this impromptu lunch we're having here today does not count as the dinner I asked if you wanted to go out to."

"So you're saying I'm still committed to seeing you again?"

"I am. Burdensome though it may be."

"I don't know," Beth said with a mock wistful tone. "I'll have to check my schedule. I'm notoriously hard to get a date with."

"That's been my experience."

"Well, you pick a time and place and then we'll just have to see."

Beth could hear the relief in Ike's voice. Heather was on the mend, home from the hospital. They were going to have to keep her on a huge dose of intravenous penicillin for the next twenty days or so, but the prognosis was for a complete recovery. She could also hear his fatigue — her partner hadn't had any sleep in at least seventy hours. When he volunteered to go out to Jill's home with Beth, she told him it wasn't necessary. In fact, she suggested that he take Sunday off as well — sleep all day if he could — and unless Beth had identified or arrested a suspect by Monday morning — unlikely bordering on impossible, she thought — the two of them could pick up the investigation at that time.

So at around noon, Beth parked her Jetta across the street and knocked at Jill Corbin-Ash's front door. A younger, preppily dressed woman who self-identified as Jill's sister, Julie Rasmussen, greeted her none too cordially and in a businesslike manner led her to a large, open room in the back of the house — an enormous TV, floor-to-ceiling bookshelves, a fireplace.

As she came in, Beth had the very strong impression that she'd interrupted an argument. The two boys slumped on either end of the brown leather couch, avoiding eye contact with each other and everyone else. Wearing an overlarge pair of sunglasses to cover her bruises and holding a glass of red wine, Jill stood by one of the bookshelves.

The icy vibe showed no signs of thawing after the perfunctory introductions, so Beth waded right in. "I wanted to thank you all for agreeing to meet with me today. I know this is a difficult time for all of you, and I don't intend to take too much of it."

Tyler, the shorter, darker one, straightened himself up a bit. "Yeah, well, excuse me, I don't want to be difficult, but I don't really get why you need to take any of it. Our time, I mean. You're investigating Dad's murder, right? And none of us had anything to do with that. I'd think that would be pretty obvious."

Beth tightened her lips and met his gaze. "Tyler, right?" she asked.

"Yeah."

"Well, Tyler, I understand the last time you all were together here, your brother and your father got in a fight."

Tyler looked down the couch, then back at Beth. "Dad was being a jerk," he said. "Drunk and stupid, thinking we'd all just ignore everything."

"Like what?"

"Oh, nothing," Tyler said with heavy irony. "Just walking out on Mom and disappearing on us. Just ruining everything. Getting in a fight doesn't mean anybody wanted him dead."

"I did," the other boy said. "Fuck him."

Beth shifted her gaze over to the lanky, dirty blond, raw-boned Eric, who sat returning Beth's stare until he looked away, shook his head, and said, "Nobody even got hurt. I took a swing at him. He took a couple of shots back. Big fucking deal."

Beth hardened her look. "I'd appreciate it if you wouldn't use profanity, Eric. And when I heard about the fight, I wondered if you thought it had resolved anything."

"Nothing was going to get resolved."

"Even after he was dead? Isn't it resolved now?"

"He's dead," Eric said. "That means it can never be resolved."

"Inspector," Jill came off her perch by the wall, "wait a minute. We all agreed to be here so that maybe we could fill you in on some of the background in Peter's life, on what might have led to his murder. It wasn't my understanding that you were going to interrogate my boys. And if you are, I think we'd like to get a lawyer on board."

"Fine," Beth said. "My intention with my questions is to eliminate you from suspicion, which ought to be easy enough, but if you'd prefer to have a lawyer around, we can do that, too. It's your call."

"Give it a rest, Mom," Tyler said. "We don't need a lawyer. Nobody killed anybody here." He turned to Beth. "Look," he said. "My dad went off the rails. He totally screwed up. I'm just glad it's over. But it's like getting a tooth pulled — it hurts a little at the time, sure, but then it's better and doesn't hurt anymore. That's Dad. I wish this hadn't happened, if only because it makes Mom so sad, but now that it has, I can't say it's a bad thing."

"He didn't deserve to be killed, Tyler," his mother said.

Eric struck back at her. "You know, that's the funny thing, Mom," he said. "I think we're going to find out exactly the opposite. The way he was, there's no chance we're the only people he screwed around with, and what I think is that somebody out there just decided they weren't going to take his bullshit anymore. So they killed him. Makes perfect sense to me. If I'd have had any guts, I'd have done it myself."

"Eric! You don't mean —"

"The hell I don't, Mom. Look what he's turned us all into, a pack of pathetic victims. And why? Do any of us know how this whole thing even started?" He brought his anger around to Beth. "And how about you, Inspector? With all this background you've been looking for, trying to get some *context,* give me a break. You wouldn't be here talking to us if you had any idea who'd killed him, would you? Well, here's some context for you: for whatever reason, my dad woke up one morning and had turned into a monster. Whoever put him down did the world a favor."

From her corner, Julie Rasmussen finally piped in. "I hate to say it, but I think Eric's right."

"No," Jill said. "He might've come around. It might have been . . ."

"There's no 'might have been' here, Jill. Look what he's done to you. What he's done to the boys. And why? He obviously didn't feel he had to give you an excuse. After twenty years of marriage? Are you kidding me?"

Jill physically withered at the obvious truth in this final onslaught. Her legs almost seemed to give way beneath her as she made her way over to one of the room's chairs and lowered herself into it. Looking up at Beth, she said, "I'm sorry. I don't know what you want from us."

There was weakness here, and great pain, and Beth had to fight down a pang of guilt as she decided to exploit it. "As I said earlier, I want to eliminate you all as suspects. A few questions and it's all over." She turned. "Like, for example, you, Tyler, you live in Chico, isn't that right?"

"Yeah." Anger and frustration emanated from his every pore. "I'm in school up there."

"Do you know what you were doing last

Monday night?"

"Yeah. I was at the Pub Quiz at UOB."

"UOB?"

"University of Beer."

"How late were you there?"

"Jesus Christ."

"It's an easy question, Tyler. How late did you stay there?"

"Pretty late. Midnight. One."

"Were you alone?"

He laughed at the absurdity of that. "Yeah, except for my roommates and about half of Chico. And I'm sorry, Officer," though he didn't sound it, "but this is complete bullshit. Why don't you talk to our lawyer, get a warrant, and rock and roll? Don't you have some homeless people to harass and beat up? Meanwhile, really, I'm so done. I'm out of here." Getting to his feet, he stomped out of the room.

Jill and Julie both jumped up, following him through the house, urging him back, but in a moment the front door slammed shut.

Beth waited until, apologetic almost beyond words, they had come back. As gently as she could she asked if any of them minded if she went on for just a few more minutes.

"Do we really have a choice?" Julie asked.

"Well, as we just saw, Tyler did. So do the rest of you."

"I'm so sorry about that," Jill said. "No one's themself around here lately. That really wasn't like Tyler. He's a good boy. It's just been so hard."

"I understand that," Beth said. "I'm not here to harass anybody. If you can spare me just a little more of your time. Eric? You're at Berkeley?"

"Yeah."

"So Monday night?"

The young man pouted, wrinkled his forehead, shot a glance at the ceiling — in all a marginally convincing display of trying to recall whatever he'd done. Finally, the answer came to him. "I was here, with Mom." He looked over at his mother. "That was Monday, right?"

"Yes," said Jill, turning to Beth, explaining. "Eric called me Sunday night just to check up on how I was doing. I probably gave him the impression that I was a little tired of being alone and he said he was sick of meal ticket food, so why didn't he come over the next night and we could have some dinner together. Which is what we did."

"Did you stay overnight here, Eric?"

"No. I had an early class the next morning so I had to be back in Berkeley. I think I left here around nine or nine thirty. Does that sound right, Mom?"

"I think so, yes. Not much later than that."

"I know I was back in the dorm by a little after ten. Does that help?"

Pretty slick, Beth was thinking through her frustration, how they'd both given themselves alibis, almost as if they had it planned. Although she did not believe that Jill had killed her husband, or conspired with Eric, she was not so sure about the possibility that Eric might have acted on his own. He was a bitter and angry young man. Nevertheless, they had pretty effectively insulated each other from her inquiries.

But not completely. On a hunch, Beth asked, "Do you have a gun, Eric?"

From the reaction in the room, Beth might as well have just fired hers.

Julie exploded. "No way!"

"That's ridiculous!" Jill said. "Of course he doesn't own a gun."

But Eric's expression told Beth that she'd hit a nerve. Keeping her eyes on him, she pressed her advantage. "You can't buy a gun in this state if you're under twenty-one, Eric. You want to tell me?"

For a long silent moment, Eric didn't move. Finally, he met Beth's eyes. "All right.

Yes. I bought a gun on the street in Oakland."

His mother turned on him in disbelief. "Eric! Why on earth . . . ?"

"To protect myself." He turned to Beth. "Berkeley's a lot rougher than people think."

"Do you still have it, Eric? The gun."

"No."

"No? What happened?"

"Somebody stole it from me. That's the truth," he said with real defiance. "I didn't have it two weeks and somebody took it."

"Where did you keep it?"

"In my room at Berkeley."

"And where is that?"

"Unit One, near campus."

"So when did it go missing?"

"Like I said, right after I got it. That's the truth, like it or not."

Jill said, "I think at this point we're going to want to call a lawyer."

"Mom," Eric said, "we don't need to worry about that. Me having bought a gun doesn't mean squat. It doesn't prove I shot anybody."

Beth decided to cut to the chase. "But did you? Did you kill your father, Eric?"

"No, I didn't kill my father. Not that I wouldn't have liked to. But whoever it was beat me to it before I could get my hands

348

on another gun and get up the guts."

"You need to stop talking right now, Eric," Jill said. "And I'm sorry, Inspector, but I'm not going to allow any more questions until we've talked to a lawyer."

26

Beth had just gotten out of her car underground at the public garage in Berkeley when her cell phone chirped with her partner calling her again — the sleep he was lacking didn't appear to be a major priority in his life.

"You're not going to believe this and you're going to like it even less," Ike said. "But Theresa Boleyn just killed herself."

"You are shitting me." Beth felt her legs suddenly go weak, and she leaned back against her car. "Tell me."

Ike ran down the details as Beth tried to get her head around this altered reality. Ike was going on. ". . . ought to be easier to warrant up and get inside her apartment, see if she's maybe got a gun hidden somewhere . . ."

"Funny you should mention."

"What's that?"

She told him. "Which is why I'm over here

in Berkeley."

"Without a warrant? You're going to need a warrant, Beth."

"Thanks for reminding me, Dad. I've got the office on it. Meanwhile, I'm here to see if I can find Eric's gun, which he says was stolen, which in turn strikes me as the tiniest bit convenient. Cynic that I am, I want to make sure it's not under his bed or something. We've got no bullet to test it against, but it would still be nice to see if the mysterious disappearing gun could help us somehow, especially if our boy lied about the disappearing part."

"So you're going to search for a gun and . . . ?"

"Talk to the roommate, hopefully before Eric thinks to call him and coach him about what he needs to say."

"Who's the roommate?"

"I don't know, but I'm going to find out."

"So you're thinking it wasn't Theresa who killed Ash?"

"I don't know if I ever thought it was. And I'm pretty sure I really don't think it now."

"Just out of curiosity, why not? She looks better for it than ever to me. She finds out Peter's having multiple affairs, so in a jealous rage she kills him."

"Jealous rage, now, was it?"

"Like it or not," Ike said. "Then when the deed is done, she tries to bluff it out for a few days until finally she can't take the guilt anymore and she walks in front of the street-car."

"Well, either that or she just lost the love of her life and she's got nothing left to live for. Which seemed more like the person she was to me. Sweet and clueless and trusting."

"And if the trust gets betrayed?"

"Then she kills herself, not her betrayer, wouldn't you think? Not saying it's impossible, Ike. I just don't see her killing anybody, much less the guy she loves. Even if he betrayed her."

"So who, then?"

"That's the question. Maybe Eric. Which means none of Peter's female connections after all. He's a bitter, angry kid with a huge chip. He admitted that he actually bought a street gun illegally. So he was definitely thinking about it. On the other hand, if his alibi holds . . ."

In several ways, Beth knew that the drive across the bay to Berkeley was pretty much a shot in the dark. She didn't know the name of Eric's roommate or if he would be in their room. She didn't know the security arrangements at the huge student housing units.

Would the dorm security people even let her speak to one of the residents? She knew that in San Francisco, on a similar errand, she could expect at least stiff resistance if not outright hostility and bureaucratic stonewalling. She had no real reason to believe that things would be different here on the other side of the bay, but (maybe in part because of the aftermath of her lunch with Alan) she'd felt like it was a good karma day, the empty afternoon had loomed before her, and she'd decided she didn't have much to lose. She might as well give the god of good fortune a chance to play a role.

But to even the odds, as she'd told Ike, she had asked her lieutenant to pitch in to work up a search warrant. She expected the call that the judge had signed it at any moment.

As it turned out, the security "officer" — a college kid working as a volunteer just inside the lobby of residential Unit One — was impressed and perhaps, more than that, intimidated by Beth's credentials. After all, she was a bona fide homicide inspector from San Francisco working on a murder that he'd actually read about earlier in the week.

353

He was happy to supply her with the name of Eric's roommate, Jon Chung. He punched in Chung's emergency contact number and gave Beth a thumbs-up when the phone picked up. A few more words established that the young man was upstairs, studying. A San Francisco police officer, the guard told him, was down in the lobby and would like to speak with him.

In less than a minute, Chung exploded out of the elevator, frantic. "Are you the cop?" he pleaded to Beth. "They're not picking up. Tell me it's not my parents."

"I'm sure your parents are fine," Beth said. "I'm not here about them. I'm sorry if I alarmed you. I should have mentioned that right away. Everybody's fine. I'm just looking for a little information on your roommate."

Exhaling, Chung put his hand over his heart and gave Beth a sheepish smile. "Wow," he said. "That'll wake you right up."

"Were you sleeping?"

"Dozing, more. Chemistry in a warm room after lunch. So this is about Eric's dad then, isn't it?"

"Yes. I'm afraid it is. And the first thing I need to ask you is this. Did you ever see Eric's gun?"

"Whoa, Jesus. You think Eric killed his

father. I can't believe you're even saying that. No, he didn't have a gun. I never saw a gun. He never talked about a gun. You're totally barking up the wrong tree."

"How sure are you?"

"Officer, our whole dorm room is maybe ten feet square. I know totally everything either one of us has in the room. If there was a gun in there, I would have known it and I would have screamed bloody murder 'cause it could have gotten us expelled."

"Okay, let's talk about Eric's father. When did you hear about that?"

Chung considered for a moment. "Last Wednesday, I think. His mom called. We were both in the room."

"How'd Eric take it?"

"Mostly weird, I'd say."

"Weird how?"

"Well, first, I mean, as soon as she told him, he kind of broke down. Crying, you know, sobbing actually. But then — it wasn't a long call — after he hung up, he was all like 'YES!' Purely relieved, if not actually happy, and he kept getting happier. Which was a little scary. I mean, your dad's dead. No matter what, it's going to hit you hard, right? Even if you had issues with him.

"But with Eric, after he got used to the idea, it was like it psyched him up. I thought that was weird. I mean, a lot of the people here pretend they don't like their parents, and maybe they don't. But Eric and his dad. I mean, from his reaction, he really hated him. And I can't say I blame him, with his dad cutting out on all of them like he did. That's pretty cold. He must have been a bastard and a half. But still, it's hard to believe somebody actually killed him, much less his own son."

Suddenly it seemed to dawn on him that he was providing information in a homicide investigation. He took a step back. "You're not here because . . . ? You don't really think it was Eric, do you?"

She gave the standard cop answer. "I don't think anything yet. I'm just asking questions. I'm interested in what time he got home last Monday night. If it jogs your memory, that was the night he went over to his mom's house to have dinner with her."

"Sure. I remember. Just last Monday?"

"Right."

Chung worked it around in his brain, then said, "It wasn't too late. Twelve thirty, one, somewhere in there."

"And you were in the room when?"

"The whole night. We got in a truly vicious hearts game that never seemed to end. It didn't break up until around midnight.

Eric showed up about a half hour after everybody left."

"Twelve thirty?"

"Sometime around then. Could have been a little later."

"You're sure?"

"Pretty much, yes."

"On a scale of one to ten?"

He considered for a minute. "I know the game was Monday night. So yeah, I'd have to go with about ten."

That's two whoppers Eric had told her, Beth thought. Two big, really important lies.

"Well, thank you, Jon. You've been a help."

"I hope I didn't get Eric in trouble."

Beth's phone rang. It was her lieutenant telling her that her warrant was good to go.

When she hung up, she told Eric's roommate that she was going to be in his room for the next hour or two. She had a search warrant and, in spite of his assurance that he didn't think that there was a gun hidden somewhere in the room, she was going to make sure.

"You really think he might have done it?" Chung asked her.

"I don't think anything," Beth said. "I'm looking for some evidence."

"Could I go get the homework I'm working on?"

"Only if I go with you and check what you take when you leave. Those are the conditions. Are you good with them?"

"Sure."

"Okay, then, let me talk to your security guy here and then we'll go on up."

27

From Berkeley, Beth came back to her desk in the Hall of Justice, where she could sit with a Diet Coke and try to get some perspective on where things stood now. It seemed, at the very least, that she had finally moved things along, and might in fact have unearthed a true suspect in Eric Ash, whom she had caught in two blatant lies about his alibi — he hadn't been back in his dorm room on Monday night by ten, but closer to one. And, if true, that gave him somewhere near three hours to meet his father under some pretext, shoot him, and dump him in saltwater.

Plenty of time.

And it certainly looked like telling her that the gun had been stolen from his dorm room in Berkeley was a second lie. If he had hidden it so well that Jon Chung didn't know about it, no intruder would likely have found it either.

Beth didn't know why Eric had admitted to having a gun in the first place — it was possible that he thought that she'd already found out about him having the gun from another source. If she did know that, him admitting it made him look more forthright and cooperative. A greater likelihood, she thought, was that he'd thrown the gun in the ocean or somewhere after he'd used it to kill his father, and he wanted to taunt Beth with that possibility.

Beyond that, though, it certainly looked like whatever else happened to the gun, it wasn't randomly stolen by someone Eric didn't know.

It was clear that, no matter what, Eric no longer had the gun. Which meant that no ballistics match was going to be possible, and so he'd arrogantly, if figuratively, waved it in front of her face. Telling her he was smarter than she was; he knew the salient facts of the case; he'd left no physical evidence; he could beat her at this game.

That attitude, she was finding, was really quite the motivator.

So, then, what had happened to the gun? She toyed with the idea of telling Eric she'd found the gun to play her own games with his head. But given that the body had been in the bay, it seemed logical to think the gun would be there, too. Knowing that she was lying to him would simply convince him further that if he just held on to his story, they couldn't touch him.

Sipping her drink, she made a few notes and then sat back in her chair. She didn't know what to do about the suicide of Theresa Boleyn. Although she didn't want to believe it, she realized that it was entirely possible that Ike was right and Theresa had killed her cheating boyfriend if, in fact, he'd been her boyfriend, in which case Theresa, too, had lied to them. They would, in fact, need another warrant to go through her apartment, car (if she had one), workstation, and so on. It was going to be an insane next few days.

In the here and now, though, the same karma that had delivered Jon Chung to her without hassle seemed to be holding. When she booted it up, she saw that her computer contained emails from two friends of Peter's stoner upstairs neighbor, Ned. The other two had already answered her emails, leaving their cell phone numbers. She had all their numbers now, and she picked up the phone at her desk and punched up the first one.

Twenty minutes later, she'd talked to three of them. They were universally cooperative and totally unhelpful. Everyone agreed that all of them had gotten to Ned's apartment early and had spent the entirety of the football game there, since he had the big TV and the beer. Where else were they going to go?

They'd all heard the ruckus from Peter's apartment one floor down, probably in the second quarter, and certainly all over before the half. None of them thought it had sounded like a fight, although there had been some loud noises for sure — the squeaking bed, cries of obvious passion. Two of the guys had found it to be hysterically funny, basically.

But all of them, to a greater or lesser degree, seemed embarrassed talking about it. One of them, Stuart Aiello, wasn't a hundred percent sure what it was because, he told Beth with a touching naïveté, he'd never heard anybody making love before, so if that was what it was, he couldn't swear to it. But none of the other guys, he said, had had any doubt, so that must have been it. Stuart didn't know why it would be so loud. He was the one who didn't find it funny — it sounded to him like it hurt.

No one had left the apartment until after the game, and they hadn't seen anybody in the hallway on their way out. By the time

362

they left, Peter's apartment was silent. No one had heard him making any other noise of any kind.

She hung up and went into the bathroom. When she came out, Ike was sitting in his chair, facing her across their back-to-back desks. "Look what the cat dragged in," she said. "What the hell are you doing here, Ike? I thought you were trying to catch up on your sleep. How's Heather?"

"She's good. She's sleeping. The fever's completely gone, thank God. Me, I'm going to wait for my regular bedtime before I crash. Otherwise I'll just wake up in the middle of the night and if I get on that rhythm, I'll have insomnia for a week or maybe a year, which I'd rather avoid. So I thought I'd just kill a pleasant few hours up here, do the paperwork on my parking tickets . . ." His already gray complexion paled, his bleary eyes resting on her. "Maybe I can forget about my last few hours."

"Theresa," Beth said. She boosted herself onto his desk. "You went to the scene."

He nodded. "I had to." He drew in a breath through tightened lips, let it out in a rush. "Even if she did kill him. Lord."

"You're positive nobody pushed her?"

"I'm sure. There were, like, twenty witnesses, maybe more. She just was in the

363

crowd and got to the curb and waited, full stop for a couple of seconds, then stepped off. Like she wasn't even aware it was coming. Or didn't care."

"More that, I'm thinking."

"It breaks my heart, I tell you. I'm getting too old for this. And what was she, thirty?"

"A little more, maybe. Too young to end her life."

"Well, I'll tell you something. If she didn't kill Ash, I want to get my hands on the son of a bitch that did. Because he killed Theresa as sure as if he pushed her onto the tracks."

Beth scratched at the top of the desk, and her cell phone rang. Plucking it from her belt, she checked the number, and told Ike, "I've got to take this." Then, into the phone, "Tully, Homicide. Is this Damon?"

While she talked to the fourth guest from Ned's party, Ike pushed himself back from the desk and crossed over to the windows overlooking Bryant Street. The afternoon was bright, and he stood, hands in his pockets, in the slanting rays of sunlight.

After a couple of minutes, Beth came up behind him. "That was the last of the *Monday Night Football* fans."

"Who?"

"Ash was getting himself laid in his apart-

364

ment a couple of hours before he was killed. I've got five kids in the apartment right above him who heard it like they were in the room."

"Who was Ash with?"

"I'm guessing his landlady. Her name is Carol Lukins, but I can't prove she was with him unless and until I get some DNA, and that isn't going to happen quick, as you know, if ever."

"And why, again, do we want to prove it was her with him? She's just another one of his girlfriends, right?"

"Of course. But she was the last one. If anybody knows what Ash might have been going to do on Monday night, she's probably the best bet. Maybe he got a phone call setting up some kind of meeting while he was with her. Maybe he just told her where he was going, or with whom. But currently, she is among our stable of liars — and remind me to tell you next about Eric Ash — but if it was Carol on Monday, there's a decent chance she can tell us something we don't know."

"I'm reminding you now," he said, turning out of the sun. "How did Eric Ash lie?"

"The alibi he carefully constructed with his mother is squishy. He told me he got back to his dorm after spending the night in the city."

"In this city?"

"The very same. Having dinner with Mom. Says he got back to Berkeley around ten. But his roommate says he didn't get in until one. No doubt about it, and it's on tape if after talking with Eric the roommate decides to change his mind. Which would of course be another lie, but there's almost too many of them to count anymore."

"Makes me think we should make something up ourselves," Ike said. "Create a different reality and put the fear of God into some of these people."

"If only," Beth said. "But alas . . ."

Suddenly Ike went still, looking over her shoulder.

She frowned, followed his gaze, saw nothing, came back to him. "What?"

"That's it," he said. "We need to start lying. Fight fire with fire."

Beth called Carol Lukins from the squad room, wondering would she mind coming downtown to Homicide for a few minutes just to clarify some of the details in her statement in person. Yes, she did mind and no, they couldn't come to her home, either. Carol wanted to know a little more what this was about, but Beth kept it vague, tell-

366

ing her they just had some follow-up queries about her tenant Peter Ash. Eventually, Carol agreed to see them if they could make it at the Starbucks a couple of blocks up on Fulton.

Beth, pumped up by this proposal because it meant that Carol was probably hiding something from her husband, allowed as how that would be all right with them.

Ike drove, and twenty minutes later they were seated with their coffees around one of the small tables in the front window. Beth had rather ostentatiously brought out her tape recorder and it sat on the table between them.

The striking, white-haired woman exuded some of the same nervous energy that may have contributed to her fainting spell last time. They'd barely begun with her name and the case number and her earlier statement when she picked up her cup, blew on it, put it back down, turned it around on the table. "I'm . . ." she said, "I'm really not sure what you're saying."

"We're talking about DNA." Ike in his bad cop voice. "You're generally familiar with DNA, aren't you, Ms. Lukins?"

"Ike." Beth reached out her hand and put it on his arm, easing him off. She came back to their witness. "Well, as I'm sure you remember, Carol, after you left Mr. Ash's apartment the other day, I had the Crime Scene Unit come up and conduct a battery of tests. They were looking for fingerprints and DNA — that is, physical evidence of people who might have been in Mr. Ash's apartment, particularly that night, since we believe he was killed later that night, so I think it's obvious why we'd want to know everything we could about his last hours."

"Obvious enough, but as I told you last time, I didn't see Mr. Ash that night." She looked anxiously at Beth, then at Ike. Lifting her cup again, she blew on it, sipped, and kept right on talking. "I didn't even see Peter, Mr. Ash, that entire weekend. My husband and I were visiting his parents down in Gilroy — his dad's had a stroke — and I didn't get back until Monday morning. Besides, if you're talking about DNA in his apartment — my DNA in particular — of course I'd expect you to find some traces of it."

"How's that?" Ike asked.

"We like to check up on all the tenants and how they're treating the units. You know, students. They can wreck things in a hurry. So we've got a clause in our standard lease that allows us to come in and inspect any of the apartments once a month by appointment. Although we're also really hands on in terms of things breaking down, so either Evan or I . . . we're in most of the apartments at least once a month for some maintenance or another. So I'd expect you to find my DNA in Mr. Ash's place, but also really almost anybody's else's, too."

"How about the sheets?" Ike said. "Should we expect to find your DNA on the sheets?"

The question hung in the air.

With a flat, disgusted, baleful look at Carol, Ike leaned in close and then turned and said to Beth, "You want to tell her about Monday night?"

"No," Carol reacted in a pleading tone. "I've already told you I wasn't there Monday night. There's no way you can . . ."

Beth held up a palm, stopping her. "Carol," she said. "Your tenant upstairs, right above Mr. Ash in number five — Ned? — he had a bunch of guys over to watch the football game last Monday night. They all — all five of them — said that they heard unmistakable sounds of lovemaking in Mr. Ash's apartment directly below them."

Carol held Beth's eyes for a long moment. She picked up her coffee and then put it down. "I don't see what that has to do with me."

Ike, bad cop all the way, let out a scornful

little laugh.

Beth spoke in sympathetic tones. "As my partner just said, Carol, among the items removed from the apartment for DNA testing were the sheets on Mr. Ash's bed."

"But how would you even know if it was mine? My DNA, I mean. Don't you need to have something to check it against?"

"People are watching too much television," Ike said.

"We did have something to check it against, Carol," Beth said. "After you fainted, that glass of water you drank from?"

"That's . . . shit. That is so sneaky. I can't believe you did that. Coming across as all nice and friendly, too."

Beth sat back in her chair, silent and unyielding. Finally, she got around to her own coffee. Ike, too, waited, content to let Carol stew in these bitter juices. The next time she reached for her cup, her hands were visibly shaking.

"Carol, talk to us," Beth said.

With a last, helpless look at the two inspectors, she drew a shaky breath. "Evan cannot know," she said. "I love Evan, but he has a temper, and he cannot know any part of this. He would kill me."

"Would he have killed Peter Ash?" Ike asked. "Do either of you own a gun?"

"No."

"No to which question?" Beth asked. "Would he have killed Peter, or do either of you own a gun?"

"Neither."

Ike came at her again. "But you said if he found out about you and Peter, he'd kill you."

"That was just a figure of speech. More likely, it would kill him. We love each other."

"So you say," Beth replied. "But then there was you and Peter."

She shrugged. "Sometimes, you know, living it day to day . . ." She hesitated. "It gets a little boring. Peter was just . . . it wasn't serious. Maybe I shouldn't have . . ." Shaking her head, she looked at Beth. "You really can't tell him," she said. "Please."

"Do you know where Evan was that night?" Ike asked.

"Evan doesn't know," Carol insisted, ignoring the question. "If he knew, I wouldn't be sitting here looking like this."

"What do you mean?" Beth asked. "Like what?"

"I mean, come on, you know. This is pure proof that Evan didn't kill Peter. Evan didn't have a clue about Peter and me."

"How do you know that?" Ike asked.

" 'Cause look at me! No cuts, no bruises.

371

He doesn't know."

"Okay, then," Ike said. "Back to where Evan was that night, Monday. Do you know?"

"He was still at his parents' in Gilroy. He thought his dad might not make it, though now it looks like he will. Anyway, Evan didn't feel he should come back up here yet, but I had to."

"Why?" Ike asked. Then, surmising. "Peter?"

She shrugged dismissively. "I don't expect people to understand," she said. "But we didn't get too many opportunities."

Beth and Ike exchanged a look. "All right," Beth said. "How about Monday night?"

"What do you mean?"

Ike was losing his patience and his temper. "She means you went to all these efforts, Carol, leaving your husband down in Gilroy with his dying father so you could get up here to get together with Peter Ash. And then it's over in an hour or two and then what?"

"What do you mean, 'then what'?"

"I mean, he just kicks you out and you're okay with that?"

"He didn't kick me out. We were done. I went home, took a bath, talked to Evan for an hour. Then I did some business on my computer . . . spreadsheets on the units. You can check that out. There'll be a record of it someplace, that I was online and when."

All right, enough, Beth was thinking. Carol Lukins was a hell of a morally challenged human being, but Beth did not believe she was the killer she was hunting. Other than the enjoyment of making her squirm, there was no point in grilling her further on that score. The real issue, the reason they'd gone through this exercise in the first place, was still unexplored. "Carol," she said, "here's the big question: Did Peter mention anything to you on Monday night about what he was doing later on, if he was planning to see somebody, or just go out, or what?"

"He was going out."

"Did he say with who?"

"No. Some friend of his."

"Did you get a name?" Ike asked.

"No. Why would I need a name?"

Beth didn't answer her. Instead, "By any chance, did he set up this meeting while you were with him?"

"You mean in his apartment? No. He wasn't, like, taking calls."

"Do you remember if his phone even rang?"

"I don't think so. In fact, I'd say definitely not."

"Good," Beth said. "We like definitely."

"So this friend he mentioned," Ike said. "Would you mind trying to recall exactly what Peter said when he told you about his plans for after you left him that night?"

"It wasn't like it was a big discussion. I'm not sure I even remember much about it."

"We'd really like you to try, Carol," Beth said. "How did the topic even come up?"

Carol met Beth's gaze, then nodded and closed her eyes. "Okay," she said. "All right." Her expression went a bit sour. "We were lying there. After, you know. Both of us feeling good, I'd say. Maybe half dozing, and I told Peter that Evan wasn't coming back that night, not 'til the morning." She stopped, opened her eyes. "Telling him if he wanted I could stay over."

"And he said?" Beth prompted her.

"His exact words?"

"Close as you can, please."

Inhaling, exhaling, Carol waited another second or two, then closed her eyes again and went on in a disappointed tone. "He said, 'That is a truly sweet offer that I wish I'd have known about sooner. But this close

374

buddy of mine texted me today and evidently he's got this serious problem he wants to talk about and I already promised him we could meet up, have a drink or two and maybe a cigar.' And I told him, 'Well, after the cigar, never mind.' " She opened her eyes. "And we had a little laugh about it. That was all it was, I'm pretty sure. I don't think he mentioned it again."

They were in the car, but Ike hadn't even started the engine when he broke the silence they'd maintained since leaving the coffee shop. "A close friend who smokes cigars," he said.

"I heard that," Beth said. "Which leaves his son Eric out of the equation, doesn't it?"

"It would seem to," Ike said. "Unless Eric met him even later. Possible, I guess, but not really something I'd bet on. In any event, I don't see Peter Ash referring to his son as a close buddy of his, do you?"

"Not in the normal course of conversation, no. In fact, never in a million years. He would have just called him his son."

"Agreed. And in the meantime, diabolical though it might seem, you notice that at no time did we actually tell the unfortunate Ms. Lukins — the tape bears it out — that we had any DNA results whatsoever, although that seemed to be the conclusion she jumped to on her own."

"I did notice that. And diabolical is the word."

Ike pulled out into traffic and shot his partner a wicked smile. "Legitimate interrogation technique. I figure if everybody else we're talking to can lie to us, and they sure do, we are completely within bounds leveling the field by inadvertently creating a false impression with total avoidance of actual mendacity and still be on the side of the angels."

"I wasn't going to put it exactly like that. But I get your point." She paused. "So what do you think?"

"What do I think about what?"

"The close friend who smokes cigars."

"What do you want me to think?" Ike asked. "I think that's a damn good lead, if in fact he came and picked Peter up at his place, and especially thinking now it wasn't Theresa and it probably wasn't Eric, and we're ruling out the happy Lukins couple, too."

"Right. So let me raise you one," she said. "What if I said we've narrowed it down to a close friend of Peter's who likes cigars and who also owns a boat?"

"Are you kidding me? I'd like it a lot. If we had anybody like that."

"I just realized that I haven't told you anything yet about a guy named Geoff Cooke, have I? Used to be an assistant DA? Now he's corporate."

"I don't think so. Has he shown up around this case? Who is he?"

"Nobody much. Just a close friend of Peter's who likes cigars and owns a boat that he berths down in the marina."

Ike shot her a disbelieving look. "This is a real person?"

"Real as a blood clot, Ike. Considered himself Peter's best friend."

"And how again did we meet him?"

"He stopped by the office a couple of days ago wanting to know how he could help us. In the crush of other events, he didn't strike me as important. I must have forgotten to mention him to you, for which I offer my profound apology. But I'm mentioning him now."

"He came up to visit you?"

"Us, really. You weren't there that day on that tired old 'my daughter's got meningitis' excuse. But did he come up to visit me? Yes."

"Checking up on us, see what we had, stay a step ahead."

"Maybe. More like 'probably' now, I'm

thinking."

"You know what this sounds like?" Ike asked.

"What's that?"

"It sounds like I'm not going to catch up on much sleep tonight after all, am I?"

"Not very likely," Beth replied.

28

Several random events conspired to frustrate the efforts of Beth and Ike in their progress on the Peter Ash investigation.

In the first place, the relative hiatus on murders that the city had been enjoying for the past six weeks or so suddenly came to an end on this Saturday night. At about the same time that the interview with Carol Lukins was concluding, Len Faro and his Crime Scene Unit rolled out on an apparent gang-related drive-by shooting in Hunters Point. They had not yet arrived on that scene when a domestic violence call in the Mission had turned deadly, the victim a Hispanic middle-aged woman with multiple stab wounds.

By the time Beth and Ike got back to the Hall of Justice at a little before five o'clock, dusk creeping in, the Homicide detail had received two more calls — a robbery had gone south down in the lower Sunset when the store's owner had taken three bullets in the chest as he'd reached for his own gun behind the counter; and a young man, possibly a tourist, had succumbed to a mugging after he'd been thrown to the ground and beaten as he'd been strolling through the Tenderloin.

These four, of course, were in addition to the suicide of Theresa Boleyn earlier in the day.

Though Beth and Ike's original plan had been to apply to the weekend magistrate judge and get a warrant to search Geoff Cooke's sailboat down at the marina in the hopes that they would have something incriminating to show him when they confronted Cooke himself, no sooner had they shown up on the fourth floor than their lieutenant appeared at their desks and assigned them to the Sunset robbery and fatal shooting. Twenty minutes after they had arrived at the Hall, they were back on the road again, this time in a city-issued vehicle.

Beth, in the passenger seat, was on the phone with her daughter, explaining the all-too-familiar scenario: ". . . so bottom line, Gin, is if you come home, don't wait up. It'll probably be awhile. Are you still down at Laurie's?"

"All day. We've been having a blast, binge-

380

ing on *Blue Bloods.*"

"Ah, cop glamour. You don't get enough of that, living with a cop and all?"

"Well, no offense, Mom, but you don't do much of the glamour part."

"Hey! That hurts. Every day I'm immersed in glamour. Just ask Ike. You want to talk to him? He's right here. He'll tell you. Here, listen up. Ike, tell Ginny how glamorous is our day-to-day life."

She held out the phone and Ike bellowed, "Way glam."

Beth brought the instrument back to her ear. "See? And meanwhile," she added, going serious, "how's Laurie doing?"

Ginny's voice went to a near-whisper. "Popcorn and gelato all day. It's like she's not even thinking about it. Like eating suddenly is more or less normal."

"Don't get her sick."

"She's already sick. This is making her better."

"Good point."

"Besides, she's developing a major crush on Danny."

"Danny?"

"Donnie Wahlberg? Tom Selleck's son on *Blue Bloods*?"

"Ah."

"Which, believe it or not, might be doing

381

her some good on the Frank Rinaldi front. At least theoretically, she's definitely finding another man attractive, and that's got to be a plus."

"It can't hurt."

"No, it can't."

Beth paused for a second. Then, "Is Alan over there with you guys?"

"No. He left around noon. He said he was going to see you for lunch. Did he do that?"

"He did."

"And how'd it go?"

"We had a nice lunch."

"That's all?"

"That's plenty at this stage, Gin. He seems like a good guy."

"He is a good guy, Mom. Cute, too, as you might have noticed."

"Not really. I don't do that superficial stuff. So listen, are you planning to come home tonight?"

"I thought I'd play it by ear. You're gone anyway, right?"

" 'Til late at least."

"So I wouldn't be abandoning you?"

"No. Not even a little."

"How about if I let you know then, one way or the other? Meanwhile, if Alan comes by here again, should I tell him you had a great time at lunch?"

"Thank you, but not necessary. He knows what kind of time we had."

"Are you seeing him again?"

"He said something about dinner sometime, but nothing is carved in stone. If he calls and asks, we'll see what happens, if anything."

"You've got to rein in that enthusiasm, Mom."

"I know," Beth said. "I'm working on it."

The Ulloa Super was anything but. It wasn't even on Ulloa Street.

A mom-and-pop market at the corner of Taraval and Nineteenth Avenue, essentially unchanged in forty or fifty years, it sported an entire aisle of cheap wine, another of food staples and snacks, mostly from the high-calorie, heavily preserved end of the spectrum, a cold bin with beer and soft drinks, some questionably fresh fruits and vegetables, candy, toiletries, paper products, and hard liquor behind the counter.

Also behind the counter, on the floor, lay the body of Emil Yarian. His assailant had shot him three times in the chest, probably from two or three feet away, across the counter. He still held the handgun that he'd grabbed to defend and protect himself, a strategy that hadn't worked out so well.

383

Four patrol officers and the sergeant from Taraval Station had secured the scene by the time Beth and Ike pulled up. After fifteen or twenty minutes, it became clear that due to the crush on the city's resources, neither the Crime Scene Unit nor the coroner was going to be making an appearance anytime soon.

Beth cocked her head toward Ike, and the two of them moved away from the other cops and under the yellow crime scene tape to the sidewalk outside. Fog was starting to reappear, swirling in from the west. A couple of TV vans had pulled up outside, and the inspectors turned and walked away in the opposite direction. "I'm going way out on a limb now," Beth said when they were out of earshot, "but my gut tells me nothing new happens here for three or four hours minimum."

Ike cast a woeful glance back toward the market's door. "Looks about right," he said. "Maybe five or six."

"And even then, what? The surveillance camera's not working. No witnesses saw anything. There's nothing in the future here but paperwork, wouldn't you say? So here's my idea. You and I get back in the car right now, and I drive you to your lovely home in the Richmond, not two miles away."

"And what do I do there?"

"Get some of that sleep we've been talking about. I'd rather have you rested on Peter Ash tomorrow or Monday than wiped out doing nothing here. And trust me, I can handle things here, whatever they might turn out to be, which isn't likely to be much. I'll be back before they even know we left."

Ike considered for all of five seconds. "Twist my arm," he said.

"I just did."

He nodded. "Let's roll."

When Beth returned to the Ulloa Super twenty-five minutes later, nothing had changed.

She checked back in with the sergeant to make sure, but he and the officers were engrossed in a college football game on the store's television over the vegetable bins, and none of them appeared to be aware that she'd been gone for a while or that Ike was suddenly missing in action. She told him that she'd just be outside in her car following up on some other cases and she'd check back in at the arrival of the Crime Scene people or the coroner, whichever came first.

Back in the car, she locked the doors behind her, leaned back against the headrest, closed her eyes and though she tried to focus, her thoughts tumbled about in her brain — Ginny, Geoff Cooke, Theresa Boleyn, Laurie Shaw, Eric Ash, Peter, Kate, Alan.

She dozed.

Coming to with a start, she didn't know where she was. The fog, now in with a vengeance, rendered the Ulloa Super as little more than a fuzzed-out neon glow from her parking space half a block down the street. Her watch read ten after eight. Retracing her steps back to the market, she grabbed a bottle of water from the cool bin and noticed that two of the officers had gone. She told the sergeant that he could get back to the station and suggested he dismiss the guys who'd been here all along and send out two other squad cars with fresh troops to hold the fort with her until the cavalry arrived.

He didn't need to be told twice.

When the rest of the police contingent had gone, Beth closed the front door after them, turned off the television, and gave it a few minutes to make sure they weren't coming back. Clearing a spot on the vegetable bin from which she couldn't see Emil Yarian's cooling body, she boosted herself up, pulled out her telephone, and punched up her best friend's number.

Fresh in her mind was the bluff — the lie — that she and Ike had played on Carol Lukins. They hadn't yet gotten any DNA results from Peter Ash's room, but she and Ike had led her to believe that they had. Meanwhile, in all the detritus floating around in her brain, while she'd dozed out in her car, Beth had retrieved the fact that there must have been one other call from the mystery woman to Peter — the very first one. And if this woman was calling Peter, maybe Peter was also calling her. And that would mean that those calls were in the still-unobtained records from Peter's cell phone. Either way, though, the mystery woman might be persuaded that in fact, Beth had been able to run that trace.

And, on further reflection, Beth realized that she didn't need the actual phone records at all. She could just pretend she had seen them, tell another lie, and run the bluff.

"Hello?"

"I don't know if I can still call you 'girlfriend.' "

"Of course you can," Kate said. "I'm glad you called. I'm so sorry about the other night. I don't know what got into me."

"It was me, too. I forget how ugly homicide investigations can be when you're not used to them. I really didn't mean to upset you."

"That's all right. Every little thing seems to upset me lately."

"Well, you had socialized with someone who was murdered. Even if you weren't close. That's upsetting enough by itself. And then your best friend starts peppering you with all these intrusive questions."

"Well, that's your job, Beth, if I'm not mistaken."

"It is." She paused. "And let me just say right at the outset here that not for one second do I think that you had anything to do with the death of Peter Ash. Really, really, really."

"I realize that now. Of course. Thank you."

"You're welcome. But Kate, I'm afraid I am still on the job and I've still got a couple of questions."

Kate's voice seemed to break up. "About me?"

"Yes. And especially kind of one big personal one." Hearing Kate's sigh through the line, Beth pressed on. "Given that I hope you know that I couldn't think you had killed anybody — ever, ever — I don't really know why you didn't feel you could confide in me and tell me the truth about you and Peter Ash. After all, did you really think I wouldn't remember?"

"Well, I don't remember mentioning it after all. So why would I think you'd remember it if I didn't?"

"There's that job thing, coming up again, Kate. Somebody tells me something, especially a fact that might be related to a case I'm working, it tends to stay in my head."

"But it wasn't a case you were working back then."

"It is now, though. And lo and behold, when it became a case, there it was, just sitting in my brain waiting to be plucked."

Silence.

"I'm talking about you and Peter."

The silence stretched out.

At last, Kate said, "The truth is I've got a huge blank spot in my memory on that day, Beth. I barely remember going to the Ferry Building at all, much less what we did or talked about, and absolutely nothing after I got shot. You're saying I told you something about me and Peter Ash?"

Here we go, Beth thought, running the bluff. "How else would I know?" she asked.

Another beat. Two beats. Three.

And finally a deep sigh, then her voice barely a whisper. "It was one day six months ago, Beth. One day. A couple of hours. And nothing since then."

Not true, Beth thought. There was at least one other call and whatever may have followed from that. But she let her go on.

"I knew that of course our . . . dalliance . . . had nothing to do with his death, but I thought if it came out that we'd been together, somebody might think that it did. Then when I saw that you were the inspector on the case . . . this sounds stupid . . . but I didn't want to disappoint you somehow."

"How would you do that?"

"By being involved in a murder, even in the most tangential way. I didn't want you to think of me that way, as anything like the kind of person you investigate." She hesitated again, then said, "I should have told you the minute I found out he'd been killed, shouldn't I have?"

Obviously, Beth thought. Of course.

But she said, "I'm not going to judge you, Kate. You're telling me now."

"It's why I was so defensive last time. I didn't want you to find out. I was so embarrassed that I'd been so stupid."

"I know that, Kate. And it doesn't mean I'm any closer to thinking you're any part of Peter's death."

"That is so good to hear. And I'm really

390

not, Beth. I made a mistake, okay, sleeping with him, but I had no reason to want to hurt him. I've just been trying to put things back together here with Ron."

"And how's that going? You seemed almost all the way back to healthy to me."

"I am, but it's not just that."

After a beat, Beth said, "He knows about you and Peter?"

"Apparently so."

"How did that happen?"

"It's a long story. He's a smart guy and he put it together. It's still a little bit the elephant in the living room."

"Poor you," Beth said with real empathy.

"No. I deserve it. I just want to have us put all of this behind us. And I'm afraid it's going to take awhile."

"You'll get there."

"Let's hope. In any event, I'm glad you called and we got this out in the open."

"Me, too, girlfriend," Beth said. "Me, too."

Beth put her phone in its holster and eased herself off her perch on the vegetable bin. She grabbed a Snickers bar from its place next to the cash register, tore it open, and took a bite. Still chewing, she then went over to the cool case, removed the night's second plastic bottle of water and, unscrewing the cap, drank about a third of it in one slug. She went around and put money in the register.

Cop glamour.

She glanced down behind her for another look at her victim.

Still dead, she thought. Cop humor.

Going around to the front and hoisting herself up onto the checkout counter, she had another bite of Snickers and sipped again from her water bottle.

All in all, she realized that she felt pretty good about the results of the day — she had gone from a wild-ass universe of suspects in the morning and now, twelve hours later, had whittled that number down to a reasonably probable two — Eric Ash with his lies, his motive, and his missing handgun, and Geoff Cooke with his Scotch, his cigars, and his boat.

Ike might harbor the thought that the tragic Theresa might still be in the picture as Peter Ash's killer, but from Beth's point of view, this was no longer a possibility worth considering. And if, in fact, that's what had happened, the case would never be solved anyway, since the only two people who really knew the truth were dead.

Likewise, after their lovemaking, after Peter had told Carol Lukins that they could not spend the night together, Beth with all her heart believed that Carol did not then in jealousy or frustration spirit Peter away in her car and shoot him. Her reluctant statement that he was meeting a close friend on a boat to drink and talk and smoke cigars rang absolutely true. It was not something she had made up on the spur of the moment, or even made up at all. She had repeated to Beth and Ike precisely what Peter had told her.

Most particularly, and to her great relief, Beth had bluffed Kate into undeniably identifying herself as the "mystery woman" in Peter Ash's past. Ever since Kate's reaction to her softball queries the other night, Beth had felt forced to consider the possibility that Kate was guilty of something serious, and possibly more involved in the actual murder of Peter Ash than she was letting on.

At the very least she was hiding something. And then, tonight, Beth had discovered what that something had been — one clandestine encounter with Peter Ash six months before. This was something that Kate wasn't proud of, true, but it was a very far cry from murder. And it also explained her defensiveness the other night — Kate had been legitimately embarrassed and perhaps afraid that any interaction she'd had with Peter Ash, at whatever remove in time, would involve her in the investigation of his murder.

Ironically, her confession about the affair had the opposite effect. At least on Beth. Whether or not it was entirely rational, Beth believed in her heart that the reason Kate had been defensive and even deceptive was the affair.

Possibly, of course, but probably not the murder.

All of which, she thought, left a relatively clear path for her and Ike to follow tomorrow. When the homicide cluster had begun tonight, they had been on their way to get a warrant to search Geoff Cooke's boat. Whatever happened with that, they also needed to follow up on the discrepancies surrounding Eric Ash's alibi and his missing gun.

After that . . .

A patrolman in uniform banged on the front door, interrupting her thoughts.

Boosting herself off the counter, she came around and saw that there were two of them, the first backup team, their squad car parked across the sidewalk right out front. She opened the door to a cold gust, let them in, flashed her ID, and asked if they'd gotten any word about how long it would be before the coroner's van or any of the Crime Scene people showed up.

"Not really," one of them told her. "They said it could be a while."

29

"Mom?"

"Mmm?"

"Are you all right?"

"I'm sure I am. Where am I?"

"Home. In your bed."

"I'm so comfortable. Do I have to . . . ? What time is it?"

"Twelve fifteen."

"No, really. You've got to be . . ." Suddenly the reality registered. Throwing off her comforter, Beth was up. "Twelve fifteen? I can't sleep this late."

"Apparently you can. And it's Sunday, anyway."

"I wish you would have woken me up sooner."

"Not my fault, Mom. I just now got home from Laurie's. We've been trying to reach you all morning, but your phone's not answering. I was starting to get worried."

"Nothing to worry about."

"No. I know. Nothing bad ever happens to inspectors when they're investigating murders. Silly me. I don't remember the last time you shut your phone off."

"Did I do that? I guess I did. It's coming back to me." With an accompanying grimace, she swung her feet to the floor and put some weight on her legs. "Aahh."

"Hurts?"

"It'll shake itself out. You want to guess what time the coroner's van showed up at my scene last night?"

"What time did you get there?"

"Eight."

"Okay, I'm going to say eleven-ish."

"Close, but not really. Try two thirty."

"Seriously?"

"I didn't get home 'til seven."

"So. Five hours' sleep, though, after all. Not bad."

"I've got to check my calls. Why were you trying to reach me?"

"Alan — you know, Laurie's brother?"

"The name rings a bell."

"Yeah, well, he came by Laurie's early and took us to Yank Sing for dim sum. He asked me if I thought you might want to go with us. I went out on a limb and said you might. Except you were obviously playing hard to get again with that whole don't-answer-the-phone thing."

"Obviously." Beth snatched up her cane, next to the bed, and stood up. "I'm going to make some coffee. I've really got to check my phone. How was Laurie this morning?"

"Still hungry after all these years, if you can believe it. She told us she feels like a new person. Compared to me and Alan, she ate nothing, but compared to the way she was, she packed it away. Shrimp lo mein, bao, duck, rice. Alan said it was a miracle."

"If it was, a lot of it is you. You realize that?"

"I don't know about that. I just think she wasn't ready to give up for good. On life, I mean. She's actually a very fun person."

"And you're actually a very good person."

Ginny shrugged. "It wasn't charity, Mom. We really just get along. Why don't I get your coffee while you take your shower?"

"Deal."

The weekend magistrate was Nancy Casey Muller, thirty-four years old, the youngest judge in San Francisco. She took her job — signing off on search warrants — very seriously, and now she was looking over her desk at Beth and Ike. The set of her jaw, Beth thought, did not bode well for a positive result on their request.

"Let me get this straight," she said. "You've got a witness whose statement is that your victim told her that he was meeting a close friend of his for a drink and a cigar after he left her."

Beth nodded. "That's correct, Your Honor."

"Maybe I missed it," Muller said, "but did your witness mention that they were having this high time together on a boat, to say nothing of the particular boat you are wanting to search?"

"Not in so many words," Ike said. "But we know that Geoff Cooke, the owner of the boat in question, considered himself the victim's best friend."

"Yes?"

"Yes," Ike said. "And we are reasonably certain, Your Honor, that our victim was shot by quote, 'a close buddy,' on a boat, then dumped into the water, from which we fished him out two days later. He would have had to be out in the current to get washed ashore where we found him. Which means a boat."

"Or offhand," the judge said, "how about the Aquatic Park breakwater off Ghirardelli Square, for one example. Or Baker Beach at low tide. Or Ocean Beach, for a couple more."

399

"Your Honor," Beth said, "if Mr. Ash was shot on Mr. Cooke's sailboat, as we believe he probably was, there will in all likelihood be evidence, blood spatter, maybe even forensics from the gun used to kill him, maybe DNA from the cigars they smoked."

"All that may well be the truth, Inspector," the judge replied. "But I see nothing that remotely rises to the level of probable cause that connects us to this particular boat. Is Mr. Cooke a suspect in this homicide? Do you have any evidence whatsoever tying him to Mr. Ash on Monday night?"

Beth shook her head. "Not yet, Your Honor."

"Well, before I bothered applying for another warrant, I would try to get to there first, as a rock-bottom minimum." Muller turned her glance toward Beth. "And while we're on this general topic, Inspector, at your lieutenant's urging, didn't I just yesterday sign off on another search warrant for you in this same case?"

"Yes, Your Honor."

"Looking, I believe, for a gun in the victim's son's dorm room over in Berkeley, the theory at that time being, I was told, that the son was a suspect in the murder and that he had admitted to buying a gun, presumably to use to kill his father, and on that admission I thought you had probable cause for a search. Does my memory serve on that?"

"Yes, Your Honor."

"And did you have any luck on that search? Did you find the son's gun?"

"No. But in fairness, as you may recall from the affidavit, Eric — the son — had told us that somebody had stolen it. I was just following up on that. If it had been in his dorm room, that would have been tremendously significant."

"But he was clearly . . ." the judge began. "You were considering him a suspect at that time?"

"A possible suspect."

"Along, now, with this Mr. Cooke, I gather. Do you have a favorite between them?" she asked with heavy irony.

"If we could check the boat, Your Honor . . ."

But the judge cut her off, emphatically shaking her head. "That ship has sailed, Inspector. Or boat, if you will."

As soon as they were back in the hallway, Ike gave Beth a sheepish look and said, "Well, I thought that went swimmingly."

"She didn't like two different prime suspects in two days."

"I don't either, but that's not to say it doesn't happen. How are we supposed to narrow down the field if they don't let us look around? I'll bet you anything he was killed on that boat."

"I'd say that's a good bet but, as Her Honor so astutely pointed out, it really could have been any boat. Or no boat at all."

"No," Ike said. "Two good buddies with boats? Does that seem possible?"

"Maybe," Beth said. "They're lawyers. Lawyers have money. Money equals boats. Peter might have had five good buddies with five boats."

"If that's true, then we'll never find him."

"Well, we certainly won't get search warrants to look at all of them, that's for sure." She stopped in her tracks. "But wait a minute."

"What?"

"Geoff Cooke."

"What about him?"

"Well, if you remember when he came by . . ."

"I don't. I wasn't there, if you recall."

"Okay, but the reason he stopped in the office was to offer his help in any way he could."

"Staying close."

"Maybe that," Beth said, "but maybe that's our cynical natures messing with our heads. How about if Mr. Cooke really just wanted to help us find whoever killed his buddy Peter?"

"That would be great if it were true."

"Well, there's one way to find out. Ask him."

"Ask him what?"

"If he'd mind if we had Crime Scene come out and search his goddamn boat. We get his permission, we don't need no stinkin' warrant."

"But how about if he did do it?" Ike asked. "We've waved a big red flag saying we're on to him. And suddenly there's a mysterious fire or a goddamn act of piracy, and all of our potential evidence goes away."

"Absolutely correct, sir," Beth replied. "But having been refused a search warrant, if we don't want to ask Mr. Cooke's permission, I breathlessly await your alternative. And anyway, if he refuses us, that kind of tells us what we want to know, doesn't it?"

"Yes, my dear," Ike said. "Now that you mention it, I believe it would."

The Cookes' living room was spacious and now in midafternoon well lit with natural light. The four of them — Beth, Ike, Geoff, and Bina — sat in leather chairs around a large coffee table. The Cookes were having gin and tonics; the cops tonic and ice, hold the gin.

As soon as they'd taken their seats, Beth outlined the reason for their visit, and Geoff drew a frown and said, "You're saying you think Peter was killed on my boat? Why on God's earth would you think that?"

Beth's explanation for this — since it essentially cast Geoff in the role of Peter's murderer — created an awkward silence.

Bina, in sudden and perhaps justified high dudgeon, put down her drink and looked around their seating in disbelief. "You're saying that Peter Ash told your witness he was meeting up with a good buddy on Monday night and then, because Geoff owns a boat, there's some connection there? Do you realize what you're saying? It's absurd and insulting."

"We're sorry you take it that way, but —" Ike began.

But Bina, in a cold fury, cut him off. "How else can a reasonable person take it? You're essentially saying that because Geoff was a close friend of Peter and Geoff also owns a boat, there's probably some connection between the two. But that makes no sense. Don't you see the logical inconsistency here?"

"We do, yes," Beth said. "We know how it looks, which is like fishing in the dark. But your husband told me he wanted to help if we needed anything."

"And that's true," Geoff said.

"So we knew this didn't sound good, wouldn't sound reasonable to either of you. But he made the offer to help. We wouldn't be here now chasing down marginal scenarios if we had more solid leads."

"I told him he shouldn't get involved," Bina said. "That you'd take it wrong and that something like this could happen."

"Like what?" Beth asked.

"Like you accusing him of being part of . . . a suspect even . . ."

"I'm sorry it upsets you, but we have very little to go on. We know Peter wound up in the water, and we believe he met with someone he described as his good buddy on the night he was shot . . ."

Geoff finally broke in. "Excuse me, and you believe that was Monday night?"

"Probably. Almost certainly. Nobody saw Peter alive after about nine o'clock that night."

"Well," Geoff turned to his wife, "I don't think we need to be upset about this, dear, for a couple of reasons." He came back to

Beth. "First, you have to know that Peter called everybody his good buddy. We'd be out having a drink and see somebody he knew and next thing you know he's introducing his good buddy Al or his good buddy Bob. And I was of course his good buddy Geoff."

Ike came forward in his chair. "You said there were two things."

"Yes. Well, the other one is that Monday night I was at my office with a deposition that went on nonstop until around one o'clock Tuesday morning. I was in the conference room with Don Watrous — Watrous Properties, maybe you know him? — and three of his attorneys. Six of us all together. Talk to any of them or all of them. I promise you I didn't kill Peter. As I told you last time we talked, Inspector Tully, he was majorly flawed, but I loved the guy. Whoever killed him, I want to help you find him."

"Or her," Bina said.

"Of course," Beth said, "or her."

She and Ike exchanged a glance. "So, Mr. Cooke, you wouldn't mind if we got our Crime Scene Unit to come down and take a look at your boat?"

He took a long sip of his drink, then put it down in front of him. "I think you're barking up the wrong tree, Inspector, but you and your team are welcome to tear the thing apart if you need to."

"It's the most ridiculous thing I've ever heard of." Bina was on the phone, telling Kate about the inspectors' visit. "Can you imagine?"

"They must be getting truly desperate to find a suspect. Beth was by here the other night, you know, too."

"Beth?"

"Sorry. I mean Inspector Tully."

"You know her? Personally?"

"Very well. We went to school together and have been friends forever."

"Well, I'm sorry to tell you, but she's not my favorite person by a long shot."

"For what it's worth, she made me a little angry the other night, too. I think she's under a lot of pressure to solve this one. She's usually great. But I've never really seen her doing her job with the police."

"So she came and talked to you? Did you even know Peter?"

"Just from your house. That one dinner party, remember?"

"Sure. But how did she find out about that?"

"I must have mentioned it in passing, I

guess. In any event, she jumped on it."

"On what, though?"

"I know. Ridiculous. Were we good friends of Peter's? How well did we know each other? When was the last time we'd seen him? And you'll love this: essentially, it came down to her wanting to know what Ron and I had been doing last Monday night, too. Although she didn't come right out and ask."

"With friends like that . . ." Bina said.

"Really. Though in her favor, she did call me back and apologize."

"I wouldn't forgive her."

"Well." Kate hesitated. "To tell you the truth, besides the long history, we've got kind of a special bond. We were in the Ferry Building, sitting together. She threw herself in front of me and took two bullets. She'd have to do something pretty awful for me not to forgive her."

Bina had no reply to that.

"Anyway," Kate went on. "If you want, I could talk to her. It might help."

"And say what?"

"I don't know. Maybe call her off from searching the boat. It seems like that's really just hassling you for no real reason."

"No no no. I don't really care about that. I am ninety-nine percent positive that the odds of them finding anything on the boat are slim to none. I'm just so furious that Geoff came down to see her and offer his help out of the goodness of his heart, and the next thing you know, they're treating us like potential murderers. Because regardless of what they say, they obviously think Geoff had something to do with it. Which is just patently absurd. I can't even really imagine what your friend is thinking."

"She's just shaking trees, Bina. I think that must be all it is."

"Well, she's shaking the wrong one."

30

Beth didn't feel even close to caught up on sleep. And Ike was possibly worse.

After they left the Cookes' home, with written permission to search Geoff's boat burning a hole in their pockets, out at the curb they put in a call to Len Faro who, after the most demanding night he and his crime scene team had faced since the terrorist attack, was not at his desk. Beth left a message for him, outlining the urgency of her request, but the plain fact remained — and they should have realized it — that the backlog of processing work on the Crime Scene Unit was enormous. Faro, with not one but four homicides yesterday, had undoubtedly put in more hours over the weekend than Beth had. She didn't hold out much hope that she would hear from him before Monday morning at the earliest. And the priority he would assign to the search of a boat that was not even a definite crime scene . . .

Getting him by Monday, she knew, was optimistic. And that was a full week after Peter Ash had been killed.

She hated the fact that this would give Geoff time to clean up any obvious evidence. But on the other hand, he'd already had plenty of time to do that. The trace evidence that the Crime Scene Unit might locate wasn't so easy to get rid of.

Statistically, with so much time having passed, she and Ike were now in the neighborhood of the murder that would never be solved.

After leaving her message for Faro, still parked out in front of the Cookes' home, Beth put in a call to the Ashes, hoping to persuade Jill to agree to another brief interrogation with the boys. Beth wanted some closure on Eric's missing gun. Jill could call her lawyer and have legal representation while they talked.

In reply, Beth got an earful of bitter abuse from Jill's sister Julie. Didn't Beth realize that they were still in mourning? Peter may have deserted the family, but the bare fact, the trauma of his murder, still hung over the house. The family was also trying to deal with the myriad details and emotions surrounding the funeral, which by the way

411

(unstated but understood, "you assholes!") was *tomorrow morning.*

Julie then gave Beth their lawyer's name, Ben Patchett, and recommended that she call him and make an appointment if she wanted to do any more interrogations with the family.

When she hung up, Ike, having checked his messages while Beth was getting chewed out, said, "That was a call from Michelle Griffin with the *Chronicle.* She was following up on Theresa's suicide and wants to know what personal relationship, if any, she had with her boss, the homicide victim Peter Ash. Was she in any way a person of interest in our investigation?"

"Shit."

"Right. So we're going to have to go check out Theresa's place, too."

"In our free time."

"Or sooner."

Beth leaned back in the car seat, her head back, and closed her eyes. "I hate to say it, Ike, but I'm running out of gas. How about you?"

"I could probably keep going, but the warning light's definitely on." Ike hit the ignition and pulled out into the street. "Really, though," he said. "Who killed that son of a bitch?"

412

Beth opened her eyes and looked across at him. "I must say that I'm really starting to like Eric. He buys a gun, admittedly, to shoot his dad. Then — forget the idea that the gun got stolen, which is an absurd lie — he does kill him, on the boat, where either he's been invited or he invites his dad to come and talk and work stuff out between them after their fight. Then he throws the gun into the bay."

"How does he get on the boat?"

"His dad gets them both on the boat."

"He's got a key to the dock? And the boat?"

"Maybe. He's Cooke's good buddy. Maybe best buddy. Maybe Geoff lent him a set of keys. We could go back around and ask him. Geoff, I mean."

"I think he's had enough of us for today."

"Ask me if I care."

"Well, I do," Ike said. "And you will, too, if we go back now and piss him off and he revokes his permission to search the boat. And now that you've brought it up, I'm done in, too."

"We can ask him if Peter had a set of keys after we get the search done."

"Good plan."

"Along with the boat, and Eric's gun, and the reporter."

413

"Michelle Griffin."

"Yeah, her. And then, also, we'll probably need to search Theresa's apartment."

"All that's tomorrow? I'm exhausted just thinking about it."

"Want me to take the wheel?"

"No. I'm good. But I'm dropping you off and then heading home without passing go."

It was a school night for Ginny and she was asleep when Beth woke up from her five-hour nap at 11:00.

In the jeans and sweatshirt that she'd slept in, Beth tiptoed past Ginny's bedroom to the living room, where she turned on the television and the late news just in time to see that speculation about Theresa's relationship with Peter, and the motive for her suicide, had made the cycle. This was not going to lower the profile on the case.

She didn't need any more reminders of work at home, so she turned off the television, went back to the kitchen, and checked the refrigerator. Tomorrow and Tuesday were, technically, her days off, and she would normally go buy groceries for the week on one of those days. So right now, the shelves were mostly empty except for condiments, juices, wilted vegetables, leftover meatloaf.

In a small den off the opposite side of the kitchen from the bedrooms, she had her computer and a wall of built-in bookshelves. Sitting down at the computer, she booted it up, looked to see that she had twenty-two emails. She didn't open any of them.

She didn't know exactly what she was doing there. Not really aware that she was thinking anything, she Googled "Alan Shaw Construction San Francisco" and his site came up — general construction, handyman, no job too small. It also had his email address, which she typed in and looked at for a while. Then she keyed in her message. "Are you awake? I need some pizza immediately."

She waited. Less than a minute later, his message came back. "Where?"

Not too surprisingly, parking wasn't much of a problem at fifteen minutes before midnight on a Sunday. She realized before she'd even come to a stop in front of Gaspare's that the place was closed up. In fact, Geary was a ghost street as far as she could see in both directions. She pulled her Jetta into the spot behind a black Ford F-150 pickup and its driver's-side door opened and Alan got out and walked back.

She brought her window down. "My bad,"

she said. "What was I thinking?"

"It didn't occur to me either."

"This is when you realize that San Francisco isn't New York. You want pizza anytime in New York, you can get it. I promise."

"We could drive out to North Beach. Some place may be open there."

"Do you want to go to North Beach?"

"Not really, but I would. If the woman needs pizza . . ."

"You are a gallant soul, but it's probably not critical."

"It appeared to be pretty serious in your email."

"Well, maybe a little."

"You're sounding like my sister. Did you have any dinner tonight? Yes or no?"

"I don't really think so. I'd have to say no. I had kind of a long day."

"I could make us a pizza in twenty minutes at my place, which is five minutes away."

"You're saying I could be eating pizza in twenty-five minutes? Get in your truck and I'll follow you."

"Really, though. Who keeps fresh pizza dough in their refrigerator?"

"Somebody who likes pizza a lot. What if the urge strikes after midnight? You need it on hand."

416

"And mozzarella and mushrooms and pepperoni and anchovies?"

"All of the above. Necessary staples for the hungry bachelor."

A silence descended.

"Not to bring attention to my marital status," Alan said. "But that's what it is, just for the record."

"That's good to hear." She tore a bite off the slice she was eating. "It would be awkward if your wife came out of the bedroom right now. Also, just for the record, I'm very glad you were awake and on your computer," she said.

He grinned at her. "I wasn't. Either one. I was dead out. My phone buzzes when I get emails and it did and I hadn't turned it off, which I normally do. In fact, religiously. But for some reason, not tonight."

"A sign," she said.

"Might have been."

"The gods making up for the time we lost before."

"Those wacky old gods," Alan said. "What are you going to do with them?" He was sitting across the table from her, taking up a lot of space in his small kitchen/dining area. "So. Shall we adjourn to the parlor? Or do you need to be getting home?"

"I can probably spare a few more minutes

before the Jetta turns into a pumpkin."

In the adjoining room, he took the wing chair, and she sat at the corner of the couch. The room was small, and they both had their feet on the ottoman. "I'm pretty damn glad that the gods left my phone on," he said. "But I've got a question."

"What's that?"

"Well, eleven thirty isn't exactly everybody's let's-get-together hour."

After a short hesitation, she said, "I wish I could explain it. You've got this aura of calm and I just felt like I needed to be around it."

"That must be the other Alan Shaw."

"No. It's this one."

His expression softening, he gave her a small nod. "That's a nice thing to hear." A beat. "So calm in your life is in short supply, is it?"

"It seems to be. Part of it is this case I'm working on, but that's not it entirely, either. I don't get it. There seems to be some connection with . . . getting shot." She huffed out a sigh. "There," she said. "Getting shot."

"Almost getting killed, in fact."

"I guess so. Yes. I think about if they'd, the bullets . . . I mean, a few inches either way . . . maybe it's that. Some of it, anyway."

"Maybe a lot of it."

"Okay. Not arguing." She went on. "And then Ginny. I keep wondering what would have happened to her. I still think, every day, if I wasn't here . . ." She looked across the space between them. "God," she said, "I so didn't want to talk about this."

"I think you do."

"I'm sorry."

"Please." He waved that off. "You're going along in life like everything's fine and then, suddenly, with no warning, everything changes. The world goes upside down. You almost die. You're in the hospital for weeks, you're going through rehab, your daughter needs to take care of you, your job feels different. And then you don't want to talk about it because you don't want anybody to feel sorry for you, or cut you any slack, but there's no place to put what you're feeling and what you're going through."

Tears in the dim light left glistening streaks down her cheeks. "Yeah," she said. "Roughly. That."

"I don't mean to be presumptuous."

"Are you kidding? You got it exactly."

His gaze settled on her face for a few seconds. Taking his feet off the ottoman, he stood up, walked back into the kitchen, and returned with a box of Kleenex, which he put down in front of her. "You're allowed to

419

feel whatever it is, Beth. As to what you're doing now that you've survived that attack, not only are you back at your rather intense job, you're raising an awesome daughter. If Laurie somehow comes out of this nightmare she's been living in, and for the first time now I'm thinking she might, it's all going to come back to Ginny, and that means you, too. Nothing would have started without you stepping in. Do you see that?"

"I suppose I do." She took one of the tissues and dabbed at her eyes. "Then why do I feel so messed up?"

"Maybe because the world you're living in now is so different than it was six months ago. I mean fundamentally. Priorities. Plans. Expectations. And really, with all that you've been through, how could it be the same? I think you're just going to have to give things some time. Get used to the new order."

"That's not really been my strong suit."

He shrugged and chuckled again. "Well, you might have to get over that one."

She looked over at him. "And so, what about my case?" she asked.

"What about it?"

"Well, time is the enemy on investigations. It won't help if I give myself some more time to figure it out. But beyond that . . ." She stopped.

"What? Tell me."

"This is what makes so little sense to me. I've worked literally dozens, maybe a hundred homicide cases. They don't usually get personal. And suddenly this one . . . it feels like it's part of all this confusion that's been eating me up, that we've been talking about here."

"About you getting shot? And the aftermath?"

"I think so, yes. Does that make any sense to you?"

"Only that it's more death, and you're obviously immersed in it."

"Which is true of all my cases."

"And maybe just now they're all catching up with you and you're getting to some critical mass. I don't know how this stuff works, Beth, but it would be more strange to me if you didn't feel these cases even more strongly now. I mean, homicide almost happened to you. Of course it hits close to home. Of course it's more personal."

She drew in a deep breath and let it out in a heavy sigh. "We had a young woman, about Laurie's age, one of our suspects, commit suicide on Saturday. It's just so damn sad."

"And now you feel it more than you used to."

"All of life, it seems like."

"That, you know, might not be all bad." He paused. "So. You're doing the Peter Ash case."

Suddenly she snapped to full attention. "How do you know that?"

"It was his secretary — right? — who killed herself. It's all over the news."

"And you're following it?"

"A little bit. As you say, the whole thing is pretty tragic. And not just the secretary. His family, too. Peter's. Everything that happened with them. I didn't know he was your case."

She held a clenched fist over her chest. "You knew Peter Ash? Don't tell me you knew Peter Ash."

"Okay, I didn't know Peter Ash." She didn't laugh at the sarcasm, so he added, "But in fact, I did."

"Did you know him well?"

"Not really." He sat on the ottoman in front of her and lowered his voice. "What's the matter, Beth? I can tell this upsets you. What are you upset about?"

"I'm not. I'm surprised, is all."

"No. You're unhappy, too. You can't kid a kidder."

She let out a sigh. "How did you know him?"

"I did some work at their house a while ago. We went out for drinks a couple of times afterwards. He was a good guy."

"Yeah," she said. "I know. A sweetheart. That's what everybody says." Closing her eyes, leaning back into the couch, she shook her head in disbelief or denial. "This is just what we were talking about earlier. How this case is everywhere in my life. No wonder it's freaking me out. And now with you . . ."

"Beth." He reached out and took her hands in his. "Listen. I have nothing to do with this case. I worked on the guy's house a year ago and haven't really thought of him since, until he got himself killed. He's no part of me, I promise you."

"I know. All right, I know. But it's just . . ," Extricating her hands, she brought them both up to her face. "I really shouldn't talk to you about this, Alan. When did you first know he was my case?"

"Never. I mean, never before just now, when you told me about the secretary. Could I please have your hands again?"

She met his eyes, let her hands fall onto her lap, did not resist when he took them. "This has nothing to do with you and me," he said. "This is a coincidence, plain and simple. Crappy timing, evidently, and a coincidence."

Letting out a breath, she said, "Do you have any idea how much we're trained not to believe in coincidences?"

"No, not really. I'm guessing the answer is 'a lot.' "

"Somewhat more than that. Remind me to tell you someday."

"I will. And I hope that means we're still likely to have a someday? Not to be pushy, but you and me?"

She tried to break a smile, but it didn't quite take. "I'm sorry. You're not being pushy. I'm being difficult, and I hate that. The last thing I want is to complicate things with us."

"This doesn't have to do that."

"Maybe it doesn't have to," she said, "but here it is."

"So what do you want to do?"

She still sat on the front few inches of the couch, her hands in his on his lap. "I want this case to be over. I don't want anybody else to die. I want Ginny to be safe and Laurie to start eating. I want you and me to see each other again. I really do, but I don't know how to make that happen. Most of all, I want to be not so fucked up."

"You're not fucked up, Beth. You've been shot. Twice. Things are in flux and maybe

424

not so easy to understand. And then in the middle of talking about how you're feeling and why all this stuff is freaking you out, you find out I knew Peter Ash. If this case was messing with your head before, that's not going to make it any better, is it? I get it."

Hands entwined, they sat facing each other in the low-watt, amber-tinted light. Alan brought her hands to his mouth and kissed them.

"I should probably get going," she said.

"Did I just drive you off?" he asked. "That kiss?"

"No. The opposite, in fact. It makes me want to stay, which is why I'd better get going."

He inclined his head. "All right."

"Before anything happens," she said, "I've got to get some of this resolved."

"Didn't I already say I got it? I get it."

"It was still fantastic pizza."

"Good. I can make it anytime you want."

This time, it was she who brought their hands up together and planted a kiss on the back of his hand. Then she let go of them, pushed up off the couch, and got to her feet. "Despite all indications to the contrary," she said, "I hope you know that I'm really not crazy."

"I never thought you were."

"Just a little confused."

"Join the club."

She met his eyes. "Would it be too forward to ask you not to give up on me?"

"No. At this stage, nothing you could do would be too forward."

She flashed him a smile of regret. "Don't tempt me." She took her leather jacket off the back of the chair where she'd draped it and shrugged into it. "I'll see you when I do?"

"It's a date," he said. "Drive safe."

31

From behind his desk, crime scene supervisor Len Faro looked at both Beth and Ike as though they were from another planet. "You guys are joking with me, right?"

"It's a small boat," Beth said. "Two or three of your people could do the whole thing in an hour or two."

"An hour or two, I like that. Where do you suppose I'm going to get my hands on these two or three people of mine? Not to mention the hour or two. Everybody's out today after the relatively insane weekend which you may remember since you, Beth, were out half the night, too, were you not? At the Ulloa?"

"I was. But this . . ."

"This," Faro interrupted, "is something you tried and failed to get a warrant on, if I'm not mistaken. Right?"

"Right," Ike said. "But now we don't need

a warrant. We've got the owner's permission."

"I'm proud of you. But the whole warrant process, you know what that's designed to do? It's designed to keep us from wasting time and budget money on wild goose chases which, guys, no offense, this is. How am I supposed to give your boat any priority over any real crime scene, which is where we think a crime has actually been committed?"

"We think that's this boat, Len," Beth said. "We believe there's a good chance that Peter Ash got himself shot on this boat."

"Well, I'll tell you what." Faro pulled at the soul patch under his lower lip. "Why don't you both go out to this boat yourselves and take a look around and see if you can find even the tiniest shred of evidence that it's a crime scene. Bullet casing, slug, visible blood spatter, a suitcase full of cash or drugs or both, anything. Maybe another body," he said hopefully. "Find another body and I can almost guarantee that we will process that boat. Eventually."

Ignoring the sarcasm, Ike said, "This isn't a drug case."

Faro shook his head, enjoying the exchange. "Never said it was. Cash and drugs are what we in the trade call an example of evidence of some kind. Which, after you get it, then go back and get yourselves a signed warrant and then I will gladly assign a squad to go have a look. But even so, it's not going to be first up on my list. It's going to be assigned in the order received, as they say."

"No." Geoff Cooke gently placed his coffee cup down in the middle of its saucer at their kitchen table. "I've been thinking about it all night, hon, and I'm not going," he said.

"Of course you are," Bina replied. "Of course we both are."

"I am not. The son of a bitch put the make on you? The balls on the guy. I can't get it out of my mind."

Bina reached over and patted his hand. "I should never have mentioned it. It really was a nonevent, Geoff."

"That's not even the point. Here we are, best fucking friends. I mean, I really believed that. And he's trying to talk you into betraying me."

"Yeah, well, maybe he didn't see that as a conflict."

"He's trying to fuck my wife and it's not a conflict?"

"Geoff. Come on. And it wasn't that crude. Maybe he was just playing a game. Maybe I misinterpreted it."

"I doubt that."

"Well, and even if I didn't, the fact remains. We absolutely have to go to his funeral."

"I'm not seeing why."

"Because the whole world knows, including little Inspector What's Her Face . . ."

"Tully."

"Whatever. She knows, and everybody else believes because you've told them, about the friendship you and Peter had, how close you'd gotten. How strange would it be if you weren't at the funeral? Why wouldn't you be there, the first among the mourners? It would not go unnoticed, particularly by Tully, to say nothing of everybody else."

"So it gets noticed? So what?"

"So you have a reputation, a good one going back forever, and that's not who Geoff Cooke is. He is a true and loyal man, and he goes to his best friend's funeral."

"Goddamn it."

"All right. Don't think I don't understand. But you've simply got to make an appearance there, Geoff, and that's the end of that story."

Even though St. John of God was a very small church on Fifth Avenue, there were more than a few empty pews for the funeral mass. Beth and Ike got there at around 10:20 and the service was already well under way, so they settled into the last row. Beth was thinking that for a guy everybody supposedly loved except possibly his murderer, this wasn't much of a turnout, with a total of probably fewer than fifty people in attendance. Beth recognized Manny Meyer and the receptionist from Peter's firm; Julie, Jill, and the twin boys; Geoff and Bina Cooke; and, very much to her surprise, Kate and Ron Jameson, along with their two children — obviously off from school — Aidan and Janey.

No Carol Lukins, she noticed, nor anyone else from Peter's apartment building. Though Beth had been more or less expecting a decent turnout of some of the many women with whom Peter had been involved, very few, if any, had actually shown up. The rest of what there was of the crowd seemed to come from the legal community — most of them, by far, men in the general neighborhood of Peter's age in well-cut business suits.

Beth and Ike stood on the sidewalk outside after the Mass ended. The priest had announced that they would be driving down to Colma for the interment, and most of the crowd, in spite of the heavy fog that clung to the street, came out the church's front doors and seemed to be waiting for direction, the limo for the casket, something.

Kate was the first one to recognize Beth. Dragging her family with her, she was soon by her side. Evincing no sign of their last uncomfortable meeting, or of their phone call, Kate fluttered about after first bussing Beth on both cheeks, getting introduced to Ike ("The famous Inspector McCaffrey who Beth just *raves* about!"), making the pro forma introductions to her family again. Though both Ron and the kids had only rarely been part of the two women's activities together, there had been enough picnics and birthdays and Christmas cards over the years to make introductions unnecessary, if not a little bit silly. Nevertheless, Aidan and Janey dutifully shook hands with Beth and Ike just like the very polite children they were.

Ron, somewhat awkwardly, came forward and gave Beth an embracing hug and an air kiss. "I can't believe how long it's been," he said to her with apparent real enthusiasm. "You and Gin have got to come by for dinner. And soon, I mean it. With your miraculous recoveries behind you — look at you both! — it's time to do a little celebrating and get back to real life."

"That sounds wonderful," Beth said.

"It does," Kate said. "You and me, Beth. And definitely Ginny and the kids for a change. Let's pick a day soon."

"Deal," Beth said, knowing that that day might be far off, if ever.

"So," Ron said, leaning in and lowering his voice. His expression now dead serious, concerned. "How's your investigation into this tragedy going? Are we allowed to ask?"

"You can ask and I can tell you it's ongoing."

"Well, at least that's better than 'stopped dead,' I'd say."

Beth smiled at him. "Better than that, yes. Though frankly, not much better."

"That's a shame. He was a good guy."

"That seems to be the consensus. But I thought you and Kate didn't know him that well."

"Not that well, that's true. But you didn't have to know him that well to pick up the charm," Ron said. "Though I guess the main reason we're here is to show solidarity with Geoff. You know my law partner, Geoff Cooke?"

"We've met, yes."

"Well, he and Peter — you probably know — they were really close. This whole thing has just devastated him."

433

"So I gather."

"I'd love it — we'd all love it if you got whoever did it."

"I would, too, Ron. We'll see."

Over Ron's shoulder, she saw Jill, still in her dark glasses, and Jill's sister Julie and a man in a trench coat over a business suit approaching with the twins. Excusing herself from Ron, she gave Ike the high sign to join her — he'd been buttonholed by Kate on some pretext — and together the two inspectors moved a few steps back from the Jamesons and turned to the newcomers, who clearly had something they wanted to talk to them about.

"Good morning, Inspectors," Jill began. "They've almost got the casket loaded into the limo and we're going to have to leave soon, but I hoped we might save us all some time and trouble." She stepped to one side, including her entourage. "This is Ben Patchett," she said, "the lawyer we mentioned the other day. Ben, Inspectors Tully and McCaffrey."

Patchett looked to be in his midfifties. He was deeply into the hired-gun role of attorney for the defense. With steel-gray, short-cropped hair and almost matching steel-gray eyes, he did not project any sort of warmth. Nodding but silent at the introduction to the inspectors, his mouth may as well have been sewn shut. Beth thought it possible that he was incapable of a smile in any setting, and certainly in this one. He did not extend his hand.

Jill, showing more strength than Beth had seen before, stepped closer, right up in her face. "All right, we're here, Inspectors. And we'll give you five minutes to ask anything you want, after which I expect never to see either one of you again."

To which her lawyer, in a barely audible voice of gravel, immediately added, "Mrs. Ash is speaking with you, much less at her husband's funeral, over my strenuous objection. In fact, I don't think any of the family should be talking to you at all, given your previous interaction."

"If I get anything wrong, he's going to jump in and save us from ourselves," Jill said. "But in the meanwhile, we were all having a discussion last night and the question of Eric's gun came up. The one that was stolen."

"Right," Beth said. "From his room in Berkeley."

"Well, that's the first thing."

Patchett cleared his throat. "Jill."

"It's all right," she assured him, then said to Beth and Ike, "He never brought it to

Berkeley."

"Well, then . . ." Ike reached into his breast pocket. "I'm going to be recording this."

"Absolutely not," Patchett said. "And have the slightest deviation in any of my client's statements be produced at trial, if it should come to that, and made to appear as an egregious contradiction? Jill, I simply can't allow it."

"It's not negotiable." Ike was matter-of-fact. "I don't want there to be any question of precisely what anyone has said."

"Well, I've already made my decision, Ben, so, Inspectors, you can tape away. None of us have done anything wrong and so we're not likely to implicate ourselves in anything. And regardless of what you might think, we really do want you to find whoever killed my husband."

Beth said, "I believe we were where the gun wasn't in Eric's room in Berkeley. So where was it?"

"In his room," Jill said. "At our house."

"So it was stolen from your house?"

"Yes."

"Do you know who took it?"

From behind the pack, Tyler came forward. "That was me. I took it."

"Really, this time," Patchett said. "No."

436

Tyler ignored him. "You remember I kind of lost my temper last time you guys were out at the house. And I left. Remember that?"

"Sure," Beth said. "You asked me why I wasn't out hassling homeless people."

He dropped his head for a moment in chagrin. "I'm sorry about that. That was stupid. I'm not usually that person. Anyway, the point is I wasn't there when you started asking Eric all about the gun. I didn't find out what all the hassle was about, why we needed a lawyer, nothing, until last night when we were trying to get all of this straight."

"So why did you take it?" Ike asked.

"Because Eric was really going to kill Dad with it, and I had to stop him."

"Okay," Beth said. "But then when it went missing . . . where did Eric hide it?"

"Our room. We both have had our secret places up there, in our room, I mean, forever. His is under the floorboards under his bed. So he started talking seriously — this was after the fight, you know? — about killing Dad. He was going to get himself a gun and kill him. So I started checking and one day, there it was."

"Come on, Tyler," Ike said. "He must have known it was you."

"Yeah, he thought that. Of course. What else is he going to think? But I said I didn't know what he was talking about. We got seriously into it. In fact, he almost strangled me, but I wouldn't give it up."

Beth got in her question. "So Eric, if you didn't know where it was, why did you lie to us about the gun getting stolen from your dorm?"

The surlier brother stood slumped with his hands in his pockets. "Because if it wasn't Tyler who took the gun," he said, "then the only other option in the house was Mom. I had to keep you guys away from her."

"Us guys? Us inspectors, you mean?" Beth asked.

"Yeah."

Clearly, Jill could still barely believe it. "He actually thought that I found his gun and used it to kill his father," she said.

"And who would blame you?" Eric said. "Nobody in the world."

"Please, son," Jill said. "Especially not here, not now. Not ever again, okay?" She walked over and put her arms around him. "It's over. I love you. This part is all done."

Eric leaned into her. He hid his face, and his shoulders began to heave, and Jill turned and walked her big son away.

"So Tyler." Testing the fragile surface of the cone of silence, Ike asked, "What happened to the gun?"

"I dropped it into the sewer."

"Any particular sewer?"

"The one at the corner down from our house."

"And when did you do this?"

"I don't know exactly. A month and a half ago? Something like that."

Beth felt blood starting to pump in her ears. With the continuing drought, there had been no significant rain in San Francisco for the past eight months at least. If Tyler was telling the truth, that gun was in all probability pretty close to exactly where he had pitched it. "Tyler," she said, "how'd you like to ride out with us right now and show us exactly where you tossed it?"

Patchett took a step forward. "Tyler, I don't really think . . ."

"No offense, sir," he said. "But I'm going. That gun didn't shoot my dad, which means Eric didn't shoot my dad, and neither did my mom."

Beth wasn't sure that any of this would prove to be true. In fact, this whole tangled scenario could be a highly orchestrated charade, but if so, it would be creative beyond her wildest imagining. She believed

439

that everything she'd just heard from the Ashes was the truth and, if nothing else, if they got their hands on Eric's gun, they would at last have their first morsel of physical evidence related to the case. Even if it turned out to be only a useless trinket, physical possession of the actual gun bought by Eric Ash to kill his father would feel like a moral victory.

"Do you guys want to go right now?" Tyler asked her.

"If you can talk your mother into you missing the rest of the funeral," Beth said.

"I'll go ask her. I just need to get this over with." He turned and started walking, and his aunt Julie fell in behind him.

Three feet from Beth, Patchett stood alone, mute and self-important. Beth caught his eye and gave him a curt nod, the twin to the one with which he'd greeted them. "Thanks so much," she said with as flat an affect as she could muster. "You've been a big help."

Back in the Hall of Justice just after lunch, they were doing a reprise of their early-morning meeting with the Crime Scene boss. "All right," Faro said. "Let's do this again and take it slow, because on a first listen this isn't going to add to your case to

440

get you on your boat."

Beth nodded. "Ike told me you were going to say that."

Faro eyed her partner. "Ike's a smart guy," he said. The gun that Eric had bought, a Taurus twenty-five caliber, tagged and bagged in a Ziploc, was sitting in the middle of his desk, and Faro now poked at it with the eraser end of a pencil. "But let's play this out, just for fun, starting with the gun. Do we know that this is the gun that killed Peter Ash?"

"No."

"Good. Do we know that it's *not* the gun that killed Peter Ash?"

"Yes."

"Absolutely?"

"Absolutely," Beth said. "This gun hasn't killed anybody, at least in the last twenty years or so."

"And we know this because?"

"Because it's a total piece of shit, Len. Eric Ash had no idea what he was doing when he went looking for a gun in Oakland, and he wound up buying a pig in a poke. Add to that, he was evidently so scared when he got it that he didn't bother hanging around long enough to shoot the damn thing to make sure it worked. Not with bullets in it, anyway. And guess what? It doesn't work. The slide is so corroded you can't even pull it back to chamber a round."

"Great," Faro said. "So this is in all probability not the gun that shot Mr. Ash. How does this get you anywhere closer to your boat? There's no way this rises to the level of evidence. Now, if you knew it was the gun that did kill him, then we might have something to talk about, but even so, it would be a reach. And this . . ." He poked at the baggie again. "Make me an argument about what any of this means. I'll be open-minded, swear to God."

"Okay," Beth said. "Before we found this gun, we'd pretty much narrowed down our suspect list to two people, Eric Ash and Geoff Cooke, our boat owner. This gun eliminates Eric. Leaving only Cooke."

"How about if Eric bought another gun?" Faro asked. "The one he actually used after the first one he bought didn't work and next turned up stolen."

"He didn't do that."

"How do you know that?"

"Because he really thought his mother might have done it. Which means he didn't do it."

Faro glanced at Ike, now growing a bit testy. "Really?"

Ike nodded, noncommittal. "I'm with my

442

partner here. She's right. Eric didn't kill his dad, with this gun or any gun. And that leaves only Geoff Cooke, who has given us permission to have your guys take his boat apart."

His patience clearly wearing thin, Faro rolled his eyes. "Seriously? You think this is going to persuade me? This is not new evidence. It's not evidence at all. It gives me no reason to okay a Crime Scene visit to this man's boat which, I might point out, is very possibly not a crime scene at all."

"But if we do find, say, a casing —" Ike began.

Faro fairly exploded. "A casing? You think you're going to find a casing on this boat?"

"I realize it's not a strong possibility," Beth said, "but at least —"

"Not a strong possibility! Holy shit, Inspector. I mean it. Holy shit." He leaned back in his chair and crossed his arms. "We've got one shot taking out Ash, isn't that correct? Bang. Once. The gun fires, the casing gets ejected out in the middle of the bay, if anything actually happened on this boat at all and it's even out in the bay to begin with. And now let's say it didn't get ejected into the bay, but landed someplace on the boat. Don't you think, since it's the only evidence tying him to the crime, that the killer is going to put in a little effort looking for it, so he can then throw it overboard? Does this not sing to you?"

"Of course," Beth said. She flashed him an apologetic smile.

"So you admit it's a near impossibility that you'll find a casing? Or anything else? And you're still hassling me about this?"

Her smile actually brightened. "We really want to get on that boat, Len. Your guys, I mean. Find whatever we find."

"I'm getting that impression, but really, guys — both of you — the troops are all taken. Get me a crime scene, I'll put people to work. Really. That's what we do here, after all. But not 'til."

When Ike went back to his desk to check in on Heather's progress back at home, Beth took the opportunity to go down to the morgue for another visit with the eccentric and brilliant medical examiner Amit Patel. Even though it didn't work, Eric's Taurus .25 had turned her thoughts to guns, and specifically to the weapon that had been used to kill Peter Ash. She didn't exactly know why she felt she needed to know this, but she trusted her instincts and did not consider for a moment that this might be another waste of her time.

444

She caught him at his desk, in the middle of a lunch comprised of a cornucopia of assorted raw vegetables with some kind of a white dipping sauce. He'd laid his paperback facedown in front of him. As Beth came in, he rose halfway out of his chair in greeting and said, "You're walking much better, Inspector."

"Every day," she said.

He sat back down. "So how can I help you? As long as it's fast and easy. Not to be rude, but as you may know, we've had a bit of a run on our services here. Five incidents this weekend."

She nodded. "I was out on one of them Saturday night. And I mean all night Saturday night. Emil Yarian."

Patel clucked. "An interesting man," he said. "Six toes. Did you know that the gene for six toes is dominant?"

"I didn't know that."

"All digits, actually. Preference for six. So why, over time, don't we all have six of everything, fingers and toes?"

"Good question."

"It is. And here is something I find truly fascinating. The trait was most common in the Mideast, ancient Sumeria, which has given us sixty seconds in a minute, sixty minutes in an hour, and so on. Six fingers.

445

Imagine if that was the norm. How different the world. In any event, Mr. Yarian was from Armenia, which I suppose is close enough, genetically." He took a bite of carrot. "But I'm thinking your question does not concern Mr. Yarian's toes."

"Actually, it doesn't even concern Mr. Yarian. This one goes back to Peter Ash."

"Yes," he said, "the floater."

"Right. I thought we could talk for a minute about the shot that killed him. It went right through, if you remember? Clothes, skin, heart, lung, back muscle, skin, out, more clothes."

"Of course. What's the question?"

"Can you draw any conclusions about the type of bullet or gun that would pack that kind of penetrating power?"

Patel popped some broccoli and chewed for a moment. "Bullet or gun?"

"Both. Either. I'd just like your thoughts."

He took another moment, thinking. "Well, what did Crime Scene say?"

Beth smiled at him. "We've kind of worn out our welcome with them."

Patel paused. "Okay. But don't expect me to offer this as an expert opinion on the witness stand."

"I don't think it will come to that."

"Let's take the bullet first. We are almost

undoubtedly talking about a metal jacket, or it does not go through and through. And even with a full metal jacket . . . well, the main thing is that if it was a standard-issue, store-bought semi-auto, for example, it would fire jacketed ammunition."

"So far, so good," she said.

Patel gave her a thoughtful look, then a nod. "But a .380 in general, metal jacket and all, with a standard propellant charge — I wouldn't bet my career on this — you're probably not going to go through and through. It's going to slow down pretty fast. I'd be hugely surprised to see it coming all the way through and out the back."

"Have you ever seen it happen?"

"I've seen jacketed bullets go through arms and legs any number of times, but I can't recall one through the middle of the body. On a full-grown man, anyway. Kids, unfortunately, yes. But a man, there's just too much to cut through, and the muscle mass is dense stuff."

Beth sat back in her chair. "So standard issue .380, standard propellant charge, what are the odds?"

"In the specific case of Peter Ash?" Patel pondered for a final few seconds. "I'd have to go with pretty darn close to zero."

"I don't care if we can't verify Eric's alibi. It's believable as all hell. He went to Top Dog and killed a couple of hours there on his laptop because he didn't want to hang out with his nerd roommate and his hearts-playing fellow nerds." Beth sat at her desk, across from her partner. "I'm personally satisfied," she went on. "Eric didn't buy a second gun and shoot his dad with it. No way, no how."

"Which leaves us back where?"

She tried to sound hopeful. "Want to go back and look at Theresa?"

He shook his head no. "It wasn't her."

"So who?"

"Anybody. Nobody. Maybe it was random. Peter was taking a jog out at the beach after he left Carol Lukins. He's running along and a new bunch of terrorists were training out there and he came upon them and they shot him."

"Yeah," Beth said, "maybe that's it."

Shaking his head again in frustration, Ike pulled his computer around and started typing.

"What are you looking for?" she asked.

"Nothing," he said. "Just dicking around."

Beth looked over at the wall clock: 3:15. Her phone chirped at her belt and she checked the screen. "Ginny out of school, checking in," she said.

"Tell her about the six-toed guy," Ike said. "That'll make her day."

32

Ginny hadn't just been checking in to tell Beth school was out. It was far more serious than that.

Laurie Shaw had left a message on her cell phone, her voice weak, even desperate: "I'm sorry to bother you but I'm not doing so well. I've been sick all day and I'm really weak. I don't know what to do and I'm kind of scared."

Ginny tried calling her back, and when she didn't answer, she put in a call to 911, and then called her mother.

In her Jetta, without the benefit of lights and sirens, it took Beth twenty-two minutes to get from the Hall of Justice to Laurie's place on Green Street.

When she was halfway to that destination, Ike called in a state of excitement to tell her that his web search had discovered that Geoff Cooke's résumé included time spent in the military. He'd been a captain in Desert Storm in 1991.

But Beth's concern at the moment was for Laurie. The significance, if any, of Ike's information seemed slight, although it did provide what felt like a little ex post facto justification for her visit to Patel. But she didn't want to rain on her partner's parade, so she told him he should follow up on that — whatever, if anything, it might mean — on his own while she dealt with this problem that had come up with one of Ginny's friends. She'd see him tomorrow.

She parked in an open space in front of the fire hydrant down by the corner and jogged at her top speed in a kind of hobble up to the ambulance, which was parked directly in front of the entrance to Laurie's apartment building. There was no sign yet of Ginny, but Beth didn't slow down. She flashed her ID at the ambulance driver, entered the building, and willed herself step-by-step up to the third floor, where Laurie's door stood ajar. Just inside, they had her on a gurney and were trying to get an intravenous tube into her rail-thin arm. With some alarm, Beth noted a bluish tinge to her skin, a pronounced, perhaps deathly pallor in her face.

The young man running the show — his

name tag read "Brian Fisk" — looked up over her body at Beth's appearance. "Who are you?"

She held up her ID and said, "A friend of hers. My daughter called you guys."

"No relation?"

"No."

"Do you know what happened?"

"No idea. She called my daughter and said she'd been sick all day."

"Longer than that, it looks like," Fisk said. "Besides the serious malnutrition, it looks like she's aspirated part of a bolus into her lungs. She's in a seriously obtunded state. We've got to get her on some fluids. When did this start?"

"I don't know. She was eating very well all weekend. A lot, actually."

"Bingeing?"

"It didn't seem like it. It seemed healthy."

"Her body wasn't used to it."

"Maybe. Probably."

"Whatever it was, she probably threw most of it up. She's really weak now, barely conscious, as you can see. Her pulse is a thread. We've got to get a needle into her stat, but her veins aren't holding up."

"Do what you need to do. Don't let me get in your way."

"Don't worry. I won't."

Backing up onto the floor's landing, she pulled her phone off her belt, scrolled down to Alan's number, the one she'd only entered into her contacts the night before.

Picking up on the third ring, he said, "This is a nice surprise."

"No it isn't."

Alan said they'd probably find her medical insurance card in Laurie's wallet in her purse. And they did. Miraculously, Beth thought, she and Alan had not let her coverage lapse, so they took her to St. Francis rather than County General. By the time they'd gotten Laurie into the ambulance, Ginny had shown up and they all drove down to the hospital in a caravan. Alan arrived shortly after they'd finished with the admission. They'd finally succeeded in getting a drip into her arm.

As her closest relative, Alan was allowed past the doors to the emergency room while Beth and Ginny sat together just outside, holding hands, mostly silent.

Until finally, Ginny found her voice. "I feel so guilty, Mom."

"There's nothing to feel guilty about."

"There is. I should have realized."

"Realized what?"

"That she couldn't just start in again like

she'd been eating all along."

"How would you know that? I didn't know it either, by the way."

"That's what I'm saying, though. I should have checked someplace."

"Why? Why should it even have occurred to you? You were being a friend. You two were having fun."

"Yeah, but I'm healthy. She's seriously anorexic, and that's a real disease at her level. You can't just treat it by getting back to eating whatever you want. At least the way we did."

"Okay, so we know that now. We won't do it again. But don't beat yourself up over what you didn't know then. It's possible even Laurie didn't know, since she had not exactly been pushing the envelope on how much she could eat and hold down. But they've got her safely here now, don't they? Also because of your quick thinking. Plus, I think you've shown her she can still have a good time in this life once she beats this thing. That's your influence, too. And that's huge, psychologically, which is half the battle."

"If she gets through this."

Beth squeezed her daughter's hand. "She'll get through it. She wants to live now."

"I hope she does."

"You wait," Beth said. "You'll see."

The waiting room doors opened. Alan looked drawn and exhausted, but he dredged a half-smile from out of somewhere. "They think they've got it diagnosed," he said. "It's called refeeding syndrome."

"Refeeding?" Ginny asked.

"Yeah. If you've been near starving and then suddenly start to eat, your body can't handle it."

"What happens?" Beth asked.

"Pretty much what we've got here, although sometimes much worse and sometimes fatal."

"Fatal?" Ginny looked to her mom.

"The laymen's version," Alan went on, "is that your metabolism gets all screwed up. But the good news is they've got her stabilized," he said. "They say they're moving her to a room soon. They're going to keep her here at least overnight, then see where they are tomorrow. I probably should be staying with her at her place when they send her home. I probably should have stayed with her last night, too."

Beth said, "I've just been telling Ginny how this whole thing with Laurie wasn't her fault. Do you want to get in line?"

Alan turned his smile Ginny's way. "She pretends to have a soft spot, but it turns out your mom is a bit of a hard-ass. Have you noticed that?"

"I do have a soft spot," Beth said. "I just ignore it most of the time."

Ginny left in an Uber to go home at 8:45. Beth and Alan lingered by his truck in the hospital's parking garage. "You know," Alan said, "seeing her today, I kind of wish Frank Rinaldi was still alive."

"Why is that?" Beth asked.

"So I could kill him."

She looked up at him with a smile. "You ever think of being a cop?" she asked. "The attitude's about halfway there."

"No, thanks. I'm happy building stuff. But I almost mean it."

"Except that, if you want to get technical, he was a victim. You can't really blame him."

"I can't? He's married and screwing around with my sister. I can blame the shit out of him. And I know what you're going to say."

"You do?"

"Sure. She was screwing around with him, too, so she is equally to blame."

"The argument could be made," Beth said.

"But she didn't know he was married when they started. He told her that he and his wife were separated and getting divorced."

"And she didn't check? They didn't have Google a year ago? Not coming down on her. Just sayin'."

He acknowledged the point with a nod. "Okay, so maybe she was dumb to believe him. And there was probably a way she could have checked. But she didn't. She fell in love. Probably not her fault. And by the time he fessed up, she was already committed." He held up a hand. "I know, I'm making excuses for her. She should have dumped him as soon as she found out, but by then maybe he was really planning to leave his wife."

"He'd half packed a suitcase the day she shot him, so I think I believe him on that."

"Still, he was married. When you're married, you don't screw around on your spouse. Right?"

"Well, that's the theory, anyway."

"I mean, if things are miserable, okay, you break up. Although one could argue that once you commit, you simply don't let that happen either."

"Don't let what happen?"

"Don't let it get miserable. And don't

457

break up, period."

"How do you do that?"

"A million different ways, all variations on the theme of keep talking, stay committed, work it out."

"Excuse me," Beth said. "For a minute there I thought we were in the twenty-first century."

A sheepish grin. "Sorry," he said. "I'm old-fashioned, I'll admit it."

"You really think people shouldn't break up no matter what?"

"No, of course not. If one of them gets violent, gets an addiction problem, that kind of thing, sure. Or you're just too damn young and don't know who you are yet. But once you're an adult and make that commitment?" He shrugged. "What I'm saying is that maybe some couples try their best and just really can't make it, but maybe a lot more of them give up too easy. Or start playing around. Which brings me back to my point."

"Which is?"

"Which is you don't start seeing somebody new before you're out of your marriage — and I mean really out, as in stopped living together, and no getting back together three or four times while you deal with all the inevitable fallout. Only when you're abso-

458

lutely sure it's completely done and you're really on your own, divorced, then you can go looking around again. But not before. Not a minute before."

"How about twenty-seven seconds?"

"Go ahead. Make fun of me."

"I'm not making fun of you. Although I do worry about a guy who won't express an opinion." She put a hand on his sleeve. "Just kidding again. In all honesty, if you want to know, I think it's endearing."

Alan broke a frown. "Endearing?"

"An old-fashioned kind of word for an old-fashioned kind of guy."

"Not exactly what I was going for. Old-fashioned, I mean."

"Well, I mean it in the best possible way. Especially for a woman who might be thinking about getting herself into a commitment."

"You know somebody like that?"

"I think I do."

"I thought we weren't seeing each other again until you got this Peter Ash case all worked out."

"We weren't. Then this happened with Laurie today and here we are. Nothing else we could have done about it, was there?"

"No. I don't see what."

"Man plans," she said, "God laughs." As

though on cue, the phone went off on her belt. She looked at the screen. "This is my partner," she said in an apologetic tone. "I've got to take it." She pushed the button. "Yo, Eisenhower. What up?"

33

The crime scene unit had already set up the kliegs by the time Beth rolled up and, as always, they illuminated the fog-bound scene pretty well in their garish glow. What she assumed to be Geoff Cooke's black Mercedes-Benz sat in the back corner of the Palace of Fine Arts parking lot under a nonfunctioning overhead light. Even from back in her own parking spot far behind the yellow crime scene tape, she could see that the driver's-side window was a spiderweb of safety glass.

She would not be surprised — in fact she expected — to see one distinct hole in that same window when she got closer.

But first she saw her partner standing alone near his city-issued vehicle. He turned at the sound of her footsteps crunching in the gravel of the lot. "That was fast," he said.

"I was motivated. Do we know for sure

that this is Geoff Cooke?"

"That license number is registered to him. He's carrying Geoff Cooke's wallet. I've taken a quick look. I'd say the odds are good."

"How'd you get him?"

"What do you mean?"

"I mean, a body in a car. How'd they know it's connected to us? Why'd they call you?"

"Ah. And therein lies a tale."

"I'm listening."

Ike spun it out for her. How on the web he'd come upon the Desert Storm connection to Geoff Cooke — whatever that meant, and he wasn't at all sure. Then, since Beth had left for the day, he had wanted to bounce some of his thoughts off a living person to get some perspective on what anything might mean, and eventually he'd gone into the lieutenant's office and tried to explain the tenuous connections between Geoff Cooke, best friend to Peter Ash, and Desert Storm, and his boat, the *Mary Alice,* which Len Faro was reluctant to go and search, even though they had Cooke's permission.

They hadn't reached any conclusions by the time the lieutenant had to go home, so Ike had returned to his desk. Feeling guilty about all the time he'd missed in the past week, he thought he'd spend a few hours catching up on his paperwork, and had gotten about two hours into it when the lieutenant had called from his home saying he'd had a call on a homicide — a car whose license plate was registered to Geoffrey Cooke. Naturally, he remembered the name with the British spelling and had called Ike first thing. And here they were.

Beth nodded, cocked her head toward the car. "Has Faro made it down here yet?"

"No."

"Well, let's go see what we've got." She led the way over to the car, stopping by the driver's-side window to verify that there was, in fact, a hole in the upper third of the spiderweb pattern. So the bullet had passed through the brain, out the other side, then through the window.

Beth and Ike crossed around to the passenger side. Both doors on that side were open. Someone was taking pictures in the backseat, but three other guys stood off a few feet, probably waiting for their boss to arrive before they did any wholesale messing with the site. Beth had a relationship of sorts with all three of these men and went right up to Rickie Grant and started in.

"So what have we got?" Beth asked.

"Looks like a suicide," Grant volunteered, "although . . ."

"Right." Beth cut him off. "But you won't know for sure until you've finished with your analysis and the ME's had a chance to make a ruling. Let's forgo all that stuff, though, shall we? I'm just trying to get a sense of this. This guy — Geoff Cooke, right?"

He gave her a tight smile. "Geoffrey. Yes." He pronounced it like the ballet company: Joffrey.

"Well, I don't know if Ike mentioned it, but he's connected to another one of our cases, Peter Ash. We don't know how. You got anything inconsistent with suicide?"

"Well, not inconsistent," Grant said, "but the passenger door was unlocked. Which doesn't prove somebody was there with him, but doesn't rule it out either."

"Okay."

"And this might be interesting," Grant went on. "The magazine is three rounds light."

"Three rounds? Does that really mean anything?"

"Depends. He put one through his head, there's one in the chamber after he fired that shot. So if he started with a full magazine, where did that third round go? And if

464

he started with a full magazine and an additional round already in the chamber, we're actually missing two. But, of course, he could have fired that shot or shots anytime. Maybe months ago, maybe last week, we don't know. Maybe wanted to make sure it fired. But it's a little odd."

"Hmm. What kind of rounds? Jacketed? Looks like it from the hole in the window."

"Oh, absolutely," Grant said. "And that's the other thing." He turned to one of his partners. "Jasper, let's let the inspectors have a look at the gun, would you?"

Jasper reached down onto the front seat and lifted a plastic evidence bag containing the weapon. He held it up for easy viewing, and Grant shined his flashlight on it.

Ike stepped forward, took a quick look. "What the hell?" he asked in a whisper.

"Yeah. Right? Let the expert tell you." Grant nodded at his colleague.

And Jasper said, "I'll have to double-check when we get it back downtown to be positive, but this looks to me like a Tariq nine millimeter, made in Iraq, popular in Desert Storm. It's basically the brother to the Beretta 951, a licensed copy but, as I said, made in sandland, so maybe not as reliable."

"Which is maybe why he tested it first," Grant put in.

Pointing to a triangle marking etched into the barrel, Jasper said, "That there's the symbol for the Republican Guard, although evidently only a few got marked."

"Cooke was in Desert Storm," Ike said.

"Well, that explains that," Grant said. He made some motion to Jasper, and the younger man pulled another couple of baggies from out of the car and handed them to Grant. "Check out the slugs," he said to the inspectors. "Jacketed. Lots of pop." He held up the other baggie. "The casing, here, was on the passenger-side floor, which is as good a place as any for it to wind up."

"Where was the gun?" Ike asked.

"Between the seats," Grant said. "He pulled the trigger, it kicked loose. Absolutely plausible."

"And no sign of another casing?" Beth asked. Then, explaining, "The other bullet."

Grant shook his head. "No. Wouldn't expect it, really. Probably shot in the long ago."

Ike asked, "Any GSR?"

"We got his hands bagged," Grant said. "But that will be a few days."

"Burn marks?" Beth asked, wanting to know if the gun went off in close proximity to Cooke's head.

"Looks like, but again, that's the ME's call."

"Okay. Is Len on his way?"

Grant looked at Beth, then over her shoulder. "It looks like that's him now."

"Why does this seem like a case of déjà vu?"

"It's really not." Beth didn't want to argue herself into a place where Faro would have to turn her down to preserve his authority. "This is a totally different situation, Len," she went on in a reasonable tone. "This morning, you were absolutely right. The boat wasn't even arguably a crime scene, there was no connection between Geoff Cooke and any crime at all. But then, suddenly, tonight, he winds up dead, an apparent suicide."

"Apparent? I'd say slam dunk. Do you have any reason to think he wasn't a suicide?"

"No. We'll know for sure when forensics is done. But do I expect any surprises? No. He probably killed himself. Which is just what this looks like."

"And why," Faro asked, "does this change anything with the boat? Where there's still no proof, or even an indication, that it's a crime scene. Am I wrong here?"

"No. But that will change when I tell you

the reason he committed suicide, which is that he knew that when we searched the boat, we would find the evidence that tied him to the murder of Peter Ash. A murder, I might add, accomplished, I would bet, by the same Iraqi-issued handgun that he brought back from Desert Storm."

Faro, hands in the pockets of his perfectly cut Zegna suit, blew a plume of vapor out into the chill. "Correct me if I'm wrong, Beth," he said, "but didn't he give you permission to search his boat himself, and wouldn't that indicate that he wasn't too worried about what we might find on it? And certainly not worried enough to kill himself over it?"

Ike finally spoke up. "He's been playing that game all the way, Len."

"What game?"

"Stay close to us. Keep tabs on the investigation. Even volunteer to help. He probably figured that if he gave us permission to search the boat, it wouldn't be half as rigorous as if we went and got a warrant and pulled the damn thing apart. No doubt he's washed it down and cleaned it up, but then maybe he came to realize that that wasn't going to work."

"Or maybe, finally," Beth said, "the guilt just got to him. He was at the funeral this morning, hanging with Ash's wife and kids. Maybe it all got to be just too much, seeing the results of what he'd done. It broke him."

Faro closed his eyes and let his shoulders settle. "You can wear a guy down, Inspector," he said. "You know that?"

"That's not my intention, Len. But this is a stone we simply need to turn if we want to close the book on Peter Ash."

"Search Mr. Cooke's boat, even though now he's dead?"

"Yes, sir."

Faro released another deep sigh. "Didn't you say he had an alibi for Ash?"

"He was at a deposition until late, yeah. But obviously, 'til not late enough. He could have met Ash any time. Midnight. Two a.m. Whenever he finished up with the depo."

Finally, Faro broke a smile. "I'm not going to win this one, am I?"

"I hope not, Len, but think of the good side."

"And what is that?"

"If you come through for me here, I'll owe you one."

"I hate this," Beth said as she pushed the doorbell and heard the deep chimes ring out within the house. Glancing to her left, she gave a determined nod to Ike, who stood at attention, his lips tight over his clenched jaw. They heard the footsteps coming toward them from within, and she stole a glimpse at her watch: 10:50.

"Yes?" Bina asked through the door. "Who is it?"

"Inspectors Tully and McCaffrey, Mrs. Cooke, if you could spare us a few minutes."

The door opened and Bina Cooke stood in front of them. Wearing running shoes and the matching top and bottom to dark blue workout clothes, she exuded a barely controlled sense of panic. "Have you heard from Geoff?" she asked without preamble. "Why are you here?" Then, giving Beth no chance to answer, "Where's Geoff? *Why are you here?*"

"Maybe it would be better if we came inside," Beth said gently.

Ike had been able to pawn off his city-issued car for Jasper from the CSU to drive back downtown, so closing in on midnight, the two inspectors were driving back toward Ike's home in the Jetta, Beth at the wheel.

"You really don't think the note makes it conclusive?" Ike asked. "Not that it wasn't already. But with the note . . ."

"It wasn't a note," Beth said. "It was an email. And I'm not saying it's inconclusive . . ."

"No?" Ike cut her off. "Hold on a minute. 'Dear Bina. Please forgive me,' " he recited from memory, " 'they're going to put it together about Peter and me and I don't want to put us through that. This is cleaner and better for you. I love you. Geoff.' "

"Yep. That's it," Beth said. "Perfectly rendered. Nice work."

"Thank you. And that doesn't sound like a suicide note to you? Or have it your way, a suicide email?"

"It has all the elements, yes. I'll admit that. I just wish it was a real note in his handwriting that he'd left at his desk or something, instead of sent on his laptop so she could get it and freak out waiting to get the news from us, or however else it came to her. Doesn't that strike you as a little cruel for a guy who supposedly loved his wife?"

"He wasn't thinking about cruel. He was thinking about protecting her."

"From what, exactly?"

"The trial. The media. His conviction. Prison time. Everything."

She suddenly realized how late it was; how exhausted they both were. It had been a grueling night and suddenly she didn't have the energy to fight over some admittedly minuscule quibbles that she might not even still have, much less remember, when she woke up the next morning. She looked across the seat at him. "What am I arguing about this for?" she asked him.

"I have no idea. You like to argue?"

"That must be it."

"And that, right there," he said, pointing out his window as they passed through an intersection, "was my turn that you just missed."

"I know. I was just testing you."

"Are you okay to get home?"

"I'm fine."

"Tired?"

"Fine."

"You could sleep on our couch for an hour or two."

"No. I'm fine."

"You always say that."

"Doesn't mean it isn't true."

"Doesn't mean it is, either."

"Well, either way, when I slow down around this next corner," she said, "you jump out."

34

At 7:30 the next morning, Ginny sat at the counter in her kitchen with a mug of coffee in front of her. When Beth came in, she told her mother that she'd already talked to Laurie in the hospital, where she'd been moved to a regular room, was off the drip, and had started an eating regimen of lots of milk, which evidently was the refeeding food of choice. She had appointments later in the morning with a nutritionist and a psychologist, but then they were planning to release her, which seemed a little soon to Ginny. What did Beth think?

"I think they probably know what they're doing. She's got to learn to manage her diet — and her life, for that matter — on her own sometime. How did she seem?"

"Actually, more embarrassed than anything. She kept apologizing for being a bother. I told her not to be ridiculous. It's not like she tried to have a meltdown. But now I'm worried that if she's going back home, it just might happen again."

"Did you tell her that?"

Ginny nodded yes.

"And what did she say to that?"

"She told me it wouldn't. She *guaranteed* me it wouldn't. She said that the thing yesterday actually was a wake-up call, telling her that she was really, truly physically sick. And she didn't want to be sick anymore. She wanted to have a life. To enjoy things again. Like food. Like we'd done over the weekend, except maybe she'd gotten carried away with the pure joy of it all. But now she knew that she just had to be aware of what she was doing until she put some weight back on, got her metabolism back under control."

"Well, let's hope. I must say it does sound promising."

"That's what I thought, too. But still . . . if she's living alone . . ."

Beth put her own mug down on the counter. "I think Alan's planning to stay with her. For the short term, at least, make sure she gets on a program and sticks to it."

"That would probably help."

"It certainly couldn't hurt."

"So." Ginny met her mother's eyes. "Do

474

you think I should still go by once in a
while?"

"No 'should' about it. You're friends. You
have fun together. Why wouldn't you?"

"Well, because I'm the one who force-fed
her over the weekend, which almost killed
her."

Beth gave her daughter a long disapproving stare. "Nobody force-fed anybody, Gin,"
she said at last. "Nobody realized how serious her situation had become. Including
me, your trained investigator mother who is
supposed to see things. We just weren't
aware of it. As I've mentioned before, you
are not to blame here. And yes, you should
definitely go by and see her if you want to.
I'm sure she'd like that a lot."

"I wouldn't be stepping on Alan's toes?"

"Alan's a big boy," Beth said. "If he's got
a problem, I'm sure he'll tell you about it.
But I predict that he'd like your company,
too."

Ginny sipped from her mug, made a face,
put it back down.

"What?" Beth asked.

"Cold coffee."

Beth shook her head, smiling. "Nice try.
What else?"

"Well, since you brought him up."

"Alan? Yes, I like him and no, we are not

an item."

"Really? Not to sound like a mom, but what time did you get in last night?"

Beth chuckled. "That wasn't Alan. It was this damn case I'm on." She filled her in on the details. "In any event," she concluded, "Alan and I seem to be on hold until this Peter Ash case settles out, which might be as soon as today."

"Why is that? Is he connected to Peter Ash?"

"No. I mean, well, he knew him slightly. But mostly it's been bad timing. Last night being a perfect example." She hesitated for a moment. "I'd like you to be okay with it, if it did become something."

"Are you kidding? I think he's great."

"I do, too," Beth said. "I think."

At 10:00 a.m., Beth was sitting at her desk in the Homicide detail doing one of her least favorite jobs, reviewing the transcript of one of her witnesses' testimony in a case they'd been working on six weeks before. In general and in theory, these transcripts were the official written record of the tape recordings that inspectors made of interviews in the field — people who had witnessed the crime or something to do with the crime.

The wrinkle was that many of these witnesses — and today's Ivan Vrotovna was a perfect example — did not speak English as their first, or even second or third language. This hardly mattered, however, because the denizens of the transcription pool often were not overburdened with too much education themselves and simply typed what they thought they heard. And God forbid they should go back and look for typos or spell-check malfunctions.

The first sentence of the last paragraph she'd read was more or less typical: "Yah was tree sometime there where I was stopping in front of bank and (inaudible) . . ."

She was deeply immersed, pondering the true meaning of this, when an object in a baggie dropped right at her elbow on her desk. She jerked up halfway out of her chair. "Jesus!" Looking up, she saw Len Faro grinning down at her.

"Sorry," he said. "Did I startle you?"

"No, not at all. Levitation is part of my regular workout."

"Where's Eisenhower this fine day?"

"Down at the morgue. The Geoff Cooke autopsy. I figured Dr. Patel wouldn't need both of us. Probably don't need him, either, if you want to know. But Ike wanted to go down. How could I ruin his fun?" Reaching over, she picked up the evidence baggie, saw that it contained one brass bullet casing. She turned it over in her hand, looked at it from the other side. "What's this?" she asked, when suddenly her eyes lit up. "The boat."

Faro nodded. "They found it under the gutter — the drain thing that runs along both sides. Stuck there under the lip. It's a miracle it didn't wash out, proving once again that God's with the good guys. And you want to hear the best part?"

"This isn't it?"

"This is good, I admit. It means somebody shot a gun on the boat, as you predicted and as I, much to my chagrin, doubted. But the best part is you'll remember we got a casing out of Cooke's car last night."

"I like the way this is going."

Faro bobbed his head again. "You'll like it better in a second. Just after you left, I gave up and sent some of my gang straight over from Cooke's suicide to the boat."

"How'd you get onto the dock?"

"Piece of cake. Cooke's key ring, still in the Benz's ignition. Dock and boat both."

"This really is divine intervention, Len."

"Tell me about it. Anyway, Jasper's not on the boat for five minutes when they find this thing, and five minutes after that, he's back with me. At first glance, the casings are

478

twins, but we've got everything we need to know for sure, so I send Jasper off to the lab with both casings and the gun for comparison."

"And you wouldn't be here right now if they didn't match up."

"Perfectly. Bottom line is the same gun shot those two bullets — one of them killing Geoff Cooke and, I'd bet on it, the other one did Peter Ash. And yes, on Cooke's boat. Oh, and I almost forgot . . ."

"There's more? How could there be more?"

"Not tied up as tight as these casings yet, but back at the boat, they luminoled everywhere, popped it with our ultraviolet magic light, and there it was, plain as day. Spatter on the side and a small pooling in the gutter."

"So blood on the boat?"

"Luminol. I love that stuff."

"What's not to love?" Faro went on. "So anyway, Mr. Cooke had tried to wash the deck down and clean the blood off, of course, but he didn't get it all because no one ever does. I'm having it expedited at the lab even as we speak, and I'm betting that the blood came from Peter Ash. But we'll know that soon enough."

Beth turned the baggie over again.

"Damn," she said. "Nice work, Len. I mean it."

"Well, a day late and a dollar short," he said seriously. "If I'd have listened to you when you first brought it up, we might have saved Mr. Cooke's life."

"Yeah. Well, it looks like he didn't want it saved, so I wouldn't lose sleep over it."

"Is this what it's going to be like to be dating a cop?"

"Is *what* what it's like?"

"You know. You set something up and then if the cop doesn't have work, you can go ahead and do whatever you planned. But if something in the line of work comes up, the date gets canceled or moved around."

"Yep. That's pretty much it. We're a pretty flexible group. But who's dating a cop who wants to know?"

"I seem to be trying to, without much luck so far."

"Maybe you should try again."

"All right. Assuming no citywide catastrophe or personal tragedy, would you like to go out this Friday night, seven p.m., to dinner someplace?"

"That was a good try."

"Thank you. So what's the answer?"

"What was the question again?"

"Smart-ass."

Beth and Ike, eleventh and twelfth in line for the Swan Oyster Depot on Polk Street, stood with their hands in their pockets against the chill — not as cold as the near-frost of the previous week, but with the wind chill it was midfifties — plenty cold enough for San Francisco. The bright sun packed all the warmth of a birthday candle on the fifty-yard line.

The Swan — one of the best seafood spots in a big seafood town — was a tradition between Beth and Ike whenever they closed a righteous murder case. Waiting in the ever-present line was always an entertainment in itself. In front of them today, they'd already met a couple from Portland, Oregon, who were celebrating their tenth anniversary and who had had their first date here. Just behind them, the self-styled Sally the Septuagenarian marched in place, keeping her feet warm (she told them), humming "The Battle Hymn of the Republic" just loud enough to be heard.

While they waited, between their interactions with their line mates, they'd already covered the continuing progress of Ike's daughter, Heather, and Alan's sister, Laurie,

481

and the burden of raising children in general.

Moving on to professional matters, due to the lack of even one witness, they had decided to refile the Ulloa Super case as inactive, at least until the next liquor store robbery presented itself with a similar pattern of facts. It turned out that the Ulloa Super's surveillance camera, when they'd fired it up again, hadn't been working anyway. Beth figured that mom-and-pop stores had one mainly for wall decoration. She'd never seen one that actually worked the way it was supposed to. The television, by contrast, always worked perfectly. Finally, on the Ulloa case, Ike pointed out the hopeful detail that they had recovered a bullet slug that might prove useful in comparison at a later date.

Beth went into a rant about trying to correct the basically unintelligible transcripts they were getting on their cases. She wondered about the possibility of giving some kind of merit-based test to determine an applicant's eligibility for the transcription pool. "You know," she said, "like the ability to type. How about that?"

"It'll never happen," Ike said.

"But it's the job."

"Right. Which means you can teach people

to do it. And this in turn means you can hire them to do it even if they've never typed in their lives."

"But there are so many people who can already actually type. Every kid in the world grows up glued to a keyboard. Why don't we test and then hire them? And by the way, I read a story the other day where eighty-seven percent of kids under twenty-five didn't know what a typewriter ribbon was. You know why? They don't know what a *typewriter* is. Maybe they think that whatever it is, it comes wrapped in a ribbon."

Ike nodded sagely. "That's like the story I read the other day that said seventy-four percent of all statistics are wrong."

Beth gave him a cold eye. "Funny," she said. Then, "Hey, we're up."

There are no tables at the Swan, just about a dozen mismatched seats in front of a counter. Everyone is elbow to elbow.

A couple of spoonfuls into her clam chowder, Beth finally got around to Ike's morning down at the morgue. "Any surprises?"

"Well, after our talk last night when you were so pissy about the note to his wife . . ."

"I was not pissy. It just seemed a little off. Sent in an email? Really?"

"Well, whatever, I went down to the

morgue with a bit of a chip on my shoulder. I wanted to make sure the body didn't have any tales to tell that might eliminate suicide."

"So you agreed with me, the whole computer suicide email thing?"

"Actually, I didn't. I thought you were grasping at straws. My opinion, that note was completely legit. But hey," he held up a finger, "I also wanted . . . hell, you know. This far along, ready to close the case, I didn't want to fuck things up by taking things for granted."

"Always a good idea. So how'd it go down there?"

"Pretty damn well. It got me past reasonable doubt, anyway. Mr. Cooke killed himself. Want me to count the ways?"

"Go for it."

"One. GSR was all over his gun hand, on the front of his shirt, every place you'd expect to find it, no place you wouldn't."

"Okay. What else?"

"Burn marks right up against the hair? Check. Trajectory of the shot through the brain? Totally consistent with self-inflicted. By the way, is it just me or is Patel a little bit out there?"

"Maybe a little," Beth said. "But I like him. So he signed off on his ruling?"

"Well, he was still on it when I left, but off the record, he said that unless he came across something truly drastic, which he didn't expect from what he'd seen so far, he was going with suicide." The waiter slid a glass filled with white wine along the counter. It stopped of its own accord right in front of Ike. "These guys are too good," Ike said. He picked up the glass and knocked back a third of it. "And though it pains me to say it, Beth, you're not so bad yourself."

"Me? I did nothing."

"Wrong. You turned Len on to the boat, where he never would have looked on his own. And which in turn closes the circle on Cooke and Ash. I mean, the casing and blood match from the luminol, both. You must admit it's about as clean as it gets."

"Still, believe me, it was just a hunch that worked out."

Ike took another sip of wine. "This false modesty ill becomes you."

Beth shrugged. "I never put it together, Ike. If Cooke hadn't done what he did, I'd still be wondering if it might have been Theresa, after all. Or Carol Lukins's husband. Or the boyfriend of another of Ash's conquests. So I'm really not considering this my masterpiece in the art of detecting. Cooke had me completely fooled."

485

"Me, too. If it makes you feel any better." Spearing some crab, he chewed for a minute.

Beth took the opportunity to get a few words in. "So," she said, "one last question and I'll leave this forever."

He looked across at her, drank more wine, swallowed. "Okay. Shoot."

"Motive."

"What about it?"

"What was it? These two guys were supposedly best friends. Why'd Cooke kill Ash?"

Ike considered. "Well, first, as we know, motive is highly overrated. Any jury in the world looks at the hard evidence we got — the gun, the matching casings, the spatter on the boat — they convict in a heartbeat."

"I'm not talking jury, though," Beth said, "since there's never going to be a trial. But just between us, what do you think?"

"I don't know. Some kind of betrayal, I suppose. Maybe with Cooke's wife. And somebody sleeps with your wife, you kill him, right? Oldest motive in the world, and we know that Ash was on the make at all times."

"Maybe."

"Okay, if you don't like that, how about this? Cooke and Ash were out hounding around together, maybe they did some

486

stupid guy thing and Cooke couldn't trust Ash to keep their secret so he had to shut him up. There's at least two motives off the top of my head. But as I say, and as you well know, we don't need motive. The evidence talks."

Beth tipped up her Diet Coke. "It certainly does," she said.

Ike looked over at her. "Do I detect a note of sarcasm?"

"From me?" Beth asked. "Perish the thought."

35

Somebody sleeps with your wife, you kill him, right?

Beth opened her eyes and was completely awake, her heart pounding in her chest. Disoriented, she could not at first place where she was. No night-light relieved the darkness in the pitch-black room.

She all but heard aloud her partner's voice as his comment at the Swan counter hovered in and around the borders of her consciousness. Those words were what had woken her up, except that in the dream they had been out in a biting wind at Crissy Field, where she and Kate used to walk.

Somebody sleeps with your wife, you kill him, right?

Her hand went to her breast, and she was somewhat surprised to realize that she was in a nightgown. She had no memory of going to bed. Or of coming home for that matter.

Now, forcing a deep breath of air into her lungs, she blew out heavily.

The dark shadows were becoming familiar. She was in her room.

Throwing off the covers, she went to move her legs off the side of the bed so that she could stand up.

But the pain stopped her and for a long moment would not let her move.

With an unconscious groan, she labored to get another breath, steeled herself, and tried again.

Her legs held her and she was on her feet. Finally, in her bathroom, she turned on the light and splashed cold water on her face. Her hands gripped the sink on both sides, taking some of her weight off her legs.

She dried her face and hobbled out to the front of the duplex where she looked down at the quiet street, then turned back and checked in at Ginny's room.

But her daughter, she remembered now as she saw the empty bed, was staying over at Laurie's. Alan was there, too, she supposed. That had been the plan, anyway.

But for Beth, the fatigue had been too great. The Ulloa all-nighter case this past weekend, then Laurie's emergency yesterday morning, and finally Geoff Cooke, which had led to formally closing the Ash case with Patel's suicide ruling they'd been waiting for. She simply had needed to go home and get some rest.

Now the digital clock on her microwave in the kitchen told her it was 4:17.

Retracing her steps through her apartment, she found herself back in her bedroom. Gingerly she lowered herself down to where she was sitting on the side of her bed, then lay on her side and pulled her blanket up to cover her.

A blessed two hours later, she threw the blanket off, forced her legs to move again, and walked into the kitchen, where she pushed the button on her Keurig coffee machine.

As she was getting dressed, Beth checked her calendar and realized that on this Wednesday morning, Ike was testifying at the trial of Raul Sanchez, whom they had arrested for the murder of his girlfriend a little over a year ago. Best case, this would tie him up all morning; it would not be unheard of for his testimony to take all afternoon as well. Or longer.

So she would be on her own.

This suited her to a T.

Although it had been Ike's question — *Somebody sleeps with your wife, you kill him, right?* — that had woken her up and set her on the path she was now planning to pursue, she also knew that he wouldn't particularly appreciate her agenda. After all, the Geoff Cooke case was closed, and that in turn closed the Peter Ash inquiry. It was now, Ike was convinced, open and shut. Cooke had killed Peter Ash because his friend had seduced his wife, and then — exact motive be damned — he had taken his own life.

But Beth didn't know for a certainty, or even believe as a strong possibility, that Peter Ash had in fact slept with Bina Cooke. And though she knew that the evidence strongly if not overwhelmingly supported the theory on which both cases had been solved and closed, she would feel much better about everything if she could just verify that one prime mover of a fact — if Peter Ash hadn't slept with Bina Cooke, or even if Geoff never knew or believed that he had, the whole thing fell apart.

She had to know.

She'd been to the Cooke home twice before, but somehow the grandeur of the place hadn't registered. Now as she got herself settled with her tape recorder at the head of the ten-foot-long mahogany table in the formal dining room, she realized that this was one of the most beautiful homes she'd ever seen.

The view off to her right through the north-facing windows was, she thought, nothing short of ridiculous — the whitecap-studded bay, the bridges, Alcatraz, the Marin headlands, and beyond. She thought that any one of the chairs around the table cost more than her monthly rent; the Murano glass sculpture of a naked woman in the far corner probably would come close to her yearly salary.

When she and Ike had last come here on Monday night to break the news about Geoff's death, Bina had been overcome first with shock and then with an overriding grief. But before they were done, she was fairly seething with open hostility — of course wanting to kill the messengers.

And there had been more than a trace of that anger when Beth had called her an hour ago, asking for another interview. But now, as Bina sat down cater-corner to her, one chair down to her left, before Beth could even lead up to her questions, Bina launched into her own alternative theory of the case, contending that it somehow had to do with Theresa Boleyn.

"I didn't think of it originally," she said, "though of course I was aware of it, the connection between Theresa and Peter. But after what's happened with Geoff . . . well, it occurred to me that her suicide might not have been exactly what it seemed, either. And I *know* that in Geoff's case — he did not kill Peter, and he certainly did not kill himself. That is just not possible."

"You're saying that Theresa . . ."

The color rising in her cheeks, Bina said, "Didn't you think she did it, too? Killed Peter, I mean?"

"Well, we did talk to her, but we hadn't gotten too far before she killed herself."

"Exactly. First, she was a suspect and then she conveniently killed herself. Doesn't this sound all too familiar?"

"So what are you saying?"

"I'm saying that when Peter's real killer realized that Theresa was a suspect, if he could cast the blame onto her, you would stop looking for him."

"You're saying you think the same person killed Peter Ash, and Theresa, and then your husband?"

Her eyes bright with what seemed almost like a kind of madness, Bina nodded. "And when that didn't work with Theresa, when the suspicion shifted to Geoffrey, for some ungodly reason, the killer tried the same thing. Except this time, it seems to have worked."

Beth scratched at a tiny blemish in the tabletop. Suddenly Bina, in her grief and panic, was exuding a kind of hysterical intensity in the telling that threatened her basic credibility. This was a woman distraught over the loss, the abandonment, of her husband, and if she could find a plausible way to deny the horrible basic truth of Geoff's taking his own life, Beth thought that she would follow that path wherever it led.

"Bina," Beth said with a conscious gentleness, "you realize that there were over a dozen witnesses who saw Theresa step in front of the streetcar that day, and nobody even hinted at the idea that somebody pushed her? Is that what you're saying you believe?"

"I don't know exactly what I believe about that. All I know is that there must have been another way he got her to do it. I don't know how. But something like that must have happened . . . And the same thing happened with Geoff."

Something like getting pushed in front of a streetcar? Beth thought. This was making no sense. Beth asked, "Do you have something to back up what you're saying?"

"Of course," Bina said. "That's why I said I'd talk to you."

"You know something about Theresa that hasn't . . . ?"

"No. Not Theresa. Geoff. Someone killed Geoff and made it look like a suicide, and of course I can prove it."

Beth reached out and put a hand over one of Bina's. "The other night when my partner and I were here, did you . . . ?"

"Did I know then what I have found since? No. I was too devastated to think, but since then . . ."

"You have found some kind of proof?"

"That's what I've been trying to say. I have to get the truth out there."

"Well, I am here now. And I'm anxious to see what you've got." Although her hope for a credible story was fading with every new word out of Bina's mouth, Beth felt she had to stay until she'd heard it all, and until she'd had a chance to ask her own questions as well.

But Bina was already on her feet. "Let me just get my folder."

A folder no less, Beth thought.

In ten seconds, Bina was back, sitting down. She opened the folder and pulled out a yellow legal pad where she had written her notes. "Okay," she said, "number one. The gun. When Geoff got back from Iraq — you know he was in Desert Storm, right?

495

Okay. When he came home, he brought back a couple of Iraqi-made semiautomatic pistols he picked up over there as souvenirs. A couple, as in two of them."

"All right."

"All right." Bina broke a tight smile. "Let's take a short walk, shall we?"

Again, she was out of her chair. Beth followed her through the professional-grade kitchen, down a hallway to a man's home office — dark leather chair and love seat, two walls of books, the faint odor of cigars. Bina had already removed some books from one of the bookshelves and now reached in and opened a small wall safe.

She took out one gun, showed it to Beth, then placed it on the desk behind her. It looked to Beth like the exact same gun that Geoff had used to kill himself.

"Don't worry," Bina said. "It's not loaded. The magazines with the bullets are in the back of the safe." Pulling out the other gun, she placed it next to the first one. "Two guns," she said. "That's all he brought home. It's all he ever had. Look in if you want and check it out."

Beth gave the safe a quick glance. No more guns.

Bina picked up the guns and put them back in the safe, then closed it and spun the combination lock. Turning, she said, "Two guns, both of them still there in his safe. He didn't have another gun. So, you're going to ask, what about the gun that killed him and Peter? Where did that come from? Okay, let's go back."

In spite of herself, in spite of the irrationality of opinions about Theresa Boleyn, Beth was getting caught up in Bina Cooke's narrative, and followed her back through the house.

At her dining room table again, Bina picked up the folder and said, "This is the so-called suicide note that he emailed me, supposedly from his laptop in his car. You've already seen this, but . . ."

She read: " 'Dear Bina. Please forgive me. They're going to put it together about Peter and me and I don't want to put us through that. This is cleaner and better for you. I love you. Geoff.' "

Her eyes glistening with tears, Bina said, "Geoff did not write this, Inspector. I've got five hundred other emails from him at least, and none of them start with 'Dear Bina.' Whenever he wrote me, he called me 'Bean.' 'Bean.' Not 'Bina.' Every single goddamn time. You can look back and check. And while we're at it, he wasn't 'Geoff.' He was 'Freddie.' I don't even remember why anymore. But the fact is, if he ever even would have written this email, which he would not have done, it would have been to Bean from Freddie. Could it be any more clear? He just didn't write this thing."

Bina, wiping the tears from her face, fairly glowed with her conviction. "Anyway, that's two elements of proof right there. One, he didn't have any third gun. And two, he never wrote that email. Here's number three: he was left-handed."

Beth cocked her head, a question.

"He was shot in the right side of his head. He is not holding a gun in his off hand and shooting himself with it. Think about it. If he's holding the gun, it's in his left hand."

Beth said nothing.

Bina, apparently spent, had found a Kleenex and was wiping beneath her eyes. Finally looking up at Beth, she forced a pathetic facsimile of a smile, her lips trembling. "My husband did not kill himself," she said. "I promise you. And all of what I've told and shown you here proves it. This absolutely proves it."

Actually, Beth knew, it did no such thing. Compared to the positive evidence — the gun from Desert Storm, the casings proving that that same gun had killed both Peter Ash and Geoff Cooke, the positive ID of the blood on Geoff's boat as Peter's — the three objections that Bina had made were not definitive. Although taken together, Beth had to admit that they were tantalizing. If Bina hadn't led off with her implausible if not impossible theory about Theresa Boleyn, Beth might have found them even more compelling.

Which brought her back to the reason she'd come here, painful though it would be to ask. "You raise some very good points," Beth said, "and I will keep them in mind if we turn up any evidence of a more positive nature . . ."

"But these are positive."

"No. Technically, they are all what we call negative evidence — the dog who didn't bark in the nighttime. In the sense that none of them help identify another possible suspect. Do you see that?"

"But they do eliminate Geoff."

"Not conclusively, they don't." Beth huffed out a breath. "Mrs. Cooke," she said. "Bina. I have a question to ask you, and I'm afraid it will make you angry, but I can't help that. Did you have an affair with Peter Ash?"

To Beth's surprise, Bina's reaction was a full-bellied laugh. When she finished, several seconds later, she wiped her eyes again.

"Why in the world would you ask me that?"

"Because it might have given your husband a reason to kill him. Out of jealousy."

Bina shook her head, still apparently somewhat amused. "Geoff didn't kill Peter, Inspector," she said. "He loved the man. That's why he came to you and offered his help in your investigation. Does that strike you as the action of a man who wanted to kill his friend?"

"But you haven't answered me."

"Oh, I'm sorry. I thought I had. No, I never had any intimate relations with Peter Ash. Although . . ." She narrowed her eyes.

"What?"

"Actually, this might be important," Bina said. "Peter did make a pass at me four or five months ago, which I decided to treat as a joke."

"All right, and . . . ?"

"And Geoff never knew about it. In fact, I didn't tell Geoff about it until last . . . let's see . . . it was last Saturday. And he was absolutely furious, that Peter had done that. He almost didn't go to the funeral because of it.

"Don't you see?" Bina asked. "That was the first he'd heard about that. If you'd seen his reaction, you'd know. He might have wanted to pick a fight with Peter then, but

Peter was already dead. I'd never seen him angry at Peter before because he never had been. That should tell you something. He had no motive to kill him, over me or over anything else."

Beth straightened up, reached over, and turned off her tape recorder. Again, Bina's information was interesting and even compelling. Beth felt that it was probably true as well. And most importantly, she believed that Bina Cooke had not slept with Peter Ash.

With that, though it was neither positive evidence nor proof of any sort, in her bones she felt the case against Geoff Cooke collapse.

At the door on her way out, Beth shook Bina's hand and thanked her for her information. She was halfway down the front steps when suddenly she stopped. She'd come here to get the answer to one simple, specific question, and she'd gotten it to her satisfaction. But in her myopia on that account, she'd lost sight of a potentially larger and more significant fact.

Turning, she trudged back up to the porch and rang the bell again, hearing the chimes echo through the house. When Bina opened the door, Beth apologized for the interruption, then asked, "What is the possibility that Geoff had more than two guns, and that you didn't know about them?"

"Zero," she said. "He only had the two. We talked about it quite a lot early on. I wanted him to throw them away a long time ago, but he wanted to keep them as souvenirs to remind him of what it had been like over there."

"In Iraq?"

"Yes. In Iraq? What are you getting at?"

"Well, just that the gun that killed him is not what I'd call common here in the city, or anywhere else in this country. What are the odds that somebody else would even have that same type of gun? I mean, Geoff was in Iraq and he had a reason to have it, but to me . . . I'm sorry, but it's more likely that he did in fact have three guns — maybe without telling you about one of them — than that some other person just happened to have the exact same type of very esoteric weapon and used it to shoot Geoff. Do you see what I'm saying?"

Bina went stiff, her eyes glazed over for a moment. "Oh my God," she said. "Ron."

It was a Thursday, not a First Friday, but given the horrific events of the past week, Ron thought that a quiet lunch in their back booth at Sam's would do them both a world of good.

He was the first to arrive and ordered his usual martini. After delivering the drink, Stefano had left the curtain slightly open and now Ron caught a glimpse of his wife as she came walking down the narrow aisle between the booths. Even after all she'd had to endure in the past couple of weeks, to say nothing of the past six months since she'd been shot, she still radiated warmth and goodness.

She was also, he realized, still and always staggeringly beautiful. Trim and buxom, with her thick, shoulder-length dark hair, today she wore a maroon sweater dress that accentuated her figure, which hardly needed it. As she came nearer, he noticed that she was wearing the solitaire black pearl necklace he'd given her right here at Sam's before all the madness hit.

He stood up and pulled the curtain back to greet her, holding her against him for a long moment, brushing her lips with a chaste kiss, then another not entirely so. "I'm so glad you decided you could come down," he said when they'd sat back down.

"You saved my life," she said. "Four hours is about all I can take with that woman."

"How is Bina?" he asked.

"Bereft. About like you'd expect. Maybe a

503

little worse."

"How so?"

Kate arranged her napkin on her lap. "She just seems in complete denial about Geoff committing suicide, as though that's going to bring him back. And they must have her on some serious antidepressant that I think is making her delusional. You know Peter Ash's secretary, Theresa? The woman who killed herself?"

"Vaguely. What about her?"

"Well, nothing really, except that Bina seems to think somebody pushed her onto the streetcar tracks. The same person, she says, who killed Geoff."

"Is there really any doubt that Geoff killed himself? Didn't they just rule it a suicide, like, yesterday or the day before?"

"Yes. But she doesn't believe it." Kate paused. "She asked me about your guns."

"My guns?"

"Your Iraq souvenirs. They are evidently the same type of gun that Geoff shot himself with."

"Right. I think I read that, the Iraqi gun connection. But I had understood it was his own gun. He had a few of them, I thought."

"Well, apparently, according to Bina, only two. And those two are still in the safe at their house."

Nodding, Ron lifted his martini glass and took a small sip. "That Bina knew about."

"Did he have others?"

"Well, at least one more that he kept in the safe in his office. I'll bet you if the police looked, they could find a couple more."

"I should tell her that," Kate said. "I really had the impression she thought it might have been one of your guns."

"You mean that I had a role in killing Geoff? That is crazy."

"That's what I told her, of course, but she was going on about the gun, even after I told her we didn't have them anymore."

Ron cocked his head. "But . . ."

Kate shook her head with some vehemence. "We don't have them anymore, Ron. I remember you turning them in downtown sometime last May or June. I know I didn't dream that when I was all drugged up. You must remember this. I'm sure you do."

Ron took a long beat, letting the import of her words settle. He leveled his gaze at her and held it until finally she gave him an almost infinitesimal nod, a whisper of a smile. He then lifted his stemmed glass again. "There was so much going on with you and the kids then, I can barely remember half of what I did."

"Exactly."

"Even so, I can't believe Bina would think I . . ."

"I can't really blame her, Ron. The case could be made, that's the point. Although of course it won't stand up. Even hearing we didn't have your guns anymore, I don't think it helped. I don't know if anything will help. She needs to blame someone. She's just devastated."

"Like we all are."

She took his hand across the table. "Speaking of which, how are you holding up?"

He hesitated and met her eyes, his lips turned up a fraction of an inch. "Poorly. I'm not going to lie to you. It's going to be a new world with him being gone. It'll take some getting used to. Not that we didn't have our differences. And I can't say I'll miss him screwing me over whenever he thought he could pull it off, but we go way back. It will take some adjustment, that's all."

"An adjustment that, I hate to say it, is probably worth it, Ron. Now that he's not there standing in your way, there's no real limit to where we can go." She reached for his hand. "But let's just give it some time. Everyone understands that your friend and partner killed himself. You could legitimately plead that you don't have the strength to get out of bed, much less go to work and kick ass."

He shrugged. "Day at a time, right?"

The curtain opened and the tuxedoed Stefano welcomed Kate extravagantly, bestowing a kiss on the back of her hand. "It has been too long. You need to come in here at least once a month from now on or we send someone to come and get you."

"I promise." Sharing a look with Ron, she said, "But I had a good excuse."

"No excuses next time," Stefano said. "White wine?"

"A chardonnay would be nice."

"On its way. And truly, it is wonderful to see you."

"You, too, Stefano. Thank you."

When he'd gone, Ron said, "You ought to try being a little more charming. See if you can get people to like you."

"I'll work on it," she said. Again, she reached for his hand. "But Bina? What about her?"

"Once she gets over the loss, Kate, she'll be fine. She comes from big money. So that won't be a problem. Though of course, if she ever needs us, the firm will step up."

Kate nodded, sighed. "So what — do you think — what did Peter really do to Geoff?"

"I don't know," Ron said, "but it must have been terrible."

She lowered her voice and leaned in toward him. "Could it have been worse than what he did to us?" Because, of course, as Kate and Ron had worked out their accommodations to what had happened, Kate's role had morphed from seductress to victim. Her unwavering story by now was that Peter had started it; she'd given in to a moment of weakness.

"We are still us," Ron said. "Maybe the real story is that Geoff and Bina weren't as strong."

"They seemed like it, though, didn't they?"

"The argument could be made. But the big question is believing that Geoff could have actually done it."

"The capability must have always been there."

"And don't forget, he did keep those guns all these years."

"Guns," she said with a tone of disgust. "Such a huge problem for our country, aren't they?"

"If you got 'em nearby," Ron said, "you go to them in a pinch. That's just the way that scenario plays out."

36

The large, open space that housed the Homicide detail sulked in a Friday afternoon lethargy, every workstation but one abandoned. Ike McCaffrey probably wouldn't have been at his desk, either, except that he'd finally gotten to appear in court and give his testimony in the Raul Sanchez murder case and he wanted to check his in-box and see what, if anything, he needed to do before he went home early. He'd also texted his partner and told Beth where she could find him if anything needed their immediate attention.

Assuming that she was doing some investigating somewhere out in the field, he had discovered that they'd picked up a gang-banger NHI — "No humans involved" — case down in the Mission, he didn't really expect to see her here at the office. But then, without hearing her approach, he looked up and here she was coming toward him. He flashed her a welcoming smile that almost immediately disappeared. "What's wrong?"

"Quite a bit, I think," she said. "Mostly me."

"In what way?"

"In the way that I am supposed to be a team player — you and me being the team — and there's some stuff about Peter Ash that I never got around to telling you. You had your issues going on with Heather's meningitis, I know, but that's no excuse. It just completely slipped my mind."

Ike pushed his chair back away from his desk, looking up at her. "Whatever it is, consider yourself forgiven. Any harm get done?"

"Well," Beth took a breath. "Geoff Cooke might have gotten himself murdered. How's that for harm?"

A muscle worked in Ike's jaw, and he nodded soberly. "I'll give it about a ten."

"Me, too."

"So, talk to me."

Beth boosted herself up on the corner of his desk. "You remember a woman named Kate Jameson? You met her at Ash's funeral."

"I don't think I could forget. Movie-star looks?"

"That would be her. She's a friend, a best friend, of mine since college. She was the one who was with me at the Ferry Building. She got shot, too. Worse than me. She almost died."

"All right."

"All right, so she'd been through some shit — a lot of shit — and I wanted to spare her any more of it." She hesitated, then came out with it. "Even after I found out she had had a thing with Peter Ash."

Out on the street, four stories down, a car's horn blared, tires squealed, metal crunched against metal. A car alarm began to squawk.

His face closing down, Ike folded his arms and leaned back in his chair.

"I should have told you as soon as I found out," Beth went on, "but you had Heather to worry about, and I somehow convinced myself that just because Kate slept with Peter didn't mean she had anything to do with killing him. I didn't think that was even remotely possible. Honestly. And since that was the case, you didn't have to know about it. I realize now, Ike, that was a huge mistake."

"You're saying now you think she did kill him?"

"No, not her. Remember when you said,

511

'Somebody sleeps with your wife, you kill him?' "

"Sure. Universal truth. So. Her husband?"

"Ron. Yes. Ron who has a set of keys to Geoff Cooke's boat because they were law partners and good pals since they were in Desert Storm together."

At this news, Ike straightened up in his chair. "You're shitting me. Tell me he had a souvenir gun."

"Two of them, actually."

"How did you get this?"

"I wanted to find out if Bina and Peter had had a thing together, which would have given Geoff his motive, right? So I called and then went by and talked to Bina Wednesday. I asked her point-blank if she'd slept with Peter Ash, and the question actually made her laugh. She also had some pretty persuasive arguments against Geoff killing himself."

"Such as?"

"Well, both of his souvenir guns were accounted for, still locked in his safe, for one example. He was left-handed, for another. Nothing conclusive, I know, but still . . . so finally, I asked her if Geoff might have had a third gun she didn't know about, because who else would have a gun exactly like the one that killed him? It didn't take her two seconds: Ron Jameson. He also had two of them. The guys used to go out together and shoot 'em. Bina had seen Ron's guns dozens of times."

"Son of a bitch," Ike said.

"Exactly." Beth shook her head wearily from side to side. "I feel like such a fucking idiot, Ike. If I'd only mentioned this Kate and Peter thing to you earlier. At least we might have started asking some of the right questions. We might have saved Geoff Cooke's life."

"You're saying Ron Jameson killed him, too?"

"With his own Desert Storm gun, yeah."

Ike brightened. "Well, hey, we've got that gun in evidence. We could . . ."

Beth held up a hand. "Already done. I went down yesterday morning and had the lab take the damn thing apart looking for fingerprints on the magazine or casings or anywhere, but guess what? Whoever loaded the gun had wiped it clean. No prints whatever. Not Geoff Cooke's, not Ron Jameson's."

"And why would Geoff have done that?"

"Right. Whereas Ron would have all the reason in the world." The partners sat in silence for a minute until Beth drew a breath, then let it out. "You want some more?"

"Sure."

"As soon as I finished up with the lab yesterday, I decided to try to get a warrant to search Ron Jameson's house and while we're at it, we luminol his clothes and search for GSR and everything else we can find."

"I'm guessing that didn't work."

Beth shook her head. "Fucking Muller said I've used up my warrant quota for this month. Where's my probable cause this time? We apparently already believe that there won't be any guns at Ron's house because, if my theory is correct, one of them is presumably in the bay and the other one is in the evidence lockup downstairs. Which leaves me searching for something that we know is not there, right? Besides which, she asks me, aren't both of these cases closed? Hasn't Dr. Patel ruled Mr. Cooke a suicide? Has that case been reopened? What the hell am I wasting her time for?"

"Sweet."

"Not. I hate that woman."

"She's not exactly my favorite, either. But where does that leave us?"

"I don't know." Beth let out a deep sigh. "But I do know it's Ron."

"And why again did he kill his friend and partner?"

"Because poor clueless Bina called Kate after we'd come by to see her that first time, when we'd asked Geoff's permission to search his boat. Kate, equally clueless, passed the word along to Ron in casual conversation, and Ron realized that if he could tie Geoff to the boat — and a couple of matching casings would do it — that would get him off the hook and tie things up nicely. What do you think?"

"I think it's pretty goddamn near perfect." He looked up at her. "So how do we collar this son of a bitch?"

"You're not going to like this, and I'm very sorry, but you know that dinner date we had for tonight?"

"I've got a reservation at A16. Really unbelievably good Italian, which I know you love more than anything. Seven thirty sharp, picking you up at seven."

"Right. But you know that whole thing we had about dating a cop . . ."

"Something's come up."

"I'm sorry, Alan, but it truly has."

"All night?"

"It's kind of open ended, and it might go pretty late. But the bottom line is that it

515

needs to happen and happen tonight."

"All right."

"You sound a little unhappy."

"I am disappointed and a little unhappy, but it's not like you didn't warn me. I'll get over it. What are you doing tomorrow night?"

"Just like that?"

"Gotta fill out that dance card if you want to dance. So, tomorrow?"

"Nothing on the agenda, but that — as we know — could change. I'm not trying to be difficult, Alan, but . . ."

"Hey! Really. I get it, but I'm going to keep asking until you tell me to stop. Do you want me to stop?"

"No."

"Good. Pencil me in, then. Seven o'clock, your place."

"Deal."

In Ron Jameson's office, his private line sounded shrilly. He checked his watch and saw that it was seven o'clock. Outside his floor-to-ceiling windows, twenty stories above the city's streets, it was pitch-black. He should really go home, he thought. Ignore this call and let it go to voicemail, and then he could deal with whatever it was over the weekend. But it was his private line, after all. Someone he knew. Someone who needed him.

Sighing, he reached for the receiver.

"Hello."

"Ron? Hello. I'm so glad I caught you. This is Bina."

"It's so good to hear from you. I'm sorry I haven't been in much contact these past couple of days, but I've just been lying low, trying to cope as best I can. Well, you know about that. And speaking of which, how are you holding up?"

"Not well at all. I'm so alone and so afraid. I don't think I'll ever hold up well again."

"I know how you feel. It's like this gaping hole."

"It is. I don't know how it will ever get filled up, if it will."

"I hear what you're saying. You just keep hoping against hope that the fog will start to lift. I've got to believe that it will, though it doesn't feel like that at the moment. But enough of all that . . . how can I help you?"

"This is . . . I know it's a little odd, but could we just talk for a few minutes?"

"Of course. As long as you want."

"It's just that I know that Geoff didn't kill himself. And I don't know what to do about it. I mean, you were his best friend. Does it make any sense to you?"

Ron let a heavy breath escape. "I know," he said. "It's so hard to accept. I think somehow that that whole connection with Peter . . ."

"No! It's not that. I don't mean to snap, but . . . I mean, this is not about Peter Ash. This is about Geoff — he really didn't kill himself, Ron. Can you honestly believe that he did?"

Another sigh. "I don't know what to say, Bean. Didn't the coroner rule on it already? Painful though it may be to understand, I thought it was completely settled."

"Not to me. I know he would never have left me like that. And then, you know, why would he have been holding the gun in his right hand? And the gun! Where did that gun come from?"

"I thought it was one of his souvenirs from —"

"No. No. No. Both of those guns are still in our safe, Ron. It wasn't one of those."

"Well." Ron cleared his throat. "Maybe he had another one locked away at the office. That must have been the one he used."

"That's not true, Ron. Why are you saying that when you know it's just not true? He only had two of them, the same as you did. The same exact type of gun. You brought

518

them all home together. You know I've seen them a hundred times. There isn't any third gun that he had. You know that."

Another silence, Then. "I don't know what you want me to say, Bean."

"It wasn't his own gun that shot him, Ron, that's what I'm saying. And who else owns a gun like that?"

"My God, Bina. What are you saying? You don't think —"

Her voice broke. Clearly, Bina was crying, close to breaking down entirely. "I don't know what to think, except it wasn't Geoff's gun. And I just wonder — please forgive me, Ron — if somehow it could have been one of yours."

A beat, then another. "Of course I'll forgive you. But the simple truth is that I don't have either of those guns anymore, Bina. I haven't had them in months. After Kate got shot, I turned them in to the city. I didn't want any more guns in my life. This was back in June sometime."

"And how do we know that?"

"What do you mean?"

"I mean, how do we know you got rid of your guns back in June? Is there any proof of that? Did you also get rid of the keys to our boat? How convenient that you can make things just disappear by saying so. But how do we know that one of those guns isn't the one you shot Peter with and then threw in the bay, and the other one isn't the one you used on Geoff?"

Silence.

"I'm thinking about this, Ron. This is all becoming clear to me now."

"No, Bina, it's —"

She all but screamed at him. "So what happened? What the hell happened that you decided to kill my darling Geoff? How did this all start? Did Peter have a fling with Kate? Is that it? Is that what this is all about? And you hated him because of that and had to kill him?"

"Bina, please. You're hysterical."

"Of course I am! I finally see what has happened here, Ron. I have to tell the police about this. Have they ever even talked to you? Can it be that they don't see it? Because I can see exactly how you did it, you murderer. You filthy, vile murderer!"

After Bina hung up, Ron sat in a cold fury at his desk for the better part of five minutes before he realized that even five minutes might be too long. In spite of the success Ron had had so far in helping to misdirect the authorities, he knew that if Bina in fact called the police, things very easily could come unraveled.

Mistakes may have been made, true; that was not impossible — and once the inspectors began looking in the right places, those mistakes might come to light.

He could not let that happen.

But he knew Bina fairly well and knew that the emotional breakdown he'd just heard on the telephone was very unusual for her. She would probably wait until she had herself in some kind of control again before she made any more telephone calls, such as to the police. And, he reasoned, this time on a Friday night, she wasn't terribly likely to speak to a living person on her call to the cops either — so he should still have some time.

But not much.

Picking up the phone, he punched the numbers and waited and, thank God, she picked up on the third ring.

"Bina, it's Ron again. Please, I need you to hear me out."

"No. I have nothing to say to you."

But she didn't hang up.

"I didn't do this," he said. "I swear to you on my mother's honor, I would never have killed Geoff. I loved him. You must know that. He was my brother and my friend. I would never have hurt him. But maybe I know who would."

"How did they get your gun?"

"It wasn't my gun, Bina. I don't know anything about the gun that they might have used."

"You're saying . . ."

"Look, I'm saying I don't know if Geoff kept you in the loop about some of these Tekkei problems we've been experiencing at work. It's been incredibly tense down here, to the point of insanity. But now you have me thinking that you may be right. He may not have killed himself. I don't know what some of those Tekkei people might have done, what they might be capable of, but I assure you that they have no qualms about doing whatever they need to get what they want. Geoff told me he was getting worried, but . . ."

"About these clients?"

"They're thugs, Bina. They pay big time, which is why we kept them on, but they are dangerous people. But the point is that I know none of it about Geoff had to do with me. None of it. And so I ask you please to let me explain everything that was going on here, that still is going on if you must know. Maybe we could get the police involved then. Get them to reopen the case. We might at least be able to put this whole tragedy in some kind of perspective."

"I don't know, Ron. I just don't know."

"I do know, Bina. You have to trust me. We've known each other for twenty-five years. I'm not lying to you. I'm beginning to understand that there may be more involved here than anybody knew about. Once we talk, you'll see what I'm saying. I could be at your house in twenty minutes. You said earlier you were alone. Would this be a good time?"

"I'm scared, Ron. I don't know what to do."

"I don't blame you. I'm scared, too. We need to understand what's happening here, Bina. Please, you have to trust me."

"Twenty minutes?"

"Or less. I'll fly."

"All right. I'll see you then."

Ron had been holding the receiver so tightly that his hand cramped around it. Carefully, he put it back in its place, opened and closed his fist. But the clock was ticking now, and he had no more time. He would refine the plan on the drive out.

He got out his keys and unlocked the lower left drawer of his desk, then reached in and picked up his Beretta 951, essentially the same gun as the two he'd picked up in Iraq. Double-checking the magazine, then racking a round, he placed the gun on his desk. He reached back down and took out the extra box of bullets and the extra magazine. He'd have to throw these away while he drove.

Closing and relocking the drawer, he stood up, put the extra stuff in his pocket, and tucked the gun in his belt. He grabbed his coat from the back of his chair, pulled it on, and headed for the door.

Both Ike and Beth thought that Bina had performed brilliantly. But it had taken its toll emotionally. After both phone calls with Ron, she'd broken down, crying. Now they had left her resting on the red leather lounge chair next to the desk in Geoff's office while the two of them sat out in the main house in the dimmed light of the living room.

"I just wanted to put the fear of God in him," Beth said. "Loosen him up at work and then hit him at home, with Kate there. Ask them both about Peter, show him his motive. Get his excuse about where his guns went. Knock down his alibis for both killings. But I never dreamed he'd actually be coming over here."

"He's got to take care of Bina," Ike said. "Neutralize her one way or the other."

"So now she's bait? That makes me more

than a little nervous."

Ike shrugged. "Hey, it evolved. Okay, it wasn't the original plan, but when he gets here, if we don't let him get near her, we're good. Bina's done her part. But my worry is this: will he talk to us if we just ambush him here and start asking questions?"

"Maybe not. Probably not. Maybe he'll panic. Or lawyer up. But whatever, he's going to be seriously off balance, if he doesn't outright slip up. Don't worry. We're going to get him. If not tonight . . ."

"All right, but I'm concerned. He's not coming over here to talk, you know?"

"Yeah, I think I'm aware of that."

"So . . . ?"

"So we play it as it lays."

And the doorbell rang, chiming throughout the house.

"Just a minute!"

Despite the firm instructions that the inspectors had given Bina to stay in the office, and under all circumstances to stay clear of the front door, here was Bina rushing directly to it, seemingly completely oblivious to the situation.

Before Beth and Ike could even stand up, Bina was already down the hallway, across the foyer, two steps from the door.

Beth muttered "Shit" as she drew her gun and, pushing herself up from the couch, ignoring the pain in her legs, charged toward the foyer.

But not before Bina reached the front door, saw the silhouette through the beveled glass, and grasped the doorknob, turning it, pulling the door toward her.

Ron Jameson stood a little back from the threshold, on the welcome mat under the porch light. "Bina," he said in a friendly tone, a small smile playing at the corners of his mouth. "I'm so glad to see you."

The door partially blocked Beth's line of sight, but as she came around the corner, she saw Bina as she started to raise her right hand, something glinting dark and metallic in her grip.

And all at once Beth realized what was happening — Bina was bringing up to fire the Tariq 9-millimeter pistol that she must have gotten out of Geoff's safe while Beth and Ike had stupidly, inexcusably, left her alone for the past twenty minutes in his office.

"Bina," she yelled. "Drop it! Drop it!"

She turned halfway to Beth, a horrified expression on her face, and froze for an instant.

Just barely enough time for Ike, coming

526

around behind her the other way into the foyer, to get his arms around her, grab for the gun, and efficiently wrest it from her as she sank to her knees and began to sob.

Ron, all solicitude and concern, came forward uncertainly and stepped over the threshold. "Beth," he said. "What are you doing here? Is Bina all right? Is there anything I can do to help?"

37

At ten o'clock on the day before Thanksgiving, Beth Tully sat on a bench facing the water across the street from the Safeway store by San Francisco's marina. The day was cool and clear and foot traffic was heavy with its usual load of joggers and walkers, strollers and dogs.

Beth was in plainclothes — black slacks, hiking boots, a black and orange Giants jacket. Under the jacket, she carried her service weapon in a shoulder holster. Waiting for Kate to arrive, she scanned the faces of people coming toward her while she tried to calm her nerves. Unconsciously, she clutched at the knotted mass, her stomach tight in the middle of her guts.

All of her instincts were telling her that she should not be here. And if she was going to meet up with Kate, at the very least she ought to have called Ike and alerted him as to her plans. But she hadn't done that.

And last night when Kate had called her, she'd taken it as the opportunity she'd been waiting for since the night at Bina's when she had finally understood.

Surely, she now tried to convince herself, Kate wasn't going to be a danger to her.

Still, though, this morning she'd barely hesitated before packing her own gun.

Kate had asked her to come by her house on Washington Street so they could start their walk from there the way they used to, but Beth suggested a public place like this bench instead, out in the open.

Not that it would really matter. But, she thought, it might.

And now suddenly Kate's actual appearance interrupted her reverie. She was across the street, waiting for the light to change on the corner. Even from a distance, she looked drawn and depressed, her hands in her jacket pockets, her shoulders slumped.

Beth stood up, caught her eye, raised a tentative hand in greeting.

Kate crossed the street and, the two women barely exchanging greetings, they fell into stride with each other, heading toward the Golden Gate. After a few steps, Kate thanked Beth for coming down to meet with her, especially when she was under no real obligation to do so.

Beth shrugged. "We've been friends a long time, Kate. Of course I'm going to come if you want to see me."

They walked on in a silence that stretched and stretched until, to Beth, it had become almost unbearable. She was about to say something — anything — when Kate finally spoke up. "You really thought it was Ron?"

"I still believe Ron killed Peter, if that's what you're talking about."

"Of course it is. What else could it be?"

"Don't fuck with me, Kate."

"There's no proof. There was never any proof."

Beth chose not to respond to that. "You know why he came to Bina's, Kate. Because she told him that she knew he'd killed Geoff. And by extension, Peter. She was going to call the police — us — and lay out all of her evidence, which was compelling. He couldn't let that happen."

"But you were already at her house . . ."

They walked on a few steps.

"I was." Beth had nothing to lose by telling the truth. "The plain fact is that we baited a trap for him, Kate, and he took the bait."

"You mean you, personally, you baited it?"

"Yes, I did. You have to understand, Kate, Ron had to be stopped."

530

"But there was nothing to stop. He wasn't going to kill anyone."

"Well, maybe except for Bina. He had a gun on him, after all. What did he need that for if he wasn't planning to kill her?"

"How about self-defense? If she was planning to kill him. Which, after all, she almost did."

"No. He came to kill her, and then after her anyone else who threatened to expose what you'd both done."

"Both?" Kate stopped and turned to face Beth. "Will you ever give it a rest, Beth?"

"I don't know if I will. Probably not."

"Even with no proof? No evidence? Even though Ron was at a deposition with four witnesses the whole night Geoff killed himself? I would have thought that would have been a little inconvenient for your theories."

"Yes, that was a surprise. Because I really did believe that Ron had killed Geoff. But his alibi totally checked out. So I had no choice but to admit that Ron didn't kill Geoff after all. But you knew that, too, didn't you? Because you killed Geoff."

"You're out of your mind, Beth."

"I think not. Why don't you tell me what you were doing that night, Kate?"

"You must be joking."

531

"Not at all, really."

"So you really believe that Ron killed Peter and that I killed Geoff?"

"I'm certain of it."

"Okay, then, tell me why?"

"Why what?"

"Well, to start off, why did Ron kill Peter? Which is what started all this."

Beth cocked her head and let out a breath. "You know this, too, Kate. Because you slept with him."

"Once, Beth. One time only. That can't have been it. And on top of it all, that was six months before Peter got shot."

"But maybe only a few days after Ron found out about it, Kate. Or maybe the jealousy was heating up for a few months and then all at once it boiled over."

"And what? It finally got to Ron and he just called Peter up one day and said they ought to get together . . ."

"From the phone in Geoff's office, yes. Don't forget that."

"I never would," Kate said. "And why not, while we're fantasizing here. Then what did he do in your make-believe world?"

"We know what he did. He took out his Iraqi souvenir gun . . ."

"You mean one of the guns he turned in to the city last summer?"

532

"Exactly, Kate. Except maybe you don't know that they keep a record of all guns surrendered to the city, and neither of those guns, or anything like them, are on the list. I checked."

"Of course you did. But again, so what? It's just more evidence that isn't there. It must be very disappointing to you. And you have to understand something else, Beth. Peter was a dangerous man," she said. "He was ruining lives."

"So he deserved to die?" Beth fixed her with a flat stare. "How about Geoff? Was he ruining lives, too?"

"He was cheating the firm, cheating us. Everyone thought Geoff was so honorable, but he stole clients from Ron, he did a lot more shady business than anyone realized."

"And he had to die, too? Because of his business dealings? I don't think so."

"No, then why?"

"Because you saw your opportunity and took it. You could make it look like he killed both Peter and himself. All you had to do was get him alone and shoot him, leave one casing in the car and plant another one — from the same Iraqi gun — on the boat where you knew there'd be traces of Peter's blood, because that's where he'd actually been shot by Ron. You got the casing you needed, by the way, from the missing extra bullet, and I'll give it to you, that was a nice touch. As long as you got us — the police — to believe the same gun killed Geoff and Peter, you'd done your job, hadn't you?"

Kate made a face. "It sounds to me, *girl-friend,* that all that evidence you talk about comes to that same conclusion. Which is why they closed the case, isn't it?"

"It isn't closed to me, Kate. It never will be, and you'll have to live knowing that."

Kate's perfect face was a study in frustration. "You can't blame me for all of this. I didn't know any of this was going to happen."

"But it did happen, didn't it?"

"So it's my fault? All these dead people? You're saying they're my fault?"

Beth said nothing.

"I'm just not willing to accept that," Kate said.

"That would be your decision. I can't help you with that. It is what it is."

Kate's eyes scanned the horizon behind Beth, as though looking for a different answer.

"And what am I supposed to do now?"

"I don't know, Kate. I can't help you with that, either. You've got to try to find a place to put it. And when I find a way to take you and Ron down, I promise you that I will."

Kate reached out a hand and touched Beth's arm. Incipient tears shone in her eyes. "I never meant for anyone to get hurt, Beth. You have to believe that."

Beth's eyes looked straight into Kate's. "As a matter of fact," Beth said, "I do believe that. I don't think it ever entered your mind that what you did with Peter would have consequences. And maybe, you know, it should have." Seconds passed, perhaps half a minute, and finally Beth simply nodded. "Good-bye, Kate," she said.

Beth turned and started back toward the marina. The thought crossed her mind that if Kate had somehow brought along a weapon, now would be when she would use it.

Hands in her jacket pockets, she kept moving.

Kate called out her name — once — but she didn't stop, didn't even pause.

She just kept on putting down one painful step after the other.

About a mile south of where Peter Ash's body had washed up on shore at the Cliff House, a lone white seagull soared over a patch of large sand dunes the size of a football field. The bird banked hard right out over the Pacific Coast Highway, floated in to a landing atop the tallest of the dunes, then jumped a few feet downhill, where it spread its wings and squawked at the couple in front of it.

Beth said, "Look at this guy. Is he shameless or what?"

"He just wants food," Alan said.

The two of them were sharing a blanket, their picnic the leftovers from the Thanksgiving dinner they'd shared at his sister Laurie's place yesterday. Down in the cup of the dunes, there was no breeze. The sun shone down from directly above them, enveloping them in an incongruous late November warmth.

Alan flung a piece of crust from a turkey sandwich out toward the begging bird. "It's his lucky day."

"Not only his."

Beth broke a sunbeam of a smile and held it long enough that the sheer force of it pulled him toward her.

A minute or so later, Alan was on his back and she was on her side, lying up against him. A few of the buttons on his shirt had somehow come undone and her hand lay flat up against the skin of his chest.

"Are you okay?" Alan asked her.

"Just a random tear," she said, wiping at

her eye. "I wouldn't worry about it." Bringing her face up to his, she lay a soft kiss against his cheek, then sighed heavily.

"I'm here, you know," he said. "Whatever it is."

She drew in another breath. "You remember our pizza night at your place? What a mess I was?"

"I wouldn't go that far."

"Actually, I don't think that's far enough. I can't tell you how disconnected and scared I was, Alan. Just generally scared of life, of terrorists, and for Ginny and her future, and of what was going to come of me."

"Scared of me, too, a little, if I remember right."

"Well, in all honesty, of every shadow on every wall."

He tightened his arm around her. "You had your reasons."

"Admittedly. I'm not denying it. But my point is, whatever the reasons were, I felt that they were beating me. I couldn't seem to shake them. And then, yesterday I'm cutting the turkey and I look around the table and there's Ginny and Laurie and you and it was like something just shifted inside me — I know that sounds weird, but that's what it felt like. And suddenly all that stuff was gone. And now here we are today, you and me . . ."

He held her against him. "It's all right, Beth. You can let it all go."

"I know," she said. "That's the amazing thing. I already have."

ACKNOWLEDGMENTS

When a writer has been fortunate enough to have established a successful series, as I have with Dismas Hardy and his universe, the idea of that writer creating a stand-alone novel outside of that series is not particularly calculated to warm the heart of his agent. So it was with more than a soupçon of trepidation that I proposed the idea of this book to my agent, Barney Karpfinger. I needn't have worried. As he has been for the past twenty years, he was the soul of enthusiasm and cooperation. Barney remains the rock of my career, and a great cheerleader for this book at every step of the process. It truly would never have been written without his input and support. Thank you, sir. You are the best.

Last year I met a fellow writer, Rob Leininger, via email. We began a near-daily correspondence during the writing of this book that was a great source of motivation and connection in this often-lonely business. I also wound up reading more of Rob's books than any other author's last year — *Gumshoe, Killing Suki Flood, Richter Ten, Sunspot,* and *Gumshoe for Two.* I recommend every one of them. He is a talented writer who deserves wide recognition.

As is the case with most of my books, this one needed a medical consult or two. For the umpteenth time I called on my friend Dr. John Chuck, who in turn introduced me to Lisa Loker, LCSW, manager of the Eating Disorder Program at Kaiser Permanente, Sacramento. Thanks to both of you for your time and expertise. Also on the medical front, I would be remiss if I didn't thank Dr. Amit Banerjee of Kaiser Permanente Vacaville, whose surgery on my back midway through the writing of this book alleviated some pretty impressive chronic pain that threatened my peace and productivity. Finally, my brother-in-law, Mark Detzer, PhD, was again helpful in clarifying some important psychological issues that arose as the story progressed. By the way, and perhaps needless to say, any medical (or other) errors that survived into the final manuscript are the fault of the author alone.

On a day-to-day basis, my assistant, Anita Boone, continues to work her organizational magic keeping the decks clear for my daily pages. Without her unbelievable competence, cheerful personality, and remarkable efficiency, I would be hard-pressed to find the time needed to devote to writing these books.

It is a lucky man who finds himself surrounded by friends, and I have been extremely fortunate to count myself among those so blessed. So here's to all the "usual suspects" — you know who you are.

As long as we can keep from killing each other over differences of opinion about various plot points, legal and otherwise, in my books, Alfred F. Giannini, Esq., is and will remain the quintessential technical consultant, as he has been for this and all of my other novels. There is no way to overstate Al's contributions to my work over the years, and I hope it goes on forever.

Generous contributors to charitable organizations have purchased the right to name characters in this book. These people and their respective organizations are: Michelle Griffin (SFCASA); Nancy Casey Muller (Yolo County CASA); and Kathy Pelz (Napa County Library Literacy Center/ Charitybuzz.com).

Taking great care of the entire social media package, including my web page (www.johnlescroart.com), blog, Facebook, Twitter (www.twitter.com/johnlescroart), is the inimitable Dr. Andy Jones (Poet Laureate of the City of Davis, California). I'd also like to thank Doug Kelly and Peggy Nauts, who have been editing my books for the past decade — thank you both for your keen eyes and sensibilities.

I am extraordinarily proud to be published by Atria Books, and I'd like to thank my publisher, Judith Curr, and my editor, Peter Borland, for giving me the opportunity to work with one of the best imprints in the world. Thanks also to Janice Fryer, Wendy Sheanin, Colin Shields, and to the efforts of the publicity and marketing departments at Atria, especially the indefatigable David Brown.

Finally, I truly love to be in contact with my readers, and I invite one and all to stop by any of the sites mentioned above and get in touch with me. I look forward to hearing from you. And thanks for buying my books!

ABOUT THE AUTHOR

John Lescroart is the author of twenty-five previous novels, including the *New York Times* bestsellers *The Ophelia Cut*, *The Keeper*, and *The Fall*. He lives in Northern California.